Praise for J. R.

...ard wields a commanding voice perfect for the genre ...
...ntriguing, adrenaline-pumping ... Fans of L. A. Banks,
...rell K. Hamilton and Sherrilyn Kenyon will add Ward
to their must-read list'
Booklist

Harley-riding angels battle a demon temptress in the
latest paranormal romance thriller from bestseller
...ard, author of the beloved Black Dagger Brotherhood
...eries ...Ward provides the combination of fun, thrills
and gratuitous sex she's best known for. Fans of the
Brotherhood, clear a shelf: your next series
addiction has just begun'
Publishers Weekly

'Powerful. Ward pulls no punches and delivers an
extraordinary paranormal drama'
Romantic Times

'Proves that J. R. Ward's talents don't stop at vampires'
Love Vampires

'[Ward] has smashed expectations and provided a new
...ovel that will captivate readers. This author's incredibly
unique style of writing, mixed with her outrageous shocks
and twists ... changed the face of paranormal romance'
Suite 101

12374870

J. R. Ward lives in the South with her incredibly supportive husband and her beloved golden retriever. After graduating from law school, she began working in health care in Boston and spent many years as chief of staff for one of the premier academic medical centres in the nation.

Visit her at www.jrward.com and her facebook page www.facebook.com/JRWardBooks

J.R. WARD

ENVY

piatkus

PIATKUS

First published in the United States in 2011 by New American Library,
A Division of Penguin Group (USA) Inc., New York
First published in Great Britain as a paperback original in 2011 by Piatkus

A CIP catalogue record for this book
is available from the British Library.

ISBN 978-0-349-40020-4

Printed and bound in Great Britain by CPI Mackays, Chatham ME5 8TD

Papers used by Piatkus are from well-managed forests
and other responsible sources.

MIX
Paper from
responsible sources
FSC® C104740

Piatkus
An imprint of
Little, Brown Book Group
100 Victoria Embankment
London EC4Y 0DY

An Hachette UK Company
www.hachette.co.uk

www.piatkus.co.uk

Dedicated to:
David B. Fox, DMD
The master smile-maker in so many ways.

ACKNOWLEDGMENTS

Thank you to Kara Welsh, Claire Zion, Leslie Gelbman, and everyone at NAL! Thank you to Steve Axelrod!

With love to Team Waud: LeE, Nath, D, Lu, Jen as well as Jake(Ken) and Cheryle, Buster (Ben) and Shanna, and Elwood (Mike) and Jenn.

With thanks to my family and all the angels in my life, whether they have two feet or four.
You all know who you are. . . .

CHAPTER
1

It was in the spring, on a dark April evening, when Detective Thomas DelVecchio Jr. learned that nightmares could in fact make the jump out of the mind and into real life.

Unfortunately for him, it wasn't exactly a news flash.

Blood was everywhere. Glossy and crimson in the moonlight, it was as if a gallon of paint had been cracked open and spastic-splashed all over not just the forest floor ... but the man who lay shredded and unmoving on a bed of decaying leaves.

At Veck's feet.

All that red shit was not a premium interior latex, however. Or an oil-based trim. Or a hearty exterior barn paint. You couldn't buy it at Home Depot or Lowe's, and you didn't clean it up with turpentine or use it in some B movie.

That was real life, right there. Leaking out all over the fuck.

What had he done? Dear God ...

Ripping off his leather jacket, he wadded the thing up, knelt down, and pressed it against the man's exposed thorax. Gurgling sounds mixed with the hard bursts of Veck's own breath as he stared down into eyes that were going opaque. Fast.

"Did I kill you? *Did I*?"

No response. Then again, the bastard's voice box was probably hanging from a branch somewhere.

Shit . . . oh, *shit* . . . it was like the night his mother had been killed.

Except in this case, he'd actually come to slice up someone.

That much he knew for sure: He had gotten on his motorcycle, driven out here, and waited in the forest for this psychotic POS to show up—all the while telling himself the lie that he was just going to take the "suspect" into custody.

His palm had told the truth. When his prey had finally arrived, his knife had been in his hand, and he'd made like a shadow in his deliberately black clothes, closing in. . . .

The Monroe Motel & Suites was only fifteen yards away, on the far side of this thick stand of brush and pines. Illuminated by piss yellow security lights, the seedy lineup of rent-by-the-night-or-the-hour was the reason both he and this sieve of a murderer had come out tonight.

Serial killers often took trophies from their victims. Incapable of forming proper emotional attachments to people, and needing physical representations of the fleeting power they enjoyed over their prey, they vested emotion in the objects or remains of the people they butchered.

David Kroner had lost his collection of souvenirs two nights ago. When his work here had been interrupted and the police had swarmed in.

So of course he would return to where he'd last been in control. It was the closest he could come to everything he'd once had.

"I've called an ambulance," Veck heard himself say, unsure who he was talking to.

Shifting his eyes, he focused on the motel's last room, the one at the end that was closest to where they were and farthest from the office. An official Caldwell Police Department evidence seal was plastered on the door and the jamb, and crime scene tape whistled in the breeze all around it. Between one blink and the next, he saw what he and the other CPDers had found there the night before last: another young woman, freshly killed and in the process of being picked over for mementos of the flesh.

More gurgling.

He looked back down. The man bleeding out beneath him was wiry and thin, but then again, David Kroner's victims had been young women aged sixteen to twenty-four so it wasn't like he needed to be built like a bouncer to get the job done. Sandy blond hair was thinning at the crown. Skin that had been white-boy pale was now going gray—at least where it wasn't covered with blood.

Diving into his databanks, Veck tried to remember what the hell had just happened. After waiting for what had felt like days, a snapping of sticks had shifted his eyes around and he'd found Kroner tiptoeing through the pines.

The instant he saw the man, his hand had gone for his knife, his body had crouched down and then he'd—

"Mother*fucker* . . ."

The headache came on sharp and fast, like someone had pounded a roofing nail into his frontal lobe. Putting a hand up, he listed to the left, and thought, well, great. When the ambulance came, the medics could treat him for an aneurysm.

At least it would give them something to do—Kroner was going to be a stiff by the time they got here.

When the screaming pain faded a little, Veck took another run at remembering . . . only to slam temple-first into the land of Excedrin and blackout drapes again. With the fresh round of agony blooming in his skull like a bright red bouquet, he closed his eyes, and considered throwing up—and while the to-boot or not-to-boot debate raged in his gut, he figured it was time to be honest with himself. As much as his short-term memory had a big-ass hole in it, the fact was, he *had* come out here to kill this perverted bastard who, as the tally stood now, had defiled at least eleven young women from Chicago to Caldwell in the last year.

Horrific, of course. But amateur night compared to Veck's own father—who'd done that in a three-month span once: Thomas DelVecchio Sr. wrote the book for guys like Kroner.

And it was precisely that lineage that had gotten Veck on the horn to not just the ambulance, but his partner at Homicide.

As much as he hated to admit it, he was his father's son: He had come to kill. Period. And the fact that his victim had been such a violent asshole was nothing but a socially acceptable filter over the real picture.

At its core, this had not been about avenging those dead girls.

And for fuck's sake, he'd known this night was inevitable. All his life, the shadow had been behind him, guiding him, seducing him, pulling him toward this very scene of destruction. So it made sense he didn't remember anything. His other half had finally taken over, and hadn't ceded control of the wheel until the violence was done. The proof? Somewhere in the back of his head, laughter was echoing, maniacal and satisfied.

Yeah, well, get your jollies on now, he thought at the stuff. Because he wasn't going to let himself follow too far in his father's footsteps—

The sounds of sirens bubbled up from the east, and got louder, fast.

Apparently, he wasn't the only person who heard the approach. A man burst out of one of the motel rooms, and raced around the hood of a ten-year-old beater that had open latticework for quarter panels. Kind of tough for him to get his keys out, considering he was yanking his pants on at the same time.

Next up on the flee-parade was a rough-looking woman

who scrambled into an old Honda Civic while pulling down her miniskirt.

Their screeching departures meant the parking lot was good and empty when the ambulance bumped in off the road and halted in front of the office.

As the passenger-side medic got out, and what had to be a manager opened the glass door, Veck whistled loud and clear. "Over here!"

The manager apparently had no intentions of getting involved and ducked back inside. But the medic jogged over and the ambulance trundled across the parking lot. And as they zeroed in on him, Veck became utterly calm—dead calm. As untouchable as the cold, distant moon that watched over the inky black night.

Fuck his dark side. He had done this. And he was going to make himself pay.

Internal Affairs officer Sophia Reilly was going like a bat out of hell in her unmarked, shooting through the backwoods of Caldwell's scruffy edges. As she rode the twists and turns of Route 149 at a dead run, the fact that she was on her way to a crime scene didn't account for the high speed: She drove fast. Ate quick. Hated to wait in lines, wait for people, wait for information.

If she could just avoid hitting a deer before she got to the Monroe Motel & Suites—

When her cell phone went off, she had it to her ear before the second ring. "Reilly."

"Detective de la Cruz."

"Hey. Guess where I'm going right now?"

"Who called you?"

"Dispatch. Your partner's on my list of things to do—so when he dials in for an ambulance and backup in the middle of the night, and says he doesn't know what happened to the victim, I get a ring-a-ding-ding."

Unfortunately, it was something she was getting familiar with. Thomas DelVecchio Jr. had been working Homicide for only two weeks, and he'd already brushed up against a possible suspension for coldcocking a paparazzo who'd tried to sneak a pic of a victim.

That was child's play to this mess, though.

"How'd you find out?" she asked.

"He woke me up."

"How'd he sound?"

"I'm going to be honest."

"You always are, Detective."

"He sounded just fine. Complained of a headache and loss of memory. He said there was a lot of blood and that he was one hundred percent sure that the victim was David Kroner."

A.k.a., the sick bastard who had been carving up young girls and saving the bits and pieces. The bastard's latest "work" session had been conducted the night before last at the motel, and been interrupted by unknowns. Following the disturbance, Kroner had escaped out a window over the toilet, leaving behind a tragically messy corpse and a truck full of specimen jars and other objects—all of which were being cataloged at H.Q. and cross-referenced nationwide.

"Did you ask him if he did it?" As a member of Internal Affairs, Reilly investigated her own colleagues' misdeeds, and though she took pride in her work, she didn't enjoy the fact that people with her job description had anything to do. Much better if everyone, including the cops, were law abiders and played by the rules.

"He said he didn't know."

Blackout while committing murder? Not uncommon. Especially if it was a crime of passion—like, oh, say, a homicide detective taking down a debased serial killer. And Veck had already proved himself to be a hothead in the protection or defense of victims. Well, a hothead period. The guy was a brilliant, very sexy hothead—

Not that the sexy was in any way relevant.

In the slightest.

"What's your ETA, Detective?" she asked.

" 'Bout fifteen minutes."

"I'm under a mile away. I'll see you there."

"Roger that."

As they hung up, she put her phone in the inside pocket of her coat, and hitched herself up in her seat. For a member of the force to be a possible suspect in a murder investigation—and going by what Veck had said to Dispatch, the likelihood of Kroner surviving was small—created all kinds of conflicts of interest. Most of the time, Internal Affairs folks dealt with corruption, procedural infractions, and investigations into on-the-job competence. But in a situation like this, members of Veck's own department were in the tight spot of assessing whether or not one of their own had committed a crime.

Hell, depending on how this went, she might need to bring in some kind of an outside panel to make the call. But it was too early for that.

It was not too soon to think about Veck's dad, however.

Everyone knew who the man was, and she had to admit that if that blood tie had not been in the picture, she wouldn't be going into this on quite as high alert ... with the worry that payback might well have been a DelVecchio, as it were.

Thomas Sr. was one of the most notorious serial killers of the late twentieth century. Officially, he had been charged and convicted of "only" twenty-eight murders. But he'd been implicated in some thirty more—and that was just what authorities in four states knew about. Chances were good there were dozens of missing women who hadn't been properly linked to him.

So yeah, if Veck's father had been a lawyer or an accountant or a teacher, she might not be quite so concerned. But the whole apple-doesn't-fall-far-from-the-tree thing had evil implications when it came to serial killers and their sons.

After she went over a squat bridge, the Monroe Motel & Suites was up on the right, and she pulled in, going past the office and the row of rooms to the far end of the parking lot

by the forest. Getting out with her backpack full of neces-
saries, the sweet diesel from the ambulance made her
sneeze hard, and in the aftermath, she caught the tang of
the pine boughs . . . as well as the unmistakable copper
sting of fresh blood.

The medics had angled their vehicle so it faced into the
woods, and in the headlights, both of the EMTs were work-
ing over the bloodied body of a Caucasian male. The vic-
tim's clothes had been cut off—or torn off—and what was
under them was a raw pastiche of too many wounds to
count.

No way he was going to live, she thought.

And then she saw Veck. The homicide detective was
standing off to the side, arms crossed, feet planted, face
showing . . . absolutely nothing. Just as de la Cruz had said.

Christ, the guy might as well have been in line for a deli
sandwich.

As she walked over the spongy bed of downed leaves
and soft earth, she felt a sudden urge to tighten her own
insides up. Although if she was honest, that wasn't just
about this crime scene. It was the man she'd come here
for, too.

On the approach, she noted the black motorcycle parked
on the fringe of the forest. It was his; she'd seen it at HQ
before. Matter of fact, she'd watched him from her window
as he mounted the thing, kick-started it, and tore off. He
wore his helmet—most of the time.

She knew that a lot of women at the station house pulled
the same stare thing, but then again, there was a lot to look
at. Between his heavy shoulders and his tight hips, he was
built like a boxer, but his face was more pretty-boy than
pugilist—or would have been had it not been for his stare.
Those cold, intelligent dark blues of his took that J.Crew–
model bone structure into all-man territory. And then
some.

Stopping in front of him, the first thing she noticed was
the blood on his black turtleneck. Spots of it here and there,
not big smudges or soaked-in patches.

No scratches on his face. Or his neck.

Clothes and hat were in good condition—nothing out of kilter, torn, or abraded. Two mud circles were on the knees of his black pants. Gun was holstered. Unclear whether he had other weapons on him.

He didn't say anything. No "I didn't do it" or "Let me explain . . ."

His eyes just locked on her and . . . that was it.

Ditching the pleasantries, she said, "The sergeant called me in."

"I figured."

"Are you injured?"

"No."

"Mind if I ask you some questions?"

"G'head."

God, he was in such control of himself. "What brought you out here tonight?"

"I knew Kroner was going to come back. He had to. With his collection impounded, he had nothing left of his work, so this is a holy site to him."

"And what happened after you got here?"

"I waited. He came . . . and then . . ." Veck hesitated, his brows going tight as a knot before one hand came up and rubbed his temple. "Shit . . ."

"Detective?"

"I can't remember." He looked her square in the eye again. "I can't remember anything after he showed up, and that's the God's honest. One minute he was coming through the woods, and the next? There was blood everywhere."

"May I see your hands, Detective?" When he held them out, they were rock steady . . . and unmarked with cuts or abrasions. No blood on the palms, the fingertips, the nails. "Did you assess the victim or intervene with him in some way prior to or after calling nine-one-one?"

"I took my leather jacket off and put it to his neck. It wasn't going to help, but I did it anyway."

"Are you carrying any weapons other than your gun?"

"My knife. It's on my—"

She put her hand on his arm to stop his reaching around. "Let me take a look."

Nodding, he pivoted on his boot heel. In the light from the ambulance, the nasty-looking blade holstered at the small of his back was a laceration waiting to happen.

"May I remove this weapon, Detective?"

"Have at it."

Taking a set of vinyl gloves out of her backpack, she snapped them on and went for the dagger. As she tugged to loosen the snap, his body didn't shift at all. She might as well have been disarming a statue.

The knife was clean and dry as a whistle.

Lifting it up to her nose, she inhaled. No scent of astringent as if he'd scrubbed it in a hurry.

As he looked over his shoulder, the torsion in his body made his shoulders seem huge, and for no good reason, she realized she was eye-to-eye with his pecs. At five-foot-six, she was of average height, but next to him she felt like she'd shrunk to miniature.

"I'm going to confiscate this, if you don't mind?" She was going to take his gun as well, but given the injuries . . . the blade was what she really wanted from him.

"Not at all."

As she took a plastic bag out of her sack, she said, "What do you *think* happened here."

"Someone ripped him apart, and I think it was me."

That stopped her, but not because she thought it was an admission of any kind—she just didn't expect anyone under these circumstances to be so honest.

At that moment, an unmarked pulled into the parking lot along with two squad cars. "Your partner's arrived," she said. "But the sergeant wants me to lead the investigation to avoid any possible conflicts of interest."

"Not a problem."

"Will you consent to my taking samples from under your nails?"

"Yes."

She shifted the pack in front again and took out a Swiss army knife, along with some smaller plastic bags.

"You're very organized, Officer," Veck said.

"I don't like not being prepared. Please hold out your right hand."

She made fast work, starting with the pinkie. His nails were cut short, but not manicured, and there was very little under any of them.

"Do you have a background in detective work?" Veck asked.

"Yes."

"Shows."

When she was finished, she glanced up . . . and immediately had to downshift from his midnight blue eyes to somewhere in his chin vicinity. "Would you like another coat, Detective? It's cold out here."

"I'm fine."

If you were bleeding from a chest wound, would you take a damn Band-Aid? she wondered. Or would you tough-guy it until there was no plasma left in your veins?

He'd tough-guy it, she thought. Definitely.

"I want the medics to look you over—"

"I'm fine—"

"That would be an order, Detective. You look like your head hurts."

At that moment, de la Cruz emerged from his car, and as he came over, he looked grim faced and weary. Word had it he'd already lost a partner a couple of years ago; he obviously wasn't psyched at the retread, even if it was for a different reason.

"Excuse me," she said to them both. "I'm going to snag one of the medics."

Except when she got over to the two men, they were in the process of transferring Kroner onto the gurney, and it was clear they couldn't spare even a minute. "What are his chances?"

"Bad," the one who was bagging him said. "But we'll do our best, Officer."

"I know you will."

The gurney's supports were extended so that the thing was at waist height, and just before they wheeled away, she took a mental snapshot. Kroner looked like he'd been pulled from the steaming wreck of a car, his face mangled as if he hadn't been wearing a seat belt and had gone through the window.

Reilly glanced back at Veck.

Lot of holes in this scene, she thought. Especially given that he believed he'd been the attacker. But there was no way to do that much damage and get cleaned up this fast in the woods. Besides, he didn't look like he'd been in any altercation at all—there was no way you could soap-and-water away bruises and scratches.

The question was . . . who had done it?

As if he could feel her eyes on him, Veck's head cranked around, and when their stares met, everything disappeared: she might as well have been all alone with him . . . and standing not fifteen yards away, but fifteen inches.

From out of nowhere, a welling heat boiled up in her body, the kind of thing that, if she'd been indoors, she'd have told herself was the result of standing under a heat duct. As it was, she justified the flush as being an adrenal response to stress.

Stress, damn it. *Not* sexual attraction.

Reilly broke the connection by calling out to the newly arrived uniforms, "Would you tape us up?"

"Roger that, Officer."

Right, time to get back to work: That brief spike of wholly inappropriate attraction was not going to get in the way of her doing her job. She was far too levelheaded, for one thing, and for another, her professional integrity demanded nothing less. She also had no intention of being on the man's very long list of adoring fans. She was going to take care of business, and leave the Moon Pie eyes to all the others.

Besides, guys like Veck didn't go for women like her, and that was just fine. She was far more interested in work than in showing her legs, puffing her hair, and competing in the date Olympics. Brittany—spelled Britnae, a.k.a. the office hottie—could have him and keep him if she wanted.

In the meantime, Reilly was going to see whether or not the son had lived up to the father's horrors.

CHAPTER
2

Under normal circumstances, Jim Heron considered himself a sore loser.

And that was with your average, everyday shit like World of Warcraft or frickin' tennis or poker.

Not that he wasted time playing any of those, but if he did, he would have been the type who didn't leave the controller, court, or table until he was on top.

And again, that was just about unimportant crap.

When it came to the war with the demon Devina, he was on fire, he was so pissed off: He had lost the last round.

Lost as in no win. As in out of the seven souls they were battling over, he and that bitch were now tied 1–1. Granted, there were still five more at-bats, but this was not the direction he or anyone else needed to go in.

He got defeated? That demon had dominion over not only the earth but the heavens above ... which meant his mother and all those good souls up there, as well as him and his fallen angel soldiers, were looking at an eternity of damnation.

And that was not, he'd recently discovered, just a hypothetical used to motivate the religious. Hell was an actual place and the suffering there was very real. Matter of fact, so much of what he'd previously written off as silly rhetoric from the holier-than-thou crowd had turned out to be dead on.

So yeah, the stakes were high and he *hated* losing. Especially when it didn't need to go down like it had.

He was flat-out rip-shit at the game. At his boss, Nigel. At the "rules."

It was common fucking sense: When you told a guy he was supposed to influence some jackass at a crossroads in his or her life, it kind of helped if you frickin' told him who was on deck. After all, it wasn't a big goddamn secret: Nigel knew. The enemy, Devina, knew. Jim? Not so much, people. And courtesy of that informational black hole, he'd focused on the wrong man in the last round and blown it.

So here he was, tied with the bitch and pissed off in a hotel room in Caldwell, New York.

And he wasn't the only one with a case of the grumpies.

Next door, on the far side of a connector, two deep male voices were doing the back-and-forth, in the key of frustrated-to-shit.

Not a news flash. His wingmen, Adrian Vogel and Eddie Blackhawk, were not happy with him, and clearly the two of them were chewing him out in absentia.

This goin'-back-to-Caldie-Caldie-Caldic wasn't so much the issue. It was the reason Jim had dragged them all here.

His eyes shifted across the duvet. Dog was curled up in a tight ball beside him, his scruffy fur giving the impression that he'd been heavily moussed and put into a stiff wind, even though he hadn't. Next to the little guy, there was a computer printout of a three-week-old newspaper article from the *Caldwell Courier Journal*. The title was "Local Girl Missing," and off to the side of the text, there was a picture of a group of smiling friends, heads close together, arms wrapped around one another's shoulders. The caption beneath the pic identified the one in the middle as Cecilia Barten.

His Sissy.

Well, not really "his," but he'd come to think of her as his responsibility.

The thing was, unlike her parents and family and friends and community, he knew where she was and what had happened to her. She was not part of the countless roster of runaways; nor had she been murdered by a boyfriend or a stranger; and she hadn't been cut up by that serial killer who, according to the *CCJ*'s Web site this morning, was at large.

She had been defiled, however. By Devina.

Sissy was a virgin sacrificed to protect the demon's mirror, that most sacred possession. Jim had found her body hanging upside down in front of the thing in the demon's temporary lair and been forced to leave her behind. It had been bad enough to know that she'd lost her life to his enemy, but then later, he'd seen her in Devina's wall of souls . . . trapped, suffering, lost forever among the damned who deserved that fate.

Cecilia didn't belong in hell. She was an innocent taken and used by evil—and Jim was going to get her free, if it was the last thing he did.

Which, yeah, was why they'd come back to Caldwell. And the reason Adrian and Eddie were pissed.

But no offense . . . fuck them.

With care, Jim picked up the article and brushed his calloused thumb over the grainy image of Sissy's long, blond hair. When he blinked, he saw the stuff covered in her blood and hanging down close to the drain of a white porcelain tub. Then he blinked again and saw her as he had the other night, in Devina's viscous prison, terrified, confused, worried about her parents.

He was going to do right by all of the Bartens. But Adrian's and Eddie's yammering was just aerobics for their pieholes: He wasn't taking his eye off the war, because he couldn't afford to lose to Devina before he got Sissy out of the well of souls. Duh.

The connecting door broke wide and Adrian, a.k.a. the

Tone-deaf Wonder, walked in without knocking. Which was exactly his style.

The angel was dressed in black, as usual, and the various piercings on his face weren't half of what he supposedly had all over his body.

"You two finished bitching about me?" Jim turned the article facedown and crossed his arms over his chest. "Or are you just having a little break."

"How about you take this seriously."

Jim got up off the bed and went nose-to-nose with his soldier. "Am I giving any indication I'm fucking around?"

"You didn't drag us back here for the war."

"The hell I didn't."

As they faced off, Adrian was undaunted, even though as a former black ops assassin, Jim knew how to drop a heavyweight like the other angel twelve different ways to Sunday. "That girl is not your target," Ad said, "and in case you haven't noticed, we're down one. Distractions are not our friend."

Jim gave the Sissy reference a pass: he made a point never to talk about her. His boys had been witness to him finding her body, and they'd seen what that had done to him—so it wasn't as if they didn't know enough. And there was no reason to vocalize what seeing her in that wall had been like. Or mention the fact that while he'd been used and abused by Devina and her minions during the last round, he feared the young girl might have seen everything that had been done to him.

Shit . . . the stuff on that "work" table was nothing you wanted even a battle-hardened man to witness. An innocent? Who was petrified already?

Besides, in actuality, the violations hadn't bothered him one way or the other. Torture, in whatever form it took, was nothing more than an overload of physical sensation—but again, no one needed to eyeball that, much less his girl.

Not that she was his.

"I'm on my way to go talk to Nigel," Jim bit out. "So if

you're finished jerking me off? Or do you want to waste my time some more."

"Why aren't you already over there, then?"

Well, because he'd been sitting on that bed, staring into space, wondering where in the hell Devina had taken Sissy's body.

Except Jim was just that flavor of asshole not to concede the point in the slightest.

"Jim, I know that this girl is a thing to you. But come on, man, we need to take care of business."

As Ad spoke, Jim looked over the guy's shoulder. Eddie was standing in the connector between the two rooms, his huge body tense, his red eyes grave, that long black braid of his over his shoulder with the tail end nearly at the waist of his leathers.

Fuck.

Adrian's loud noise was the kind of shit you could argue with. Or punch—which had happened before. But Eddie's steady, nonconfrontational routine didn't offer you a target. It was a mirror that simply reflected your own dumbass behavior.

"I've got this under control," Jim said. "And I'm going to see Nigel right now."

The archangel Nigel was in his private quarters in Heaven when the summoning came through.

It was about time to get out of the bath anyway.

"We are due for company," he said to Colin as he rose from the scented water.

"I shall stay herein—the bath is the perfect temperature." With that, Colin stretched in a languorous arch. His dark hair was damp from humidity and curling at the ends, his regal, intelligent face as relaxed as it ever got. Which was not terribly so. "You do realize why he's coming."

"But of course."

Crossing over the white marble and pulling aside the coral-and-sapphire drapery, Nigel stepped out and was careful to resettle the heavy velvet-and-damask weight. No one needed to know who joined him in his bathing suite — although he suspected Bertie and Byron had an idea. They were, however, far too discreet to say anything.

Drawing on a silk robe, he did not bother to clothe himself in anything more formal. Jim Heron was going to care naught about his apparel, and given how this was likely to go, returning to the bath was going to be necessary.

With the pass of a hand, Nigel called the angel forth from the earth below, gathering Heron's corporeal body up and coalescing it here in his private quarters.

On his silk-wrapped chaise longue, as a matter of fact.

The savior looked utterly ridiculous on the raspberry expanse, heavy arms and legs flopping off the sides, his black T-shirt and beat-to-hell blue jeans an offense to such delicate fabric.

Heron came into his head a split second later and jumped to his feet, ready, alert . . . and none too pleased.

"Ice wine?" Nigel inquired as he went over to a French bombé chest, the marble top of which served as a bar. "Or perhaps a dram?"

"I want to know who is next, Nigel."

"So is that a 'no' on the tipple?" He took his time choosing among the Baccarat decanters, and when he poured, it was slowly, steadily.

He was not some dolt of whom to make demands, and Heron needed to learn some manners.

Nigel pivoted and took a sip. " 'Tis light and refreshing."

"Fuck the wine."

Nigel let that one stay where it lay, and just stared at the savior.

When the Creator had appeared unto Nigel and Devina, and explained that there would be a final contest, both sides had had to agree to Heron's being the one on the field with the seven chosen souls. Naturally, each opposite wanted its values represented, and the end result was that this massive, war-minded angel standing afore him had equal amounts of the good and evil in him.

Nigel believed, however, that the fact that Jim's slain

mother was within the walls of the manse here would be the tipping factor, and he still thought that was true. Moments like this, however, made him question the very foundation of this terminal game they were all playing.

The angel looked ready to kill.

"You have to tell me who it is."

"And as I have said before, I cannot."

"I lost, asshole. And she cheated."

"I am well aware of the lines she has o'erstepped, and if you recall, my advice to you was to let her do what she will—reprisals shall come."

"When."

"When they do."

Heron did not like that answer, and he began to pace about the ornate tent with its drapes of satin and its Oriental rugs and the low bedding platform—around which, Nigel realized too late, two sets of very different clothes were scattered.

Nigel cleared his throat. "I cannot risk having an overturn that goes against us. I have stooped to Devina's level too much already by giving you Adrian and Edward. If I help you any further, I chance forfeiture of not just a round, but the entire contest. And that is unacceptable."

"You know who the soul is, though. And so does Devina."

"Yes."

"And that doesn't strike you as seriously uneven? She's going to go after them herself—probably already has."

"By the established and agreed-upon rules, she's not allowed to interact with the souls. She, as with myself, is supposed to influence you to influence them. Direct contact is not allowed."

"So why haven't you stopped it?"

" 'Tis not my purview."

"Oh, for fuck's sake, Nigel, grow a set—"

"I assure you, his balls are just fine."

At the dry interjection, both Nigel and the savior turned to the draped archway that led into the bath. Colin hadn't

bothered with a robe, but was standing there unapologeti-
cally nude.

And now that he had everyone's attention, the archan-
gel tacked on, "I'll also ask you to watch your language,
mate."

Heron's brows shot up, and there was a moment of ten-
nis matching, whereupon his head went back and forth be-
tween the two of them.

Nigel cursed under his breath. So much for decorum.
And privacy. "Ice wine, Colin?" he said gruffly. "And may-
hap some robing?"

"I'm fine."

"True enough. But your lack of modesty offers you no
better cover than the temperate air in this tent. And I have
a guest."

A grunt was all that came in manner of reply. Which was
Colin's way of proclaiming that there was no reason to be a
stuffy old tart.

Lovely.

Nigel turned back to the savior. "I am sorry that I cannot
grant you what you seek. Believe that."

"You helped me with the first."

"I was permitted that license."

"And look at how number two turned out."

Nigel hid his agreeing concern behind a sip of his glass.
"Your passion is laudable. And I will tell you that your re-
turn to Caldwell is well-served."

"Thanks for the tip. There are two million people in that
goddamn town. Hardly narrows it down."

"Nothing is arbitrary, and there are no coincidences,
Jim. In fact, there is another who shall seek what you do,
and as the separate quests unite, you will find the next
soul."

"No offense, but that doesn't mean shit." Heron glanced
at Colin. "And I'm not going to apologize to the talk police
for that. Sorry."

Colin crossed his arms over his bare chest. "Suit your-
self, lad. And I'll do the same."

Read: Maybe I'll pop you now. Or maybe later.

The last thing Nigel needed was a fistfight in his quarters as undoubtedly that would bring the other archangels, as well as Tarquin at a full gallop. Hardly the intermission one looked for.

"Colin," he said, "do go soak your head."

"I'm wet enough, thank you."

"That is a matter of opinion," Nigel muttered before addressing Jim again. "Go forth and have faith that you will be where you should and do what you must."

"I don't believe in fate, Nigel. That's like picking up an unloaded gun and thinking it'll shoot something. You've got to put the bullets in the chamber yourself."

"And I am telling you there are greater things at work than your efforts."

"Okay, wonderful, so put that on a Christmas card. But don't try to feed that bullshit to me."

Staring into the hard face of the savior, Nigel knew a flash of fear. With this attitude, there was yet one more thing stacked against the angels prevailing. And yet what could he do? Heron had no patience or faith, but that did naught to change the rules of the game or the likelihood that the Creator would inevitably redress Devina's liberties.

At least the latter worked in their favor.

"I believe we are through," Nigel said. "Nothing favorable shall come from our continued conversing."

There was a dark, rather evil moment during which Heron regarded him with a kind of fury.

"Fine," the savior said. "But I don't give up this easy."

"And I am the mountain that will not be moved."

"Roger that."

In between one blink and the next, that angel was gone. And it was not until silence rang out within the tent that Nigel realized he had not been the one to send Heron on his way. He had done that himself.

He was becoming stronger, wasn't he.

"Do you want me to go down and watch over him," Colin said.

"When I agreed to him as the chosen one, I thought there were enough reins to hold him. I truly did."

"And so I say, shall I depart and watch o'er him?"

Nigel turned to his dearest friend, who was so much more than a colleague and a confidant. "That is the purpose of Adrian and Edward."

"Stipulated. But I worry where his growing competence will take him. We are not on a good path with this."

Nigel took another sip of his wine and stared at the empty space that Heron had just inhabited. Though he kept silent, he had to agree. The question was, what to do, what to do . . .

CHAPTER
3

Down below, in the cold woods next to the Monroe Motel & Suites, Veck stood in the direct glare of the ambulance's headlights, his partner de la Cruz on his right, his buddy Bails on the left. Spotlit as he was, he felt like he was onstage as Kroner was rolled out from the trees on a gurney.

Except there was only one person looking at him.

Internal Affairs officer Sophia Reilly.

She was standing off to the side, and as their eyes locked, he wished they were getting together under different circumstances—again. The first time he'd been introduced to her had been because he'd corked that paparazzo.

This shit made one sucker punch look like a day at the beach.

The thing was, he'd liked her the moment he'd shaken her hand, and that first impression had only been reinforced tonight: The detective in him had so approved of her questions just now, as well as the way she'd looked him over, like even if he'd been bullshitting her—and he hadn't—she would have known.

But they had to stop meeting like this. Literally.

Over at the asphalt lip of the parking lot, there was a

thunch as the medics shut the double doors of the ambulance and then the vehicle backed out, taking the illumination with it. As Reilly turned to watch the departure, she was in the shadows—until she clicked on a flashlight.

Before she came back over, de la Cruz leaned into him and spoke softly: "Do you want a lawyer."

"Why would he need a lawyer," Bails snapped.

Veck shook his head at his buddy. He understood the guy's loyalty, but it was a shitload more faith than he had in himself at the moment. "It's a fair question."

"So do you?" de la Cruz whispered.

Officer Reilly circled around the blood pool, wending in and out of the trunks and branches, small sticks snapping under her feet, the sounds loud in his ears.

She stopped in front of him. "I'm going to have follow-up questions tomorrow, but you can go home now."

Veck narrowed his eyes. "You're letting me go."

"You were never in my custody, Detective."

"And that's it."

"No, not at all. But you're through here tonight."

Veck shook his head. "Listen, Officer, that can't be—"

"The CSI people are on the way. I don't want you here when they go through the scene because it represents a potential compromise to their work. That clear enough for you?"

Ah. And he should have guessed. It was dark here in the woods. He could easily pick up or manipulate evidence from the ground without anyone knowing, and she'd been trying to give him a gracious way out.

She was smart, he thought.

She also happened to be beautiful: In the reflected glow of the flashlight, she was stunning in the way that only a natural, healthy woman could be—with no heavy makeup to gunk up her pores or weigh down her lids, and no greasy, slippery gloss on her mouth, she was utterly un-fake.

And that heavy dark red hair and that deep green stare weren't exactly hard on the eyes, either.

Plus there was her take-no-shit attitude . . .

"Fair enough, Officer," he murmured.

"Please report to the sarge's office at eight thirty a.m. tomorrow."

"You got it."

As Bails muttered something under his breath, Veck prayed the bastard kept his opinions to himself. Reilly was just doing her job—and being damn professional about it. The least they could do was pay her the respect back.

Before his buddy could spout anything else, Veck clapped palms with Bails and nodded at de la Cruz. As he went to walk off, Reilly's low, serious voice broke out through the night.

"Detective."

He looked over his shoulder. "Yeah, Officer."

"I'm going to have to take your gun. And your badge. And that knife holster."

Right. Of course. "Badge is in the leather coat over there on the ground. Do you want to do the honors on my nine and strap?"

"Yes, please. And I'll take your cell phone, too, if you don't mind."

As she stepped in close, he smelled her perfume. Nothing fruity or flowery or, God forbid, that vanilla shit. Nothing he could place commercially, either. Shampoo, maybe? Had she gotten the call just when she'd been stepping out of the shower?

Now, there was a picture. . . .

Wait a minute. Was he *actually* fantasizing about his co-worker . . . five feet from a murder scene? While he was a suspect?

Wow.

Yup, that was all he had on that one.

Reilly put her flashlight in her mouth, and then her bright blue gloved hands reached forward. As he lifted his arms to help her get to his waist, a subtle tugging registered in his hips, the kind of thing that he would have felt if she'd been taking off his pants—

The electric bolt that shot down into his cock was a

surprise—and Christ, he was glad that beam was flashing right at his chest and not in a southerly direction.

Man, this was so damned wrong—and unlike him. He didn't hit on colleagues, whether they were admin assistants, fellow detectives . . . or Internal Affairs officers. Too much hassle when the inevitable end to the one-night stand came—

Dear God, where was his head at?

Not on reality, apparently.

It was almost like the magnitude of what had happened on that patch of red-stained leaves over there was so great, his brain was seeking shelter in any topic other than the giant, bloody elephant in the forest.

Then again, maybe he'd just lost his mind. Period.

"Thank you, Detective," Reilly said as she stepped back with his weapon and leather holster. "Your phone?"

He handed it over. "You want my wallet?"

"Yes, but you can keep your driver's license."

When the handoffs were finished, she tacked on, "Further, I'll ask you to remove your clothing at home, bag it, and turn it in to me tomorrow."

"No problem. And you know where to find me," he said, his voice gruff.

"Yes, I do."

As they got ready to part, there was no coy duck of her chin and flash of the eyes. No hair flipping. No brush of the hip. Which, okay, would have been ridiculous under the circumstances—but he had the sense that the two of them could have been at a club by the bar and she wouldn't have pulled any of that obvious crap anyway. Not her style.

Shit, she really did just keep getting more attractive by the minute. This kept up and he was going to end up asking her to marry him next week.

Har-har, hardy-har-har.

On that note, Veck turned away from her for the second time. And was surprised to hear her say, "You sure you don't want a coat, Detective? I've got an extra flak jacket in my trunk, and it's going to be cold on that bike of yours."

"I'll be fine."

For some reason, he didn't want to look back. Probably because of the peanut-gallery combo of de la Cruz and Bails.

Yeah. That was it.

At his BMW, he threw his leg over the seat and grabbed his helmet. He hadn't worn the damn thing on the way here, but he needed to conserve body heat—and as he pulled it on, he half expected de la Cruz to wander over to revisit the lawyer issue. Instead, the venerable detective stayed where he was and spoke with Officer Reilly.

Bails was the one who came up. The guy was in gym clothes, his short hair spiky, his dark eyes a little aggressive—no doubt because he didn't like Reilly taking over. "You sure you're okay to get home?"

"Yeah."

"You want me to follow you?"

"Nah." Likely the guy would anyway. He was just that way.

"I know you didn't do it."

As Veck stared at his buddy, he was tempted to unload everything—the two sides to him, the split that he had felt coming for years, the fear that what he'd worried about had finally happened. Hell, he knew he could trust the guy. He and Bails had been at the police academy together years ago, and though they'd gone their separate ways, they'd stayed tight and in touch—until Bails had recruited him to come up from Manhattan to join the Caldwell homicide team.

Two weeks. He'd been on the force here for only two frickin' weeks.

Just as he opened his mouth, a van pulled behind to other CPD cars, announcing the arrival of Team Nitpick.

Veck shook his head. "Thanks, man. I'll see you tomorrow."

With a swift punch of his boot, he kick-started the engine, and as he pumped the gas, he glanced back to the scene. Reilly was kneeling by his jacket, going through its pockets. Just like she was going to do with his wallet.

Oh, shit. She was going to find—

"Call me if you want me to come over, man."

"Yeah. I will."

Veck nodded at Bails and eased his bike off the shoulder, thinking he really didn't need her to see the two Trojans he always kept in that inside slot behind his credit cards.

Funny, being a slut had never really bothered him before. Now, he wished he'd tied it in a knot years ago.

When he got out to the proper road, he gunned the bike hard, and went roaring off. As he rocketed through 149's twists and turns, he leaned into the corners, ducking down tight over the handlebars, becoming just another aerodynamic part of the BMW. With his lick-split velocity, winding turns became nothing but quick jogs left and right as he and the bike wagered on the laws of physics.

Given that he was betting everything he had at this speed? He'd be lucky if he left anything big enough to bury.

Faster. *Faster.* Fast—

Unfortunately, or fortunately, he wasn't sure which, the end for him did not come in a screeching rip into the trees to avoid a Buick or a Bambi.

It was a Polo Ralph Lauren outlet store.

Or specifically, the light right before the place.

Pulling out of the tunnel vision he'd enjoyed made him feel strangely disoriented, and the only reason he stopped at the red was that there were a couple of cars in front of him and he was forced to obey the traffic laws or ride over their roofs. The goddamn light took forever, and the lineup he was in moved at a snail's pace when it finally got its green on.

Then again, he could have been popping sixty-five on the highway and it would have felt like he was twiddling his thumbs.

But it wasn't like he was trying to run from something. Of course not.

Passing by Nike, Van Heusen, and Brooks Brothers, he felt as empty as the huge parking lots, and there was a part of him that wanted to keep going ... past this retail fringe, through Caldie's suburban maze, out around the skyscrapers, and over the bridge to God only knew where.

The trouble was, everywhere he went ... there he was: Geographical relocation wasn't going to change the face in the mirror. Or that part of him that he'd never understood, but never questioned. Or what the fuck had gone down tonight.

He must have killed that sick bastard. There was no other explanation. And he didn't know what Reilly was thinking in letting him go. Maybe he just needed to confess. ... Yeah, but to what? That he went there with the intent to kill, and then he—

The headache that plowed into his front lobe was the kind of thing you couldn't think around. All you did was groan and close your eyes—not the best move when you were on a bike that was basically just an engine with a padded seat screwed to it.

Forcing himself to focus on the road and nothing else, he was relieved when the cranial thumping eased off and he pulled into his development.

The house he lived in was in a neighborhood full of teachers, nurses, and sales reps. There were a lot of young kids, and the yards were maintained by amateurs—which meant in the summer there was probably going to be a lot of crabgrass, but at least the shit would be mowed regularly.

Veck was the outlier: He had no wife, no kids, and he was never going to bust out a Toro or a Lawn-Boy. Fortunately, he had the vibe that the neighbors on either side of his postage stamp of a yard were the type to cheerfully encroach with their blades.

Good people. Who had told them they felt safer with a cop next door.

Showed what they knew.

His two-story house was about as fancy and unique as a penny from the seventies. Which, as it turned out, was the last time the place had been wallpapered.

Pulling up to the garage, he dismounted and left his helmet hanging from the handlebars. There wasn't a lot of crime in this area—so his mowing neighbors were getting a bum deal on a lot of levels.

He went in the side door, passed through the mudroom and walked into his kitchen. Not a lot of Food Network going down in here: all he had were a couple of empty pizza boxes on the counter, and some Starbucks dead soldiers clustered around the sink. Half-opened mail and loosely stacked reports were on the table. Laptop was closed down for the day next to a Valpak coupon book he was never going to use and a cable bill that was not yet overdue but probably would be because he sucked at paying shit on time.

Always too busy to write a check out or go online to pay.

God, the only difference between this place and the office downtown was the fact that there was a king-size bed upstairs.

On that note, Officer Reilly wanted him to get naked, didn't she.

Snagging a Glad trash bag from under the kitchen sink, he went upstairs, thinking he was going to have to hire a cleaner to come once a week so that he didn't end up with cobwebs in every corner and dust bunnies going IVF clinic under the couch. But this was no home and was never going to be. Pine-Sol and 409 four times a month didn't get you cozy.

Although at least the occasional chick he brought in would have somewhere halfway decent to get re-dressed in.

His bedroom was at the front of the house, and all it had in it was that big bed and a bureau. His boots, socks and pants came off quick. Turtleneck was the same. As he peeled off his black boxer briefs, he refused to think of Officer Reilly handling them. Just was not going to go there.

Heading into the bath, he turned on the shower, and as he waited for it to get warm, he stood in front of the mirror over the sink. No reflection to bother with—he'd covered the glass with a beach towel the day he'd moved in.

He was not a fan of mirrors.

Lifting his hands, he held them out palms down. Then flipped them. Then looked under his nails.

It appeared as though his body, as with his mind, was empty of clues. Although you could argue that no scratches, no blood, no gore on him was an indicator—and no doubt what the fine Officer Reilly had noticed and acted on.

Man, this was the second time in his life he'd been in this situation. And the first . . .

No reason to think about his mother's murder. Not on a night like tonight.

Stepping into the shower, he closed his eyes and let the spray fall down his head and shoulders and face. Soap. Rinse. Shampoo. Rinse.

He was standing in the steamy, wet heat when he felt the draft: Sure as if someone had opened the window by the toilet, the blast of air shot over the top of the plastic curtain and brushed across his skin. Goose bumps came when called, popping out across his chest and shooting down his legs and back.

The window hadn't been opened, however.

And this was why he'd removed the glass wall of the shower and covered that built-in mirror over the sink. Those two things had been the only changes he'd made to the house, and the unimprovement had been for his own sanity. He'd been shaving for years without his reflection.

"Get the fuck away from me," he said, closing his eyes and keeping them that way.

The draft swirled around his legs, feeling like hands roaming over his flesh, going higher, fondling his sex before hitting his abdomen and his pecs, up to his neck . . . his face. . . .

Cold hands ran through his hair—

"Leave me alone!" He threw out his arm and shoved the curtain aside. As warm air greeted him, he bore down at his core, trying to kick the intruder out, kill the connection.

Stumbling over to the counter, he braced his arms and leaned down, breathing hard and hating himself, hating this night, hating his life.

He knew damn well that it was possible, if you had multiple personality disorder, for a part of you to break free and act independently. Sufferers could be completely unaware of the actions their body had taken, even if it involved violence—

As that headache started kicking his temples like tires again, he cursed and dried off; then pulled on the flannel shirt and NYPD academy sweatpants he'd slept in the night before and left on the back of the toilet. He was about to go downstairs when a quick glance out the window held him in place.

There was a car parked across the street about two houses down.

He knew every vehicle in the neighborhood, all the trucks, vans, SUVs, sedans, and hybrids, and that shadow-colored, late-model American nothing-much was not on the list.

It was, however, exactly the kind of unmarked that the Caldwell Police Department used.

Reilly was having him surveilled. Good move—exactly what he would have done in her position.

Might even be her in the flesh.

Hitting the stairs, he hesitated at the front door, drawn to go out in his bare feet, because maybe she, or whoever it was, had some answers from the scene. . . .

With a curse, he pulled himself out of that bright idea and headed for the kitchen. There had to be something to eat in the cupboards. Had to be.

Pulling them open and finding a lot of shelf space and nothing more, he wondered exactly what grocery-fairy he thought had magically come and delivered food.

Then again he could just throw some ketchup on a pizza box and chow down. Probably good for his fiber intake.

Yum.

Two houses down from Detective DelVecchio's, Reilly was behind the wheel and partially blinded.

"By all that is holy . . ." She rubbed her eyes. "Do you not believe in curtains?"

As she prayed for the image of a spectacularly naked colleague to fade from her retinas, she seriously rethought her decision to do the stakeout herself. She was exhausted, for one thing—or had been before she'd seen just about everything Veck had to offer.

Take out the *just*.

One bene was that she was really frickin' awake now, thank you very much—she might as well have licked two fingers and shoved them into a socket: a full-frontal like that was enough to give her the perm she'd wanted back when she'd been thirteen.

Muttering to herself, she dropped her hands into her lap again. And gee whiz, as she stared at the dash, all she saw . . . was everything she'd seen.

Yeah, wow, on some men, no clothes was so much more than just *naked*.

And to think she'd almost missed the show. She'd parked her unmarked and just called in her position when the up-stairs lights had gone on and she gotten a gander at the vista of a bedroom. Easing back into her seat, it hadn't dawned on her exactly where the unobstructed view was going to take them both—she'd just been interested that it appeared to be nothing but a bald lightbulb on the ceiling of what had to be the master suite.

Then again, bachelor pad decorating tended to be either storage-unit crammed or Death Valley–barren.

Veck was obviously the Death Valley variety.

Except suddenly she hadn't been thinking about inte-rior decorating, because her suspect had stepped into the bathroom and flipped the switch.

Hellllllllo, big boy.

In too many ways to count.

"Stop thinking about it . . . stop thinking about—"

Closing her eyes again didn't help: If she'd reluctantly noticed before how well he filled out his clothes, now she knew exactly why. He was heavily muscled, and given that he didn't have any hair on his chest, there was nothing to obscure those hard pecs and that six-pack and the carved ridges that went over his hips.

Matter of fact, when it came to manscaping, all he had was a dark stripe that ran between his belly button and his . . .

You know, maybe size did matter, she thought.

"Oh, for chrissakes."

In an attempt to get her brain focused on something, anything more appropriate, she leaned forward and looked out the opposite window. As far as she could tell, the house directly across from him had privacy shades across every available view. Good move, assuming he paraded around like that every night.

Then again, maybe the husband had strung those puppies up so that his wife didn't get a case of the swoons.

Bracing herself, she glanced back at Veck's place. The lights were off upstairs and she had to hope now that he was dressed and on the first floor, he stayed that way.

God, what a night.

She was still waiting for any evidence that came from the scene, but she'd made up her mind already about Kroner's injuries. There were coyotes in those woods. Bears. Cats of the non–Meow Mix variety. Chances were good that the guy had come walking through there with the scent of dried blood on his clothes and something with four paws had viewed him as a Happy Meal. Veck could well have tried to step in and been shoved to the side. After all, he'd been rubbing his temples like he'd had pain there, and God knew head trauma had been known to cause short-term memory loss.

The lack of physical evidence on him supported the theory; that was for sure.

And yet . . .

God, that father of his. It was impossible not to factor him in even a little.

Like every criminal justice major, she'd studied Thomas DelVecchio Sr. as part of her courses—but she'd also spent considerable time on him in her deviant-psych classes. Veck's dad was your classic serial killer: smart, cunning, committed to his "craft," utterly remorseless. And yet, having watched videos of his interviews with police, he came across as handsome, compelling, and affable. Classy. Very non-monster.

But then again, like a lot of psychopaths, he'd cultivated an image and sustained it with care. He'd been very successful as a dealer of antiquities, although his establishment in that haughty, lofty world of money and privilege had been a complete self-invention. He'd come from absolutely nothing, but had had a knack for charming rich people—as well as a talent for going overseas and coming back with ancient artifacts and statues that were extremely marketable. It wasn't until the killings had started to surface that his business practices came under scrutiny, and to this day, no one had any idea where he'd found the stuff he had—it was almost as if he'd had a treasure trove somewhere in the Middle East. He certainly hadn't helped authorities sort things out, but what were they going to do to him? He was already on death row.

Not for much longer, though, evidently.

What had Veck's mother been like—

The knock on the window next to her head was like a shot ringing out, and she had her weapon palmed and pointed to the sound less than a heartbeat afterward.

Veck was standing in the street next to her car, his hands up, his wet hair glossy in the streetlights.

Lowering her weapon, she put her window down with a curse.

"Quick reflexes, Officer," he murmured.

"Do you want to get shot, Detective?"

"I said your name. Twice. You were deep in thought."

Thanks to what she'd seen in that bathroom, the flannel shirt and academy sweats he had on seemed eminently removable, the kind of duds that wouldn't resist a shove up or a pull down. But come on, like she hadn't seen every aisle in his grocery store already?

"You want my clothes now?" he said as he held up a trash bag.

"Yes, thank you." She accepted the load through her window and put the things down on the floor. "Boots, too?"

As he nodded, he said, "Can I bring you some coffee? I don't have much in my kitchen, but I think I can find a clean mug and I got instant."

"Thanks. I'm okay."

There was a pause. "There a reason you're not looking me in the eye, Officer?"

I just saw you buck naked, Detective. "Not at all." She pegged him right in the peepers. "You should get inside. It's chilly."

"The cold doesn't bother me. You going to be here all night?"

"Depends."

"On whether I am, right."

"Yup."

He nodded, and then glanced around casually like they were nothing but neighbors chatting about the weather. So calm. So confident. Just like his father.

"Can I be honest with you?" he said abruptly.

"You'd better be, Detective."

"I'm still surprised you let me go."

She ran her hands around the steering wheel. "May I be honest with you?"

"Yeah."

"I let you go because I really don't think you did it."

"I was at the scene and I had blood on me."

"You called nine-one-one, you didn't leave, and that kind of death is very messy to perpetrate."

"Maybe I cleaned up."

"There wasn't a shower in those woods as far as I saw."

Do. Not. Think. Of. Him. Naked.

When he started to shake his head like he was going to argue, Reilly cut him off. "Why are you trying to convince me I'm wrong?"

That shut him up. At least for a moment. Then he said in a low voice, "Are you going to feel safe tailing me."

"Why wouldn't I?"

For the first time, emotion bled through his cool expression, and her heart stopped: There was fear in his eyes, as if he didn't trust himself.

"Veck," she said softly, "is there anything I don't know."

He crossed his arms over that big chest of his and his weight went back and forth on his hips as if he were thinking. Then he hissed, and started rubbing his temple.

"I've got nothing," he muttered. "Listen, just do us both a favor, Officer. Keep that gun close by."

He didn't look back as he turned and walked across the street.

He wasn't wearing any shoes, she realized.

Putting up the window, she watched him go into the house and shut the door. Then the lights in the house went out, except for the hallway on the second floor.

Settling in, she eased down in her seat and stared at all those windows. Shortly thereafter, a massive shadow walked into the living room—or rather, appeared to be dragging something? Like a couch?

Then Veck sat down and his head disappeared as if he were stretching out on something.

It was almost like they were sleeping side by side. Well, except for the walls of the house, the stretch of scruffy spring lawn, the sidewalk, the asphalt, and the steel cage of her Crown Victoria.

Reilly's lids drifted down, but that was a function of the angle of her head. She wasn't tired and she wasn't worried about falling asleep. She was wide-awake in the dark interior of the car.

And yet she reached over and hit the door-lock button. Just in case.

CHAPTER
4

As the demon Devina wandered up and back across cold concrete, her path was not straight, but full of curves. Winding in and out of rows of bureaus, the discordant *tick-tock*ing of hundreds of clocks drowned out the *clip-clip* of her Louboutins.

Everything had been given a place here, her collection safely moved into the basement of this two-story office building. The location was perfect, just outside of Caldwell's downtown, and to appear legitimate and uncontroversial, she projected an illusion that a human resources firm took up the space above where she was pacing: As far as people were aware, a hustling, bustling business had rented the place to accommodate its expansion.

Stupid humans. As if in this economy anyone was hiring or could afford hand-holding when it came to filling jobs.

Pausing by a Hepplewhite bow front that had been made in Providence, Rhode Island, in 1801, she ran her hand over the mahogany top. The original finish was still on the piece, but then again, she'd kept the thing safe from sun and water damage since she'd bought it over two hundred years before. In its drawers were baskets full of buttons and rows of spectacles and jumbles of rings in boxes. The other bureaus had similar objects, all personal items fashioned out of various metals.

Aside from her mirror, this collection of hers was the most precious thing she had. It was the tie to her souls down below, the tethering security she needed when she felt insecure or stressed-out here on earth.

As she did now.

The problem tonight, however, was that for the first time since she'd started hoarding aeons ago, she was not calmed, nor reassured, nor eased. Walking around this repository of objects, she was summarily unaided by the addiction that had long proved to be so useful.

And what seemed even worse? This evening should have been "a seminal moment," as her therapist called them, a time to center herself and savor her accomplishments: She had won the last round against Jim Heron, and even though he and Adrian and Eddie had infiltrated her previous lair, she had safely gotten her things installed in this new, secure facility.

She should have been fucking ecstatic.

But shit-on-a-shingle, even the scent of fresh death drifting over from the bathroom gave her no pleasure: To protect her mirror, she needed so much more than what ADT or Brinks monitoring had to offer, and the new sacrificial virgin she'd strung up over her tub was bleeding out nicely—getting ready to be useful, not just decorative.

Everything was going her way, at least on the surface, and yet she felt so . . .

Ennui, she believed it was called . . . and what a lovely name for such a crappy, unmotivated state.

Maybe she was just exhausted from setting everything up after the move. She had about forty bureaus full of acquisitions from all eras of humanity, and whenever she was forced to reestablish herself in another place, she was compelled to touch every single object one by one, reconnecting with the essence of the victim that lingered in the metal. She had yet to start on the contact ritual, however, and was a little surprised at herself. Usually, she could focus on nothing else until she fractured time, stepped into the space between minutes, and completed the lengthy process.

She supposed her therapist would have seen this as progress, considering the compulsion was typically prompt and undeniable: These precious items, from ancient Egypt to Gothic France to the Civil War and the present here in the States, were what tied her to home when she was so far away.

Still, there was no panicky rush to snuggle up with what was hers for eternity. All she seemed to want to do was mope around and pace.

It was all Jim Heron's fault.

He was just too defiant. Dominant. Extraordinary.

He had been chosen by her and that supercilious son-ofabitch Nigel because Heron was equal parts good and evil—and as she had learned through the ages, when it came to mankind, evil always won. In fact, she'd assumed that drawing him over to her side would be nothing but a tedious bore, the kind of thing she had done to men and women since time had cast its first hour so very long ago.

Instead . . . it was she who had been sucked in and seduced.

Heron was just so . . . unownable. Even when he had turned himself over to her and she had been playing with him, her minions swarming him, her true nature revealed . . . he had been unbowed, unbending, unyielding.

And that strength made him unattainable.

She had never known that before. From anyone.

The thing was, it was in her very nature to take over: She was a perfect parasite, niggling her way in and replicating her essence until what she had entered became hers forever.

Heron's challenge to her was intoxicating, a slap in the face, a breath of fresh air. But it also seemed to deflate the importance of everything else.

Pulling open a drawer, she took out a thin gold bracelet that had a little dove charm dangling off of it. The inscription on the inside was in cursive and just precious. From parents to a daughter. With a date from the year before. Blah, blah, blah.

She hated the name Cecilia. She really did.

That irrelevant virgin ... what a thorn in her side. The purpose of that Barten girl had been to protect the mirror. Now the little shit had some kind of connection with Jim—

Just as she was going to crush the fragile memento, a waft of warmth went through her, as if a lover's touch had passed not just over her flesh, but through to her very bones.

Jim.

It was *Jim*. Calling to *her*.

Ditching the bracelet, she hip-checked the drawer closed and ran down the row to an ornate floor-length mirror that functioned only to check her appearance. As she went, she changed her form, assuming the body of a gorgeous brunette who had gravity-defying breasts and an ass with more ledge than a bookshelf.

Fluffing her hair, she smoothed her black skirt, and decided the hem was too long. Willing it upward, she pivoted and flashed her smooth thighs and perfect calves.

Suddenly, she was *alive*.

Well, *alive* wasn't technically correct. But that was what it felt like: In the space of a moment, her mood had gone from buried to flying.

Except she was not going to be stupid about this.

Confident of her hemline, her neckline, and her hairline, she went into the bathroom.

"How do I look?"

She did a little twirl in front of the young man who was hanging upside down over her tub. Except he didn't have anything to say, even though his eyes were open.

"Oh, what the hell do you know."

She bent down and dipped her fingertips into the blood that had been steadily draining out of his carotid artery. Impatient with the delay, she quickly traced around the doorjambs and the floor, going back and forth to the tub to get more. The purity of his essence formed a seal that was better than any security alarm any human could ever create—plus, the process rid the world of one more mortal creature.

Made her job easier.

Closing herself in with Mr. Chatty, she turned to face the ancient mirror that hung in a mangy frame that had rotted out centuries and centuries ago. The leaded-glass surface had a constantly shifting reflection, waves of dark gray and black swirling around a background the color of a rug stain. The thing was a hideous portal, and the only way for her to get to her well of souls.

"Hang out," she told the stiff. "I'll be back."

Stepping through the surface of the mirror, she was pulled into a vicious suction, and she gave herself over freely, the body she assumed going taffy through the wormhole. On the far side, she emerged at the base of her well, spit out of the tempest, but requiring no time to recover.

As she patted her hair, and smoothed her tight skirt, she thought how stupid it was not to have a mirror here.

Then again, she didn't care what her minions' opinions were, and her souls ... oh, her lovely souls ... well, they had other things on their minds.

Tilting her head back, she looked up at the miles of shiny black walls that rose up from the stone floor. The tortured damned writhed against the confines of their viscous prison, faces and hips and knees and elbows straining for a freedom that they would never attain, their woeful voices multi-layered and muffled.

"How do I look?" she shouted upward.

The chorus of moans rose in reply, but told her absolutely nothing.

For fuck's sake, couldn't she get a witness somewhere? Anywhere?

After a last double-check of herself, she granted access to Jim, summoning him forth. And as she waited, her heart beat triple-time, a flush charging every inch of her skin with an electric sizzle. But she was not going to show it. Cool. Keep it cool.

Jim arrived in a swirl of mist, and her breath caught.

The chosen savior was the very best of the male sex. Built big and lethal, his body was an instrument of warfare, but it was also made for fucking. Raw, pounding . . .

"You want me," she said in a low voice.

His eyes narrowed, and the hatred in them did more for her libido than the best plate of oysters anyone had ever served up. "Not like that, sweetheart."

Oh, how he lied.

Swaying her hips, she went over to the worktable and trailed her fingertips across the pitted, discolored surface. Memories of him tied down naked, his legs spread and his sex glistening from use, made her breathe deep.

"No?" she said. "You called me. Not the other way around."

"I want you to tell me who the next soul is."

Interesting. "So Nigel turned you down when you asked him, did he."

"Didn't say that."

"Well, I find it hard to believe you'd come to me first," she muttered bitterly. "And you think I'm going to tell you?"

"Yeah, I do."

She laughed in a violent burst. "You should know what I'm like by now."

"And you're going to tell me."

"Why in the world would I . . ."

His hand lifted to his heavy chest and slowly, oh, so slowly, drifted down his stomach. . . .

Devina swallowed hard. And then her mouth went totally dry as he cupped himself between his legs.

"I have something you want," he said roughly. "And vice versa."

Well, well, well . . . She wanted to be with him, yes, but this was even better than voluntary coupling. He was going to have to force himself to have sex with her, sacrificing his flesh to her for information . . . in front of his dear, sweet Sissy.

Devina looked up to her wall and found the soul he was

so goddamned concerned with. Willing the girl downward, she leaned back against the table.

"Exactly what are you proposing."

"Tell me who it is and I'll fuck you."

"Make love to me."

"It'll be fucking. Trust me."

"A rose by any other name . . . But I'm not sure." What a lie. "That's very valuable information."

"And you know what *I'm* like."

Oh, she did, and she wanted him again. Wanted him always.

"Fine," she said. "I'll tell you who it is, and in return, you will give yourself to me whenever I want you. You will be at my beck and call."

His eyes narrowed again in that way they did, turning into slits that made him look like a predator.

And then there was only silence. As the quiet stretched out, she held tight. He was going to come around, and oddly enough, she had Nigel, the tight-ass rule abider, to thank for it. If that archangel had breathed the name of the soul, this wonderful sacrifice wouldn't be getting made.

"Done."

Devina began to smile—

"With a caveat." As she froze the expression, he said, "I'll be with you now and you give me the name. Then we'll see if it's the right one. At the end of this round, if you didn't lie . . . you've got me. Whenever you want me."

Devina growled. Fucking piece of shit free will. If she could just own him properly, he wouldn't get a vote at all. But that was not the way it worked.

Although there were still loopholes to be had, she told herself. Ways to shade this so that she didn't give too much away and yet managed to have him regardless.

"Do we have a deal," he demanded.

Walking forward to him, she focused over his shoulder at the small shape in the wall that she had called down for a close, ringside seat at what was going to happen.

As Devina stepped into that hard body and rose up onto

her tiptoes, she reveled in the utterly rigid flesh she brushed against. Into Heron's ear, she whispered, "Take off your pants."

"Deal or no deal, demon."

He was unbending before her, perfectly capable of denying her, not just now but in the future: Even though he was right in front of her, he was completely untouchable.

Except as he'd said, they both had something the other wanted.

"Take off your pants." She stepped back, ready to enjoy the show. "Do it slowly—and we have a deal."

"What the *hell* is he doing up there?"

As Adrian barked out the rhetorical, he didn't expect a response from his roommate. Then again, you could drop a Lexus on Eddie's combat boot and maybe you got an *ow*. More likely the angel would just blink and kick the sedan off his big toe.

Frankly, the strong-and-silent bullshit got to be annoying.

"It's been two hours." He stopped at the foot of the bed Eddie was sprawled out on. "Hello? You tracking at all? Or were you planning on sleeping through this round."

The lids on that red stare lifted. "I'm not sleeping."

"Meditating. Whatever."

"I wasn't meditating."

"Fine. Psychically manipulating energy fields—"

"You make me dizzy when you pace. It's vertigo diversion."

He didn't buy that for a second. "Would it kill you to get worried once in a while."

"Who says I'm not."

"I do." Adrian ran his eyeballs down his buddy's long, still body. "I feel like rolling in a defibrillator and paddling your ass."

"What am I going to do, Ad? He's going to come back when he does."

Images of Nigel, the dandy, going galactically stoopid all

over Jim came to mind, and made Adrian wonder if they'd need to plan a memorial service. That archangel up there might pass his time playing croquet and polo, but that didn't mean he couldn't rip into a guy—and Jim had left here with a whole lot of throw down on his mind.

Maybe the bastard had gotten what he was looking for.

Adrian started up with the pacing again, but the hotel room didn't offer much in terms of floor space. He supposed he could go down to the bar—

Next door, there was a creaking sound. Like someone had sat down on the bed. Or opened and closed something.

Reaching behind to the small of his back, Ad withdrew his crystal knife. If it was just some human breaking in to steal a laptop, he wasn't going to need what was in his palm. But if Devina had sent over a minion or two to distract them, the weapon was going to come in handy.

Pushing the connector open an inch or two, he leaned in.

A black shirt came flying out of the bathroom. Then a pair of beat-to-shit jeans.

Boot.

Boot.

The shower started running and then there was a hiss, like Jim hadn't waited for the water to warm up first.

Shit. He hadn't just been to see Nigel, had he.

Reholstering his dagger, Adrian shoved the door wide, walked through and sat on the other angel's bed.

God knew there was no reason to ditch the duds and hot-water it right after you met with the archangel. Poor bastard must have been to Devina's—and nobody needed two guesses to figure out what had happened.

Listening to the sound of Jim washing the stank of the demon off, Adrian was weary to the point of blurry-vision exhaustion. This path the savior was on? Been there. Done that.

Lost his mind over it.

That was the thing with Devina. She got into you. Even though, in the beginning, you thought you were the one in control? Eventually, what you were making yourself do with her, for reasons that sounded entirely sane, ate at you until she was inside your skin and driving your bus. It was how she worked, and she was very successful at it.

When Jim eventually stepped out of the bathroom, he stopped with the towel stretched across his back, one arm up, the other down. There were scratch marks on his thighs and abdomen, and his sex hung low, as if it had been used hard and left for dead.

"She's going to eat you alive," Adrian said.

The angel who was responsible for saving everyone and everything shook his head. "The hell she will."

"Jim—"

"She's going to tell us who the soul is." Jim wrapped the towel around his hips. "We're meeting her tomorrow morning."

Holy. Shit— "Wait, she didn't give the info to you now?"

"Tomorrow morning."

Ad just shook his head. "She's fucking with you—"

"She'll show. And she'll tell. Trust me."

"She's not a reliable source. And this is not the way to win."

"So you liked last round's outcome better?"

Well . . . fuck.

Jim went over to his black duffel and took out a pair of fatigues. As he turned away and pulled them on, that massive back tat of his, the one featuring the Grim Reaper in a graveyard, distorted and then refound its shape.

Maybe Jim was tougher.

Which would be a slap in the balls, and something Ad would admit only over his own steaming carcass. But if the guy could hold it together . . . if he could somehow sustain himself . . . then they had the best weapon in this fight because the demon had a jones for the guy. Bad.

Jim went over to the jeans he'd tossed out of the bathroom and rifled through the pockets. When he stood back up again, he had a square of folded paper in his hands.

Hands that shook ever so slightly.

As the guy carefully brushed off the thing, even though

there was no lint on it, Adrian scrubbed his face and wished a Lexus would fall on his own head: He knew damn well that had to be the article on that girl they'd found hanging over Devina's tub—the virgin Jim was obsessed with.

Tougher his ass, Ad thought. They were fucked.

They were *so* fucked.

CHAPTER
5

Veck woke up on his living room sofa. Which was sort of a surprise, because he didn't have one.

As he rubbed his eyes against the cheerful spring sunlight, he was amazed that he'd taken the desire to sleep closer to the fine Officer Reilly as far as dragging the POS in from his man cave of a family room.

Sitting up, he looked out into the street. The unmarked was gone, and he wondered when she'd left. Last he'd checked, she'd still been out there at four a.m.

Groaning, he gave things a stretch, his shoulders cracking. Details from the night before filtered back, but he instinctually stayed away from the Monroe Motel & Suites part. He already felt like hell; he didn't need to add a headache to the steaming pile of fuck-me he was rocking.

When he stood up, he had to rearrange an obscene morning erection—which gave him another thing to studiously ignore. He had a feeling he'd been wrapped up in a fairly raunchy and totally spectacular dream about him and his Internal Affairs shadow. Something about her riding him raw . . . he'd been mostly clothed; she'd been completely naked—

No, wait, she'd had her badge and her gun and her hip belt on.

"Fuck . . ." As his cock kicked hard, he put in a prayer for another round of short-term memory loss, and cursed at the porn cliché.

Then again, he could now see why guys found that shit attractive.

Given the direction his brain was heading in, he wasn't sure that adding caffeine to the mix was a good plan, but his body needed the lift. Too bad he'd discovered he'd lied to Officer Reilly: after coming back inside from talking to her, he'd realized he'd run out of Folgers.

Upstairs, he showered, shaved, and put on his working uniform of slacks and a dress shirt. No tie for him, although a lot of the detectives wore them. No suit jacket; he didn't wear one unless it was leather and of the biker or bomber variety.

Downstairs, he got his backup coat out of the closet, grabbed the key to his bike, and locked things up. As he walked over to the BMW, he was dogged by the night before, but also feeling too light: No cell to check for voice mail. No badge in his breast pocket. No gun in his holster. No wallet on his ass.

Officer Reilly had all of that. And his BVDs.

Squeezing on his helmet and mounting up, the morning was too frickin' bright and shiny for him—and this was without the sun being fully up. Hell, given the squint he was rocking, it was a good thing his bike knew where he was going.

De la Cruz had introduced him to the Riverside Diner just the other day, and already Veck wondered how he'd managed without the greasy spoon. Heading for the place, he took the surface roads in, because even at seven forty-five, the Northway was going to be crowded.

The dive was right on the shores of the Hudson, only about four blocks from HQ—and it wasn't until he pulled into the parking lot full of unmarkeds that he second-guessed his destination. Chances were good that half the force was sucking java inside, as usual, but it was too late to go anywhere else.

Just before he went in, he palmed up seventy-five cents and grabbed a *Caldwell Courier Journal* from the dispenser box outside. There was nothing about last night on the first page above the fold, so he flipped the thing over, looking for an article—

And there was his name. In bold.

Except the reporting wasn't about him or Kroner. It was something on his old man, and he quickly avoided the piece. He hadn't kept up with the charges, the trial, the death row sentence, anything that had to do with his father. And gee whiz, when he'd been taking criminal justice, he'd been sick the day they'd covered the case.

The rest of the first section was clear, so was the Local, and naturally, there was nothing in the Sports/Comics/Classified caboose. The lack of coverage wasn't going to last, however: Reporters had access to the police blotter, and the story was probably on the television and radio news already. A homicide detective so prominently associated with the mauling of a psycho? That shit sold papers and justified ad prices.

Pushing open the glass door, he went into the Riverside's cacophony with his face buried in the nonheadlines of the Sports section. The place was packed, and as loud and hot as a bar, and he studiously didn't make eye contact with anyone as he scanned around for a free stool at the counter or an empty booth along the edges.

Nothing was vacant. Damn it. And he wasn't about to join a table of CPDers. The last thing he needed was a lot of questions from his colleagues. Maybe he should just go on to HQ and hit the vending machine—

"Morning, Detective."

Veck glanced over to the right. The fine Officer Reilly was sitting in the booth closest to the door, her back to him, her head cranked over her shoulder to look up at him. There was a cup of coffee in front of her, a cell phone in her hand, and a whole lot of no-nonsense on her face.

"Care to join me?" she said, motioning across her table.

She had to be kidding. There were about a dozen members of the force staring over at them—some more surreptitiously than others.

"You sure you want to be seen with me?"

"Why? Do you have terrible table manners?"

"You know what I mean."

She shrugged and took a sip from her cup. "Our meeting with the sergeant is in about twenty minutes. You'll be lucky to have a seat by then."

Veck slid in opposite her. "I thought in Internal Affairs you guys always worried about propriety."

"This is just two eggs over easy, Detective."

He put his newspaper aside. "Fair enough."

The waitress came over with her pad out and her pencil ready. "What'll it be."

No reason to look at a menu. Riverside had every omelet, egg, and toast known to man. You wanted pie for breakfast? A BLT? Cereal, oatmeal, pancakes? Fine, whatever—just order quick and eat fast so someone else could get a seat.

"Three scrambled. Hard. White toast with butter. Coffee. Thanks."

The waitress smiled at him, like she approved of the efficiency. "Comin' up."

Annnnnd then he was alone again with Reilly. She'd had a shower and changed into a professional skirt-and-buttondown combo. The jacket that went with the outfit was folded neatly beside her on top of her coat. Her dark red hair was once again pulled back from her face, and she had just a little lipstick on for makeup.

Matter of fact, as she put down her coffee cup, there was a half-moon of pink where she'd put her mouth. Not that he was looking for details on her lips. Really.

"I have a preliminary report from the field," she said.

Huh ... those eyes weren't just green, as he'd assumed before. They were hazel-ish, made up of a unique combination of colors that merely appeared green from a distance. "I'm sorry, what did you say?"

"I have last night's prelim."

"And?"

"No other weapons were found in the area."

He kept his relief to himself out of habit.

And before he could comment, the waitress put down his coffee and Reilly's breakfast: a bowl of oatmeal with a side of toast. No butter.

"Is that whole-wheat?" he asked.

"Yes, it is."

Of course it was. She probably had a light salad for lunch with a protein, and one glass of wine, if that, with a dinner that was all about root vegetables, grilled chicken, and a low-glycemic-index starch of some kind.

He wondered what she thought of the heart attack special he'd ordered.

"Please don't wait for me," he said.

She picked up her spoon and added a little brown sugar and cream. "You want to know what I think happened?"

"Yeah, I do."

"It was a wild animal attack and you got knocked in the head in the process."

He brushed his face. "No bruises."

"Could have fallen backward."

Matter of fact, he thought maybe he had? "But no bumps. And then my coat would have been dirty all over."

"It is."

"Only from when I put it on Kroner."

She lowered her spoon. "Can you verify that? How do you know when it got soiled if you can't remember anything? Besides, your head was killing you last night, and P.S., you're doing it again."

"Doing what?"

"Arguing with me about this. As well as rubbing your temple." As he cursed and relocated his hand to his mug of coffee, she smiled with an edge. "Guess what, Detective? You're getting yourself checked out at HQ right after our meeting."

"I'm fine." Christ, he could hear the bitch in his own voice.

"Remember what I said last night, Detective? That's an order."

As he sat back and drank some of his wakey-wakey, he caught himself checking out her ring finger. Nothing there. Not even a circular indent as if something *had* been there.

He wished she was sporting a solitaire and a band: He didn't do wives knowingly. Ever. No doubt he'd been with a couple in his long history of anonymous hookups, but it had been only because they hadn't told him.

He was a man-whore with standards, don't you know.

"Why aren't you suspending me?"

"Again with the negative."

"I don't want you ruining your career over me," he muttered.

"And I have no intention of allowing that to happen. But there is no evidence that you were responsible for the attack, Detective, and plenty that says you weren't—and I really don't get why you keep pushing me on this."

As he stared into those eyes of hers, he heard himself say, "You know who my father is, don't you."

That put her in pause-mode for a moment, her triangle of unbuttered fiber goodness halfway back down to her plate. She even stopped in midchew.

But then the fine Officer Reilly recovered with a shrug. "Of course I do, but that doesn't mean you tore up somebody." She leaned in. "But that's what you're afraid of, aren't you. And that's why you keep playing devil's advocate."

The waitress picked that moment to show up with his steaming plate of cholesterol, and the arrival was a conversational lifesaver if he'd ever seen one.

He salted. Peppered. Forked up and sucked down.

"Would it help if you talked to someone?" Reilly said quietly.

"As in a psychiatrist?"

"Therapist. They can be very helpful."

"This from personal experience, Officer?"

"As a matter of fact, yes."

He laughed in a hard burst. "Somehow I wouldn't think you're the type who needed one."

"Everybody has issues."

He knew he was being a bit of a shit, but he felt naked, and not in a good way. "So what's one of yours."

"We're not talking about me."

"Well, I'm getting tired of being up onstage all by my little lonesome." He polished off half a piece of toast in two bites. "Come on, Officer. Spill something about yourself."

"I'm an open book."

"Who needs a therapist?" When she didn't respond, he leveled his stare at her. "Coward."

Eyes narrowing, she eased back and pushed her half-full bowl away. He expected some witty retort. Or, even more likely, a smack-down.

Instead, she reached into her pocket, took out a ten-dollar bill, and put it between them. "I'll see you in the sergeant's office."

With subtle grace, she scooched out, taking her coat, purse, and cell phone with her.

Before she took off, Veck snagged her wrist. "I'm sorry. I was out of line."

She disengaged the hold by putting her phone in her bag. "See you shortly."

After she left, Veck pushed his own plate away, even though there was a good egg and a half left.

Not even nine in the morning . . . and he'd already won the asshole-of-the-day prize. Fantastic—

A draft passed over the back of his neck, prickling the hairs at his nape and making him crank around toward the door.

A woman had come in, and she was as out of place as a Ming vase in the Target housewares department. As her perfume drifted over, and she swizzled out of her fur jacket, there was an audible pause in the diner's fifty or so conversations. Then again, she'd just exposed some Pamela Anderson breasts to half the CPD.

As Veck checked her out, he supposed he should have been attracted to her, but instead, that cold shaft tickling down his spine made him want to take out a gun and point it at her in self-defense.

And how fucked up was that.

Leaving a twenty of his own, he bailed on the rest of his breakfast and hit the door. Stepping outside, he stopped. Glanced around.

The back of his neck was still going, his instincts screaming, particularly as he glanced at the round windows of the diner. Someone was watching him. Maybe the chippie with the Hustler body, maybe someone else.

But his instincts never lied.

Good news was, it appeared he'd be getting his weapons back later this morning. So at least he could legally protect himself again.

As Jim pulled into the Riverside Diner's lot on his Harley, some guy on a sweet BMW bike tooled off with a roar.

Adrian and Eddie were right behind him on their rides, and the three of them parked together in the far corner by the Hudson's shore. As he dismounted and looked at the place Devina had named for a rendezvous, he thought, Well, isn't this special. He'd been at this very same dive with his first soul.

Guess Caldwell was a hotbed of activity for the damned.

Then again, maybe she just liked the java here and was going to tell him the soul in question was somewhere else.

Heading over to the entrance, his boys were giving him the silent treatment—not a news flash on Eddie's part, but a miracle on the other angel's. No way that was going to last with Ad, though.

The diner was crowded, noisy, and smelled like coffee and melted butter. Hell of a place for Devina to pick—

And there she was, way to the left, sitting at a booth and facing the door with a shaft of sunlight pouring in through the window next to her. The warm yellow rays illuminated her face perfectly, like she was about to be photographed, and he thought of the first time he'd seen her at that club, standing under a ceiling fixture. She'd been glowing then, too.

Evil had never looked so hot, but unlike the other men, who were staring over the rims of their mugs and all but drooling like dogs, he knew what she really was—and he wasn't so distracted by the slipcover that he didn't notice she threw no shadow: As bright as the illumination that struck her was, there was no dark outline on the tabletop or the Naugahyde beside her.

For a split second, he had an image of the two of them together from the night before. He'd tried to fuck her from behind on that table, but she'd insisted on doing it face-to-face. Frankly, he'd been surprised that he could get it up, but anger had a way of making him hard. At least with her.

As he'd departed that sweaty, rough scene, he'd looked around at her walls, imagining Sissy stuck in the tangle of the damned. He prayed his girl couldn't see out of it. God, to think she might have . . .

But enough of that. Coming up to Devina, he put a block on any thoughts of Sissy or sex with the enemy or even the game itself.

"So who is it?" he said.

The demon peered over the top of her *Caldwell Courier Journal*, her black eyes doing a quick circuit of his body and making him want to take another shower—this time with a belt sander.

"Well, good morning, Jim. Won't you sit down with me."

"No goddamn way."

The guy in the booth in front of her glared over his shoulder. Like he didn't approve of Jim's tone or language around a lady.

She only looks like one, buddy, Jim thought.

Devina put the paper down, and went back to her buttermilk pancakes and her coffee. "Do you have a pen?"

"Do not fuck with me."

"Little late for that. Pen?"

As some people tried to get past, Jim and the boys had
to turn sideways while Eddie outed a Paper Mate some-
thing or other and handed it over.

Devina uncapped the thing with her long, manicured
hands. And then she folded the paper to the crossword
puzzle.

"What's a five-letter word for—"

"Damn it, Devina, cut—"

"—antagonist."

"—the shit."

"Actually, Jim, 'the shit' is seven letters. Although I am,
aren't I." Devina began carefully filling in a word. "I be-
lieve 'enemy' is the word I'm looking for. And you're ei-
ther sitting down with me—alone—or you're going to
stand there until your legs rot off and you fall over in the
aisle."

More with the careful printing. Wonder if she was work-
ing on another word for "pain in the ass."

Jim glanced at his boys. "I'll be right out."

"Good-bye, Adrian," Devina said, with a wave. "I'll see
you soon, though—I'm quite sure."

The demon didn't say anything to Eddie. Then again,
she liked to get a rise out of people, and Eddie was as un-
leavened as matzo.

Which Jim supposed put him and Adrian in the hot-
cross-bun department.

As the two angels took off, Jim slid into the booth. "So."

"Would you care for some breakfast?"

"Who is it, Devina."

"I hate to eat alone."

"You could hold your breath until I join you—how
about that."

Her black eyes became direct. "Must we fight."

At that, he had to honestly laugh. "It's the reason we're
here, baby."

She smiled a little. "I think that's the first time I've heard
you do that."

Jim cut the sound right off as a waitress came over with a coffeepot. "Nothing for me, thanks."

"He'll have coffee and the waffles."

When the waitress looked at him like, *Come on, make up your damn mind*, he shrugged and let it go.

After they were alone again, Devina just went back to her puzzle.

"You can't have a shot with me unless you get talking."

There was a pause, as if the demon were thinking of some way to prolong the meeting. Eventually, she tapped the newspaper with the tip of Eddie's pen.

"You read the *CCJ*?"

"Sometimes."

"It's a treasure trove of information." She made an elaborate show of picking up the first section. "You never know what you might find."

Flattening the thing and spinning it around to face him, she stared across the table.

Jim looked down. Three big articles. One on a new school districting plan. Another on emerging minority businesses. And a third on . . .

The nib of Eddie's pen pointed to the last article.

"I believe I have completed my part of the agreement," she drawled.

The headline read: "DelVecchio Execution Scheduled."

Jim quickly skimmed the article and thought, Shit, *that* was the soul?

Just as Devina went to retract the pen, he flashed out a hand and locked a hold on her wrist, keeping it in place.

The nib of the Paper Mate was actually on a name within the article—and it wasn't the DelVecchio serial killer guy. It was the man's son . . . Thomas DelVecchio Jr.

A detective on the Caldwell police force.

Jim glanced across the table at his enemy and smiled with his incisors. "Tricky."

Her lashes lowered demurely. "Always."

Done with her and the time suck, Jim got up and took the pen with him. "Enjoy my waffles, sweetheart."

"Hey, how will I finish my crossword puzzle?"

"I'm sure you'll find a way. See you soon."

Jim stalked out of the diner and beelined for his wing-men. When he came up to the bikes, he held the Paper Mate up to Eddie.

"Your pen." As the angel went to take it back, Jim held on to the thing. "Metal casing around the nib. Next time, give the bitch a Sharpie."

As Jim went to sling a leg over his hog, Adrian asked, "What did she say?"

"Looks like we're going into the land of cops and robbers."

"Oh. Good." Ad mounted his own bike. "At least I speak the language there."

CHAPTER
6

When Reilly walked into HQ, it was through the back door and down the cinder-block hallway that dumped out into what was supposed to be the newly renovated, inspiring and uplifting lobby. Unfortunately, the bronze statue of Lady Justice with her scales and her sword was a modern interpretation of the classic Greco-Roman prototype, and the blindfolded goddess looked like melted cheese. Old, brown melted cheese.

The circular walk around her and the spotlights shining down from the open loggia above just provided greater visual access to the hot mess. Then again, most of the police personnel, district attorneys, and defense lawyers striding through were too busy to worry about the decor. Headquarters had a lot going on: The secured dropoff and central processing for arrests was to the right, along with the jail itself. Records was to the left. Up at the top of the curving stairs were the offices for Homicide and Internal Affairs, as well as the squad room and locker room. Third floor was the new lab and the evidence lockup.

Reilly hit the stairs two at a time, passing a couple of colleagues who were going slower than her. But as she stepped off on the second-floor landing she lost her momentum. The wide-open area up ahead had a bank of desks where the pool of admin support people worked. Front and center among the young men and women? Brittany spelled Britnae, a.k.a., the Pneumatic Office Hottie.

The blonde had a hand mirror up and was running her fingertip under one heavily MAC'd or Bobbi Brown'd or Sephora'd eye. Next move was to fluff the curls. Last was to smack her lips and pout.

All the while, she was bending forward and flashing her double Ds to . . . herself.

Evidently pleased with her paint job and landscaping, Britnae turned her wrist and checked one of those little itty-bitty watches some women wore, the kind that had linked bracelets and tiny mother-of-pearl faces.

She probably had baskets of bangles, and dangly earrings that hung from a little stand, and a closet full of pink stuff.

Reilly's closet looked like Marilyn Manson's. Assuming he'd been reborn as an accountant. And she didn't do jewelry. Her watch? Casio. Black and shockproof.

Three guesses who Britnae was getting ready for . . . and the first two didn't count: The girl had been panting after Veck since the day he'd come through that door two weeks ago.

Not that it was Reilly's business.

Before someone booked her for being a creepy-ass stalker, she hurried along to the IA division and went to her cubicle. Pretending to be alert, she signed into her computer, but as she went into her e-mail, everything had been translated into a foreign language. Either that or her brain had forgotten English.

Goddamn DelVecchio.

Calling *her* a coward? Just because she wanted to keep things professional? He didn't know half the hell she'd been through. Besides, she'd been trying to help him . . .

Made her want to feed the guy his breakfast with her size nine.

Getting with the program, she called up the report she'd

filed via e-mail early this morning and double-checked her work, going through the whole document from beginning to end.

When her phone rang, she reached for the receiver without having to look up. "Reilly."

"Thomason." Ah, the lab upstairs. "Just wanted you to know that I think Kroner's injuries were the result of teeth."

"As in . . ."

"Fangs, specifically. I met up with the medics last night at the ER and was there as Kroner was intubated, stitched up, and transfused. I had a good look at those neck and facial wounds. When a knife is used in an attack like that, you tend to get very clear boundaries on the lacerations. His flesh had been torn—which was what I saw when that tiger ate that trainer last year."

Well, that sealed the deal, didn't it—and made her worried about what might be loose in those woods. "What kind of animal are we talking about?"

"That I'm not too sure of. I took some tissue samples— God knows there were plenty to go around—and we'll find out what kind of saliva was left. I'll tell you this, though: Whatever it was? We're talking big, powerful . . . and pissed off."

"Thanks so much for calling me this fast."

"No problem. I'm going to catch a couple of Zs and get back to work. I'll be in touch."

After she hung up, she typed out an addendum to her report, hit ctrl-P and then sent the document as an attachment to the sergeant on e-mail. Gathering her file and cell phone, she went to stand by the printer as the pages licked out of the machine.

At least she had some evidence to back up what she'd told the sarge before breakfast this morning.

On that note, she thought about the diner. She probably shouldn't have asked Veck to join her. He was right; it did look bad, but more to the point, they could have avoided that unpleasant exchange. Which had hurt, actually.

Not that it should have. Casual comment over coffee when he was being inappropriate? Shouldn't have bothered her. At all.

Or maybe it was just her being allergic to the word *coward*.

Yeah, that was it.

Veck went through the lobby of headquarters like a cold draft, shooting around people, rushing across the floor. He hit the staircase and took the stone steps two at a time.

When he got to the second-floor landing, he headed left, but he wasn't going to his office. Internal Affairs was where he was—

From out of nowhere, something pink and blond stepped in his path. "Hi!"

As he looked down at the girl, he thought . . . now he knew what tornadoes felt like when they came up to a trailer home: absolutely nothing. He'd just as soon mow her over to get to Reilly, if that was what it took.

"Hi!" she said again, like a one-note bird.

Man, too loud, too cheerful, too much flowery perfume. And what was with the lip gloss? Any more of that shit and she could give her own car an oil change.

"Hey. 'Scuse me—I'm late."

Unfortunately, she decided to take up ballroom dancing with him, jogging right when he did, and then left. When he stopped, she took a deep breath, or arched her back, or maybe hit some kind of air compressor, because suddenly she became Jessica Rabbit with the cleavage.

If she showed any more breast tissue, she'd be getting a goddamn mammogram.

"So," she drawled, "I was wondering if you want some coffee . . ."

Tea . . . or me? he finished in his head for her.

"Thanks, but I'm late for a meeting." Sidestep.

Counterstep. "Well, I could bring it to you?"

"No, thanks—"

She put her hand on his arm. "Really, I don't mind—"

The fine Officer Reilly picked that moment to come out of IA. And what do you know, she didn't hesitate or show any change of expression—but then again, why in the hell should it bother her that he was getting the come-on from someone?

As she passed by, she nodded at him and said hi to his nemesis.

"I've got to go," he said, beyond done with the delays.

"I'll come see you later," Britnae called out.

"Reilly," he hissed. *"Reilly."*

The woman he was actually after stopped in front of the sarge's office. "Yes?"

"I really am sorry. For what I said. That was out of line."

Reilly switched her file over to her left arm and smoothed her hair. "It's okay. High-stress time. I understand."

"It won't happen again."

"Wouldn't matter to me if it did."

On that note, she pivoted on her sensible heel and pushed into the waiting room.

Okay . . . ouch. But he couldn't blame her.

Instead of following her inside, he just stood there like a plank as the door shut in his face, preoccupied by wanting to kick his own ass. Next thing he knew, the scent of fresh coffee announced that his partner had come up to him.

José de la Cruz looked tired, but alert, which was the man's SOP. "How we doing?"

"Shitty."

"You don't say." He handed over one of the two coffees in his mitts. "Drink this. Or maybe mainline it."

"Thanks, man."

"You ready?"

No. "Yeah."

As they went into the office, Reilly glanced over to good-morning de la Cruz, then went back to talking to the sarge's assistant.

Veck parked it on one of the old-school wooden chairs that were lined up against the wood-paneled walls of the sergeant's outer office. Drinking the coffee, he watched Reilly and noticed all kinds of minute details about her: the way she fussed with her right earring, like the back was loose; how she tended to bend her leg and tap the toe of her shoe when she was making a point; the fact that when she smiled, she had a gold filling on an upper molar that flashed ever so slightly.

She was really attractive. Like, *really* attractive.

"So, I tried to call you last night," de la Cruz said quietly.

"My cell's at the lab right now."

"You really should get a landline."

"Yeah." He looked at his partner. "Guess they didn't find much out there in the woods."

"*Nada.*"

They sat side by side, drinking out of those paper mugs with the card deck suits on them. The coffee tasted awful, but it was hot and gave him something to do.

"You thought about killing Kroner, didn't you." As Veck shot a glance over, the other detective shrugged. "I saw you with that paparazzo, remember. I was the one who pulled you off of him. Lot of anger."

Veck resumed staring at Reilly, glad she was deep in conversation. Nodding in her direction, he said softly, "She doesn't think I did it. I'm getting the impression you do, however."

"Didn't say that."

"Don't have to."

"Nah, I saw the shape Kroner was in. Saw you, too. That's an equation that doesn't add up."

"So why bring up intent?"

"Because I think it's on your mind."

Veck made a noncommittal noise. "If she recommends that I stay on active duty, are you going to have a problem with that."

"No, but I think you shouldn't be out on the streets alone right now."

Funny, he felt the same way. And wasn't that a bitch. "We gonna be grafted at the hip, then?"

The sarge opened his office door and stuck his gray-haired head out. "Let's do this."

Reilly unplugged from the assistant, and Veck and de la Cruz followed her into the larger office beyond. The conference table in the far corner was big enough to seat everyone comfortably, and she took the chair farthest away from Veck—which meant she was right across from him. No eye contact; no surprise.

Fucking hell.

"So I've read the report you e-mailed me," the sergeant said to Reilly. "Anything else?"

"Just this addendum which I also sent through." She passed copies around, and then entwined her fingers together and sat back. "I stand by my conclusions."

The sarge looked over at de la Cruz. "Anything to add?"

"No. I've read the report as well and it says it all."

"Then I'm prepared to agree with Officer Reilly." The sergeant stared hard at Veck. "I like you. You're my kind of cop. But I won't keep anyone under the badge who's a danger to others. Reilly here's your new partner—I can't spare de la Cruz for the probational hand-holding period I'm laying on you. Which is a month, minimum."

Reilly showed no reaction to the reassignment, but she was a professional, wasn't she.

"Can I work on Kroner?" Veck asked.

"Not on your life. You'll be focusing on cold cases for the next thirty days, as well as meeting with Dr. Riccard."

Ah, yes, the departmental shrink. And in the silence that followed, he knew everyone was waiting for him to groan, but he wasn't a *Lethal Weapon* wild card, damn it.

Yeah. For example, he couldn't dislocate his shoulder, he didn't live on the beach with a dog, and he wasn't rocking a death wish. You're welcome.

"Okay."

Sarge seemed a little surprised, but then he knocked on his table with his knuckles, which Veck took as the guy's way of expressing satisfaction. "Good. De la Cruz, I want to talk to you. The pair of you—we're done."

Reilly was up and out of the office faster than a bullet,

but two could shoot that quick. Veck got right on her tail, and he caught her in the outside hallway.

"So how's this going to work," he said.

That was all he had. The apology route hadn't worked, and somehow he didn't think thanking her for the report was going to fly, either.

She shrugged. "I'll wrap up what I'm working on this morning, and then we'll focus on cold cases."

"For thirty days."

"Thirty days." She didn't look enthused, but neither did she seem to dread the prospect. Which told him she was not an easy poker target if they had downtime. "I'll see you at one o'clock in your department, Detective."

"Roger that, Officer."

As she walked off, she made some notes in her file, her head buried in work. A couple of guys from the beat passed her and looked her way, their focus lingering, as if they were hoping to catch her eye. She didn't look up, though. Didn't notice.

Veck sure as hell did. And found that he wanted to perform an optical adjustment on the bastards.

"You left this in the sarge's office."

Veck turned. De la Cruz had come out and had Veck's coffee.

Well, this wasn't awkward. Nope.

"Thanks, man." Veck palmed the paper mug and took a draw from the rim. The shit was now lukewarm, its only redeeming factor gone. "Well, it was nice working with you."

"Same." José put his palm out. "But who knows, maybe you'll be reassigned to me in a month."

"Yeah." Somehow, though, Veck had a feeling his days with the CPD were numbered.

They walked back to Homicide together in silence, and when they opened the door to the department, every single detective in there looked around the gray partition walls of his or her cubicle.

Veck saw no reason to sugarcoat things. "On duty. Off Kroner. With Reilly."

A lot of nodding came back at him, and, man, he appreciated people being cool. Then again, these were decent folks doing a hard job on a shoestring budget, and there wasn't a lot of time for bullshit. Besides, good or bad, after he'd coldcocked that paparazzo, he'd earned a lot of respect.

As everyone returned to work, José clapped him on the shoulder and headed off to his own desk.

Veck didn't waste time. He parked it in his chair, signed into the computer, and checked his e-mail.

Cold cases, huh. That was a pretty goddamn broad category.

Going into the departmental database, he called up all missing persons reports. Which were technically cold cases, weren't they, assuming they were still open. Initiating a search, he leaned back and let the computer do its thing. The fact that the data screen he used just happened to be women aged sixteen to thirty who'd been reported in the last, oh, say . . . three weeks? When Kroner happened to be busy in the area?

Wasn't that a coincidence.

CHAPTER
7

At twelve o'clock, Reilly left the station house on foot and headed into deep downtown. The day was glorious, the April sun so bright and warm that it chased away the bite of the fifty-five-degree air. She was not the only one taking advantage of the weather. People were out on the sidewalks and crosswalks in droves, clogging traffic while they strolled with sodas or ice cream in their hands, or carried their take-out to the lip of a fountain or the contour of an iron bench in the park.

After six months of icy-cold darkness, upstate New York was panting for some sign that winter's back had finally been broken—and this beautiful lunch hour was not to be squandered.

Ostensibly, she was taking a break so she could clear her head before she saw Veck again. Her strides, however, had a purpose and direction she refused to look too closely at.

The Galleria Mall was yet another downtown revitalization project, but unlike so many attempts, it had actually succeeded. Anchored by a Macy's and a shiny new Barnes and Noble bookstore, the four-block stretch of 1920s office buildings had been closed to everything but foot traffic, given an attractive, unifying face-lift, and become the locus of high-noon retail therapy for thousands of cubicons like Reilly.

Except unlike a lot of her cohorts, this was the first time she'd ever walked the stretch of Bath & Body Works, and Talbots, and the Gap. . . .

When she stopped in front of the next store in line, she blinked in the pink glare that came through all the glass.

Oh, no. Nope. This was not her—

A woman came out with two big bags swinging from her hands, and a smile as wide as a freeway on her face.

"Sale!" she said to Reilly. "Yay!"

Her voice was so high it was like she was breathing out helium. Although maybe that was because it looked like she was wearing a bustier under her coat.

Reilly shook her head. Sale or no sale, this was not her kind of—

Annnnnnd somehow she was in the store.

Holy. Crap. She'd never seen so much underwear in one place in her whole damn life.

Victoria's Secret was not for the faint of heart . . . or the big of butt, she feared, wondering exactly how long it had been since she'd hit the gym.

High school. No . . . maybe it was elementary.

Boy, all the lace was intimidating. As were the pictures of the Photoshop'd models who had been blown up to beyond life-size.

And to make matters worse, the place was packed with women who were not Reilly's demographic. These were all chippies in their early twenties, snatching up thongs and demi-cups and peekaboo somethings or another. Even the slouchy, sweatpantsy stuff looked like it was meant to be stripped off by the teeth of some quarterback—

"Hi, can I help you?"

Reilly winced. "Ah . . ."

The saleswoman was a gorgeous African-American who probably looked good in every single thing that hung on the little hangers or was folded on the tables, and in comparison, Reilly felt like a pasty, freckled stretch of please-let's-do-this-with-the-lights-off.

"I'm good, thanks—"

"We're having a sale."

"Yeah, I saw someone come out of here with a couple of bags." Which, considering how small everything was, meant the chick had bought five hundred, maybe six hundred sets of stuff.

"Are you looking for anything in particular?"

Reilly was about to shake her head no, when her mouth opened of its own volition. "I want to feel like a woman, instead of a police officer. I'm just . . . really frickin' tired of myself and my job right now. Do you know what I mean?"

Oh, shit, what was she saying?

And P.S., this had nothing to do with Brittany, spelled Britnae.

The saleswoman smiled. "I do. And you've come to the right place."

Reilly glanced at a tiger-print teddy and wasn't so sure about that. "I don't think I've ever bought lingerie before—nothing I own matches, and I think a couple of my bras are from the Civil War. Maybe the Revolutionary."

"Well, I'm Ralonda." She put out her hand. "And I can take care of you."

"Reilly. I mean . . . Sophia." As they shook, she muttered, "Do you have a pysch degree, by any chance?"

"As a matter of fact, that's what I'm going to school for over at SUNY Caldwell."

"God, you are perfect."

"Hardly." Ralonda smiled again, flashing beautiful white teeth. "Let's get you measured and I'll bring you some things."

One hour and six hundred seventy-two dollars and forty-three cents later, Reilly left with three bags full of things. As she headed out the door, her chin was up and she found herself smiling at two girls who were peering in through the windows.

"They're having a sale," she said to them. "Better get in there. And ask for Ralonda—she's the best."

As they scurried inside, Reilly marched back to the station house feeling curiously light in her shoes. Then again, maybe the slightly padded cherry red bra with matching red panties she'd put on and kept on had antigravity properties, lifting not just her cleavage, but her entire body.

Made you wonder what the astronauts had on under their suits.

As a horrific image of Buzz Aldrin in a set of hot pink itty-bitties lit up her mind, it dawned on her that walking into HQ with her VS bags and a bounce in her step didn't exactly send the right message—especially given that she was partnering with Veck for the next month.

Sneaking around the outside of the station house, she made it to her car and stashed the contraband in her trunk, as opposed to the backseat.

This time, as she went in through the back and passed by the guard in the lobby, she was painfully aware of herself, wondering whether anyone knew what she had on under her clothes. Nobody paid her any unusual attention, though, which suggested that among the numerous talents of the various members of the force, it appeared as if X-ray vision was not one of them.

First stop was her office. Quick check of voice mail and e-mail. Then it was grab a pad and head for Homicide. And what do you know, her growing confidence in the concealing properties of cotton and wool took it on the chin as she opened the door into the department.

Everyone looked up, including Veck.

Right. Now she knew why folks hated those dreams where they walked naked into a room full of people. She'd never had a nightmare like that before, and as she put her pad up to the front of her breasts, she wasn't in a big hurry to hop on that learning curve.

But then people just waved and helloed, and she nodded and helloed back while heading over to Veck. The cubicle next to him was empty of everything but a computer and a phone, and as she sat down, she kept her yellow-and-lined right where it was.

Veck eased back in his chair in a way that made his chest look huge against his white button-down. "All settled back in your office?"

"Yes. What are we working on today?"

He nodded to his computer screen. "I've found something to pass the time with. I was waiting for you to come over—thought we'd go do some recon in the field, and double-check some witnesses."

"Good. What's the case."

"I'll tell you about it on the way across town. Mind if we take your car? I've only got my bike."

"Ah . . ." Surely there could be no reason for him to look in her trunk. "Sure. Yeah. That's fine."

"Thanks, Officer. Or should I call you 'Detective' for the next four weeks?"

As they stood up together and she found herself eye-to-pectoral with him, she knew it was time to kick her inner Britnae to the curb. "Reilly is fine."

For a moment, his lids dropped low, and she could have sworn that he muttered under his breath something like, *She sure is.*

But no doubt it was her new underwear making her hear things.

"Wait a minute—that is *not* a homicide cold case."

As they came up to a red light, Veck got nailed with a hard stare from his new partner . . . and that was an incredible turn-on.

Shifting in his seat, and praying that the arousal he'd abruptly popped would deflate before they reached their destination, he made it his business to keep his voice level and completely groan-free. Although, for fuck's sake, if this was an indication of what the next four weeks were going to be like?

He was in trouble.

"She's technically a missing person—"

"There's no 'technically' about it. There's no body."

"If you'll let me finish?"

"Sorry." As the light turned green, she hit the gas. "But I have a feeling where this is going, and you're not getting anywhere near the Kroner case."

We'll see about that, he thought. "I got a call from one of the FBI field officers this morning. He's been working on the case of this missing girl, and he wanted to know if there was any new information. I told him I'd be happy to go back through what we've got—"

"The FBI can do its own—"

"No reason not to be collegial. Or to assume that there's a tie with Kroner."

She frowned. "What's the FBI's angle?"

"I didn't ask. Maybe it's interstate." Because maaaaybe it was part of the Kroner investigation—which was why he didn't ask.

"Just so we're clear, if there's a nexus with Kroner, we're out."

"Got it." He reached into his breast pocket and took out a three-page disposition form. "Cecilia Barten, age nineteen, missing for just over three weeks. Last seen leaving her home to go to the Hannaford supermarket on Union Avenue. Surveillance cameras picked up nothing, thanks to a power surge that knocked out the feed from the lot and from the exit of the store."

"And we're starting where?"

"Her parents' house. I just want to see if there's anything that was missed. Her mother is expecting us—hang a right here."

Reilly hit the directional signal and followed through on the turn, heading into a neighborhood that was a good click or two above where Veck lived. Here, the houses were a little bigger and better planted. No cars parked on the street, and he imagined that there were newer sedans and station wagons in all those attached garages. Probably not as many minivans—although this was the land of the soccer mom, so maybe he was wrong.

"Okay," he murmured, looking at the colonials. "Four ninety-one. Ninety-three. Five . . . here it is."

Reilly pulled over to the curb in front of 497. After canning the engine, they got out into the sunshine and—

The car that pulled up behind them was a gold SUV with blackened windows, and what got out of it was a whole lot of federal agent: The three men were in plain clothes, and as they came up, the one in the lead, with the dark blond hair, flashed his credentials.

"Jim Heron. We spoke on the phone. These are my partners, Blackhawk and Vogel."

"Thomas DelVecchio."

As they shook, Veck felt a strange kind of charge, and he stepped back. "This is Officer Reilly. You want to come in with us?"

The agent narrowed his eyes on the house. "Yeah. Thanks. My partners will wait out here."

Good idea. It would be hard to fit the three of those boys in a front hall smaller than a football stadium.

As they went up the brick walk to the front door, one of those seasonal flags waved casually in the spring breeze. The thing was pastel and had an egg on it that was half lavender and half pink with a bright yellow band around the middle.

Easter had come at the end of March this year. Right around the time the daughter had gone missing. No doubt the flag had been forgotten . . . or perhaps they were praying for a resurrection of their own. Either way, ruination had come to this house, even though it still had four walls and a roof: This girl was dead. Veck knew it in his bones, even though he wasn't one for prescient shit.

Doorbell.

Wait.

Wait.

He glanced back at Reilly. She seemed sad as she leaned back and scanned the windows on the second floor—and he wondered whether she was trying to imagine which one had been Cecilia Barten's. Behind her, Heron was doing an excellent impression of a statue: towering and unmoving, his eyes were focused on the front door as if he were seeing through it into the house.

Veck frowned. There was something off about the guy. Clearly not competence, however; the agent radiated a militaristic precision about everything from the way he flashed his creds to his walk to how his body settled at rest. Still . . . what the fuck was it—

The door opened with a soft creak and the woman on the other side looked like she hadn't slept or eaten well in a long time.

"Good morning, ma'am, I'm Detective DelVecchio. This is Officer Reilly and Agent Heron."

Everyone flashed their credentials.

"Please come in." She stepped back and motioned with her arm. "May I get you anything?"

"No, thank you, ma'am. We appreciate your taking the time to speak with us."

The house was beyond spotless and smelled of Pine-Sol and Pledge. Which suggested Mrs. Barten cleaned when she was stressed.

"I thought maybe we could talk in the living room?" she said.

"Please."

The room was done in keepsake and heirloom, with wallpaper that had flowers on it, and two couches that did not. As Mrs. Barten sat in an armchair, and everybody else took a sofa cushion, Veck got a good look at the woman. She was in her late forties, with a lot of blond hair that was pulled back and twisted around a scrunchie, and a long, thin body that had needed the weight she'd recently lost. No makeup, and she was still pretty. Stare was empty, however.

Shit, where did he start.

"Mrs. Barten," Reilly cut in, "can you tell us about your daughter. Things she liked to do or was good at. Memories?"

Glancing over at his new partner, he wanted to mouth a thank-you.

Especially as some of the tension left the woman's shoulders and the hint of a smile appeared. "Sissy was—is ..." She collected herself. "Please forgive me. This is hard."

Reilly moved closer to the armchair. "Take your time. I know this is a lot to ask of you."

"Actually, it helps to talk about her. It takes me out of where we all are now."

In a halting voice that gradually gained momentum, stories started to roll out, painting a picture of a highly intelligent, slightly shy good girl who would never have walked into trouble if she'd seen it coming.

Yup, Cecilia Barten had most definitely been murdered, Veck thought to himself. This was not one of those drug-related runaways, or an abusive-boyfriend-gone-haywire nightmare. Stable family. Happy young woman. Bright future. Until destiny's equivalent of a car crash had slammed into her life and wiped it out.

"Mind if I look at the pictures over there?" Veck said when there was a pause in the narrative.

"Please."

He stood up and went across to the built-in bookcases on either side of the bowed windows that faced the street. Two kids. The other was a younger sister. And there were shots from graduations and birthday parties and track meets and field hockey games ... family reunions and weddings ... Christmases.

He was curiously in awe at the display. Man, this was the very best that "normal" had to offer, and for no particular reason, he thought of how, growing up, his house had had none of this stuff—the happy times or the photographs to show it off. The moments that he and his mom had had to share were nothing you wanted other people to see. Nothing you wanted to remember, either, for that matter.

He reached out and picked up one of the five-by-sevens. Cecilia was standing next to her father, her arm through his, her hand resting on the back of his.

She was mostly like her mom, only a little like her dad. But the lineage was clear.

"...called home?" Reilly said.

Veck retuned in to the conversation.

"That's right," Mrs. Barten said. "She left around nine. I'd just had my foot operated on—hammertoes...." For a moment, the woman appeared to ruminate, and he was willing to bet that she was thinking about how much she wanted to go back to the time where all she had to do was worry about the way her shoes fit.

And maybe she was blaming herself, too.

She shook her head and refocused. "I was pretty immobile. I'd given her the shopping list and...she called from the store. She didn't know whether I wanted green or red peppers. I wanted the red ones. I was making..." The tears came and were blinked away sharply. "Anyway, that was the last time anyone heard from her."

Veck returned the photograph to the shelf. As he went to sit back down next to Heron, he frowned. The man was staring at the victim's mother with the intensity of a film camera, like he was reading and recording every twitch of her eye and purse of her mouth as she spoke.

As Veck's radar started pinging like crazy, it was unclear whether it was about the missing girl or her sad, lovely mother or this massive man who looked like he could start a fire with that hard, burning stare of his.

"If I can interject," Veck said, "did she have any boyfriends?"

From the corner of his eye, he saw Heron's hands tighten on his thighs, cranking down tight.

"No. She had friends that were boys, of course, and a prom date here and there...nothing serious, though. At least, not that she told me—and she was generally open about her life."

Those hands released abruptly.

"Do you have anything you want to ask," Veck said to the agent.

There was a long stretch of silence. Just before it got

truly awkward, the man said in a deep, low voice, "Mrs. Barten, I'm going to bring her home to you. One way or another, I will get her back for you."

Veck recoiled, thinking, Shit, don't go there, buddy. "Ah, what he means is—"

"It's all right." Mrs. Barten clasped the base of her throat. "I'm not fooling myself. I know that she's . . . not with us anymore. A mother feels the cold in the heart. We just want to know what happened and . . . have a chance to lay her to rest properly."

"You will have her back. I swear it."

Now Mrs. Barten choked up—and why wouldn't she. The guy was like a warrior with the vengeance routine, more avenger than agent.

"Thank you . . . all of you."

Veck discreetly checked his watch. "If you'll excuse me and my partner, we're going to head over to the supermarket. The manager said he was leaving early today."

"Oh, yes, of course."

Agent Heron helped Mrs. Barten up by taking her hand. "Would you mind if I take a look at her bedroom?"

"Sure—I'll lead you right up." She turned to Veck and Reilly. "If you need to go now, you can always come back."

"Thank you," Reilly said. "We'll do that."

"And we'll see ourselves out the door," Veck murmured.

As Agent Heron and the victim's mother hit the stairs, Veck paused in the front hall and watched them ascend together. A window on the landing above cast illumination on them, the shaft of sunlight hitting them both square on the face and acting as a beacon for their—

Wait a minute.

Veck glanced over into the living room . . . where the golden rays were pouring in from the west.

Impossible. You couldn't get that effect from opposite directions, front and rear of the house.

"What is it?" Reilly said softly.

Veck swung his eyes back to the staircase. Heron and Mrs. Barten were nowhere to be seen, and the light on the landing was gone now, too, the window showing nothing more than the budded branches of the maple tree behind the house and the clear blue sky above it.

"I'm going up there," he told his new partner. "Just for a minute."

CHAPTER
8

As Jim followed behind Sissy's mother, he was out-of-body overwhelmed. In a dim corner of his mind, he knew he had to keep tabs on Veck, but this opportunity was not going to smoothly present itself again anytime soon.

Turning the corner at the head of the stairs, the volume of the house was cranked up to Slipknot levels. Everything from the subtle creak of the carpeted floor beneath his boots to the soft talk down below in the foyer to his own breath in the back of his throat, it all seemed to scream in his ears.

Abruptly, Veck appeared behind them and made some kind of an I'm-only-here-for-a-minute comment. Jim nodded at the guy—and promptly forgot he was even there.

"Sissy's room is this way."

The three of them went to the right, and when Mrs. Barten hesitated at the closed door, Jim raised his hand to put it on her shoulder . . . and then couldn't quite make the contact.

"Would you like us to go in alone?" he asked.

Mrs. Barten opened her mouth. But then just nodded. "I haven't been in there since . . . that night. It's the way she left it."

At that moment, the phone rang, and there was visible relief in Sissy's mom's face. "I'll just go get that. Feel free to open the drawers and the closet, but if you have to take something, will you let me know what it is?"

"Absolutely," Veck answered.

As she hurried across the landing and disappeared into what he assumed was the master bedroom, Jim cracked the door.

Oh . . . the scent.

Slipping inside, he closed his eyes and tried not to feel like a letch as he breathed in deep. Perfume. Body lotion. Dryer sheets.

It was . . . extraordinary.

And he did not belong in this room. He was an adult male who had done things that shouldn't even be passing thoughts in a room like this—and the representations of those evil deeds were in the ink that covered his back. Plus he had weapons on him. And then there was that shit he'd pulled with the demon the night before.

He felt like a stain.

As Veck did his own recon, Jim opened his lids, and went over to the built-in desk by the front window. The flat stretch and shelving were painted white, but the chair was a blue to match the gingham drapes and the striped wallpaper. Carpet was an area rug with braided fringe. Bedspread was a quilt made from different strips of blue and white fabric. Handmade. Had to be.

The books that were lined up were orderly and girlie. She liked Jane Austen, but there was also a whole shelf of Gossip Girls—probably left over from when she was thirteen. Couple of 4-H ribbons, red and blue. Track trophies.

On the desk there was an Apple laptop along with two textbooks, one on calculus and the other on . . . advanced trigonometry?

Huh. His Sissy might well be smarter than he was.

There was also a magazine. *Cosmopolitan*—from this month.

Okaaaay, the cover with the word *ORGASM* in seventy-four-point hot-pink print didn't exactly jibe with the rest of this land of innocence and schoolwork . . . but then, she'd been growing up, hadn't she.

Pivoting, he all but ran into the foot of the twin bed.

Shit, now he knew why her mother didn't come in here. That blue quilt was pulled back and the pillows still dented as if Sissy had just been napping.

"I'm going to take off," Veck said. Which made Jim wonder how long they'd been in the room.

"See you soon," Jim said with distraction.

"Roger that."

When he was left to his own devices, Jim's hand shook as he reached out to touch the sheets. Brushing what had touched her skin, he thought about Devina and what that demon had done to this girl . . . and her family.

Adrian and Eddie were wrong. If they wanted him focused on the war, this was exactly where he needed to be. This was motivation to win if he'd ever seen it: Sissy was never going to lie in this bed again. She was not going to finish whatever article she'd been reading. And no more crunching numbers. Ever. But he could at least find her a better place to wait for her parents' and her sister's passings so they could all be reunited for eternity.

And then he could make Devina pay a thousand times over.

On the bedside table, there was a white alarm clock, another magazine—*In Touch* this time—and the remote to her little white television. He had the feeling that even though she was in college, she came back on a lot of weekends, and a peek into the closet confirmed this. Given the number of blouses and pants and skirts and dresses, it didn't look like the thing had been mined for favorites, but instead was on the ready. Plenty of shoes on the floor.

He left the bureau's drawers alone, because he wasn't sure which one held her . . . underthings, as it were. Probably either of the top two, but he was not running the risk of guessing wrong. He was a voyeur here already, because he'd come not in hopes of finding something that helped him help her. God knew, there was nothing on earth that could do that. Instead, he'd just wanted to . . . be close to her.

Right. Fine. *This* was the sort of shit that Ad and Eddie were worried about.

On that note, it was time to go. Again, he didn't know how long he'd been here. Could have been two minutes or two hours, and the last thing he wanted was Sissy's mother feeling like she had to knock on the door to see if he was okay or whether he'd already left.

He wasn't going to take anything, even though there was a temptation to hold on to an object, a focal point . . . something of Sissy's. Her family had lost too much, however, and he wasn't about to graft anything more from them.

Jim took a last moment to look around, and then he made himself leave. Out in the hall, he closed the door and listened. Sissy's mother was in the room across the way, talking quietly, her voice cracking.

Jim took the stairs down and waited discreetly in the foyer by the front door. Leaning to the side, he looked into the living room at the pictures by the big windows. The one that grabbed him and got his feet moving was a close-up of Sissy. She wasn't looking at the camera, but off to the side, and she wasn't smiling. She was deep in thought, and the expression on her face was nothing girlish, everything . . . survivor.

She looked iron willed.

"She had no idea the camera was on her."

Jim straightened and glanced at her mother. "No?"

Mrs. Barten came over and picked up the frame. "She always smiled if she knew there was a camera around. When her father took this, she was watching her teammates in a game—she played field hockey. She'd sprained her ankle and she was on the bench . . . and she wanted to be out with them." The woman looked over. "She was tougher than she appeared to be."

As their eyes met, Jim took a deep breath and thought, Thank God—that was going to keep her sane until he got to her.

Mrs. Barten tilted her head to the side. "You're different from the others."

Time to go. "I'm just like everyone else."

"No, you're not. I've met more officers, detectives, and agents in the last three weeks than I've seen on *Cops* over the course of my whole life." Her stare narrowed. "Your eyes . . ."

He turned to the door. "Detective DelVecchio will be in touch—"

"I want to give you something."

Jim froze with his hand on the knob and thought, Bad idea. He was too hungry for whatever she had to offer. "You don't have to."

"Here."

As he turned around to give her a "no, thank you," he found her reaching behind her neck. What came forward in her hands was a delicate gold chain.

"She wore this every day. I found it on the counter in her bathroom—she'd taken a shower and forgotten to put it back on . . . anyway, take this."

Dangling from the chain was a delicate winged bird made of gold. A dove.

"Her father gave it to her on her eighteenth birthday. It was part of a set."

Jim shook his head. "I can't. I'm—"

"You will. It's going to keep your eyes the way they are now, and our family needs that."

After a moment, he brought his hands forward, replacing her fingertips with his own. The necklace and charm weighed nothing at all. And it barely fit around his throat. But the thing went on like a dream even though the clasp was tiny and his hands were big.

As he dropped his arms, he stared down at her.

"What are my eyes like," he said hoarsely.

"Destroyed."

CHAPTER
9

The Hannaford supermarket was about five miles away, but it took Reilly some time to get them over there. Between the traffic and the red lights, she was beginning to think that the pair of them were going to spend eternity in the car.

Or maybe the buzzing in her head was what made it seem like forever.

"What's on your mind," Veck said.

Tightening her hands on the wheel, she readjusted herself in the driver's seat. "If it turns out that Cecilia Barten is one of Kroner's victims, we have to let her go. Are you prepared to do that?"

"Yeah. I am."

As she looked over, her new partner's jaw was tight, his big body tense.

"You sure about that." Because she wasn't.

"Yeah. I am."

Are you a hardheaded sonofabitch who's likely to do what he damn well pleases even if it screws a direct order? Yeah. I am.

Just as she pulled into the parking lot and started on the spot hunt, her phone went off. "Officer Reilly. Uh-huh, yes—not a big surprise. Really? Okay, and thanks for the update. Yes, please keep me informed."

She hung up and plugged them into a vacancy between an older silver Mercedes and a blue truck.

Twisting sideways in her seat, she said, "Kroner's barely hanging on. They don't expect him to live."

Veck's harsh face gave nothing away. "Shame. Maybe he knew what happened."

"And the analysis is in from the samples they took off him—there is saliva residue, but the readings are not one hundred percent clear as to the source. There appear to be similarities with both cougars and wolves. Hard to say for sure, but the animal hypothesis continues to look directionally correct."

He nodded and cracked his door open. "Mind if I have a smoke before we go in."

So maybe he was having a reaction, after all. "Sure."

They got out, and Veck came around to the back of the car, easing against the trunk and taking out a pack of Marlboros—as if a man like him would smoke anything else? As he lit up, she did her best not to think about all the bras and panties that were separated from the seat of his pants by nothing but some layers of sheet metal.

He was careful not to exhale anywhere near her or in a direction she was downwind of. "Bad habit," he muttered, "but no one lives forever."

"Very true."

Leaning against the trunk herself, she crossed her arms over her chest and looked up toward the sun. The warmth on her face was a benediction, and she closed her eyes to enjoy it.

When she eventually opened her lids again, she was shocked.

Veck was staring at her, and there was an expression on his face ... a sexual speculation that she was almost sure she was reading incorrectly.

Except then he looked away quick.

Not something you did if you were thinking about work.

Abruptly, the spring day's temperature shot up into the tropical, and now *she* was the one staring at *him*. Well, "ogling" was another word for it.

As he brought the cigarette up to his lips, his mouth parted and then he was sucking, the tip flaring orange, his fore- and middle fingers briefly releasing the shaft. Oh, hell's bells, she thought. Smoking was a deadly, nasty habit she didn't approve of . . . so it was unsettling to realize all those old Humphrey Bogart movies had not been insane when they'd done close-ups like this. There was just something undeniably erotic about the whole thing. Especially as the smoke eased out of his mouth and briefly shadowed his laser-like navy blue eyes and his dark cropped hair.

She looked away fast before she got caught—

"So?" he prompted.

"I'm sorry, what?"

"I asked what you think."

Right. How to answer that: *I think all the cherry red I'm wearing under my clothes is warping my brain. Because I'm finding the idea of straddling you against this car and riding you like a cowgirl with her hat over her head pretty damn appealing.*

"I need more information before I can form an opinion." *So how about lighting up another one of those bad boys and dropping your pants*— "Oh, God—"

"Are you okay?" he said, leaning in and putting his free hand on her arm. "You didn't eat much breakfast—did you get anything for lunch?"

You're all but sitting on three bags of what I had on my hour off, big daddy.

"You know"—she cleared her throat—"I probably should eat something."

And so help her, God, if her brain coughed up anything even remotely like whipped cream on some part of his body, she was putting in for a transfer away from herself.

"Let's go inside," he said, snuffing out his Marlboro on the heel of his shoe.

Good idea. And note to self: No downtime with her temporary partner. Ever.

They walked over and went through the automatic doors, passing the lineup of carts in the foyer and entering the supermarket proper.

When Veck paused and looked around, she nodded to the right. "The manager's office is this way."

"You shop here?"

"These stores are all laid out pretty much the same."

As they walked together, he said, "I probably should know this one by heart. My house isn't far from here."

"So this is where you buy your groceries?"

"My coffee and cigarettes—healthy, huh."

He sure looked to be in great shape. "You can always change your habits."

"You know, I quit for a while. The cigs, not the caffeine."

"What made you take it up again?"

"Coldcocking that photographer."

Ahhh, so he did have emotions. "There's a lot of stress in your job."

"Have you ever been a smoker?"

"No, and I don't really drink. I'm not big on vices."

Then again, she could be working on one for shopping.

And that was the last thought she had on any off-work subject. As they went over to customer service, she put aside all distractions, her game head coming back online as she imagined Mrs. Barten's daughter coming here to this store to help out her mother . . . only to have what should have been a routine trip for groceries turn into a nightmare.

Maybe because of Kroner.

As she got ready to flash her badge to the manager, it was dangerously satisfying to imagine Veck, or even that hard-ass Agent Heron, beating the ever-loving hell out of the guy. But that was not the kind of justice that was going to be served to the serial killer. And she wasn't fooling herself: It would not be a surprise to find out Sissy was on Kroner's list of victims, and that possibility was absolutely why Veck was interested in the case.

But Reilly played by the rules. Always had, always would.

First sign this poor girl was one of his victims? They were turning her case over to de la Cruz, and she was dragging Veck's attention to something else.

Even if it killed him.

When Veck next checked his watch, it was four thirty. The manager was a slow talker, and the digital recordings from the security cameras took a while to review; there were also a bagger and two cart sweepers to interview. No new information, but damn, he and Reilly worked well together.

She knew just when to come forward, and as with Mrs. Barten, she had a way of putting people at ease—which meant they talked more. Meanwhile, he tended to scope out the environment, and assess all the things folks weren't saying, but were showing in their faces.

Outside the customer service counter, he shook the manager's hand, and then Reilly did the same.

"Thank you for your time," she said to the guy. "We really appreciate it."

"I don't think we helped you at all." The man pushed his square glasses up higher on his nose. "Now or before. I feel awful about the whole thing."

"Here's my card." She passed it over. "Call me anytime— I'm available twenty-four/seven. And truly, you've been open and honest—that's all you can do."

Veck handed his card over as well and then he and Reilly headed for the exit.

"Have dinner with me," he said abruptly. After all, a second shot at sharing a meal had to go better than their first. Provided he didn't behave like a defensive asshole again . . .

In response, all he got was a slowdown in her stride and a long hesitation. And then an "Ah . . ."

Not a good sign, so he backed the invite up with a valid rationale: "We need to go through the file together in light of the four hours of interviews we've done. Might as well

eat at the same time—and I know you've got to be starved
by now."

Man, check his shit out. Smooth, casual. Perfect.

He stopped at a huge display made up out of bags of
nacho chips, jars of salsa, and a refrigerator bank full of
cheese. "I'll cook for you. Mexican—that's my specialty."

Actually, that would be comparatively so: he didn't
know jack about fiesta-anything, but considering this lay-
out, he had more to go on than any other style of cooking:
Ordering takeout was the only expertise he had in the
kitchen. But come on, if he hit this setup? Nabbed a box of
Tacos-for-Dummies in the Ortega aisle? How could he
fuck it up?

"We should probably keep things professional," she
hedged.

"It's not a date, I promise. You're way too good for that
and I'm not that lucky."

As her eyebrows shot to the heavens, he let the com-
ment stand. It was the truth and they both knew it.

"So what do you say, Officer? The only spice will be in
the salsa."

That got him a true smile, her lips curling upward. "I do
like Mexican."

"Then I'm your man."

For a moment, they just looked at each other. Then she
spoke slowly and carefully, "Okay, but where?"

"My place."

Walking past her, he snagged a cart and raided the shit
out of the nachos display. Talk about manna from above:
All the ingredients were lined up, so there was no choice
involved. This was just the preamble, however, and he
headed for the hanging sign with MEXICAN FOOD on it.

"Are you staring at me, Officer?" he said, as he felt her
eyes on him.

"I'm just . . . surprised, that's all."

"About what?"

Docking their cart in front of shelves full of bright yel-
low boxes, he waited for her answer.

"Tacos or enchiladas?" When she didn't reply to either inquiry, he reached for a meal-in-a-box. "Tacos it is."

Quick scan of the back. Lettuce. Cheese—he checked in the cart and decided they needed more. Tomatoes.

Roger that. "Where's the produce section?"

"Down and to the left. But you need hamburger."

"Yeah, good call."

The meat counter and freezers ran down the rear of the store, and as they passed by the trays of ground beef, he snagged a flat of four percent lean organic—because she was probably an all-natural kind of eater. When they got to the land of greens and gourds, it was a case of tomato, tomato, and a head of iceberg in a bag.

"Talk to me, Reilly," he said quietly.

"You just . . . you don't strike me as a man who needs luck with the ladies."

"You'd be surprised." As he piloted them toward the line of checkouts, going by the deli and the salad bar, he felt like explaining himself for some reason. "Look, my father's well-known for an evil reason, and people are attracted to me because of the notoriety. The women are not like you. Either they've got tattoos in stupid places and piercings all over themselves and dumb-ass, overdyed hair or they're Barbies who want to 'save' someone or are hungry for a safe walk on the wild side. Then there are the ones who seem normal, but turn out to have pictures of my father in their purses, and letters they want me to get to him—it's a fucking mess, to be honest. I've learned that I can't trust anyone, but the good news is that I'm never surprised anymore."

He pulled their cart into a U-serve and began swiping stuff as Reilly handed him things. "But like I said, you aren't in any of those categories," he finished.

"Definitely not." She passed over the bag of tomatoes. "I'm sorry, I had no idea."

"There are worse things to get saddled with." Like his blood tie to that maniac father of his, for instance. Hell, the groupies who wanted to fuck him just because of his name were bad, but the fact that he had that killer in his very marrow was the true nightmare.

"Are you going...in the middle of next week?" she asked.

"I'm sorry?"

"To the execution," she said gently.

Veck froze with the yellow Old El Paso box in his hand. "It's going forward?"

"If the governor doesn't issue a stay. There was an article in the paper today."

Ah, yes, the three columns he'd skipped at the diner. "Well, I hope they fry the bastard. And no, I'm not going. I have to see that son of a bitch every time I look into a mirror. Enough is enough."

He took his wallet out and snagged his ATM card.

"Here, let me give you some—"

Veck shot a stare over his shoulder. "The man should pay. I'm traditional like that."

"And the woman can damn well make a contribution. I'm a realist like that."

As she shoved a twenty-dollar bill into his palm and leveled her eyes at him, he knew he wanted to kiss her—and not just in his fantasies: He wanted to know what it was like to pull her in close and take a taste of that no-nonsense mouth of hers.

Not going to happen.

Refocusing on things that weren't going to get him written up or rightfully slapped, he swiped his card, punched in his PIN, and waited for the transaction to go through. After he snagged the receipt and threw it out, they headed for the exit, where he left the cart with the others and grabbed the bags.

As they walked back over to her car, he murmured, "You're quiet. Did I say too much."

She glanced up at him as she hit her remote and unlocked everything. "About your father? God, no... anytime you want to talk about him, or anything else, I'm happy to listen."

Veck believed her. Which was a miracle of its own. "Thanks, but you've just heard all I'll ever say on the matter."

Just as he reached for the trunk release, she went for the rear passenger door and said, "Wait, here, put the groceries—"

"I'll just throw them in—"

As the top rose on its own, he got a gander at three big Victoria's Secret bags.

He couldn't help it: His eyes shot over to her and scanned up her body . . . all the way to her brilliant red cheeks.

Which told him that chances were good there wcren't a whole lot of fuzzy pajamas and fluffy bathrobes in those damn bags.

"Uh . . . backseat," he muttered, "yeah . . ."

"They were having a sale," she said as he shut the trunk.

He was getting hard again. Right now. Shit.

After the groceries were in the car, the pair of them got in their respective seats and she started the engine. The seat belt cut into his erection, but he figured the damn thing deserved the pinch. He had no business fantasizing about a fashion show.

The fine Officer Reilly was into *that* stuff?

Man, he needed a smoke—

"Shit," he said.

"What?"

"We have to go to your place to do it." With a curse, he amended, "Dinner, I mean. Do *dinner* at your place—I don't have any pans."

As they stopped at the light that led out of the parking lot, she glanced over . . . and started to laugh. Before he knew it, he was smiling.

"You don't know how to cook anything, do you," she said.

"I'll be lucky if I can get the box of tacos open." He put up his forefinger. "But I'd still like to make you dinner, if you're game."

Shaking her head, she smiled. "Okay, but can you do me a favor?"

"Name it."

"Can you forget what you saw in my trunk?"

His eyes drifted to her mouth and then went farther down to the pale column of her throat and . . . "I'm sorry," he said darkly. "That I can't do."

She inhaled on a sharp suck, as if everything he was thinking was showing in his face.

"Fuck," he breathed. "I mean, yeah, of course. Consider it done. Totally forgotten."

A loud honk sounded behind them, and she jumped before hitting the gas.

Well, this was going smoothly. Maybe he'd top off the night by burning her frickin' house down.

CHAPTER
10

During his years as a black ops solider, Jim had learned that good intel was mission critical in any assignment. Of course, back when he'd been working for Matthias the Fucker, his job had been killing people, and that was not the situation with his new boss or his current targets. But a lot of the principles were the same, however.

And the stakes were even higher.

Sitting on his bed in the Marriott, with his Dell propped on his thighs, the *Caldwell Courier Journal's* Web site was front and center on the screen, and the headache he had was not from the glare.

His work was cut out for him. Assuming Devina hadn't lied about the soul.

Last night Thomas DelVecchio Jr. had been in the woods with a guy who he'd been investigating—business as usual for a homicide detective, right? Wrong. The wrench in the works was the fact that David Kroner, believed to be a serial killer, had been driven back to town in the business end of an ambulance. Where he'd been all but tomato sauce.

And that was just the start of the fun and games. After spending nearly two hours combing the Net, Jim knew enough to fill a book about DelVecchio ... and the guy's dad.

None of it was good news.

"Damn, Dog," he muttered.

Dog let out a little chuff and put his paw on Jim's forearm, as if offering support.

The question was, where was the crossroads with DelVecchio? Had it been in those woods last night?

No, because then Jim would have lost before they'd gotten started, and he had to imagine that was outside the scope of the rules. Didn't mean Devina couldn't have given that a shot, though.

And on that note. "Where are you, bitch ..."

The demon was somewhere in all this, working behind the scenes, trying to pull strings so that DelVecchio the younger would get in deep with her.

The route could be through the father. Retyping the guy's name into Google, Jim went on another surf of the Web, and what he found made him question whether humanity was worth saving: Web site after Web site of hero worship, blogs on the bastard—oh, look, role-playing based on his killings. Artwork for sale on eBay. Autographs.

The guy was his own cottage industry—but it wasn't going to last, apparently. He was due a lights-out in Connecticut very, very soon.

Then again, maybe he'd live forever in infamy: There were round-the-clock vigils going on outside the prison. No doubt that collection of protesters wouldn't stop the execution, but they were an indication that the bastard might be even more of a celebrity once he was in the ground.

According to the *CCJ* archives, the elder DelVecchio had done most of his killings in New York and Massachusetts, and the first of the AP reports on the victims dated all the way back to the mid-nineties, when an initial body had been found in ... Caldwell, New York. It had taken about three years of seemingly random butchering for the authorities to kick in that they had a serial killer on their hands. Part of the lag was the fact that he had left bodies in multiple states and the disparate investigations had been carried out with varying degrees of competency by local police. But the other thing was, at least in the beginning, DelVecchio had made it his business to hide the remains well—and creatively.

The dots had been connected, however, and then it had become a race to catch whoever the killer was. The ass slapper was that DelVecchio had been in the public eye the whole time, a dealer of antiquities—and not just trinkets or fakes. He'd been at the top of the heap with that one, importing statuary and artifacts and tablets from Egypt and the Middle East.

Handsome motherfucker. Even had an article in *Vanity Fair* on him—which went into some detail. Apparently in between the trips overseas, and the parties at the Met, DelVecchio Sr. had managed to get some woman pregnant. The son had been born on the father's birthday twenty-nine years ago, but there had been no family life to speak of. No other children.

Although there had been contact of a sort: Turned out the murder of that woman had been the key to DelVecchio's eventual capture, the first link that had brought the chain he'd been making together. The rest was history, so to speak.

"I-inn-r?"

Jim looked up over the laptop. Standing in the open connector, Adrian had a pizza box between his mitts and half of a six-pack of beer hanging from his teeth.

"Oh, yeah. Thanks, man."

Eddie came in behind the guy with a second box. "He got his with everything—and the damn bait."

Ad parked it on the bed and put the beers down. "They're called anchovies, fool."

The "whatever" went unsaid between the pair of them. Jim fed Dog first, giving the little guy some crust of the non-Adrian pie. Going by his stubby tail, the grub was more than good enough.

"So how do we know Devina didn't lie to you?" Adrian

said, before he bent a slice in half and put the pointy part in his mouth.

"This hot mess is right up our alley." He switched over to the article about the execution and turned the laptop around. "Meet the guy's dad. And wait, there's more."

As they ate, he showed them some of the sites and capped it off with the write-up online about Junior's little trip into the woods with the serial killer. While his wingmen read, there was the appropriate amount of *fuckin' hell*s, which was satisfying.

He finished his third slice. "We need to find out what happened in those woods last night."

"Article says DelVecchio has no memory."

Jim glanced over at Eddie, a.k.a. teacher of tricks. "That's where you come in. I want into that guy's mind, and you need to tell me how to do it."

Ad shrugged. "Personally, I'd just use a hacksaw, but—"

"There are potential consequences and side effects," Eddie said carefully.

"Like what?"

"Well, worst case . . . he could end up like Adrian."

"Hey—"

Jim cut the angel in question off. "Tone-deaf. Needle freak."

"Sex fiend," Eddie added.

"That would be '*god*.'" Ad cracked open a Bud. "And I keep telling you people, I'm not tone-deaf."

"We've been through this before." Eddie wiped his mouth. "If you can't hear how off-key you are, how would you know?"

"I'm not off-key."

"Yeah, you are," Jim and Eddie said together.

Before this argument got out of hand, Jim got serious with Eddie. "So tell me what I need to know."

"You're going to have to explain what you're looking for first."

Jim took a long pull from his can of beer. "I want to know where Devina is in all this. What her angle's been and which way she's likely to take shit. That's what I'm after."

And given what was doing with the father? He had his suspicions already.

Naturally, Veck had to see what was in the trunk, Reilly thought as she pulled into her driveway.

The universe just couldn't pass up an opportunity like that to get her a good one.

While her garage door went up, she glanced over at her partner. "Let me guess . . . you like to carry the groceries, as well as pay for them."

"Yeah, I do." He looked across the seats. "Like I said, I'm old-fashioned. But if you want to do the duty, I'll step back."

And that was why she didn't have a problem with him.

Besides, he could handle the food while she grabbed the VS in the trunk: However embarrassed she was, she wasn't going to leave that stuff behind. There was no pretending the disclosure hadn't been made, but more important, there was no reason to hide. She was a grown-ass woman and she could buy herself—

As the voice in her head grew more strident and defensive, she wondered who exactly she was talking to.

Probably her father.

Cutting off the ridiculous rant, she parked the car. While Veck got out and grabbed the Hannaford bags, she headed around the butt of the sedan, popping the trunk and keeping her chin up as she fisted all of her lacy-and-lovely and led the way into her kitchen.

"Wow," he said looking at the walls. And the drapes. And the counters.

"I should have warned you."

The good news about the rooster-themed nightmare of a kitchen was that it usually made people stop and look around, so she had the chance to tuck her bags around the corner, out of sight.

"I don't think I've ever seen . . ."

With a nod, she was grateful he didn't finish that one, although it wasn't like he had to. ". . . so many cocks in one place" had been let fly with reliable, if cringing, frequency.

"The little old lady who lived here before liked them." Oh, God, that sounded awful. "Ever since I moved in here two years ago, I've been meaning to get out a razor blade and start picking at the corners. But there's always some kind of work that keeps me preoccupied."

Although seeing it from his eyes made her wish she'd focused a little more. The wallpaper's pattern had three alarmingly exaggerated roosters in different poses, like they were bodybuilders competing for a trophy. Color scheme was brown, red, and cream, with green tufts of grass beneath their tripart feet. And somehow, even though the stuff had been on the walls for a good twenty years, it had retained an eye-popping vividness.

"Is it me or do their eyes follow you?" Veck asked as he put the bags on the counter.

"No, they're watching you, all right. Done wonders for my diet—I feel like I'm eating with an audience, and I haven't had chicken in here since last May."

"This is like *The Birds*."

"Except farm-themed. I know." As she went over and opened the cupboard under the stovetop, she said, "The fact that I'm getting a little used to it scares me—like maybe they've hypnotized me? By the way, pans are down here. Bowls under there and knives in those drawers by the dishwasher."

"Thanks."

As he took off his coat, his big shoulders rolled in a way that should have been only about the de-clothing, but somehow got morphed in her mind into something naked and panting.

Time for a distraction, she thought as he started to unpack.

"Hey, why don't I print out the case file while you get started with the food?" she said.

"That'd be great."

"It may take a little while. My printer's ancient."

"We've got the time."

Evidently: Going by the way he was concentrating on the chips bag, he was about to perform brain surgery with the help of her microwave. And okay, wow. The cool, impassive, handsome-as-hell routine was sexy, but this consternation made him approachable. Well, that and the way he'd opened up about the dating thing. She'd never once considered the groupie angle—but then, even good-looking people could be pursued for the wrong reasons, couldn't they.

In her office down the hall, she logged into the CPD database, fired up the report, and stood by the printer, ready to perform the Heimlich when the thing got jammed—which it did. Twice.

The first hint that all wasn't well at the other end of the house was the unmistakable nose-wrinkling aroma of burning meat. Second was an explosion of cursing. Which kept up until she headed back with the copies.

Lot of F-bombs.

And then the smoke detector went off.

Holy smokes was right. Whatever was in the pan on the stove—the hamburger meat, most likely, but with Veck, maybe it was the nachos—needed a fire hose. But he was on it, heading for the sink with the mess, putting it in there, and not turning the water on yet. And he was instantly over at the screaming unit on the ceiling, fanning the detector with a dish towel without having to get up on his tiptoes.

"I think one of the roosters jacked up the heat," he shouted.

"Wouldn't surprise me."

She hid a smile as she put the papers on the table and got a gander at what he'd laid out on a plate: Shreds of orange cheese had bonded at the molecular level with the layer of Santitas.

Only one thing to do now, she thought.

Heading for the phone, she said, "What do you like on your pizza, oh, mighty fanner."

"Pepperoni and sausage."

"Good call."

As she dialed up the local joint, she glanced over. The bottom of his shirt had ridden up, and she got a clear flash of the black waistband of his Calvins . . . as well as a stretch of taut skin that had that dark line running down from his belly button.

It took no time at all for her brain to segue back to the bathroom scene from the night before. One instant and she was there, seeing his body naked—

"Oh, yeah, hi." She turned away quickly. "This'll be for delivery. Yup, that's me. Large pepperoni and sausage. Yup. No, no drinks . . . No, I don't want a second pizza for free. . . .No, no wings . . . No, thanks, we don't need— No cinnamon wedges, either." For God's sake, it took longer to shut them down about the "deals" than for them to make, box, and drive out the damn pizza. "Great, thanks."

Hanging up, she squared her shoulders and pivoted around again—

Veck was standing right behind her, his lids at half-mast, his body so much larger that it appeared when he was five feet away from her.

She didn't move. Neither did he.

"Do you believe confession is good for the soul?" he said darkly.

"Yes . . ."

"Then I have something I'd better tell you."

Oh, God, this was why they told you not to mix business and pleasure: As their eyes met, she was not thinking about the case. She was thinking she might have to do a little admitting of her own.

I saw you naked last night and you're beautiful.

"What," she breathed.

I want you even though I shouldn't.

Swallowing hard, she said, "Tell me . . ."

CHAPTER
11

Veck knew he shouldn't answer his partner, and he sure as hell shouldn't have come around to stand this close to her. The right move would have been to start cleaning up the mess he'd made with the food—instead of creating another one.

Except he'd seen her staring at his body, and the expression on her face had been a hard, driving hunger. Surprising? Yes. Satisfying? Could be if they followed up on it.

The trouble was, that was not the kind of thing you could tidy up with soap and hot water.

"What?" she whispered.

"I want to . . ." The word was so crass that he kept it to himself.

"Say it."

He leaned in and put his lips by her ear. "You know exactly what I want."

"And I want you to say it."

"You sure about that. It ain't nothing nice."

Before he could retreat, she reached out and put her hands on his hips. Her touch was light as a shadow falling across his body, but he felt the burn all through him. And

one thing was certain, if she drew him to her? She was go-
ing to know *exactly* what was on his mind.

The hold on him tightened. "Tell me."

His voice dropped to a growl: "I want to *fuck* you,"

As she moaned a little, he kept going. "I want you na-
ked. Under me. And I want to be inside you." He dipped
down and ran his mouth over her neck. "But I know you
specialize in conflicts of interest, so you are damn familiar
with all the reasons this is a bad idea."

Cue her backing away. Or him stepping off.

Neither of them moved.

Shit, his body was teetering on out of control, his erec-
tion pounding to get free and do what it did best. Which
meant that if they were going to do the right thing here, the
strength had to come from her.

"Slap me," he groaned. "Push me away . . . for God's
sake, lock yourself in the bathroom or something. Because
if you don't, I'm going to—"

"Kiss me."

God, the tone she used: That was a command, right
there. And who was he to disobey an order? Especially
from a superior?

Veck reached out and wrapped an arm around her waist.
With a hard, impatient pull, he yanked her against his body.
Next move was to take out the tie in her hair and throw it
on the ground.

Man, she was edible with that stuff not pulled back, the
red weight down around her shoulders, looking like it was
more than ready to have a man's hands in it.

As he gripped the nape of her neck and locked on, he
was damned aware that he was dominating the hell out of
her, taking control of her body, holding her like he meant
to shove her onto her kitchen table and kneel between her
legs so he could suck on her sex.

But then again, that was what he wanted to do to her.

"I'm sorry," he said, aware that he was apologizing not
only for what he was about to do, but for all the shit racing

through his mind, all the down-and-dirty he wanted to put them both through.

And then he sealed their fate by sealing their lips.

Her mouth was soft under him—and so were her breasts against his chest and her hips against his cock . . . she was soft and hot, the kind of thing he wanted to seep into and stay in awhile. But even as his pelvis curled in and his erection pulsed, in the back of his mind, he knew that conflict of interest was not the biggest problem they had. As much as he was pretending to be back to normal, he was ripped raw on the inside, between the shit in the woods and the update on his dad.

And he was worried Reilly looked like exactly the kind of Band-Aid he needed . . .

It was the last logical, decent thought he had.

As he penetrated her with his tongue, his arms tightened up and his lower body arched again, the squeeze and stroke on his cock juicing him even further. And that was before he felt the shudder that went through Reilly. Clearly, she was right there with him, especially as her nails bit into his shoulders and her thighs split, giving him an opening to push one of his legs through.

With an internal curse, he shifted her around and eased her down on the table, on top of the paperwork she'd just printed out. Images of her with her legs over his shoulders and him licking up the center of her core made him think he might have done some false advertising with his F-bomb.

Well, not false, really. He was just adding a very vital tourist attraction on the way to the big event.

His palm swept down to the outside of her thigh and he lifted her leg, rubbing himself even closer to where he ultimately wanted to be. Breaking the suction of their mouths, he buried himself in her neck, nipping and licking.

"Let me see you," he groaned into her throat. "Let me . . ."

Inside, another voice said.

Abruptly, he lost his rhythm, pulling out of the spiral and looking up. Now his heart beat for a different reason.

"What is it?" she said.

His eyes flashed around. Except there were no shadows darting around her rooster kitchen. No creaks of floorboards or squeaking hinges. Nothing staring in through the windows.

After a moment, his adrenaline faded, and he became aware once again of where they were and what he'd been doing with her.

Maybe it had just been a really loud internal thought.

Which considering what had happened with Kroner the night before didn't make him feel better at all.

Her hand came up and lay on his cheek. "Are you okay?"

"No." He refocused on her face. Felt her body beneath his own. Heard her deep breaths. "But I don't want to stop. You're real to me . . . and I fucking need that right now. I need . . . you right now."

She was not like the other women he'd had: Her smart eyes saw too much, knew too much. Hell, he'd been naked in front of her from the first moment he'd met her— and that should have sent him running in the opposite direction. Instead? He just wanted the shit out of her.

"Then take me," she said, pulling her shirt free of her skirt.

He didn't give her more than a split second to change her mind: as he had with her lips, he dived in, running his hands under the opening she gave him, making contact with a whole lot of warm female skin. And then the buttons came free as if they had the same objective he did: all-access.

He reared up when the last popped open. . . . Holy fuck.

Red lace. Intricate red lace over a set of perfectly pro-portioned breasts.

Which meant that through the little cutouts, he saw her nipples, tight and straining.

"Do you like what I bought today?" she asked hoarsely.

"Not bad." He cleared his throat as his voice cracked. "Not bad at all. But what's underneath is even hotter."

With smooth grace, her hands went up and traced the

bra's thin, bright straps . . . then drifted down to the hard tips that, as she arched, begged for him.

On a growl, he shoved up her skirt and maneuvered himself between her legs, spreading them further with his hips as he went for what had caught his eye: Drawing her into his mouth through the amazing bra, there was the rasp of the lace against his tongue, but also peek-a-boos of the pink, tight flesh beneath.

Wasn't long before that was so not enough.

With a rough, impatient hand, he tugged the cup down, revealing her nipple.

"Fucking hell . . ." he bit out. "You are—"

Uninterested in him talking: in a rush, her fingers grabbed onto the back of his head and brought him downward to her breast. As he sucked her in, she jacked up off the table, and that movement, that jerking, demanding shove snapped what last restraint he had. All at once, he took over, pushing one of his arms under her and lifting her further, using his other hand to go right between her thighs, to that heat behind her hose and her panties.

He rubbed her sex, his palm hitting the top, right where she needed—

"Veck!"

The sound of his name was all about the more, more, more. And he was going to give it to her. Switching sides, he bit the other half of the bra and pulled it down with his teeth, before he suckled on her opposite nipple.

This still wasn't enough, though. He needed full-contact naked. Here, now—

The moan that rippled up and out of her was just the kind of agreement that he needed to hear.

Christ, this was going to happen, he thought. This was going to *happen*.

Veck was totally dominant.

Reilly hadn't expected anything less, but what was a surprise was how much it turned her on. Part of it was her sense that if she got uncomfortable with how far they'd gone, he'd pull back in a second. But the other half was the way he handled her, the confidence, the power, the erotic possibility that came from his mouth and his hands and his intense, hot eyes.

No doubt he'd started out with a natural talent for sex . . . and developed it over the years.

Abruptly, as if he read her mind, his stare flashed up to hers and locked on while he flicked her nipple with his tongue . . . and as his lids lowered, she knew he wanted her to watch him.

What a sight it was. He'd pulled down the other side of her bra and was working her there, licking and sucking as his flat hand pushed into her. God, he was big—all over: His erection was a long, thick ridge rubbing against her inner thigh, his shoulders were so huge she couldn't see anything past them, and his lower body was taking up all the room between her spread legs.

With her breasts pushed up by the bra he'd pulled down, her shirt wide-open, and her skirt up around her waist, the next logical undoing was the thin nylon covering her legs, and she popped her pelvis off the table, feeling that circling palm of his press harder into her. Dipping her thumbs into the elastic waistband, she scooped the hose down and ducked her hips, the constriction slipping onto her thighs.

"I'll take it from there." Veck eased back, his eyes on fire as he stared at her body. "Mmm . . . right where I want to be."

As he smiled like a predator, she brought her knees up to help as he stripped the hose off slowly. And it wasn't until the thin wisps were free of her feet that she had to wonder how far this was going to go. Was she really going to take what they'd started to the conclusion they were both gunning for?

If that was a "yes," there were practicalities to deal with.

But, crap, what a buzz kill the condom discussion was—and, yeah, now she knew why people made dumb choices when it came to sex. All the things that truly mattered, the things that were going to sting after these intense minutes were over and done with, the things she'd have to live with, maybe forever ... were nothing more than distant echoes she could barely hear, spoken in a language she didn't want to translate.

Fifty thousand years of evolution knew what was up.

With a surge, Veck came back to her mouth, kissing her deep as his hands drifted downward—

The curse that shot up her throat was more vibration than sound: His hand was back between her legs, brushing over her inner thigh, heading for the match to the bra he'd already seen and dominated.

"Veck!" she barked again as his touch slid to that center strip of satin.

He was careful, putting just enough pressure on that sensitive place, stroking her in a tight circle that made her body go both utterly loose and unbearably tense.

Screw the panties, she wanted nothing between them ... and yet the silk barrier was not all bad, the seam at the top adding another dimension to the rhythm he'd fallen into. And he didn't stop kissing her mouth or her neck or her breasts, until she felt as though he was all over her, surrounding her, taking her even though they had yet to become fully joined.

With a quick shift, he lifted his torso from her, and pushed his hips into her sex, locking their bodies together. Then curling his lower spine, he ground into her, stroking her with his erection as he looked down at the connection.

God, his face was dark with hunger, that cool reserve of his gone, that impassive mask blown to hell and gone by the driving need that locked his jaw.

They *were* going to do this, she realized.

Which was a shock. In her life, choices were made based on data screens of *should* and *have to* and *better not*. This hot sex was definitely in the last category ... and yet she wasn't going to stop it.

They were going to do it safely, however—although not in a bed. This table was working just fine.

But there were things she wanted to get a better feel for first.

Reaching down her body, she took her palm and slid it between them—

Veck's head dropped back. "Fuuuuuck …"

Perfect sentiment: His erection was even bigger than she imagined, and it kicked against her palm—

The sound of the doorbell was loud as a gunshot.

And yet for a moment, she couldn't comprehend what the hell the noise was, or why she should care.

Veck recovered his senses first. "Pizza."

"Wha …t?"

With quick, logical thinking, he reached over and canned the lights so that whoever had brought their pepperoni and sausage didn't get a floor show. Then, with efficient hands, he pulled her shirt back together, tugged the hem of her skirt down, and reached into his pants, rearranging his arousal so his fly didn't look like a circus tent.

"I'll take care of it," he said in a level voice. Like nothing had happened. At all.

As he walked off for the front door, Reilly sat up slowly, her head swimming and her body shaking. Holding her blouse together, his brisk return to normal made her feel totally out of control—and then she shifted herself off the table, and the papers on the Barten case fell to the floor.

The flurry of individual pages formed a kind of carpet at her feet, and they were just the kind of mirror she needed to see herself clearly in: Across town, there was a whole family mourning for a daughter they knew they had lost, and instead of focusing on their pain and her job … she was hooking up with a man she had no business getting within ten yards of.

Couldn't get a better conflict of interest than this one. It was frickin' textbook.

Fumbling with the buttons on her shirt, she did them up fast and then bent down to pick the copies of the report up. As her hair fell into her face, she thought, where was her scrunchie?

Who the hell knew.

Tucking the tangled mess behind her ears, she pulled the printouts together with careful hands, reordering the pages, separating everything back into two piles, hers and Veck's.

Separate was better.

Had she lost her mind?

Down the hall, the deep rumble of a thank-you was followed by the front door shutting and his heavy footfalls coming back toward the kitchen.

Standing up fast, she put the two stacks of papers on the table and kept her eyes on them. She couldn't look at him. Just didn't have the strength at the moment.

"I think you'd better go." Her voice didn't sound right, but then, she didn't feel right.

"Okay. I'll call a cab."

Crap. His bike was back at the station house, wasn't it.

With a silent curse, she muttered, "That's all right. I can drive you—"

"No, a cab is better."

She nodded and brushed the front page of the report ... right where Sissy's vital stats and disappearance date were listed. "We'll go through this in the office tomorrow morning."

"Yeah." As he pulled on his coat, the soft sound of fabric on fabric was loud as the doorbell. "I'm sorry."

She crossed her arms over her chest and nodded again. "Yeah, me, too. I don't know what got into me."

But she damn sure knew what would have if dinner hadn't arrived in the nick of time.

Moments later, he was gone, and he shut the door behind him so quietly it didn't make any sound.

When she finally looked over her shoulder, all she saw was the pizza on the counter. Uh-huh, right, like she was eating anything right now.

The box went right into the fridge.

On her way out, she passed the table and found her panty hose on the back of a chair. Her scrunchie, on the other hand, was on the floor by the archway into the little dining room. Leaning over to pick the thing up, she went eye-to-eye with the Victoria's Secret payload.

And realized that her bra was still waaaaaay out of place.

She left the bags where they were and fixed the immediate problem with a couple of jerks and a whole lot more cursing.

As she headed for the stairs, she thought, tomorrow she was wearing her old boring cotton underwear to work, thank you very much.

CHAPTER
12

"Question. Is it still B and E if you don't actually break anything to get inside?"

Adrian let that little ditty fly just as Jim and the boys took form in Thomas DelVecchio Jr.'s front hall—and all things considered, the angel could have come up with a much worse comment. Or broken into an ear-destroying, off-key rendition of "Take Me Out to the Ball Game."

Jim had never spent so much time praying for plugs and muffs.

At least the bastard didn't try to rap.

"Well?" Ad said.

"Look, we don't even exist," Jim muttered. "So you could argue we're not really here anyway."

"Excellent point. Guess it's legal."

"Like it would bother you if the shit weren't."

The house was decorated in exactly Jim's style: functional, nothing special, lot of empty floor space. The problem? Not a lot of personal effects, and they needed one that had some metal in it. Preferably gold, silver, or platinum. If they could get just an object with enough of Veck's imprint on it, they could use that as a connection to get into the man's brain from a remote location: According to Eddie, it was too risky to do it one-on-one in person. Not with Devina around.

"Let's split up," Jim said. "I'll cover the second floor."

As Ad and Eddie fanned out, he mounted the stairs two at a time. The master bedroom took up one whole half of the second story, although that sounded more impressive than the reality, because the total square footage of the place wasn't more than twenty-one hundred, maybe twenty-two.

"Christ, here much, buddy?" he muttered.

There was nothing in the room but a big bed and a crappy bedside table with a lamp on it. No alarm clock—guy probably used his cell phone for that. No landline telephone, but why would you need one? Requisite flat-screen screwed into the wall with the remote in the tangled sheets.

Some dirty clothes were in a plastic bin in the corner, socks and boxer briefs hanging off the sides as if the thing were drooling black cotton. Closet revealed . . . shit actually on hangers, which was better than the duffel bag shuffle Jim had lived with for years. On the back of the door, there were a couple of belts with metal fittings, but there had to be something better he could use.

He headed for the bathroom. All the lights were off, but the guy didn't believe in drapes, so there was enough from the streetlights to go by—

As soon as he stepped into the squat, tiled room, the back of his neck went wild, ants crawling over his skin.

Devina.

"Where are you," he said, turning in a tight circle. "Where the hell are you . . ."

The demon had been here—he could sense her presence lingering in the air, kind of like the stench of garbage hanging onto a trash bin even after the thing had been emptied.

And didn't this lend a little credibility to Devina's reveal at the diner.

As he turned to the sink, he frowned. The mirror was covered with a towel, and the tickling at his nape grew more intense as he reached up and pulled the terry cloth down.

Nothing except an eighties-vintage medicine cabinet sunken into the drywall. But the glass-front face of the thing was utterly contaminated.

Had she come through it somehow? he wondered.

The instant his fingertips made contact with the reflective surface, he retracted his hand. The medicine cabinet was icy cold.

Shit, Veck knew something was after him, didn't he. Why else drape the thing? The question was, how far was that demon into him?

"What did you do to him, bitch."

Replacing the towel, Jim opened the vanity drawers, rattling the backup deodorant and the extra toothpaste and the nail clippers—hey, maybe they would work. Except they were hardly something the guy would have an emotional connection with—

Light swept across the front of the house, blasting through the window Jim was standing in front of, and reminding him that he hadn't bothered to go invisi.

Disappearing himself, he looked out of the window. Directly below in the driveway, Veck got out of a Yellow Cab.

Jim ghosted away from the master suite and drafted down the front stairs, becoming nothing but a disturbance of the air. Over in the kitchen he found that Ad and Eddie had done as he had, and the three of them waited together, forming nothing more than a warm pocket in the far corner of the room.

She's already in him, he thought to his boys.

I can feel her from here, Eddie sent back.

At the far end of the front hall, the door opened and closed, and got locked. Then some heavy-ass feet came down toward where they were standing.

"Fucking ... hell ..."

The cursing continued as Veck entered the kitchen, tossed his keys and ripped off his jacket. Next move was to go to the refrigerator and grab a longneck. Cracking the lid

and drinking hard, it was clear he'd had a whole lot of bad
night wash over his transom—

Abruptly, the man leveled his head, lowered the beer,
and looked directly where they were all standing.

He shouldn't be able to sense them, much less see them.

None of them moved. Including Veck.

And that was when Jim looked on the linoleum floor
behind the detective . . . and noticed that the guy threw two
shadows.

Single light source? Two opposite patches at his feet?

Keeping quiet, Jim pointed to the ground, and his wing-
men nodded.

Veck reached out with his long arm and flipped a switch
so that more lights came on. Then he glanced all around.

"Fucking . . . hell."

Obviously, that was the guy's theme song, and but for
the fact that it might encourage Ad into a vocal riff, Jim was
thinking of humming a few bars himself.

With a shake of the head, Veck went back to his beer,
sucking it down on a oner. Leaving the dead soldier on the
counter, he got two more and walked out of the room.

Destination: living room couch.

Jim and his boys drafted after him, but kept their dis-
tance. Veck was either extremely intuitive or polluted
enough to have a radar screen for the angels.

Knowing their luck, it was the latter.

Sitting down, the detective disarmed, removing a re-
spectable autoloader as well as a nasty knife. And then he
unclipped his badge.

His shiny, gold-and-silver police badge.

The man held the thing in his cupped palm for the lon-
gest time, staring at it as if it were a crystal ball that he
could see into . . . or maybe a mirror he was trying to see
himself in.

Put it down, buddy, Jim thought. Finish up those beers,
lie the fuck back, and take a little nap. I promise I'll return
it when I'm done.

Veck followed the orders well, putting the badge with

his name and serial number on it by the weapons, swallowing the beers one after the other, and then leaning back against the cushions.

His eyes closed a moment later. It took a while longer before those hands went lax on his thighs and fell to the sides, but then slow, deep breathing was the confirmation—and the cue to get what they needed and go.

Jim extended his hand at waist level and went Jedi on the badge, levitating it up off the bare floor and drawing it through the still darkness to him. The instant his palm came in contact with the object, the same cold from upstairs registered, Devina's evil dwelling in the space between the molecules of the metal.

Eddie's caution had seemed over-kill—until now. Given the strong signal the badge was giving off, you didn't want to get caught with your pants down if you were working on the thing.

Jim nodded toward the window, and just like mist disappearing, the three of them were up and out of there.

Across town, in the thick of Caldwell's urban core, the St. Francis Hospital complex was a mammoth operation that glowed like the Vegas strip. Under its some twenty different roofs, lives started and ended by the thousands every year, the fight against the Grim Reaper waged by every kind of doctor and surgeon and nurse there was.

Devina was well familiar with the place: Sometimes those humans in white coats and green scrubs needed a little help to make sure the job got done properly.

And usually that meant death, but not always.

The demon entered the emergency room wing through its electronic front door. Wearing her banging-hot skin of female flesh, she got all kinds of stares from the collection of fathers and frat boys sitting in the waiting room. Which was why she didn't take the shortcuts she could have. Ghosting through glass, steel, or brick was efficient, but lame: She loved being gawked at. Ogled. Hit on. And the burning glares of the other women, all those hate-filled, envious eyes? Even better.

Finding Kroner in the rabbit maze of wards and floors and units was a piece of fucking cake. She'd been inside of him for years, helping him hone his skills and supporting his obsession. He'd been born a sick little shit, but he'd lacked the courage to act on his impulse—and that shriveling impotence had worked in her favor. Nothing made somebody who was hardwired like him more violent against attractive young women than his own deflated pencil dick.

The ICU in question was seven levels above where she'd come in, and she took her time going to elevators, strolling along, checking out the nurses' uniforms.

Snooze. Baggy, badly printed cotton with no cleavage showing on top and saggy asses on the bottom. What the hell did they think they were doing with that look?

When she finally got to the banks of metal double doors, she caught a ride up the building with an orderly and an old man on a gurney. The geezer was out like a light, but the pusher gave Devina not just a once-over, but a thrice-over.

No doubt he would have made it to a fourth and a fifth if the doors hadn't opened at her floor.

She tossed him a smile over her shoulder as she stepped out, just for shits and giggles.

And then it was time to get down to business. She had the option of assuming a mist and swirling over the polished floor, but that would have caused a panic. And she could have gone straight-up invisi, but that was a failure of originality in her book: She had passed many a century enjoying the interplay with humans, disguising herself among them, nipping at their heels and brushing up against them—or going farther than that.

No reason to pass up the opportunity for some fun tonight, even though she was working. After all, her therapist was urging her to find greater balance in her life.

As she zeroed in on the unit in question, she went down

a corridor that was hung with photographs of various heads of departments.

Very helpful, as it turned out.

She stopped by several, noting the features and the accessories, the name tags and titles, the white coats and the striped ties or formal blouses.

It was like shopping for a new outfit. And she came with her own tailoring service.

Stepping around a corner, she glanced up and down the hallway to make sure she was alone, and then she fritzed out the security camera above her, sending it just enough of an electrical surge to knock it cold without exploding the thing.

Then she assumed the visage and white coat of the chief of neurology, one Denton Phillips, MD.

The guise was a bit of a saggy disappointment compared to her luscious brunette suit of flesh. The man was some sixty years old, and although he was handsome in a well-preserved, snotty-white-guy kind of way, she felt ugly and badly put together.

At least it was better than what she really looked like, and a not-for-long proposition.

As she went back out into the main corridor, she strode like a man, and it was a shot in the arm to see the respect and fear in the eyes of the staff she passed. Not quite as entertaining as lust and envy, but enjoyable nonetheless.

No need to ask where Kroner was. He was a beacon easily followed—and she was not surprised to find a uniformed officer seated outside his private room.

The man rose to his feet. "Doctor."

"I'll just be a minute."

"Take your time."

Not likely—she had to work fast. She had no idea what Denton Phillips, MD, actually sounded like, and there was no way of being sure she got his height correct—which was what happened if all you had was a picture to go by: Now would not be a good time to run into any colleagues who would know better—or worse, the man himself.

The intensive care unit Kroner was in had curtained glass walls, and even from the outside, you could hear the hiss of the medical equipment that was keeping him alive. Sliding the door back temporarily, she pushed aside the bolts of piss-green fabric and stepped in.

"You look like shit," she said in a male voice.

As she walked to the bed, she let the visual lie of the good doctor slip away, showing herself as the beautiful woman Kroner had first met a decade ago.

There were tubes going in and out of every orifice he had, and the tangle of wires coming off his chest made him look like some kind of human switchboard. Lot of bandages and white gauze over gray skin. Lot of bruising. And his face looked like a Mylar balloon, all red and shiny, stretched out from the swelling.

This was not the end that she had planned and worked for. DelVecchio was supposed to have given in and killed the bastard before Heron even got wind of who the next soul was. Unfortunately, her stringy, sicko sacrificial lamb had been slaughtered by someone else.

For fuck's sake, it was obvious he wasn't going to make it. She was not a doctor—she just played one from time to time, natch—but that pallor alone made her think of morticians.

It wasn't too late for the bastard, though. And after this little whoopsie, she was not taking any chances with the outcome of this round. Time to get a little more aggressive, especially given the deal she'd struck with Heron.

"Not your time to go yet." She leaned over the bed. "I need you."

Closing her eyes, she misted out over the man's body, blanketing him, and then seeping inside of him through his every pore. The power innate in her filled his depleted tank, reenergizing him, pulling him out of the death spiral at the same time it healed and strengthened him.

And to think humans relied on crash carts. How rudimentary was that?

Kroner's eyes popped open just as she was retracting

herself, and as she reassumed her shape beside him, he focused on her.

Love shone out of his gaze.

Pathetic, but useful.

"Live," she commanded, "and I shall see you soon."

He tried to nod, but there was too much going on with the intubation thingy in his throat. He was going to make it, however. As she glanced up at the monitoring equipment, his heart rate settled down into a steady rhythm and his blood pressure regulated. Oxygen number came out of the seventies and into the nineties.

"Good boy," she said. "Now rest."

Raising her hand, she put him in a deep, healing sleep, and then she reassumed the image of the good old Dr. Denton.

Get in, get out, get gone.

She left the glassed-in room, nodded to the guard, and then strode down the corridor, passing the sycophants and suckups who all but dropped to their knees in her path. Which was enjoyable. To the point where she was tempted to parade around the hospital for a while just absorbing the experience of being the man.

But again, the last thing she needed was to run into anyone who actually knew the guy. And, more important, she had an appointment with her therapist first thing in the morning, and she needed to pick out what she was going to wear—which could take hours.

Which was why she needed a fucking shrink.

Time to run.

CHAPTER
13

Angel Airlines, those sets of iridescent wings that Jim was still getting used to, returned him and his boys to the Marriott in the blink of an eye. In the pair of rooms, they converged in Jim's half, with Dog doing a little circling dance now that the band was back together.

"So what am I doing?" As Jim put the question out there, he wondered how many years it was going to take before he didn't have to ask it of Eddie anymore. Probably a few. This job had come with no training, dire straits, and horrifying implications.

Perfect Monster.com listing, yup, yup.

"Get quiet," Eddie said, "and hold the badge. Imagine that DelVecchio is sitting in front of you, facing you with his hands on his knees and his eyes meeting yours. As always, the more specific the vision is, the better this will work. See yourself reaching forward and placing your fingertip on his forehead, and know that this connection will give you the power to pull the memories from him even though you aren't actually touching him. It's all in the mind."

"Ba-dum-bum," Adrian capped off.

Settling on the bed, Jim held the badge in his palms and

felt like an utter ass. Back in his days as an XOps soldier, or hell, even earlier, when he'd just been a punk-ass civilian, he'd never been into this transcendental, belly-lint-staring, yogi maharishi-whatever crap. He supposed with enough go-arounds like this he might get used to it, but he was always going to be a doer, not a downward-dog kind of guy.

Whatever, though.

Concentrating on the badge, the thing felt like an ice cube against his skin, with all the piercing cold, just none of the dripping water. And it would have helped if he knew DelVecchio a little better, but he did what he could to see the man: the dark hair, that handsome-as-sin face, the cold, smart blue eyes—

From one moment to the next, what he pictured became something he suddenly actually saw in 3-D, as if he'd been staring at a TV and an actor had stepped through the screen to sit in front of him.

Except the shit was all wrong.

The man had two faces.

Jim shook his head, like maybe that was going to clear up the problem. Didn't help. The primary visage was DelVecchio's . . . and so was the other one, like a double-exposed photograph.

Something told Jim not to go any farther.

He did, anyway.

Reaching out, he put his imaginary finger on the imaginary forehead of the primary DelVecchio—

The moment contact was made, a live-wire jolt shot into him, stopping his heart and jerking his body. Then, as if he were a tuning fork, a reverberation took root—and took over. Beginning with the fingertip and vibrating down his hand and his wrist and his arm, what started as a subtle tremor became so violent, he literally shook apart . . . until there were two fingertips, two hands, two wrists, two arms, with him going between the extremes like a flag ripping back and forth in a gale-force wind.

He was vaguely aware of someone yelling his name, but there was no chance of responding. He was in a fight for his immortal life, the blurring threatening to destroy him—and he was just about to lose his grip on himself completely when the DelVecchios separated until they were distinct identities linked together only at the hips and lower body.

The one on the right was smiling, and it was not the detective. It was the older DelVecchio from the newspaper article, the one with the stained soul and the evil acts.

The son of a bitch was loving this destruction.

Fucking hell . . . Jim had a terrible feeling he was not walking away from this.

Adrian knew the shit was going to hit the fan the instant Jim's hands started to vibrate around the badge.

Not normal.

And then streaming black smoke curled up out of the cupped link of Jim's palms, coalescing and then encasing the angel's grip on DelVecchio's shield. The shaking started as nothing more than a slow back-and-forth, but quickly that motion evolved into a violent rattling until the badge dropped out of Jim's hold, and bounced on the short-napped carpet.

For a split second, he thought that was going to stop it, but the smoke no longer needed the external source: Jim's own hands and arms had become the base from which the quaking infection sprouted.

"If it gets to his heart, we've lost him," Eddie ground out.

Which was the cue to get moving. Adrian and his best friend leaped up at the same time and went in opposite directions. As Eddie gunned for the connector to their room, Ad jumped on the bed behind Jim. Bracing himself, he knelt down and locked his arms around that big chest, positioning the grip as high as possible, to form a physical barrier against the onslaught.

He knew the moment the tide hit him—icy cold wafted across his skin, so frigid it registered as a burn. Opening himself up, he gave the rush a different area to contaminate, offering another target . . . even if it meant sacrificing himself.

But the shit wasn't interested in him; he was barely a speed bump as the tremors headed downward for Jim's pecs.

The saving grace they needed was that solution of lemon, white vinegar, hydrogen peroxide, and witch hazel, and good thing Eddie was always prepared. He came flying in from their room with a bucketful of the stuff, moving so fast it sloshed out, splashing his leathers and his World Wildlife Foundation T-shirt.

The angel swung back and then hit them with a splash, soaking their upper bodies along with the bed. And then it was cue the evac: with an ear-numbing screech, the evil took off in rush, leaving only a stinky smolder that wafted off Jim's wet head and chest. In the wake of the departure, the savior collapsed forward, going so limp the only thing that kept him on the bed was the hold around his torso.

"Easy there," Ad muttered, as he lay the guy out flat.

Jim opened his eyes and blinked like he wasn't sure what he was seeing.

"It's the ceiling," Ad provided. "How you doing?"

"I didn't get . . . any intel . . . from Veck."

"And guess what—you're not trying again."

"What the hell . . . was that? I feel like I've been in a turbine."

Eddie sat down next to them, settling Dog on his lap. "Devina's already in DelVecchio at a very deep level."

"Goddamn it . . . can she not cheat? Just for once." Jim fingertipped the front of his wet shirt, pulling the second skin free of his chest. "And shit, I feel polluted."

Adrian went to the bathroom and grabbed some towels. When he came back, he draped one over Jim and did a little work on his own head.

He didn't mind a hard fight, as long as it was a fair one— and this business with Devina going outside the rules was getting ridiculous. Meanwhile, Jim had all but sold himself to that demon for information, and to top it off? Nigel, their coach, didn't seem in a big hurry to throw a protest upstairs.

The whole thing sucked ass.

Reaching down, he snagged the badge and shoved it in his pocket. When Jim looked like he was going to protest, it was a case of whatever-buddy: "Sorry. You're going to need some time before the stank is fully out of you. Touch this now? We're going to have the same problem all over again, only worse." He pointed his finger right into Eddie's face. "And fuck. You."

'Cause it was obvious there was going to be a round of no-you-don'ts from the angel.

"I'm just going to take the badge back." Kinda. "DelVecchio wakes up with it gone and he's going to feel like he's losing more of his mind. You want that? Good. Glad you agree."

Before either one of them could tune up again, he went into his and Eddie's room, and stripped down—with a struggle. Leathers were tough to get off in the first place, but with the lemony wash? Like frickin' glue.

"Swear to me," Eddie said from the doorway, "that you will not touch him. In any way."

Adrian pulled on a fresh pair of fatigues and snagged the badge from his other pants. "Swear to God."

The sound of someone trying to cough his liver up was exactly the conversation ender they needed. Jim was in for a hell of a ride, and although Eddie didn't look like nurse-maid material, the bastard was great at it—something Ad had learned firsthand.

"I'll be back before you know I'm gone." Adrian smiled. "Trust me."

Eddie just rolled his eyes and went back into the other room, no doubt to hold a wastepaper basket under Jim's heaving.

In the blink of an eye, Adrian was on the front lawn of DelVecchio's little slice of home-sweet-home. The wind had come up and was blowing from the north, and the cold, crystal-clear Canadian air that came from over the border tingled in his sinuses.

No reason to knock. He just shifted himself into the living room, where DelVecchio was still asleep on the couch.

Placing the badge on the floor next to the guy's gun and holster, Adrian knelt down and reached out a hand. Passing his palm over DelVecchio's face, he lulled the man into an even deeper sleep, soothing the poor bastard.

The resulting trance revealed the truth: unfettered by consciousness, the extent of Devina's possession was obvious: she was all over every inch of him.

They might be too late already, Ad thought as he started to circle his hand over the guy's head.

"Hey, my man," he whispered. "I want you to go back to last night. Into the woods. Go back to the woods. Into the woods by the motel. In and among the pine trees. You've parked that bike—which, P.S., would it kill you to go old-school? A Beamer? Really? You might as well be straddling a Cuisinart." When DelVecchio's brows twitched, Ad figured a debate on motorcycles could wait. "You've parked that Eurotrash POS and you're walking through the forest. You're looking for Kroner. You're waiting for Kroner. Tell me what you're doing."

Ad kept up with circling. "Talk to me. What are you doing—"

"I'm going . . . to kill him."

The words were soft and spoken through a mouth that barely moved.

"With what," Ad prompted. "Tell me everything, buddy."

"My . . . knife. I have . . . my knife with me and I'm . . . waiting. . . ." DelVecchio frowned again, but this time it seemed more like he was staring off into the distance even though his eyes were closed. "I know he's going to show."

"And when he does—what do you do?"

While Ad waited for the answer, he prayed for a miracle. He'd seen the report on the news so he knew that someone had done a serious number on that Kroner character. If somehow it could be anyone other than Veck, at least they'd be headed in a better direction.

"I palm my blade . . . and I step forward. I'm . . . going to kill him. With my knife." The guy's right hand twitched at his thigh, then formed a fist as if gripping a dagger. "I'm going to— There's someone else here."

DelVecchio held his breath and didn't move at all on the couch, just as he must have done out in the woods.

"Who." When there was no reply, Adrian wanted to shake the guy's box of marbles to clear up the cognitive jam, but instead just continued circling his palm. "Who is it?"

DelVecchio seemed to struggle at that point, shaking his head from side to side and wincing. His hand crawled up his chest and rubbed his temple. "I can't . . . remember . . ."

Someone's been inside his chrome dome already, Adrian thought. Patching over the memories.

Fucking hell. There was only one species on the planet that could do that—and was also capable of tearing a human male apart with its teeth—

"Vampire."

As the word came out of DelVecchio's piehole, Adrian cursed. Yup, great. Just what they needed at this already crowded party.

With the way things were going, who was next? The Easter Bunny and the Tooth-frickin'-Fairy?

Nah, not their luck. More like Wolfman Jack and the Mummy.

CHAPTER
14

When the following morning came, Reilly woke up right before her alarm clock went off, and it was hard to know whether that was a good or a bad thing.

She'd been in the middle of an erotic dream, one that had put her and Veck back on the kitchen table. Except there had been no *pizza interruptus* this time. She'd ended up totally naked, with Veck on top of her, the two of them on a wild ride that—

Her clock's buzzer started yapping like a Yorkie.

"Shut. *Up.*"

As she silenced the damn noise, she decided, "good thing" on the early wake up. Even though her body felt cheated, those were hardly the images she needed to go into HQ with.

Shower. Blow-dry. Dress—with white cotton underneath her clothes, thank you very much.

Grabbing her travel mug, she was in her car and heading into work just in time to hit the traffic on the Northway. And what do you know, being stuck in gridlock with hundreds of other morning commuters was exactly the kind of forced introspection she didn't need.

God, mothers were right about so much: Brush your

teeth and floss before bed even when you're exhausted; wear a hat when it's cold even if you think you look like an idiot; eat your veggies even if they're boring, because you need the fiber and the vitamins.

And don't get involved with coworkers even if they are hot as hell and have magical hands and lips.

As she rolled along at a snail's pace, her mind rode a seesaw that tilted between what had been playing through it as she'd woken up, and the nightmare that had been last evening when the sex had stopped short and sanity returned.

Talk about your polar opposites—

When her phone went off, the first thing she thought was, Please let it not be my mom. The pair of them were close, but they'd never had a psychic connection, and now was not the morning to start.

Except the screen wasn't showing home. "Detective de la Cruz?" she said as she answered.

"Morning, Officer. How are you?"

Frustrated. On so many levels. "Stuck in traffic. Yourself?"

"Same crap, different direction."

"You have coffee?"

"Better believe it. You?"

"Yup. So this is almost like being at the office."

There was a sipping sound and then a swallow. "So I have news."

"And here I thought you were calling just to say good morning."

"Kroner's turned around."

Her grip on the wheel tightened. "Define 'turned around.'"

"His doctors just called me and they're floored. Sometime last night, everything changed. His vitals are steady and strong, and get this: He's frickin' conscious."

"Holy . . . I have to talk to him."

"They're not prepared to accommodate a lot of visitors, but they're allowing us to send one representative over there. And it's my recommendation that you not be the one who goes in."

"Why the hell not?"

"You are his target. White woman, in her twenties—"

"I'm late twenties."

"—and so I think we could get farther with a man—"

"I can handle him."

"I want him to talk, not get distracted by all the things he wants to do to you."

Well, wasn't that a gruesome thought.

"I'm not saying you shouldn't get with him. It's just this could be our one and only shot to hear his side of things. I don't trust things that can't be explained, and his doctor doesn't have a clue why the bastard is still alive—much less awake."

Reilly cursed, but it wasn't like she couldn't see his point. Besides, he wasn't a chauvinist.

Then again, there could be another angle—although she felt like a shit for bringing it up. "Any chance you don't want me to hear what he has to say about DelVecchio?"

"I am not protecting Veck. If he committed a crime, he will be dealt with just like anyone else—trust me. And I will let you know immediately when my guy gets out so you can follow up. Okay?"

It was hard to doubt the logic, and impossible to doubt the man.

"I want to know everything."

"You will, Officer. I swear it on my mother."

"Call me."

"Soon."

As Reilly hung up, she tossed the phone onto the empty seat beside her. The good news, she supposed, was that they were going to find out what the hell had happened in those woods—theoretically. Serial killers were not necessarily known for candor when they were finally caught.

Changing lanes and putting her directional signal on, she got ready to take her exit. And once she was off the highway, she made better time, although it turned out the delay with the traffic had been a good thing. When the graceless heft of headquarters finally loomed up ahead, she was ready to get to work—and see Veck.

They'd had one slipup. Fine. But it didn't have to be repeated, and she wasn't going to let it affect the job she did. There was a lot at stake, and she was not about to be distracted or get sloppy and unprofessional just because she was attracted to her partner.

Sissy Barten, and the other victims, deserved so much better than that. And the likes of Kroner required nothing less.

"You look like shit."

Veck glanced up from his office computer's screen. Bails was standing in front of his desk with a satisfied expression on his face and his jacket in his hand.

"Thanks." Veck eased back and wanted a cigarette. "And you look like someone just gave you—"

"A blow job, right?"

"I was going to say 'a winning lottery ticket.' What's doing?"

"Guess who's wakey-wakey."

"Given the BJ reference, I don't want to know."

"Kroner."

Veck sat forward. "Impossible."

"Well, then, de la Cruz is talking out of his ass, because he just told me to go down and see what the bastard has to say. Guess he rallied last night."

Veck burst out of his chair before he knew his thighs had gone to work. But it was a waste of vertical impulse: He was going nowhere. At least not in an official capacity.

Veck parked it again. "Fuck."

Bails leaned in, his face dead serious. "I'll take care of you. I'll tell you everything. Which reminds me—you won't believe the evidence taken from Kroner's impounded truck. The cataloging alone is going to take another day, at least—there's so much of the stuff. Cross-matching it to victims? You're talking a year, probably. At least the FBI is being cool and actually working with us instead of against us."

Shit, he needed to check in with that agent.

Veck took a suck off his coffee mug. "I can't believe Kroner's alive."

"Miracles happen."

"I guess you could call it that."

"It is. He's going to set you free, my friend. Trust me."

Veck wasn't at all sure of that, but whatever. Offering his knuckles for a pound, he said, "Go get 'em, brother."

"You got it. I'll call you when I'm through."

As the guy turned to leave, Reilly appeared in the doorway. She looked composed, professional, serious . . . all those things that someone in a business environment should be. Between one blink and the next, however, he saw her undone on her kitchen table, head back, breasts exposed, panty hose off, and skirt around her waist.

Veck rubbed his aching head. He'd woken up with a pounder at the temples, the vague tendrils of a terrifying dream lingering in his mind—and that wasn't the half of it. He'd had the eerie conviction that someone had been in his house during the night. He'd checked the doors and windows, though—all good; no break-ins. Nothing out of place, either.

After Bails nodded to Reilly and took off, she walked over. "Good morning."

"Morning." Veck glanced around. Nobody was paying any attention to them, and that seemed like a miracle—he felt like they both had neon signs around their chests that read, WE HOOKED UP LAST NIGHT. But apparently only he and Reilly knew the damn things were there, because she was surreptitiously looking at his fellow detectives, too.

"You ready to go through the Barten file?" she said, as she put her things on the desk next to his and handed him a printout.

The pages were neat, bundled, clipped at the corner. Clearly reprinted.

Swiveling his chair toward her, he wondered what had

happened to the two reports from last night. No doubt she'd had to throw them away after they'd been crushed underneath two heaving bodies and then shuffled off onto the floor.

He rubbed his head again. "You hear about Kroner?"

"De la Cruz called me."

"I'm surprised you're not going in to interview the guy."

"Oh, I will. You can bet your life on it." She unclipped her stack and spread out the various stapled sections. "So as I was reading through this, something bothered me."

He caught himself staring at her mouth and wanted to kick his own ass: Not only was it inappropriate, but it felt disrespectful.

"What's that?" *I'm sorry about last night.* "Where are you in the report?"

"The anonymous tip line section. Page two—there was a caller who said he saw Sissy get into a black car at the Hannaford."

"Got it." *I shouldn't have put you in this position.* "Yeah, no follow-up, though. Guy didn't leave his name."

"I've been thinking about what her mother said about her. Sissy doesn't strike me as the type to do something like that. She was not someone who would get into the car of a stranger."

"Maybe the tip was wrong, or a lie." *I wish I could tell you I don't want you, but I can't.* "Wouldn't be the first time, and with no follow-up possible?"

Now her eyes fully met his. "But that's the thing. Why weren't there other people who saw her after she walked out the door into the parking lot? She left her car there, right? Why didn't anyone else see what happened when she left—especially if there was a struggle? There were employees retrieving carts, customers coming and going. If we assume Sissy had to be forced into a vehicle, someone should have seen a struggle, or something out of the ordinary."

Scanning the other tips, he nodded. "Yeah, and the layout of that supermarket . . . there's nothing across the street or to either side, really. It's set off the road, so it's not as if she would go walking off anywhere."

"Someone should have seen something."

Christ, it was almost like what had happened to him with Kroner: nothing but aftermath ... surrounding a whole lot of blank hole.

Maybe there was something in the Caldwell water that was making people forget.

"Let's start at the beginning," he said, reordering his pile. "And take it one step at a time."

As he thought about Bails talking to Kroner, he took out his cell phone and put it on the desk in case the guy called in.

Sissy Barten definitely fit the profile of the killer's victims, and was one of only two reported missing persons in the city who did: Kroner had never gone for males, children, or anyone over thirty, and the other girl who was on the list had been reported as gone almost a month ago, so she might well be outside the time scope.

Sissy was it, Veck had a feeling.

Sissy was his way back into the Kroner case.

CHAPTER
15

"**B**ut I *didn't* touch him."

Jim was naked and shaving in his bathroom as the argument that had started up between Ad and Eddie hours ago continued next door in their room. It was kind of like having a TV on in the background—only their version of commercial interruptions were showers, dressing, breakfast runs, etc.

He got the impression the pair of them had done the back-and-forth forever. They were damn good at it, too ... very creative. And to think he'd once been impressed with his own F-bombing.

"Next time, be more specific," Adrian added. "You can't smack my ass on this one."

"Did you stop to think that what happened to Jim could have gotten into you? There was no one to help you."

"I didn't fucking touch him!"

Dog was ringside for the show, sitting in the open connector, his scruffy head going left and right as one of the boys spoke and the other followed up. The little guy seemed perfectly happy to just hang and play witness to the volleying. Maybe he thought it was the live version of an Animal Planet show; who knew.

Shaking his head, Jim braced his palms on the counter and leaned into the mirror. Last night's go-around with that badge had been a wake-up call. Devina had tricks and minefields he still had to learn about . . . and there was no question that Veck was sucked up into all this—

". . . vampire."

Jim frowned and leaned back, putting his head out into his room. Had he heard that right? Neither of his boys seemed like *Twilight* fans, although with Adrian, you never knew where the hell the lines were drawn. And ordinarily, he would have let it go. But he hadn't believed in angels, either . . . until he frickin' became one.

"You saying I need to invest in garlic?" he shouted out.

Dog repositioned himself so he could keep his eyes on everybody.

Before a response came through the doorway, Jim's cell phone went off on the bedside table. Going over and grabbing the thing, the screen announced that the call was from a 518 area code.

Good morning, Detective DelVecchio.

"Heron."

"This is Veck. How are you and your colleagues?"

Recovering from all kinds of fun and games with you last night. "Good. Yourself?"

"We've been going through the casework on Cecilia Barten. Do you guys have anything we don't?"

Jim had been prepared for the info request—it was SOP, and the kind of thing he'd have been able to field if he'd actually been an FBI field agent. "I'm not sure. You want to meet and I'll take a look at what you've got?"

"Good call."

"There's not a lot to go on." Devina wouldn't have left dangling threads, and given all that she could manipulate, the cleanup job around the abduction had to have been spectacular.

"Yeah, I know. There were no witnesses—how in the hell could there have been no witnesses?"

Because his Sissy had been taken by a demon, that was why.

Not that she was his.

"Listen," the detective continued, dropping his voice. "I think she's connected to Kroner. Can you double-check your files on him, too?"

"Absolutely." Jim didn't especially like lying, but he had no problem with it when shit called for a fallacy. "I'll see what I can dig up. Lunch?"

"Yeah. Riverside Diner?"

"See you there at noon."

Putting aside the whole vampire thing, Jim walked around the end of the bed and stuck his head through the connector. "We have a date with the good detective."

Eddie and Adrian looked over, and instantly both of them frowned.

"What's around your neck?" Ad demanded.

"At twelve," Jim said, "which means you have another couple hours to argue while I get back on the Internet."

As he backed out and went for the pants he'd left on the chair, they followed him into his room.

"What's up with the necklace?" Ad barked.

Even though Jim was flashing his ass, he decided getting a Hanes undershirt on was more of a priority. He didn't want them to see Sissy's little strip of gold, thank you very much—

"We are fucked," Adrian muttered. "We are so fucked."

Jim yanked the shirt over his head. "Thanks for your vote of confidence—"

"She is not your problem! She's just some girl, get over it."

Wrong thing to say in the wrong tone on the wrong morning.

Jim flashed over to the guy and jammed his face into the other angel's. "I spent part of yesterday afternoon staring into the eyes of that *girl's* mother. So before you write her off as nothing special, I suggest you go over there and see for yourself how much she *does* matter."

Adrian didn't back down. "And I suggest you get your priorities straight. There've been a hundred thousand pretty, innocent victims in this conflict, and yeah, that's tragic, but it's also reality. She's just the most recent one I've seen—you gonna pull this shit with every chick you come across? This is war, not a goddamn dating service."

Jim bared his teeth in a snarl. "You holier-than-thou mother*fucker*. Don't you *ever* pretend to know me."

"Then do us a favor and know yourself!"

Jim stepped back. And glanced at Eddie. "Get him away from me—and keep him there. We're done."

Adrian tossed a, "Yeah, whatever," over his shoulder and walked back into their bedroom. A moment later, a door slammed shut.

Jim yanked his leathers on commando, and in the silence, he wanted to scream.

"He's right," Eddie said.

Shooting a glare over his shoulder, Jim bit out, "And you can leave, too. I don't need either one of you."

There was a beat of quiet and then Eddie's brows slowly lowered, cranking down over those red eyes . . . that suddenly started to glow.

Jim took a step back, but not because he was afraid he was going to hit the guy. More like he realized he'd thrown a match on some gasoline.

Eddie Blackhawk pissed off was not something to fuck around with.

In a voice that warped as if it were a radio going in and out of frequency, the angel growled, "You want to be an island? Good luck with it—I saved your cock and balls last night, and that wasn't the first time. You think Adrian's the problem in this? Take a look in the mirror, you'll get further."

On that note, Eddie pivoted on his heel and shut the connector, locking it in place. Then a brief flare of incandescent light suggested the angel had taken off the old-fashioned way.

Wheeling around, Jim picked up a cheapo chair, raised the thing over his shoulder, and got ready to throw it at the door.

Except he paused as he caught a glimpse of himself in the mirror over the dresser.

His face was flushed with fury, his eyes glowing icy blue in the same way Eddie's had gone Christmas-light red. His T-shirt was stretched tight across his bulging chest and shoulder muscles, and Sissy's delicate necklace was cutting into the cords of his neck.

Slowly lowering the chair, he leaned into the glass and checked the tiny gold links. Any more of that and he was going to break the thing, just split it right in half.

"Dog, I'm going out for a little bit."

When there was no chuffing reply, no pawing at the calf for attention, no pair of scruffy ears popping up over the far edge of the bed, he pivoted around.

"Dog?" Jim whistled through his teeth. "Dog?"

Maybe the little guy had gotten locked in over at Eddie and Ad's. Going to the door, Jim went to spring the lock with his mind—

No luck.

No Dog, either.

He was alone.

For a moment, he had a head scratcher, a kind of what-the-fuck-just-happened-here. But then he shut his connector and dead bolted it. All things considered, this split had been inevitable. He and Adrian had gotten into a fistfight within forty-eight hours of officially working with each other, and all that oil/water had continued to simmer below the surface. And yeah, Eddie was cool, but Jim had the sense he could lap the guy when it came to the magic—so he couldn't say he felt compromised.

It was neater this way. Cleaner.

Besides, when he'd been under Matthias the Fucker at XOps, he'd always worked alone, so this was also business as usual.

He was used to this.

Partners, whether professional or personal, were just too goddamn messy for the likes of him.

CHAPTER
16

"I *beg* your pardon."

Up on the lawn outside of Heaven's castle, Nigel looked across the linen-draped table and nodded at a Royal Doulton plate. "I should like the scones, please."

"That is *not* what you said." Colin sat back in his dainty chair, his black eyebrows down over eyes that were full of curses.

Their two dining companions—well, three if you counted the Irish wolfhound—stopped in midsip ... or sniff, in Tarquin's case. Nonetheless, Bertie delivered the plate in question, his fair face full of compassion, as was his way.

Suffice it to say, however, that no matter how glorious the pastry on the bone china was, tea was ruined.

"Nigel, what the hell have you done."

"I shall thank you to not address me in that tone, Colin."

"And you can pop off with the etiquette. What do you mean, you've been to see the Creator."

Nigel broke open his fresh currant scone, and breathed in the waft of sweet steam that rose up. Indeed, they did not require sustenance, but to deprive oneself of this pleasure on a technicality was absurd.

Byron pushed his rose-colored glasses up higher on his nose. "I am sure he had his reasons, did you not."

Unlike Colin, who was a hardheaded bull, the other two would merely wait for whatever Nigel chose to impart. Bertie, with his soft heart, and Byron, with his eternal optimism, were more delicate creatures than that other one, capable of demonstrating the virtues of restraint and patience in abundance.

Colin, however, would perhaps inquire but once more. And then he would start pounding the tabletop.

So naturally, Nigel took his time with his butter knife.

And naturally, one could feel the heat from the other side of the table sure as flames atop hardwood.

"Nigel. What has transpired."

He replied only after his first bite had been chewed thoroughly. "I believe we have discussed the other side's predilection for . . . how shall one put it . . . the creative readjustment of reality—"

"She's a cheater and a whoring liar," Colin spat.

"Must you be so blunt." Nigel put the scone down, his appetite gone. "And may I remind you *again* that we, too, have broken the rules? Our hands are likewise unclean, old friend, and—"

" 'Tis but a patch on what she hath wrought—"

"You shall desist the interruptions. *Now*."

The pair of them glared at each other in unbroken, unwavering silence . . . to the point where Nigel knew well he would be sleeping alone this night—and that was more than fine with him.

"Are we finished arguing?" Nigel patronized.

Colin opened his mouth, then shut it with a clap.

"Good. Now, as I was saying, the Creator was aware of the transgressions—on both sides." Nigel tested the temperature of his Earl Grey tea, expecting, and finding, that it was perfect. "But I acknowledged our derelictions and the fact that it is hardly fair of us to demand things of Devina that we are not prepared to honor as well."

"Her nature is as it always has been," Bertie said quietly.

"She cannot help who and what she is. Surely the Maker knew this from the start."

"I think so, yes." Nigel took more of his tea. "There was no surprise at any of it. In fact, I received the impression . . ." Nigel chose his words carefully, as one should never speak for the Creator of all things good and evil. "I almost believe it was all expected. Her violations. Our attempt to provide aid to Jim in the form of Adrian and Edward. All of it."

"And the outcome of your query is?" Colin barked.

"Unknown as of this moment. The Maker did impart news of the most unfortunate kind, however. As I was leaving, I was informed that there has been a fracture of goodwill among Jim and Edward and Adrian."

"Oh, they mustn't fight," Bertie murmured.

"Since when?" Colin demanded.

Nigel placed his china cup precisely in its saucer. "It just happened, evidently."

Colin's brows tightened once again which meant he was thinking. Never a good thing. "What transpired?"

"The Creator did not say, and it is not my place to inquire." And how he wished he could impart the same restraint to the archangel's heart. "But it is clear Jim is on his own."

Which was a disastrous course. The savior was strong, but had no experience in the ways of this ancient war. He was now a sitting pheasant to that demon's proverbial birdshot.

"But I do believe the Maker is going to take action," Nigel concluded.

"Against us?" Colin asked.

"We shall wait and see."

There was nothing to promise his colleagues, no faith to install in them by virtue of conversation. Once one presented something to the Maker for consideration, the matter was out of one's hands, and there was no way of predicting how the dominoes lined up would fall.

"I am going down there," Colin announced. "Heron can't be alone."

Why can everyone not adhere to the rules, Nigel thought. Just *once*.

As he picked up his teacup and held it with his pinkie extended, he realized anew that if there was one thing that could be depended upon, it was Colin's passion: For all that he was the intellectual among them, the truth was, by nature he was fiery, his cognitional control naught but a hard-won overlay covering his true constitution.

"Nothing to say, Nigel?" Colin charged bitterly. "No, 'oh, no, you may nots'?"

Nigel focused on the castle that loomed in the near distance, and when he finally spoke, it was in a low voice that, coming from another, he would have termed as saddened. "We have an opportunity to seize this game. I would ask that you consider the action I just took—it would be foolish to follow it up—immediately—with precisely the kind of violation I presented for the Creator's redress."

"Conservatism is the cousin of cowardice. I say, if the Creator has known all along of Devina's infringements, then action could have been taken against her back in round one. That nothing has been done speaks to a condoning stance, and we should therefore be proactive in this instance." The archangel tossed his napkin onto the table. "You are not so powerful as you think, Nigel. Or do you believe yourself so important that only after you approached a response would be marshaled?"

In the silence that followed, Nigel found himself exhausted with all things and all bodies: Jim had brokered a deal with Devina. Colin was on the verge of going rogue. The demon was running amok.

The last round had been lost, and there was little hope for this current one.

"If you all will kindly excuse me." With care, he pressed his linen napkin to his mouth and folded it with precision. Laying it neatly beside his plate, he rose to his feet. "I believe I have done enough entreating with logic and you shall do what you will. I can only ask you to be cognizant of the larger implications." He shook his head at his old friend.

"I expected to battle with the demon. I never considered that I would end up locking horns with the savior or the likes of you at the same time."

He did not wait for a response, but vaporized himself back to his quarters.

Standing in privacy amid the colorful satin and silk, he felt as though he had been cast into the cold galaxy and was floating through space, going end over end ... alone and directionless.

There was a good chance they were going to lose the war. With things fracturing down upon the earth as well as up here in the heavens, there was nothing to offer in contest to Devina's scheming, and she was exactly the sort to expose and exploit this weakened state.

When he had first entered the arena with the demon, he had been so confident of victory. Now all he could see was loss.

They were going to lose. Especially given that he should have stood up to Colin just now, but instead had caved in out of tiredness.

For a long while, he stood in the place where his feet had stopped, his lungs struggling for breath he did not need, and yet seemed panicked at the prospect of not having. Eventually, he walked over to his ornate mirror and sat before the reflection of himself. With a soft curse, he let his outer image smoke off until all that was left of him was all that he truly was: an iridescent, rainbowed light source that glowed with every color of creation.

He had lied to himself, he realized.

From the start, he had believed that this war was about saving the souls in the castle—and though that was a driver, there was another truth hidden behind his heroic mantle and purpose.

This was his home. These quarters here, the time he spent with Colin, his meals and sport with Bertie and Byron. Even Tarquin's kind brown eyes and lanky limbs were a sight to nurture and sustain him.

This was his life and he had love for it all, down to the

wet footprints Colin left on the rugs after a bath, and the wine they had together when all was silent and still, and the way even the imagined skin they both assumed felt against the other's.

He was an immortal who in this moment knew the mortal terror of loss.

How did the humans do it? Going through their so-short lives, not knowing for certain when the people they loved would be taken from them . . . or whether there was in fact a place for anyone on the other side.

Perhaps that was the point, however.

Indeed, he had passed too much time to calendar blithely going through his "days" and "nights" taking for granted that all was as he would wish it to be forever. It was only now, when he was confronted with a vast, black death, that he realized how beautiful the bright colors of this existence were.

The Maker was a genius, he thought. Infinity resulted in insolence. But transience was the way one treasured what one had been given.

"Nigel."

It was not Colin but Byron who stuck his head in between the flaps of purple and red. The archangel was tentative in his interruption, and it was a surprise that he had not announced himself.

"I have been calling for you," he said.

Ah, that explained it.

Nigel reassumed his form, recasting upon himself flesh and bone and re-covering the body with the white afternoon suit he had donned for tea.

As he met the eyes behind those rose-colored glasses, in truth, he would have preferred an audience with Colin's anger. Or even Devina's duplicity, for that matter. The last thing he was interested in was Byron's eternal faith and optimism.

"My dear boy," Nigel said, "perhaps we could do this another time?"

"I shan't be long. I've just come to tell you that Colin has decided not to go down."

Nigel rose and went to the chaise lounge by the bed. Stretching out, he found it a struggle to remain corporeal. He was tired, oh, so very tired, even in the face of that which should have relieved him.

"We shall see how long that reticence lasts," he murmured.

"He has taken to his own quarters."

The subtext was that should Nigel want to speak with the archangel, that would be the place to find him, and the field report, as it were, was rather dear of Byron, actually. And not really a surprise. It was impossible for Byron and Bertie not to know how close Nigel and his second in command were, but everything was handled with discretion.

This appearance, however, was Byron's way of saying that he was worried about the pair of them.

The optimist. Worried.

Indeed, things were in a very bad way.

"Colin is in his quarters," the archangel repeated.

"As he should be." After all, they had been spending their time together herein, but "officially" they lived apart.

Upon the smooth reply, Byron removed his tinted glasses, and when his iridescent eyes lifted, Nigel could not recall the archangel ever without those rosy lenses. "Forgive me for being blunt, but I think you should perhaps go speak with him."

"He may come to me."

"I knew you were going to say that."

"Any chance you approached him first?" The silence answered that one. "Ah, but you are kindhearted, dear friend."

"No, that is Bertie."

"And you. You always see the best in people."

"No, I am surrounded by good people doing their best. In fact, I am a realist, not an optimist." Abruptly, the angel's face glowed with the power of knowledge. "Your nature and Colin's are one and the same. My hope is that you will both realize this and unite once more."

"So you are a romantic, too, then. Bit of a contradiction for a realist."

"On the contrary, I want to win, and our chances are better for prevailing if you are not distracted by a broken heart."

"My heart is not broken."

Byron replaced his glasses upon his pert, straight nose. "And I ask unto you . . . to whom you are lying."

With a bow, he ducked out of the tent.

In the silence that followed, Nigel became utterly frustrated that there was little to do save tally herein for the Maker's remark.

And how galling to think he was also awaiting Colin's arrival with an apology.

Mayhap he should not hold his unneeded breath for that one, however.

CHAPTER
17

"No, thanks—I think I'll let you have lunch with that agent on your own."

As Reilly answered his question, Veck paused in the process of pulling on his leather jacket. The pair of them had been working steadily through the morning, going line by line through the Barten reports, and he'd been surprised at how well they'd stuck to business.

The shit from the night before had been put firmly on the back burner, it seemed—at least for her. On his side? Hell, yeah, it was still on his mind, and he would have loved for that to be because he was looking for a break in conversation to slide in another lame-ass apology.

Instead, it was because he wanted her. Still.

Even more, actually.

God, he needed a cigarette. "I'll see you back here in an hour, then."

"It's a date—ah, plan, I mean."

At that, she bit on her lip with her clean white teeth, like she was shutting herself up or punishing her mouth for the "date" reference.

There were much better things to do with that part of her body.

Cursing under his breath, he left the Homicide department before that bright idea got any airtime, and instead of taking the main stairs, he went down the back way: He was not interested in getting stuck at the Britnae barricade, or in running into any colleagues. And as soon as he was out of HQ, he stopped, lit up a Marlboro, and checked the sky. The sunshine that had prevailed the day before was buried beneath a thick cloud cover, and the wind was cold and damp.

Good thing he was up for a brisk walk.

Five minutes of striding later, he was at the diner. Agent Heron was outside the front door, leaning against the building, smoking. He was wearing a lot of leather, looking more like a biker than a federal agent. Then again, maybe he was off duty and into riding.

Veck frowned. Christ, for some reason he had a hazy memory of one of those agents bitching about his BMW. Except when had that happened?

Maybe he'd just dreamed it.

"A cigarette at the right time is better than food," Veck muttered, as they shook hands.

"Amen to that."

"Bad day?"

"You got it."

"You wanna just walk it out?" Veck nodded to the sidewalk. "Chain-smoking seems more appealing than the BLT I'd planned on ordering."

"Good idea."

They hit the concrete path together and kept their speed at a meander. Beside them, the Hudson River was the same murky color as the sky, the surface getting choppier toward the middle from the wind.

"Brought you a copy of our report," Veck said, putting his cigarette between his teeth and taking out the papers that he'd folded in half. "But you've probably already seen most of it."

"Never hurts to take a second look." The documents went into Heron's breast pocket. "I want to help."

"And I could use whatever you've got. This case is fucking frustrating."

"I hear you."

And that was all they said for a while. Cars whipped along to the right of them, honking at one another from time to time. An ambulance went by at a dead run with sirens blaring. A thicket of bike riders wearing Saran Wrap suits and aerodynamic ice buckets on their heads ripped past, pedaling like they were being chased.

Unlike the rest of the world, he and Heron stayed in slow-mo.

"You're easy to talk to," Veck said on the exhale, his smoke drifting up over his head.

Heron laughed. "Haven't said much."

"I know. I like it. Shit, this Barten case is killing me. None of it makes any sense, to be honest."

"Yeah."

Veck glanced over. "By the way, where's your team?"

"Not here."

Well, duh. And clearly that was a closed subject.

At that moment, Veck's phone went off, and he jacked it right up to his ear. "DelVecchio. Yeah? Really. Shit . . . no kidding."

He felt Heron look over . . . and as the guy did, the strangest warning tickled over Veck's nape.

Last night . . . in his kitchen . . .

Veck's feet stopped and he finished the Bails report about Kroner on autopilot, his eyes locked with Heron's.

He'd always had good instincts about things, but this was deeper than intuition or hunches. This was fact, even though he didn't understand the hows or whys.

After he hung up, he just kept staring at the FBI agent. "You know, I think someone was in my house last night."

Heron didn't bat an eye—there was no reaction in his hard face at all. Which was a tell in and of itself, wasn't it.

"I don't know, maybe I was dreaming."

Bullshit. It had been Heron. As soon as Veck had walked

into his kitchen, he'd had exactly the same sense of being watched by the eyes that were meeting his now.

The question was, why would the FBI be tracking him?

Then again, file that one under *well, duh*: His father was being executed in Connecticut in a matter of days. Maybe they were worried he'd go copycat or something—and yeah, the Kroner incident helped soooo much on that front.

And although law enforcement wasn't allowed to officially single out and suspend people just because of what they looked like or who they were related to, they sure as shit could work the back angles.

Then again, they could be protecting him. From his father, or his father's followers. In that case, though, they'd just come forward and tell him, wouldn't they.

"So what did you think of Bob Greenway," Veck murmured. "The manager from the Hannaford where Cecilia Barten was last seen."

"As you said, not much to go on."

"You aren't here for the Barten case, are you."

Heron took a drag on his Marlboro. "The hell I'm not."

"The manager's name is George Strauss. Have you even read the file?"

The agent didn't blink. Didn't seem to care in the slightest that he'd been caught in at best a lapse of memory, at worst a lie. He remained utterly self-contained, as if he had seen and done things so much worse than a mere bending of the truth, he couldn't give a fuck.

"You want to tell me why you were in my house last night?" Veck said, tapping his cigarette into the air.

"It is not inaccurate to say I've taken a special interest in you. And it is very accurate to say that Sissy Barten's disappearance is a big fucking deal to me."

Veck frowned. "So what the hell is going on? Does it have anything to do with my father? Because in case you're not aware of it, I don't really know the guy, and I hope they do the world a favor and off the bastard."

Heron leaned down, lifted one boot, and stubbed out

the tip of his coffin nail on the heavy tread of his combat. After he put the butt in his back pocket, he tapped out a fresh stick from his soft pack.

He lit the thing with the efficiency of a long-term smoker. "Lemme ask you something."

"You could try answering some of my shit first, thank you very much."

"Nah. I'm more interested in you." The guy took a suck and exhaled. "You ever feel like there's another side to you? Something that follows you around, lurking under the surface. Maybe every once in a while it comes out, taking you in a direction you don't want to go in."

Veck narrowed his eyes as his heart kicked once in his chest and then stopped dead. "Why the hell would you ask me that?"

"Just curious. It would be the kind of thing you don't want to see in a mirror, for example."

Veck took a step back and pointed at the guy with his coffin nail. "Stay the fuck out of my house and away from me."

Heron just hung where he was, feet planted in the middle of the sidewalk. "It would be the kind of thing that makes you wonder what you're capable of. Reminds you of your old man so much, you don't like thinking about it."

"You're fucking crazy."

"Not in the slightest. And neither are you."

"You should know I'm good with a gun. And I don't care if you're a federal agent—assuming you didn't lie about that, too."

Veck pivoted away and started walking, fast.

"Look down at your feet, Thomas DelVecchio," Heron shouted out. "Take a good look at what's doing. And then you call me when you get scared enough. I'm the only one who can help you."

Fucking loony-ass motherfucker.

Motherfucking loony-ass bitch.

It took him no time at all to get back to HQ, and he blasted up that front stairwell, gunning for his computer. As he blew into the Homicide department, all he got for a greeting was a lot of ringing phones—everyone was out to lunch or working a case somewhere in town. Which was good news for his colleagues.

Sitting down at his desk, he got the number of the Federal Bureau of Investigation's local field office, and dialed in.

"Yeah, hello—this is Detective DelVecchio over at Caldwell Homicide. I want to speak with Personnel. Yup. Thanks." He picked up a pen and began twirling it in and out of his fingertips. "Yeah, DelVecchio at the CPD—I want to see if you have an Agent Jim Heron anywhere in your system, including out of state. I have my badge number if you want it." He recited the numbers. "Uh-huh, that's right. The guy I'm looking for is Agent Jim Heron. Yeah, that's how you spell it, like the bird. A man approached me yesterday with what looked like bona fide credentials, identified himself as an agent working on a missing persons case, and came with me to interview the family. I just met with him again and I want to verify who he is. Yup. Just call me, I'm at my desk."

He hung up.

One Mississippi. Two Mississippi. Three Mississippi. Four Miss—

His phone rang. "DelVecchio. Hey, thanks—really. Go fig, no one at all by that name. Yup, he's six-four, maybe -five. Blondish hair. Blue eyed. Looks like soldier. He had two other men with him, one with a braid, another with a lot of metal on his face. The credentials were legit, though, right down to the hologram. Thanks—yeah, please, I'd like to know if you find anything—and I'll let you know if he shows up again."

As he hung up the phone, he thought he should have known. He should have fucking known—and he should have apprehended the guy right there by the river. That talk about shadows, though, had thrown him—

"Are you okay?"

He glanced up. Reilly was standing next to his desk, a little McDonald's bag in one hand and a short soda in the other.

"No, I'm really fucking not." He shifted his eyes to the computer screen, because he knew he was glaring. "Remember that FBI agent from yesterday?"

"Heron?"

"He's a fake."

"A fake?" She sat down beside him. "What do you mean—"

"Someone broke into my house last night." As she gasped, he kept going. "It was him. Probably his two buddies, too—"

"Why didn't you tell me? And why the hell didn't you report it?"

He started rubbing his temples, and thought, Well, at least this headache was the normal stress kind. Nothing but tension—

Abruptly, he jacked around.

Except there was nothing behind him, no one staring at the back of his head or lining up a gun muzzle with his skull. It was just an empty room cut up by cubicles that were filled with computers and phones and empty office chairs.

Unfortunately, his instincts told him there was another layer to it all, one that, although his eyes couldn't measure it, was as real as anything he could touch and feel.

Just like last night in his kitchen. Just as it had been down by the river ten minutes ago.

Just as it had been his whole life.

"What is it?" Reilly asked.

"Nothing."

"Your head hurts?"

"No, it's fine."

Veck casually got up and walked all the way across the department to the banks of windows that looked out over the street below. Making like he was just glancing outside at the sky, he focused his eyes on the glass and braced himself.

No shadows in it.

Thank fuck. Mirrors were usually the surest way to see what was lurking, but windowpanes could do the trick.

Goddamn it, he was losing his mind.

Turning back around, he passed through what seemed like a warm draft as he returned to his chair.

Reilly put her hand on his arm. "Talk to me. I can help."

He rubbed his hair and didn't bother to smooth it back into place. "Last night, when I got home, I knew there was someone in my house. There was no obvious break-in, but it was just . . ." Okay, now he was starting to feel crazy as he heard himself talk. "I wasn't sure until I went to meet with Heron. Something about the way he was looking at me . . . I knew it was him, and he didn't deny it. Fucking hell, I should have expected something like this so close to my father's execution."

"What . . . I'm sorry, what does your father have—"

"Like I said before, he has fans." More with the hair scrubbing. "And they've done scary shit. They can't get close to him, but I'm out in the general public and they find me. You can't fucking imagine what it's like to discover your new roommate is a devil worshiper, or that chick who hit on you at the bar is covered with tattoos of your old man's face. Especially *my* old man." He cursed low and hard. "And believe me, those are only the less creative examples. I should have known something like this was going to happen right now, but I don't believe in paranoia. Maybe I damn well should, though."

"You can't blame yourself about Heron. I saw his ID. It absolutely looked legitimate."

His eyes shot to hers. "I took that man into a *victim's* home. To meet her goddamn *mother*. Oh, for fuck's sake . . ."

Veck shoved his chair back on a sharp push and got up. As he paced down the row of empty cubicles, he wanted to hit a wall.

And naturally, at that moment, his cell phone rang.

* * *

Reilly stayed in her seat as Veck accepted a call.

He looked awful. Stressed. Exhausted. And it dawned on her that he hadn't had anything to eat at her place last night, and probably, given how "lunch" had gone, hadn't done himself any favors at noontime, either.

"Really? Yeah, she's with me. Uh-huh . . ."

As twelve kinds of noncommittals floated over, he walked around in a tight circle, free hand on his hip, head down, brows tight. He was wearing his uniform of black trousers and a white shirt with no tie, and through the pocket of his button-down, the red stripe on his pack of Marlboros showed.

The cubicles in the Homicide department, like the ones over in IA, were no taller than chest height, and as with her colleagues, the detectives here decorated their workspaces with pictures of kids and wives and husbands. A couple of the females had small plants. Nearly all had special mugs they used for coffee, and pinned up Dilbert cartoons, and ads with stupid mistakes in them.

DelVecchio's was utterly bare, the cloth-covered, thumb-tack-friendly walls empty of anything but the holes left behind by the last inhabitant's life display. And she had a feeling it had nothing to do with the fact that he had just started working here. Usually, when someone new came in, putting up their stuff was the first thing they did.

Veck hung up and glanced over. "That was de la Cruz. I also spoke with Bails."

"As did I."

"So you know Kroner thought it was an animal that attacked him, and that he ID'd me as the man who came and called nine-one-one."

"Yeah, I do. And I think you should believe it."

"Believe what."

"That you didn't hurt him." As he made a dismissive noise, she shook her head. "I mean it, Veck. I don't understand why you're so persistent, even in the face of evidence to the contrary."

"People can be wrong."

"Not at a face-to-face distance. Unless you think those wounds were somehow created from across the parking lot?" When he didn't say anything further, she knew better than to beat a dead horse. "Heron needs to be reported."

"For impersonating a federal agent, yeah. But I doubt I can prove he was in my house." He sat back down and went through his phone. "At least I have his cell phone number in here."

"I'll file the report," she said. "You need to take the rest of the afternoon off."

"Nah. I'm good."

"That wasn't a request."

"I thought you were my partner, not my superior."

"Actually, if we go by rank, I am on top of you." With a wince, she wished she'd phrased that differently. "And I can also take care of the paperwork about what we did yesterday."

"Thanks, but I'll do it."

She turned to check her e-mail. "You're taking the afternoon off, remember."

When there was no response, she thought maybe he was gathering his things up. She should have known better.

He'd just leaned back in his chair and was staring at his computer monitor. No doubt he wasn't seeing anything on it. "I'm not leaving. I just want to work."

And that was when she realized he had nothing. No one to go home to. No one in his life—he'd left the "next of kin" slot unfilled in his HR file, and his emergency contact was that Bails guy. Where was his mother? she wondered.

"Here, eat this," she said, putting her Micky D's bag in front of him. "It's just a cheeseburger, but you look like you could use some calories."

His hands were surprisingly gentle as he picked up the gift. "I don't want to take your lunch."

"I had a big breakfast."

He rubbed the wrinkled part between his eyebrows. "Thanks. I mean that."

As he took out the yellow-wrapped package and made efficient work of the burger and the large fries, she found herself sliding back into step with him, even though neither of them were on their feet and walking.

But then, partnerships were like that. At times the gears interlocked smoothly. Others? It was all grind and squeal. And it wasn't always clear why or when things returned to being at ease.

Although in the case of last night, it was very damned obvious what had thrown them off.

Clearing her throat, she said, "How'd you like to try dinner again."

Going by the way his head whipped around, she might as well have dropped a bomb in his lap as opposed to the golden arches.

"You're serious," he said.

She shrugged, making like she was nonchalant. "My mother was mortified I went fast-food for lunch and is insisting I head over there tonight. Actually, I think she would have made me drop by even if I'd had roughage and tofu— the urge to cook comes over her from time to time, and as an only child, the extra mouth matters. Mom cooks big, if you know what I mean."

He fingered up three fries, chewed them down, and wiped his mouth with a napkin. "You sure you want to do that."

"I asked, didn't I?"

He focused on the red carton. "Well ... then yeah. I'd like that. A lot."

As Reilly got busy texting her mom, he said, "I promise to be on my best behavior."

The dark bass in his tone suggested he wasn't just talking about table manners, and she knew it was the kind of vow she should take as well. It took two to tango, and God knew she'd been right there with him in her kitchen.

Then again, she wasn't wearing anything Victoria would go hush-hush about. So they were probably safe.

Probably.

"Okay, how do you spell 'Heron,'" she murmured as she pulled up a blank incident report on her screen.

There was the briefest of pauses. And then he said quietly, "Just like the bird."

CHAPTER
18

As night fell, Adrian was drunk ... but not horny.

The two didn't always go together. It was very possible for him just to be horny—for example, whenever he woke up, he was usually ready for some action as well as stone-cold sober. However, very rarely did he float a couple of beers without getting that itch that had to be scratched. And it wasn't that he ever got piss-faced drunk—he wasn't sure that was possible. But angels could get buzzed, and generally speaking, that led to all kinds of hi-how're-ya.

As he put down yet another empty longneck, he counted on his fingers. "Wait, was that six? Or seven for us?"

For once, the other angel was keeping up with the pound-backs. Ever since the pair of them had walked through the Iron Mask's front door an hour ago, the guy had been going one-for-one with Ad's pace.

"Eight," Eddie muttered, as he held up his hand for the waitress.

The woman immediately nodded and headed for the bar. She'd been good: moved fast, kept her eyes open, and didn't seem interested in cutting him and his boy off.

As Adrian waited for the next round to be delivered,

he sat back in the crushed-velvet booth and surveyed the dark, moody crowd. Out of habit, rather than necessity, he guessed it was time to switch modes from drinking to fucking.

Such a romantic, wasn't he.

At least he knew he'd find something. This Goth club was the sort of place he felt perfectly comfortable in—the cast of characters, from the bartenders to the waitresses to the people filing past, were all his people: not a pink, paisley, or preppy POS in sight.

And usually it took him no more than a minute and a half to find a worthy candidate. Tonight? Even the chippie with the butt-length black hair and the Marilyn Monroe and the satin bustier wasn't capable of getting his ass off the couch.

Come to think of it, he wasn't even hard.

Fucking Jim Heron.

The waitress showed up with the next set of longnecks, and Eddie leaned forward to put yet another twenty on her tray. He passed Ad's bottle over and settled back.

"I think we need to get busy," Eddie said.

"As in . . ."

At that moment, Rapunzel of the night paraded by, shakin' that ass, and Eddie's eyes followed the show, burning deep red.

Well, wasn't this a role reversal. Typically, Ad was the scout.

"Why don't you do some business." Adrian sucked half his beer on a oner. "I'll watch your Bud."

The long-haired woman paused just past where they were camped out and looked over her shoulder. Given her expression, she might as well have just laid herself naked on a table for them.

"You sure?" Eddie asked.

"Yeah, I'm just going to hang."

"I won't be long."

"Take your time." Hell, the night was long. Maybe a couple more in him and he'd be ready. God knew Eddie could go for days straight, so they could still double-team something.

As Eddie rose to his feet, his erection was obvious—and the kind of thing that Enzyte guy from the TV, Bob, took all those pills to sport. And as the female who'd caught the angel's eye got a proper look at him, she practically levitated out of her bustier, her hand creeping up to her throat ... and drifting down to her cleavage.

You can cut the seduction, sweetie, Adrian thought. You got him.

And he was going to be spectacular.

Eddie always was.

"Have fun," Ad muttered.

"You know where to find us if you change your mind."

As Eddie took off, Ad finished his beer ... and, as time crawled by, went to work on his buddy's.

"You didn't find her attractive?"

The low drawl made his skin crawl.

And he refused to look to the left. "Evening, Devina."

The demon sauntered through his field of vision and took Eddie's spot in the booth. From out of the corner of his eye, he saw that she was in a stunner of a black dress, the kind that made more sense for a fancy-schmancy cocktail party at some mansion ... the kind that parted to show so much leg that the garters holding her stockings up made a brief appearance.

"You don't fit in here, Devina."

"I know, I'm too good for this place—happens to me all the time." As the waitress came over, the demon smiled. "A glass of white wine if you have it. And put it on his tab."

"Don't have a tab," he cut in.

"Then he'll pay cash."

Adrian felt the first stirring in his cock, but it wasn't sexual. It was anger toward the enemy. Man, he was never aroused by her the proper way, but she did make him hard.

Was it the same for Jim?

"So where is your third wheel," the demon asked. "I believe you are missing one part of your tripod."

The good news, he supposed, was that Devina couldn't be in two places at once. So the girl getting banged in the bathroom with Eddie definitely wasn't her. And wherever Jim was, the enemy wasn't with him, either.

"What brings you here," he asked.

"No comment on my inquiry?"

"Nope."

"Ah, well . . . I'm looking for you, actually. Flattered?"

"Not in the slightest."

"I thought you might need some company."

He opened his mouth to say he was good and she could fuck off, but then he thought about Jim out there on his own. No doubt the motherfucker was still working the angles with DelVecchio, charging forward without them. With that damn necklace around his throat.

And here they were, sitting on their asses, stalled out like a couple of bitches.

Adrian forced his head toward Devina. As she smiled at him, her perfect white teeth glowed even in the darkness, and he couldn't help remembering all the fun things they'd done together.

Real laugh riot.

His gut churned.

And the grinding got worse as she inched closer to him. "I've missed you."

"I doubt that. I know you've been busy."

"With Jim, you mean?" She leaned in, her perfect breasts pushing against his upper arm. "Jealous?"

"Yeah. Abso seething."

Her ruby red lips brushed his ear. "You don't lie very well, but you are a very good lay."

"And the opposite would be true of you."

At least that offended her enough so she pulled back. "That is *so* untrue. I am a fantastic fuck."

He laughed on a hard exhale. Typical—she didn't even care if she was called out on the other shit.

The waitress delivered the wine, and though he could

have been a prick and made the demon pay, he was afraid of dragging the poor human with the cocktail tray into this mess. Ponying up a twenty, he was relieved to see the woman go on to other people.

Devina eased back into the booth and ran a delicate finger around the foot of the wineglass.

What the hell was she doing here? he thought. She was a vicious bitch, but she didn't kibitz. And she'd just had Jim, for chrissakes, so it wasn't like she was desperate for sex.

"So where is Jim?" Devina asked over the rim of her chardonnay. "Back with your boy, doing some silly piece of ass?"

Adrian frowned. She made the statement sound like it was rhetorical, but he could see through her falsely casual routine: She didn't know where the savior was, did she. Jim was blocking her.

Somehow, the bastard had figured out a way to go truly invisi, so to speak.

Holy. Shit.

Adrian smiled. "You could go see for yourself."

Her eyes slid away. "I'd rather be with you."

Liar, he thought. "I'm touched. But I don't think that's the truth, is it."

"I'm choosing to sit with you now."

"Yes, you are, aren't you."

Her stiletto bounced at the end of her foot as she kicked her lower leg with impatience.

"You know, Adrian, you ever get bored with being a Goody Two-shoes, you could come over to my side."

"Because you have cookies, right."

Those black eyes returned to his own. "And so much more."

"Well, I'm on a diet. Sorry—but thanks for the invite."

Devina licked her lips. "Temptation is good for the soul."

"Only from the way you look at things." He finished off

Eddie's beer and got to his feet. "Now, if you'll excuse me, I think I'm going to go back and take a little ride."

"Running from me, Adrian?"

"Yup, that's right. I'm flat-out scared of you."

"Wise of you, angel mine."

"I'm not yours, bitch."

"Wrong, oh, so very wrong." Her eyes gleamed with all the tortures of hell. "I'm inside you, Adrian. I'm right in there, wrapped around your heart."

"I'll tell Jim you said hello."

"I'm inside you, angel, and you know it. It's the reason you're getting up and walking away."

"Nah. I just want to be with a real woman, not a fake one."

As her face paled, Adrian turned his back on her and sauntered away, but somehow, it didn't feel like he'd really left her.

It didn't feel as though he ever left her. And that meant . . . she was probably right.

As he approached the bathroom, he wasn't worried about protecting himself from her wrath. She wasn't going to do anything with this many humans around. Too messy when it came to cleanup. Besides, it was too obvious. If she was going to get him back, she'd be more creative about it.

I'm inside you, angel, and you know it.

Shoving that voice right out of his head, he easily found the bathroom his buddy was in—and not just because there was a whole lot of female moaning going on. He could sense his best friend clear as day—which made him realize that Devina wasn't the only one who couldn't find Jim: He wasn't picking up on the savior, either, which was a shocker. He'd been so pissed off at that guy when they'd left that morning, he'd just wanted away from him. But now . . . as he reached out, there was nothing.

So where the hell was Jim?

Even as the thought occurred, he smacked a lid on the

what-the-fuck: that demon was like a weather vane when it came to sensing things so the best course was to go about their business like there was nothing wrong. No rift. No infighting. Just Adrian and Eddie burning off some steam while Jim was cloaked and working the war.

Devina would realize there was nothing worth mining for here and go about her business.

Adrian didn't knock on the door. No reason to. A moment after he leaned against the jamb, Eddie cracked the seal and it was a case of slipping in and relocking.

The woman's bustier was off and there were breasts everywhere. Like Ad, she had both nipples pierced, and there was a stainless-steel chain linking the tips.

Impressive set. And the boobs weren't bad either.

Her skirt was up around her waist and her ass tucked in tight to Eddie's hips, her back and long hair against his pecs. His leathers were still in place, but it was obvious given the way she was arched that the buttons were free and a whole lot of penetration was going on.

Adrian sat down on the toilet seat facing them and reached up, pushing her breasts together, the little chain getting long because of the lack of distance. Before he ducked his head and started in on those nipples, he met his best friend in the eye, and relied on the centuries they'd spent together to fill in the blanks.

They had to stay in here and pretend all was okay.

And it was more than a little worrisome that Eddie, who usually had the best radar, had not caught wind of the demon's arrival.

There was the briefest of hesitations—which indicated that the message had been received. And then Eddie resumed the fucking, drawing his body back and then doing a resheathe. His face was harsh, though, and not because he was ready to come.

The woman didn't get that the vibe had changed, however. She just moaned and kicked her head back, offering her mouth to Eddie as she looked at the big palms framing her chest. As Eddie sealed their lips, Ad squeezed what he'd palmed up and then went in with his tongue, flicking one of the stainless-steel hoops; then sucking it and the start of the chain into his mouth. While he worked her nipples, he burrowed under the leather skirt, going up, up, up to the wet sex that was being used. As he found the chick's clit, it was not a surprise that she had a ball hoop through the hood—actually, it was a ho-hum cliché.

Of course she had one. And her belly button would be pierced. And maybe she had some dermals on her ribs or down her spine.

Yawn.

His heart was so not in this. It was just another fuck in another bathroom with another hard-core nothing-special.

As Eddie fell into a driving rhythm, his balls smacked back and forth, hitting Adrian's hand, and because Ad couldn't care less about the chick, he grabbed what his friend had and gave them a good twist—which guaranteed that at least someone other than the woman would have an orgasm.

Eddie barked out a curse and locked hard into the female's body, his hips kicking, his sac going tight. The woman cried out, as if the violent jerking inside her had kicked off her own little joyride, and their faces grimaced and then relaxed and then grimaced again. When Eddie eventually withdrew, his dripping erection slid across Adrian's palm, and knowing damn well his friend had another three or four rounds in him, Ad gripped that hard length and stroked it as he went back to sucking the woman's breasts and letting his forearm rub her core.

He was utterly dead as he went through the motions, making them both come again, taking over the session as he stayed sitting on the toilet.

Spinning the woman around, Ad eased her down onto her knees in front of Eddie and opened her mouth with some subtle pressure at her jaw. Grabbing the back of her head, he guided her to his friend's glistening cock, working her as he slipped a grip around to Eddie's ass.

The two of them were into this, so he upped the pace, bringing Eddie in and out faster, forcing her to take more and more of what she was panting for.

He knew Eddie liked the hookups better if he was there. That angel trusted no one, and sex was better if you felt safer. Granted, the guy never completely let go, but he was more likely to relax a little if Ad was around, and looking up into the mirror over the sink, he watched his friend. Eddie had bitten down on his lower lip and closed his eyes, his head falling back, his heavy braid swinging as he held on to the doorjamb and the wall on the other side to keep his balance.

It was getting time for another orgasm. Ad knew his buddy's body as well as he knew his own, so he stopped the furious in-and-out and gripped Eddie's erection, pumping it off as the female waited for the payload like a porn star, mouth open, puffy lips licked in anticipation.

Sometime between the stroking and when the female's face got glossed, Ad felt Devina leave the club. And it wasn't a mirage. Her physical presence was not fakeable.

But she lingered, anyway.

As Eddie panted in recovery, the female on her knees ran her fingers over her cheeks and brought them into her mouth. Sucking them in, she dropped her lids and stared up at Adrian, all wouldja-do-me.

Staring down at her, he tried to draw in a breath, but there was a weight on his chest that refused to be budged, and for some reason, the only thing he could see was the tail end of all that fake black hair of hers pooling on the dirty bathroom tile.

Her frantic, sex-starved eyes belied her fragility: There was a lost soul behind her desperate stare, an emptiness that reminded him too much of himself.

Up above her, there was a paper towel dispenser stuck to the wall, its offering like a tongue lolling out of its dull silver head.

Taking her chin in his palm, he held her face with care and snapped a white towel free. With careful strokes, he cleaned off her delicate, pale skin.

"Not tonight," he said hoarsely. "Not tonight, baby girl."

She blinked first in confusion, and then in sadness. But that was what happened when you were forced to stop and see yourself clearly: Not all mirrors were made of glass, and you didn't always need your reflection to take a good, hard look at yourself. The truth was something you wore sure as the suit of flesh that bound and gagged your soul until you were set free, and you couldn't ignore it forever.

Leaning forward, he snagged her bustier from the sink's counter, and like a child she held her arms up so that he could bind her naked breasts.

In attending to her, he felt as though he were taking care of the most broken part of himself . . . and all the while, Eddie played witness with his red eyes.

"Go on, now," Adrian said when he'd done up the last of the fasteners. "Go home . . . wherever that is."

She left on unsteady feet, but not because of the sex or the drinking, and as the door shut, Adrian settled back on the loo, put his hands on his thighs, and stared at the floor.

I'm inside you, Adrian. I'm right in there, wrapped around your heart.

It was a strange night to realize his disease, but then, as was probably typical, when you lived with something a long time, you got used to the symptoms that told you what you had was fatal.

He had the cancer. In him. It had started growing long ago, this tumor no one could see. He'd let Devina in that first time he'd bartered something of himself for something he needed in the war, and she'd been taking over ever since then, inch by inch.

He had nothing to pull him out of the oblivion that was coming for him, not even Eddie.

And damn them all, she was doing exactly the same thing with Jim.

Looking up at his best friend, he heard himself say, "I'm dying, Eddie."

Eddie's tan skin went gray, but he said nothing. Hell, no doubt the only surprise to the guy was that Ad actually brought it up.

"I'm not going to live to see the end of this war." Ad cleared his throat. "I'm just ... not going to make it."

CHAPTER
19

As Reilly pulled her unmarked into the driveway of a nice-looking clapboard colonial, Veck ran his hand across his jaw and wished he'd had time to hit a razor before they'd left HQ. Then again, a five-o'clock shadow was the least of his problems. He was well aware he had bags under his eyes and was sporting a lot of lines that he hadn't remembered from even a week before.

He glanced over at his partner. "Thank you for this."

She smiled in such an open and honest way that he was momentarily immobilized: Reilly was definitely not one of those women who needed drugstore crap on her face to get a glow on—it was all about who she was inside, not what was up with her cheeks and her eyelashes. And this expression? Pretty much made him weak in the knees.

He knew the reason for the radiance, too. He had a feeling it was because she loved where they were and who they were going to eat with: the farther away they'd gotten from work, and the closer to this house they'd become, the lighter and more delighted she'd appeared.

"Have your parents lived here long?" he asked as they got out.

"All my life." She looked around at the big oak in the yard and the little white fence at the sidewalk and the cherry red mailbox. "It was an awesome place to grow up. I could walk to school through my backyard, and there were half a dozen of us all in the same grade within a six-block radius. And, you know, my dad was superintendent of schools—still is—so I felt like he was with me every day, all the way up to college. Nice thing, believe it or not."

The street was not unlike the one the Bartens lived on, come to think of it. Very middle-class, but in the best sense of the term: These were people who worked hard, loved the crap out of their kids, and no doubt had neighborhood block parties and miniparades for the kids on the Fourth of July. Hell, even the occasional dog bark was audible nostalgia for him.

Not that he'd ever known shit like this.

"You ready to come inside?" she asked.

"Yeah, sorry." He headed around the car. "What does your mom do?"

"She's an accountant. They've been together forever—met in college, went to grad school at SUNY Caldwell at the same time. He was getting his PhD in education and she was trying to decide between number crunching and teaching. She picked the numbers because there was more money in it—and then found out she really loved the corporate stuff. She took early retirement last year and does a lot of volunteering around financial planning—well, that and the cooking."

As they hit the slate walkway and approached the glossy black front door, he realized this was the first time he'd met a woman's parents. Okay, yeah, it wasn't under the context of a "date" situation, but, man, now he knew why he didn't get close to anyone. Reilly was going to say his name, and her lovely mom and dad were going to get that frozen expression on their faces as they connected the dots.

Shit, this was a bad idea—

The door burst open before they got to it, thrown wide by an African-American woman who was tall and thin and had an apron over her jeans and turtleneck.

Reilly raced forward and the pair of them hugged so close, red hair mixed in with precisely executed dreads.

Then Reilly eased back. "Mom, this is my new partner—well, for the month, at least. Detective DelVecchio."

Veck's eyes went back and forth between the pair. And then catching himself, he quickly stepped forward and offered his palm. "Ma'am, please call me . . . Tom."

The handshake was brisk but warm, and—

"Where's my girl?"

The deep voice that boomed out of the house was something that Veck would have associated more with a drill sergeant than a school superintendent.

"Come in, come in," Mrs. Reilly said. "Your father is so excited you're eating with us."

As Veck breached the threshold, he got a view down a hallway to the kitchen, but it didn't last. A six-foot-four man stepped into the space and took it all up, his shoulders set like a mountain range, his stride long as one of Caldie's bridges. His skin was dark as night and his eyes were black . . . and missed absolutely nothing.

As Veck thought about The Kitchen Incident from the night before, he nearly pissed himself.

Reilly ran ahead and threw herself at her father, obviously confident she'd be caught and held with ease. And as she put her arms around him, they didn't go far—the guy had to top out at around two fifty, maybe two seventy-five.

As the man hugged her back, that laser stare locked on Veck. Like he knew everything his dinner guest wanted to do to his daughter.

Oh, shit . . .

Tucking Reilly under his arm, her father came forward and put out a palm that was big as a hubcap. "Tom Reilly."

"You both have the same name," Reilly's mom said. "It's meant to be."

Veck blinked for a sec.

Reilly laughed. "Didn't I mention I was adopted?"

Fuck the adoption. He didn't give a shit what color her parents were, or how it had happened. He was just praying that her father never, ever found out what had happened on his little girl's dining table the night before.

"Detective DelVecchio," he said, leaning in for the shake. "Sir."

"Pleased to meet you. You want a drink?"

"Yeah, that'd be great." Maybe they could just run an IV of Johnnie Walker into his arm.

"Game's on."

"Oh, yeah?"

Just as Reilly's mom was shutting the front door, Veck glanced outside onto the lawn. That feeling of being watched dogged him still—to the point where he wondered if you couldn't catch paranoia like a cold.

Maybe someone with a persecution complex had coughed on him.

"This way," her father said, like he was used to leading people.

Shaking himself back into focus, Veck fell in line with Reilly and the four of them walked back into a wide-open stretch of modern living, where the kitchen and the family room were all in one big space. The plasma screen was tuned to ESPN, and he knew instantly which chair was her father's—it had the *New York Times*, *Sports Illustrated*, and the remotes lined up next to it on a table. Armchair beside it? *The Economist*, *The Joy of Cooking*, and the phone.

"Sam Adams okay?" Mr. Reilly asked from the bar.

"Perfect."

"Glass?"

"I'm a bottle man."

"Me, too."

As Reilly and her mom chatted up a storm, Veck sat down with the other Tom in the room and thanked the good Lord that the television was on. It gave her father something to stare at other than him.

Veck accepted the lager that was handed over, brought it to his mouth and took a swallow—

"So have you and my daughter set a date for the wedding yet?"

The choking came fast and furious as air and beer fought for lane space in his throat.

"Daddy!"

As Reilly started in on the oh-no-you-didn'ts, her father threw back his head and laughed. Clapping Veck on the shoulder, he said, "Sorry, my man, you looked so damn stiff I had to loosen you up a little."

Veck did his best to grab some oxygen. "Hypoxia—good strategy."

"Thought so." The guy twisted around toward his wife and daughter. "He's going to be fine. Not to worry."

"Don't harass the guest, honey," her mother said from by the stove. Like the guy was a lion playing with a piece of meat.

"Fine—but if he doesn't start breathing normally again, I'll give him CPR." Mr. Reilly leaned in. "I also know the Heimlich. So you're safe with solid food, too."

"I'm so relieved," Veck said dryly.

Jim stood outside the pool of light thrown by the house, watching Veck and Reilly with what had to be the woman's parents. The bunch of them ended up at a square table, sitting down to what looked like Italian food. Lot of talking. Lot of laughing.

Veck was a little reserved, but that was probably SOP for the guy—especially given that it was clear he was interested in his partner: He was all about the clandestine looks, shooting them across that table when people were focused elsewhere.

This was everything that was good in the world, Jim thought. This was the Barten house without the tragedy, a happy family just going about their business in the world. And this blissful, simple existence was exactly what Devina loved to destroy.

This was what everyone had to lose.

Jim cursed and rubbed the back of his neck. Shit, maybe his boys had a point, maybe he was getting too distracted with the Sissy thing. It didn't feel like that was the case, but that was Eddie and Adrian's point—if you were all up in your head about something, you lost your judgment.

But come on, he *was* focused on Veck. He was with the guy: Devina so much as sneezed in that detective's direction, Jim was going to be on her like a plague.

So how was he not working this? How was he compromised?

He went for his smokes, took out a coffin nail, and lit up. He was utterly cloaked, so it wasn't as if anyone was going to see the orange glow.

Man, think of the damage he could have done in XOps if he'd had all these bells and whistles back then—and now he knew why God didn't give people superpowers. Humans were dangerous enough as it was. . . .

Time ground by, although he knew that from his watch, not any kind of stars or moon. The cloud cover was thick and the grumble of thunder off in the distance made him wonder whether he could be not just invisible, but waterproof—

From out of the corner of his eye, he caught a shadow darting from tree to tree. The thing was low to the ground and moving fast, exactly the way Devina's minions liked to roll up into a fight.

Falling into a defensive stance, he reached for his weapons—and found *none*.

Fucking hell, fucking perfect. Here he was in the 'burbs without backup, with nothing but a house frame and some clear glass windows to keep the target out of the demon's reach: Because, friggin' hothead that he was, he'd left without his gun.

At least if Eddie and Adrian were here, the three of them could divide and conquer.

Not compromised, his ass. He'd been so caught up in the drama that he hadn't taken care of himself, or Veck.

Shit.

The shadow moved to another tree . . . and came out onto the lawn.

Jim frowned and eased up. "Dog?"

As a little happy bark rippled over to him, it was clear that what he was seeing was not a mirage: More than the information his eyes provided, in his chest, he knew that was his animal.

"What the hell are you doing here?"

As the wiry-haired stray came over, his limp hampered him only a bit, and Jim was abruptly reminded of the first day he'd met the dog at that job site.

Where Jim had died for the first time.

That had been the start of it all, hadn't it. And he'd had no idea where it was going to take him.

Sinking down on his haunches, he gave Dog some good stroking. "Are Eddie and Adrian here?"

The chuff that came back at him seemed like a "negs" if he'd ever heard it.

"Well, I'm glad you are."

Dog planted his butt on the ground at Jim's feet. Even though the creature was smaller than him by about a hundred and ninety pounds and nearly six feet, Jim had the sense that he was being protected, not the other way around.

"You're not really a dog, are you."

There was a stretch of silence. Then another chuff—which seemed rather noncommittal.

"Didn't think so. You going to tell me where you went?" The animal sneezed and shook its head. "Okay, I respect your privacy."

That got him a paw on the leg.

Jim parked it on the grass and stroked Dog's rough, scratchy fur. Refocusing on the dinner that he could see but not eat, on conversation he could witness but not hear, on warmth he could sense but not feel, he knew he was nonetheless not alone.

And as rain started to fall, he was surprised at how much that mattered.

CHAPTER
20

Gary Peters had always thought he was a lot like his name: nothing special. There were millions of Garys in the nation—same for the Peters thing—and his physical appearance was no more dynamic. He'd somehow managed to avoid a beer gut, but his hair was thinning, and now that he was creeping up on the big four-oh, he was at the crossroads of buzzing the stuff all off. Face was mashed potato white, eyes were dirt brown, and it was debatable whether he had any jawline—or whether he was just neck from cheek to collarbone.

Bottom line? He was the flyover guy, the one women didn't see between the spanked-out metrosexuals and the athletes and the Richie Riches.

Which was why the sight of Britnae hipping into his desk and looking at him like . . . well, like *that* . . . was a bit of a shocker.

"I'm sorry." He shook his head. "What were you saying?"

She leaned in . . . and good God, those breasts . . .

When she eased back again, he had a feeling that she'd spoken, but he had no idea what— " 'Scuse me, phone." He reached over and picked up the receiver. "Caldwell Police Department—intake. Yup. Uh-huh. Yeah, he's booked and processed. Yeah, sure—I'll get a message to him that you'll be in in the morning."

He made some notations in the log and turned his attention back to Britnae. Who'd decided to sit up on the corner she'd perched against.

Her skirt had been small to begin with. Now he believed it was a micromini.

"Ah . . . what?" he said.

"I asked you when your break is."

"Oh, sorry." For chrissakes, that was like getting "what's your name?" wrong. "Not for a while. Hey, don't you usually go home at five?"

"I got stuck undoing a payroll screwup." As she pouted, her already puffy lower lip went right into pillow territory. "It's so unfair—and I have another hour ahead of me, at least, and it's so late."

He glanced at his clock. Eight p.m. He'd just started his new ten-hour shift of checking in prisoners and evidence, so this was early for him. Then again, he got to go home at six in the morning, and her department had to be here at eight thirty a.m.

She leaned in again. "Is it true that all of the Kroner stuff is here?"

"You mean upstairs in Evidence? Yeah, it is."

"Have you seen it?"

"Some of it."

"Really?"

There was something totally cool about the way her eyes widened a little and her hand went to the base of her throat.

"It's pretty nasty," he added, feeling his chest get bigger.

"Like . . . what is it?"

Her hesitation told him that she wanted to know, but didn't at the same time. "Bits and pieces . . . if you get my drift."

Her voice dropped to a mere whisper. "Will you take me in there?"

"To the Evidence room? Oh, yeah, no, I can't. It's only for authorized personnel."

"But you're authorized, aren't you."

"And I'd like to keep my job."

"Who would know?" She tilted forward even farther. To the point where he imagined that if he sat up a little straighter, they'd be kissing.

Afraid of making a fool out of himself, he moved away, pushing his chair back.

"I wouldn't tell," she whispered.

"It's not so simple. You have to sign in and out, and there are security cameras. It's not like a break room."

He could hear the petulance in his own voice, and abruptly despised his balding, half-assed self. Maybe this was the reason he never got laid.

"But you could get me in ... if you wanted to." Her lips were absolutely mesmerizing, moving slowly as she enunciated the words. "Right? I know you could, if you wanted to. And I wouldn't touch anything."

God, how strange was this? He'd expected to come into work and just do his thing like he did every night. But here it was, this ... crossroads.

Did he Gary Peters it? Or did he grow a set and actually *do* something with this hot chick?

"You know what? Let's go."

He stood up and double-checked that his keys were on his belt—which, of course, they were. And what do you know, he had a reason to go up to the third floor. During the night shift, there was only a skeleton crew on at HQ, so he was the one responsible for walking any stuff upstairs— and Hicks and Rodriguez had just brought in two grams of pot that had been sealed and signed for.

"Oh, my God," she said, leaping off the desk. "For real?"

His chest went back to feeling thick rather than hollow. "Yeah. Come on."

He put up his break sign, the one that told people to hit him up on his remote if they needed to book anyone or log in evidence, and then he opened the door for her.

As she passed by and he smelled her perfume, he felt taller than he had been when he'd come into work, and it was great. And he knew there was a really good chance of getting away with this. The Evidence staff had been working around the clock for days on the Kroner stuff, but they'd finally decided they needed to sleep, so there would be no one up there. And damn right Britnae wasn't going to touch anything—he was going to make sure of that—so there was going to be no need for anyone to check the security tapes.

Risky? Little bit. But at worst, they'd reprimand him—he had the cleanest record for attendance and performance of anyone in intake. Because he had no life. And Britnae was never going to approach him again.

Sometimes you just had to be something other than a Gary Peters behind the desk—

Britnae jumped up and hugged him. "You are so cool!"

"Ah . . . you're welcome."

Shit, what a dumb ass he was. And thank God she didn't hold onto him for long because he nearly fainted.

Except you know what, he did feel cool as he led the way, taking her up in the elevator to the second floor and then insisting, like he was 007, that they hit the stairs for the rest of the way. At the top landing, he opened the fire exit, and listened. Nothing. Not even cleaning people. And down at the end of the hall, the lights in the forensics lab were off.

"I've never been up here before," Britnae whispered into his sleeve as she gripped his arm.

"I'll take care of you. Come on."

They tiptoed down the hall to a heavy steel door marked EVIDENCE—AUTHORIZED PERSONNEL ONLY. Using his keys, he unlocked the thing and pushed the way into an anteroom where the check-in was. His nerves perked up as he went over to the desk where the receptionist sat during normal business hours, but as he logged in and registered, he knew he wasn't going to turn back now.

"Oh, my God, I'm so excited!" As Britnae put her hands on his upper arm and leaned into him, like he was her protector, he didn't bother hiding his smile, because she couldn't see his face.

This was . . . very cool, he thought as he started to enter the cannabis into the system.

As Devina rubbed herself against the officer's body, she did this sad sack Gary Peters guy a favor by putting the security camera in the corner to sleep. It was fun to pretend to be the office ditz, and the idiot desk jockey was eating up the lie, but the ruse needed to begin and end with the pair of them tonight.

He wasn't going to remember this tomorrow morning: In order for this to work, the status quo had to be preserved.

"Okay, let's go in," the guy said as he logged off the computer.

Using Britnae's high-pitched voice and Kardashian, fake-ass, California pronunciation, she said, "Oh, my God, I'm soooo psyched. This is too real!"

Blah, blah, blah . . . but she got the tone right, because she'd been casing headquarters for quite a while now. And it wasn't like the vocabulary was a stretch—add OMG to any one noun and one verb and that was that.

Over at the second bolted steel door, Gary Peters swiped his pass card through the reader on the wall, and then the lock disengaged with a *clunk*.

"You ready?" he said, all Big Man.

"I don't know . . . I mean, yes!"

She bounced a couple of times and then resumed breast-iculating on his arm as she held his hand. And while he soaked up the show, she thought, What a dumbass.

The instant they walked inside the massive storage facility, the cat-and-mouse routine took a backseat to her mission. On some level, she was pissed off at this diversion, but then again, she supposed she would have had to do something like this anyway.

Jim Heron's disappearance was forcing her hand, though, and she hated that.

She just couldn't fucking believe there was no sign of him. First time that had happened with an angel, and she knew only one thing for sure—he hadn't backed out, or given up. Not in his nature. The war was still going on, and she had a soul to take over—and there were ways of guaranteeing that he showed himself.

The guard led her down the long rows of floor-to-ceiling shelving that were set at various heights and filled with boxes and bags of an incalculable variety of shapes and sizes. Everything was clearly cataloged and indexed, little hanging tags and mounted alpha-numerical signs delineating some sort of system.

What a collection. What organization . . .

Devina had to stop and take it all in. "This is *amazing*."

The idiot officer got all proud and shit, even though he was just a cog that worked in the larger machine. "There are tens of thousands of pieces of evidence here at any given time. Everything is referenced by case number and logged into the computer so we can find things efficiently." He started walking again, heading for the recesses of the place. "There are exceptions, though, like with Kroner, because there's just so much associated with the case."

As she followed, she stared up and around at all the objects. What. A. Turn-on.

All the way in the back, there was a bank of empty tables with chairs, like the place was a cafeteria serving up inanimate objects for consumption.

"Detectives and officers are allowed to come in and take more pictures or reexamine things or pull evidence for court. The lab also takes the objects down the hall from time to time, but they have to return the evidence. Kroner's stuff is over here. Do *not* touch anything."

Around the back of a six-foot-tall partition, there was a temporary workstation set up with tables, chairs, computer and photographic equipment, as well as bins of empty plastic bags and rolls of adhesive labels. But that wasn't the interesting stuff. Running along low-slung shelves that were eight or nine feet long, there was a lineup of bar-coded bags that had jars and jewelry and other things in them.

Her little minion had been a busy, busy boy, hadn't he.

"Usually, evidence is logged in down at intake, or in the lab if it's human remains, but there was so much taken from that impounded truck, they had to set up a temporary processing unit here. All the tissue samples were done first, because they were worried about preserving them—but it turned out Kroner knew exactly what to keep the stuff in."

Of course he had. He wanted to have parts of his victims with him always.

"There's a lot of other objects here." The officer lifted a white sheet that covered a huge, shallow box.

Ah, yes, exactly what she had hoped to find—a tangle of T-shirts, jewelry, purses, hair ties, and other personal effects.

Taking it all in, she felt truly, deeply sorry for Kroner. She knew exactly where his obsession was coming from, the way you didn't want to lose what you had worked so hard for, the way you treasured your connection with the objects. And it was even more difficult for him, because unlike herself, he didn't have a way to keep his victims forever—and now he had lost his collection.

Abruptly, Devina struggled for breath.

He had *lost* his precious objects, and here they were, under the aegis of humans who touched them and recataloged them and might possibly, someday in the far future, throw them away.

"Britnae? Are you okay?"

The officer appeared right by her side, hitching a hold on the image of the secretary's arm.

"Sit down," she heard him say from a distance.

As the room started to spin, Devina did what she was told and put her head between the knees that were not her own. Throwing out a palm, she gripped the edge of the table as if she could hold on to consciousness that way.

"Shit, shit . . . here, let me get you some cool water."

As the officer shot off, his footfalls went at a dead run down the stacks, and she knew she didn't have a lot of time. With a shaking, clammy hand, she took out the gold earring she had brought with her from her own collection. Tears waved across her vision as she realized anew that she was going to have to give the thing up if she wanted to progress this round with Heron—and DelVecchio.

The prospect had seemed so reasonable, so dealable, back when she'd been in her private place, surrounded by hundreds of thousands of trophies. What was one earring from a dead virgin? She was keeping the other half of the set—and she had more objects to remember that fucking Sissy Barten with.

Now, though, sitting next to the carnage of Kroner's keepsakes, she felt like she was sending one of her very souls out into a sea of unknown and permanent loss. But what choice did she have? She had to flush out Heron, and just as important, she had to set up the endgame—

Abruptly, the image of the hot blond secretary-type began to disintegrate, Devina's true form emerging through the slipcover of young and pink and human, her dead, ropy flesh and curled gray claws cradling the cheap-ass bird earring.

For a moment, she didn't care. Too shaken by her own hoarding instinct, she couldn't marshal any urgency at the fact that the officer would soon be returning and then she'd have to either infect him or kill him—neither of which she had the energy for.

Except she had to pull herself together.

Forcing herself to think, she called up a vision of her therapist, picturing that roly-poly, fully actualized, post-menopausal tree hugger who not only had an answer for everything ... but seemed to know what the fuck she was talking about.

Devina, the anxiety is not about the things. It's about your place in this world. ... You must remember that you don't need objects to justify your existence or make yourself feel safe and secure.

More to the point, unless she got her shit together, and planted the earring, she was going to compromise her larger goals even further.

You've already lost once, she reminded herself.

Two deep breaths ... and another. Then she looked

down at her hand and willed the image of young, dewy flesh back into place. The concentration required gave her a headache that lingered after she was back to being who she wasn't, but there was no time to dwell on the thumping at her temples. Standing up on legs that were about as solid as soda straws, she stumbled over to the box of objects. Flipping up the corner of the drape, she planted the dove earring and then skated back to the seat the officer had put her in.

Just in time, too.

"Here, drink this."

She looked up at the guy. Going by his face, it appeared as if the Britnae ruse was still working: One thing you could guarantee about humans was a total freak-out if they got a gander at the real her.

"Thank you," she said hoarsely as she reached forward ... with a hand that had pink-polished fake nails. But how long was that going to last?

She drank the cold water, crumpled the paper cup, and tossed the thing into a trash bin under the table. "Please ... can you help me out of here? Now?"

"Absolutely."

He dragged her up from the chair, throwing a surprisingly sturdy arm around her waist and bearing most of her weight.

Down the long rows. Out through the locked door thanks to that pass card. Into the corridor beyond.

The elevator was a blessing, even if the descent made her feel even dizzier.

The plan, she told herself. Work the plan. This was the sacrifice that was necessary to bring everything back where it needed be.

When they were in his office, he seated her in one of the plastic chairs next to his desk, and brought her a second glass of water. Which helped clear her head a little more.

Focusing on the officer, she decided she would not only let him live; she would give him a little present.

"Thank you," she said to him, meaning it.

"You're welcome. Do you have to drive home?"

She gave that a pass, and leaned forward. Mentally reaching through the stale air, she grabbed onto his eyes and wheedled into his brain, strolling along the metaphorical hallways of his mind, viewing casually the evidence on his private shelves.

Just as she had planted the earring, she inserted a knowledge in his brain that he was a Casanova beyond compare, a guy who, in spite of his modest looks, was wanted by women and therefore confident and manly around them.

It was the kind of thing that was going to get him laid. Because unlike men, who were visual creatures, women tended to go more for what was in between the ears.

And self-possession was sexy.

Devina left shortly thereafter, taking with her the memories of what they'd done and where they'd gone. Her act of charity both disgusted her and made her want to thumb her nose at the insufferable Nigel.

Just as a nun with the purest heart imaginable could still curse on occasion, a demon could in rare instances be moved to show compassion.

But it made her feel like she needed a shower to get the stank off.

CHAPTER
21

"I think I'm in heaven."

Reilly hid a smile as Veck stared with awe at the slice of apple pie her mother had put in front of him.

"You really made this?" he said as he looked up.

"From scratch, including the crust," her dad announced. "And not only that, she can do your taxes with her eyes closed and one arm tied behind her back."

"I think I'm in love."

"Sorry, she's taken." Her dad pulled her mom in for a quick kiss as he got his plate of dessert. "Right?"

"Right," was the answer spoken against his mouth.

Reilly passed a quart of vanilla ice cream to Veck. "À la mode?"

"You betcha."

Turned out Detective DelVecchio was a good little eater. He'd had seconds on the *Vitello Saltimbocca* and the *Linguine con Pomodoro*. Not a big salad guy, but that was not a surprise. And it looked like dessert might well be a twofer also.

Although his capacity to savor her mother's cooking wasn't all she was impressed with: He'd held his own against her dad. Jokingly and with respect, he'd made it clear he wasn't a pushover, even though Tom Reilly had been known to scare elected public officials half to death. As a result?

"And, yeah, Veck, I agree with you," her father announced. "There's a lot out there that needs changing in the system. It's a hard balance between prosecution and persecution—especially among certain racial and ethnic groups. Socioeconomic, too."

Yup, the full approval had been bestowed on her partner.

As talk sprang up around the subject of profiling in law enforcement, she sat back and watched Veck. He seemed so much more relaxed than she'd ever seen him.

And man, he was handsome.

A half hour and another serving of pie later, Veck helped bring the plates to the sink and hopped on drying duty. Then it was time to coat up and head for the exit.

"Thanks, Mom," she said, hugging the woman who had always been there for her. "And Dad."

Going over to her father, she had to tiptoe it to put her arms around him, stretching high and not making it even halfway around his shoulders.

"I love you," he said, holding her tight. And then in her ear, he whispered, "Nice guy you got there."

Before she could return a he's-not-actually-mine, handshakes were being passed around and she and Veck were out the door.

As she was backing out into the street, they both waved and then it was all over.

"Your parents are incredible," he said, as she drove them away.

A flush of pride in her family made her smile. "They are."

"If you don't mind my asking . . ."

When he didn't turn to look at her, and he didn't finish the sentence, she had the sense her answer was important to him, but that he wasn't going to force her to reply.

"I'm more than happy to talk about it." As rain started to fall, she pulled up to a stop sign and put her wipers on. "My parents had always worked with at-risk youth and crisis centers—starting before they'd even met. There's one run by the Catholic Church downtown, and after they were married, they used to spend Saturdays there, crunching the books, soliciting donations, helping with the displaced families. The woman who gave birth to me and I came into the place after her and one of her three boyfriends got into a fight and she lost the sight in her left eye." Reilly glanced over. "I saw it happen. It's my first memory, actually."

"How old were you?" he asked tightly.

"Three and a half. She was fighting with him over a dirty needle, which was nothing new, but then she just snapped and went after him with a knife. He shoved her away in self-defense, but she kept coming at him until he hit her. Hard. She told the cops he beat her, and they took him to jail. And that's how we ended up in the shelter—it was his apartment that we were staying in." Reilly hit her directional signal and headed over for the entrance onto the Northway that was down by the high school. "Anyway, we were staying at the place my parents volunteered at, and the woman who gave birth to me stole some things from another family, so that was the end of that. We went to stay with her other two boyfriends for about a week and then ... she took me back and dropped me off at the shelter. Just left me."

Veck met her in the eyes. "Where is she now?"

"Not a clue. I never saw her again, and I know this is going to sound bitter, but I don't care what happened to her." She came up to a stoplight and hit the brakes. "She was a liar and an addict, and the only nice thing she ever did was leave me—although to be honest, I'm pretty sure it wasn't for my benefit. I was probably cramping her style, and she had to know that killing a child was the kind of no-no that would guarantee her life behind bars."

At that point, it was time to merge onto the highway—which was fine, because this was the hard part of her story.

Little break, little breath, as she found a space for them in the traffic.

"Boy, the rain's really starting to come down," she said, speeding up the wipers.

"You don't have to finish."

"No, it's okay. The real nightmare is what would have happened if my parents hadn't taken an interest in me. That's what still scares me to this day." She checked in the rearview mirror, changed into the fast lane, and hit the gas. "My parents happened to be working that day—and I just stuck to them like glue. I'd loved my father from when I'd met him before, because he's just so big and strong, with that deep voice—I knew he'd protect me. And my mother always gave me cookies and milk—and played with me. Almost immediately, I was determined to go home with them, but they were trying to conceive at that point and, gee whiz, weren't necessarily all about some drug addict's baby.

"That night, and for a week afterward, they tried to find the woman and talk sense into her, because they knew that once a kid gets into the system, it can be hard to break out of it. When they finally found her, she didn't want me—and she said she'd sign her rights away. They came back later that evening and sat with me. I wasn't supposed to be staying at the shelter, because you needed your guardian there, but my mom had been camping out with me so I could have a bunk. I remember knowing they were going to tell me I had to go, but one more day turned into two ... which turned into another week. I was really well behaved, and I had the sense my dad was working on something. Finally, they came back and asked me if I wanted to stay with them for a little bit. He'd gotten them cleared as foster parents by pulling strings like only he could." She glanced over and smiled. "Little bit turned into twenty-five-plus years. They officially adopted me, like, a year after I moved in."

"That's awesome." Veck returned her smile, and then got serious again. "What about your biological father?"

"No one knows who he was—including the woman who birthed me, according to my parents. They told me much later, when I was grown up, that she'd maintained it was one of two exes of hers—both of whom were in jail for dealing drugs." She sped up her wipers. "And listen, I know I sound ... angry in places. I guess I just struggle with the whole addiction-is-a-disease theory. With a pair of addicts as my biological basis, there's a statistical probability that I'd end up like them, but I didn't go that route—I knew it was a door I shouldn't open, and I never have. And yeah, you could argue that my parents provided me with opportunities my biological mother never had, and that's true. But you make your own destiny. You choose your way."

For a while there was just the beat of the wipers and the subtle rush of water whipping down the underside of the car.

"I'm sorry, I probably said too much."

"No, not at all."

Reilly glanced over and had the sense Veck was back in his own past. Staying quiet, she hoped he'd open up, but he kept silent, elbow propped on the door, hand massaging his jaw.

From out of nowhere, a massive black SUV roared by in the middle lane, the Escalade splashing up gallons of water over Reilly's hood and obscuring the view.

"Jesus," she said, easing off on the gas. "They must be going a hundred."

"Nothing like a death wish to cut your travel time."

The vehicle dodged right, then left, then right again, jogging by other cars like a football receiver on the way to the goal line.

Reilly frowned as she imagined Veck on his bike in this downpour with that kind of maniac on the road. "Hey, are you going to be able to ride home in all the rain? This is getting dangerous."

"Nah, it's no problem."

Cursing to herself, she was not at all sure of his read on the situation. And the fact that he was stupid enough to get on that rocket of his in this sort of weather really didn't put her in her happy place.

*   *   *

As Veck sat next to Reilly, he found himself thinking about his father . . . and his mother, too—although the latter was someone he couldn't dwell on. How ironic. DelVecchio Sr. was almost always on his mind, but his mother—

"I think I'd better take you home," Reilly said. "This is nothing you need to be going through on a bike."

"I had no idea about your past," he heard himself murmur. "And I wouldn't have ever guessed it. You're so totally put together."

There was a pause, as if she had to change conversational lanes in her head. "Well, a lot of it is my parents. By example and in actuality, they are who I wanted to be and who I became. It always wasn't easy though. For a long while, I was worried that if I wasn't perfect, they'd return me like a defective toaster. But then I wrecked my father's new car on my learner's permit—tested that theory pretty damn well, and guess what? They kept me anyway."

Staring at her profile, he said, "I don't think you give yourself enough credit."

"The only thing I did was take advantage of the good example that was in front of me."

"And that's tremendous."

When she turned into his neighborhood five minutes later, he realized she'd taken her own advice about him and his bike and the weather.

The brakes squeaked slightly as she stopped in his driveway, and abruptly, the rain hitting the roof of the car sounded like Ping-Pong balls.

"I think we're having some hail," he said.

"Yes." She stared through the front windshield. "Bad storm."

"No thunder."

"No."

The wipers flopped back and forth, clearing the view only momentarily.

Eventually, he looked over at her. "I want to kiss you again."

"I know."

He laughed a little. "Am I so obvious."

"No . . . I want it, too."

Then turn your head, he thought. All you have to do is turn your head and I'll take it from there.

The rain fell. The wipers slapped around. The engine idled.

She turned her head. And focused on his mouth. "I *really* want it."

Veck leaned in toward her, and pulled her to his lips. The kiss was very slow and very deep. And as her tongue met his, he was well aware he wanted something more from her than just sex, but if he'd had to name what the hell it was, he'd have been out of words. Ultimately, however, the definition didn't matter. Not in the interior of this unmarked, parked in his driveway, with the storm on the outside of the car.

What they both needed had nothing to do with talking.

God, she was still so soft beneath him, soft skin, soft hair, soft scent, but it was the tough inner core of her, the resilience and the single-mindedness, that really turned him on. The idea that she was such a survivor, that she was so strong and clear with who she was and where she was from, made him respect the shit out of her.

And what do you know . . . that was sexier than anything that came in a Victoria's Secret bag.

With a surge of his torso, he tried to get even closer, but the steering wheel bit into his side, and blocked him. The caveman in him actually growled as he gave it another shot, but he got nowhere near where he wanted to be.

Which was naked and on top of her.

On a curse, he eased back. In the reflected brightness of the headlights on the garage door, her beautiful face was illuminated clearly, the pattern of the rain on the windshield playing across her features, spotting them up before the wipers cleared away what looked like tears.

He thought of her with her family, so happy and at peace.

He thought of her, period.

"I'm going to go in alone," he said abruptly.

Veck didn't wait for a response. He was out of that car a split second later, and he hotfooted it over to the front door of his house, not because of the storm, but because he could see too clearly into himself.

"Wait!" she called out as he palmed up his keys.

"Go back to your car," he muttered in a rough, hungry voice.

Rushing over to him, she shook her head. "I don't want to."

With that, she lifted up her hand and pointed it in the direction of her unmarked. As she hit her remote, the locks punched down and the blinkers flared.

Veck closed his eyes and let his head flop back on his spine, the rain hitting his forehead and cheeks. "You come in here, I'm not going to be able to stop."

Reilly's reply was to take the keys out of his hand, unlock the dead bolt, and subtly, inexorably push him back into his house.

Just as with the kiss in the car, he took it from there.

Kicking the door shut, he unleashed himself, grabbing her and yanking her against him, holding her hard, taking her mouth again. And she attacked him right back, locking her arms around his shoulders, pressing herself against him.

The couch.

He'd moved the couch.

Thank fuck.

It was a shuffle to get over there, and the fact that he was taking off her wet coat and his, and then both of their gun holsters, didn't make the going any easier. But soon enough he was maneuvering her down so she was stretched out on the cushions ... and he mounted her, all but jumping on top of her body.

The kissing was heavy-duty desperate, the kind of thing where their teeth hit every now and then, and he didn't want to stop to breathe, even though his lungs were burning from lack of oxygen—especially as she started clawing at his shoulders.

He was not nice to her button-down.

Without breaking their lip-lock, he took its lapels in his fists and split the damn thing from collar to hem, popping free all kinds of pearly white UFOs that sailed through the air and bounced off the carpet.

Her bra underneath was buff colored, and nothing but simple cotton that looked spectacular over her breasts. And what a relief not to have to worry about whether he'd rip delicate lace.

As he went for the uncomplicated front clasp, she was breathing fast and hard, and the undulation of her ribs under her skin was one hell of a turn-on—that was nothing compared to when he sprang the bra and those modest cups snapped to the sides.

"You're amazing," he groaned as he took a proper look at her . . . something he'd cheated himself out of the night before.

Oh, man, her breasts were heavier than they appeared with her clothes on, fuller and rounder—which made him wonder whether she didn't deliberately wear tight bras to constrict them. And what a waste that was.

Then again, the idea of any other man ogling her like this made him want to go for his gun.

Palming up what he had revealed, he got another surprise that he'd missed in his hurry back in her kitchen. She was all natural, a gift from God, undoctored by insecurity or vanity. And the heavy, supple weight of her made his cock throb—reminding him how long it had been since he'd been with a woman who didn't have hard-as-rock implants.

Pushing her together, her nipples were tight and erect, and he bent down, sucking on one and then the other. Then he nuzzled the undersides of what was in his hands.

So he was a breast man, after all, he thought as his hips rolled against her legs. Who knew.

Or . . . maybe he was just a Sophia Reilly man.

"You are so fucking beautiful," he growled as he went back to work on those pink tips.

As desperate as he was to get in her, he was so capti-
vated by her upper body, he just explored her, licking at her
and touching her and watching her respond. Somehow her
thighs parted—maybe it was his knee, maybe her need;
who gave a shit—and then the two of them were flush
where it counted most.

Pushing himself up with his arms, he started to grind
against her, his erection rubbing against her core. In re-
sponse, she arched in the most erotic way, her chest rising
as her spine torqued, her fingernails biting into his fore-
arms.

As he pumped against her, her breasts swayed to the
beat and got him drunk, his body numb and hypersensitive
at the same time—except he missed her lips. Resealing
their mouths, he knew he was close to the edge of no-
control . . . and then he felt her hands tugging at his shirt.

Guess he wasn't the only one.

Abruptly, he lost his patience with his clothes, and what
covered his chest was gone a moment later, ripped off like
hers had been.

"Feel me," he bit out, as he arched back over her.

He kissed her hard as her hands went everywhere, trac-
ing over his muscles, grabbing his shoulders, streaking her
nails down his ribs.

More.

"Can I get you naked?" he said.

"Yes . . ."

She lifted her hips and went for her belt at the same
time he rose over her. And she did such a good job on those
pants, he just sat back and watched as a pair of white cotton
panties made an appearance.

When she had trouble going any further, because hello,
she had a two-hundred-pound man looming over her, he
helped her draw the slacks down her long, smooth legs.

Oh, man . . . he thought, running his hands up and down
her thighs. She was lean, and gently muscled, and he found
himself imagining that he was spreading her wide, and dip-
ping his head—

204 J. R. Ward

Snapping, he lunged at her, stretching out on top of her once more and pumping himself against her. His plan? Ease his way south and take those panties off with his teeth. Then he was going to spend a while making sure her body was good and ready for him. With his lips and his tongue and his fingers.

Turned out he had a little gentleman in him after all.

Yeah. That was it. Not because he was dying to taste her—

Except then she went for his belt.

He froze, and put his hands over hers, stilling her.

"If that comes off," he said roughly, "I'm not going to be able to wait for more than a split second."

With Veck's massive body poised above her, Reilly's brain was focused on one and only one thing—and that was getting his pants down.

"I don't want to wait."

"You sure?" His voice was so guttural, it was nearly inaudible.

In reply, she shifted her hand between his thighs and palmed his sex. The instant the connection was made, he cursed on an explosive exhale, and his body bucked against her, the soft material of his pants doing nothing to hide that rigid length.

"I want to see you," she demanded hoarsely.

Not something she had to ask twice: With fast, violent hands, he went to work on his fly, and she was the one who pulled at the waistband. Then they were working together on his boxer briefs to free his—

His erection jutted straight out from his hips, and the lids of his eyes went low as he watched her take him in.

Holy . . .

Well, she could use a thesaurus's worth of terms for "magnificent," couldn't she. And it was safe to say that if she'd been impressed when she'd seen him in his bathroom that first night, or when she'd felt him through his clothes in her kitchen, fully revealed and ready to roar, she was blown away. And his sex wasn't the only sight worth seeing: His chest was just as smooth and muscled as she remembered, and his abdominals were amazing, a tight double row of ridges that led down to his pelvis and his—

"Fuck—"

As she gripped him, palm to skin, he shuddered violently, and she loved the sense of power that came from rocking his world. And oh, God, he was thick and long, pulsing and kicking against her hold as she stroked him.

She was never going to forget this, she thought, this sight of him above her, teeth bared, head back, huge chest straining as he struggled for control. It was the hottest thing she'd ever seen. And exploration was a virtue, for sure ... but she wanted him in the deepest way before she took the time to learn his ins-and-outs.

Although phrased like that ...

"Your wallet?" She'd seen what he kept in there when she'd handled his billfold out in the woods—and the sight of those condoms had embarrassed her then. Now, she was grateful, because Lord knew she didn't have anything of the sort. And there was no need to dwell on the reason a man would always have to be prepared. Besides, it wasn't as if she didn't know about that side of him. She'd witnessed the Britnae effect, thank you very much.

"Now," she barked.

Yet another thing she didn't have to ask twice about. As he found his slacks and got out his wallet, she lifted her butt and swept her panties down and off—so that she was ready when he brought up his hand, a condom held between his fore- and middle fingers.

He paused, like he was giving her a chance to look hard at the thing.

She didn't hesitate. She sat up and took the foiled packet from him, biting into it and ripping it open.

He groaned and then said, "I can put—"

"No, let me."

Practicalities had never been so erotic. She handled him well, stroking his great length as she covered him, until he was arched back and bearing his weight on his arms. As she worked him, his eyes burned, and when she pulled him down on top of her, he growled ... and kissed her the way she was learning he always did—with a dominance that came from a man knowing precisely what he could do to a woman.

She positioned him at her core, and in spite of how desperate she was for this and how much he obviously wanted her, he was slow and careful as he pressed inside. Good thing, too. Her body was ready—but that was a relative term, given the size of him.

Gloriously relative—the stretching was electric, and she spread her legs further, tilting her hips up, easing his way.

And then they were together.

In contrast to the fury that had gotten them to this point, everything now slowed down. With his slick tongue, he licked at her lips, the lazy laps tantalizing her as he waited for her to adjust. And then she moved her hips, curling her spine, creating an insane frisson.

The hiss he let out was followed by another groan. Then he fused his mouth to hers and got going, keeping the rhythm unhurried and even. Mirroring him, she countered his thrusts with her own, the sex gaining a momentum that took her at once out of her body and deep inside herself.

The house was quiet; what they were doing was loud. From the creak of the sofa, to the subtle rasp of the cushions, to their breath ... everything was amplified until she wouldn't have been surprised if people could hear it downtown.

Faster. Harder. Even deeper.

His body became a heavy, pistoning machine, and she held on, swept up in the maelstrom, gripping his back first with her hands, then with her nails.

She came with a savage burst so powerful, she was surprised she didn't snap in half. And he followed immediately, his hips spasming into her as violently as she clenched onto him internally.

It was a long while before the roar in her ears subsided, and as it did, the silence in the house rushed forward.

In the wake of the passion, reality returned: she became acutely aware that she was completely naked, and Veck was in her body . . . and she had just had sex.

With the man who was her partner. With the detective she was supposed to be overseeing. With the person who she'd spent a number of hours with . . . who was nonethe less a stranger.

A stranger she'd brought to her family's house.

A stranger she now had to add to her very short list of the number of people she'd been with.

What had they just done?

CHAPTER
22

A drian and Eddie wasted more of the night in that booth at the Iron Mask, drinking Buds out of longnecks and turning down the women who trolled by.

Neither of them said much. It was like what had happened in the bathroom had sucked the conversation right out of their voice boxes. And another round of sex was out of the question.

As he sat beside his partner, Ad waited for something inside of him to kick in and get him back into the groove.

Annnnnnnnnd . . . nothing was coming to him.

The thing was, you could fight the enemy with your knives and your fists, but your own soul was nothing to wage war against, because there was no chance of winning that one. You also couldn't square off in the ring against reality, either—no target to hit. Unless it was a proverbial brick wall with your head.

So he just sat in the club, watching the crowd, drinking but no longer getting drunk.

"Do we go back to the hotel?" he finally asked.

As he waited for an answer, he was acutely aware of how much he relied on the other angel to be the voice of reason, to make the right decisions, to get them headed in the correct direction.

What the fuck did the guy get from him?

Apart from sex, that was—and tonight Eddie had proved he didn't need that service, either.

Waah, waah, waah, Ad thought. He kept this up and he was going to get his panty card stamped.

"What I really want is an audience with Nigel," Eddie muttered, "but he's blowing me off."

Ad looked over. "Have we been fired again? 'Cause no shit, this is not our fault. Jim's the one with the problem, not us. He gave us the boot."

And all because of that damn virgin of his.

Man, if he could do one thing over since he'd met the savior, it would be to have kept the guy out of Devina's lair. Yeah, sure, the Sissy issue was a tragedy. But what it was doing to Jim was worse. One girl, one family, versus the whole of the souls in the hereafter? Cruel math for the Bartens, but it was what it was.

Ad ran a hand through his hair and felt like screaming. "Listen, I can't stay here anymore."

The grunt that came out of Eddie was either agreement, hunger, or beer that hadn't settled well.

"Come on," Ad declared, getting to his feet.

For once, Eddie was the one who followed him, and to-gether, they weaved in and out of the crowd, zeroing in on the door. On the other side of the exit? Rain. Cool air. Nighttime in a city that was no different from any other on the planet on an evening that was no different from so many they had passed together.

Shit, maybe they needed to get with Jim and . . . chill this out. Nothing good was going to come of the savior fighting on his own.

Walking off from the club, they went in no direction in particular. Sooner or later, they were going to have to find a place to crash for the night: Unless they were welcomed up in Nigel's territory—and it looked like that wasn't happening anytime soon—they needed to rest. Immortal was immortal only up to a point when they were down here. Yeah, they didn't age, but they were vulnerable in some ways and very much subject to the eat, sleep, bathe rules—

The attack happened so fast, he didn't see it coming. And neither did Eddie.

His partner just let out a curse, grabbed his side, and went down like a tree, falling sideways onto the wet pavement of the alley.

"Eddie? What the fuck?"

The other angel moaned and curled into a ball . . . leaving behind a shimmering smudge of fresh blood on the dirty asphalt.

"Eddie!" he screamed.

Before he could drop to his knees, maniacal laughter echoed up into the cold, wet darkness.

Adrian's response was delayed by nothing but a breath. He wheeled around and unsheathed his knife, expecting to face Devina. Backed up by a minion. Or twelve.

All he got . . . was a human. A fucking piece-of-shit human. With a switchblade in his hand and the wild eyes of a junkie staring out of his shrunken-head skull.

More laughter leaped out of the man's gaping mouth. "The devil made me do it! The devil made me do it!"

The homeless man lifted his knife over his shoulder and lunged forward, gunning for Adrian with the kind of super-human strength that only the crazy had.

Ad sank down into his thighs. His normal move would be to tuck and roll, and come up from underneath, but not with Eddie on the ground: He needed to keep his fallen friend in the corner of his eye . . . because the guy was not moving, not going for a weapon, not . . . oh, shit, not *moving* . . .

"Come on, Eddie—shake it off!" Switching his crystal dagger to his left hand, Ad focused on the forearm of the possessed harpy, waiting for the right moment—

He caught the flailing limb on the downstroke, at the perfect second to change the switchblade's trajectory and redirect it back at the bastard. And the course correction should have been easy as pie, with the weapon making an arc that avoided contact with Ad's major organs and terminated in the gut of the attacker.

No. Go.

The wiry body controlled by the haywire mind slipped from his grip like Ad was trying to hold on to a gust of wind.

And that was when he realized that Eddie wasn't going to get up on his feet.

Like the harpy could read his mind, laughter bubbled out of the lost soul, sounding like piano keys hit randomly with a heavy hand, nothing but sharp, discordant noise.

The fucker was practically flying over the ground as it came at Adrian again, knife over his shoulder, skin peeling back from that face that was more skull than flesh.

Ad had no choice but to focus on his attacker and protect himself. Eddie was as good as dead on the pavement if Ad didn't survive this and get him to safety. There was no losing this one.

Crouching down at the last moment, he tackled the piece of shit, pile-driving the harpy back against a building. As impact was made, a blazing pain above his kidneys told him that that knife had broken skin and gone in a hell of a lot deeper, but there was no time to worry about a leak. He reached up, caught that wild-card arm, and nailed it to the wet brick. Locking the limb in place, he stabbed upward with his dagger once.

All that maniacal laugher got replaced by the high-pitched scream of pain.

He stabbed again. And a third time . . . a fourth, a fifth.

Somewhere along the line, it dawned on him that he'd become just as unleashed as the harpy, but he didn't stop. With vicious, jabbing power, he drove that crystal blade into the man's torso over and over until he stopped hitting ribs because he'd broken them all, and instead penetrated nothing but a wet sponge of desecrated tissue.

And still he kept going. No longer pinning the man to

get control, instead, he held the bastard up so he could continue stabbing.

The fun and games finally stopped when his blade hit the brick wall, the crystal carving its way into whatever building he had killed against.

Ad was breathing hard as he let his weapon fall to his side. Blood was everywhere, and so was the harpy's intestinal tract—matter of fact, the bastard was nearly cut in two, his spine the only thing that was linking his hips to the top half of his body.

From out of slack, flappy lips, gagging noises interrupted the steady stream of plasma that blocked the air the man was still trying to get down his throat.

That was going to stop soon, though.

"The devil . . . made me . . . do it. . . ."

"And she can keep you," Ad growled—before he stabbed the harpy right between the eyes.

There was a terrible screech as Devina's essence exploded out of the eye sockets of what had once been a street-lost addict, the black smoke coalescing, coming together, preparing an assault of its own.

"Fuck!" With a great leap, Adrian threw his body into the air and went sailing. Eddie's prone, injured figure was his landing pad, and he covered the angel's body with his own, becoming the shield that was all that could keep Devina out of his partner's flesh.

Bracing for impact, he thought to himself, Well, I hadn't expected to be this right, this soon.

About the death thing, that was.

At least Eddie was going to pull through. It was going to take more than a poke to down him for good. Wounds, after all, could be fixed—they had to be.

As Jim stood with Dog on the sidewalk outside of Veck's house, he was aware that he was taking a backseat approach to the soul in question, just following the guy from place to place and biding his time until Devina made the next move.

It was fucking painful as shit.

He was much more comfortable assuming an aggressive stance, but wait and see was sometimes the name of the game. Although, damn, the weather could be better. The rain was continuing to fall and he sure as hell could do without the windchill.

Could do without having to studiously ignore what was going on inside the house, as well.

Of course the pair of them were having sex.

Duh.

He'd caught the start of the fun and games just before they'd gone inside, so it was obvious what the next move was: Their chemistry was off the chain, and generally speaking, that was not the kind of stuff you walked away from.

Jim crossed his arms over his chest and hunkered in, all the hot-'n'-heavy making him think about the women he'd been with. Huh. Did Devina count as one? Only if she was in the brunette flesh costume, he supposed. Without it, he probably had to start an "animal" category.

But whatever. Regardless of species, he'd never once been with someone he gave two shits about. The fucking had been a participatory kind of masturbation for him—and maybe, if he was honest, a head game with the chippies. He'd enjoyed getting them off, the sense of control over them being better than anything they'd made him feel in return.

His sex life was over now, though, wasn't it. What he had with that demon couldn't possibly count—that was fighting in the war, just with a different set of fists and elbows. And it wasn't like his lifestyle encouraged frickin' dating. Although . . .

An abrupt image of Adrian and Eddie hooking up with that redhead in the hotel room in Framingham, Massachusetts, filtered down like it had rained into his head. He saw Eddie stretching over her while Adrian had looked dead behind the eyes as he went to join them.

Devina had done that to the angel. Put that emptiness in his stare.

Fucking bitch.

Taking out a Marlboro, Jim lit the thing and inhaled.

Veck was a lucky man to be with the woman he wanted. Jim was never going to have that. Even if he got Sissy free of—

"Fuck me," he muttered on the exhale.

Had the shit with that girl gone so far that in some ridiculous part of his brain, he was actually thinking of her as not just "his" as in a responsibility kind of way? But really "his"?

Had he lost his frickin' mind? She was like nineteen, and he was a hundred and forty thousand years old at this point.

Okay, maybe Adrian and Eddie were right. What was doing with that girl *was* a distraction. Yeah, he'd tried to package it to himself in all sorts of this-is-cool verbiage, but he'd so been lying. And naturally, when his partners had forced him to look at his head-in-the-sand, he'd thrown it back at them and huffed off like a little bitch.

A scratching at his leg brought his head down. Dog had curled into a sit at his feet and was pawing at his calf, looking worried.

"What is it—"

Jim's phone went off, and even before he grabbed it and checked the screen, he had a premonition of tragedy.

Accepting the call, all he heard was labored breathing. Then Eddie's voice, weak and broken. "Trade . . . and Thirteenth. Help—"

The pealing laughter in the background was all kinds of bad news, and Jim didn't waste a moment. He left Dog on the sidewalk and whisked away to downtown, praying that blink-of-an-eye would get him there in time.

The address was irrelevant; all he had to do was zero in on the essence of his boys . . . and he got there just as Adrian took his crystal dagger and nailed some crazy-ass, bleeding bastard right between the eyes.

Devina.

Jim didn't need the screech to know that something evil

was coming out of that bag of flesh, and there was nothing on hand to stop it from getting into Eddie: The angel was down and then some, tucked into a tight ball, cell phone in what was now a lax hand.

Without stopping to think, Jim threw himself in the direction of the defenseless angel, hurling his body through the air—at the same time Adrian did.

Ad landed first.

And then Jim covered them all, without much hope of protecting anyone—

The strangest thing happened: His body dissolved into light, the same way it had when he'd been furious with Devina during the last round. One moment he was in his corporeal form . . . the next he was pure energy.

Blanketing the angels beneath him. Keeping them safe.

The minion, demon, whatever the hell it was, hit with all the impact of a golf ball on a car hood, boinking off, leaving not even a dent behind. Immediately, it came again, to the same effect. Annnnnd a third time.

There was a long pause that Jim didn't buy a moment of. He could sense the presence circling them, searching for a way in.

All the while, it was clear Eddie was bleeding. The smell of copper was too bold to be from the body over by the alley's brick sidewall. Hell, maybe both of the angels were injured.

Time to end this bullshit.

Jim retracted himself, rising up into a column of brilliant light that nonetheless illuminated nothing of the grungy environs and threw no shadows. Squaring off at the evil, he focused everything he had on the smoky stain in the air—

And blew the fucker apart.

The explosion had no flash, but the screech was as loud as an SUV braking on dry pavement, and then there was a strange, pattering follow-up on the ground, as if sand were being poured out of a satchel.

Jim resumed his corporeal form and knelt over his boys. "Who's hurt?"

Adrian groaned and rolled off his best friend, his hand clasping his side. "Him. Stabbed in the stomach."

Ad had clearly been nailed as well, but Eddie was the one who wasn't moving. Although at least when Jim touched the angel's shoulder, the guy flinched.

"How you doing?"

When there was a whole lot of no-answer, Jim glanced around. They needed to get off the streets. This was a busy area of the city at night, and the last thing he wanted was for some well-intentioned kibitzer to 911 the sitch. Or worse, for a mugger to come by. Or a policeman on patrol.

"How about you?" he asked Adrian as he measured the other end of the alley.

"I'm fine."

"Oh, really." Office buildings. Warehouse next to them. "Why are you wincing like that?"

"Constipation."

"Yeah. Right."

There was no chance they could go back to the hotel. They needed more privacy than what they'd get there, and anyway, there was no way he could carry Eddie through the frickin' lobby: Even though he could camo them both, the guy would still leave a trail of blood.

Then again, it was all a moot point because there was no flying with that kind of weight. He needed to find them shelter close by.

"You mobile?" he asked Adrian.

"Depends. Walking? Yeah. Flying? Don't think so."

Jim scooped his arms under Eddie's prone body. "Brace yourself, big boy. This is gonna hurt."

With a surge, Jim threw the muscles of his thighs into service and hefted the angel's weight off the damp pavement. In response, Eddie groaned and tightened up, which was a bene, as it made the guy easier to hold on to.

Also meant the bastard was still with them.

Before Jim could start walking, Eddie's cell phone hit the ground and skittered away, knocking into Adrian's combat boot.

The angel bent down and picked it up. The screen was glowing and the transparent wash of blood across it made the thing throw off red light. Pushing his wet hair back, Ad said, "So he called you."

"Yeah." Jim nodded at the bank across the street from the alley's opening. "We're going in there."

"How."

"Through the front door." As Jim began striding forward, he muttered to Eddie, "Damn, son, you weigh as much as a fucking car."

The shuffling behind told him that Ad was along for the ride. Likewise with the hoarse commentary: "A bank? That place is going to be more than locked. So short of—"

As they came up to the entrance of the glass-enclosed lobby, the interior lights went off, the security system disengaged, and the front door ...

Opened. Wide.

As soon as they were inside, everything righted itself except for the lights and the motion sensors.

"How did you pull that off?" Adrian breathed.

Jim glanced over his shoulder. The angel behind him looked like a train wreck: face too pale, eyes too wide, blood on his hands and dripping down his wet muscle shirt.

"I don't know," Jim said softly. "I just did it. And you need to sit down. Right now."

"Fuck that—we have to treat Eddie."

True enough. The trouble was, in this situation ... Eddie was the guy he'd go to to ask what the hell to do.

Time to start praying for a miracle, Jim thought.

CHAPTER
23

Veck felt the change in Reilly immediately: Even though he was inside her, mentally, she had put her clothes back on, stepped out of his door, and driven away.

Shit.

Moving a hand down between their bodies, he held on and pulled out. "I know what you're thinking."

She rubbed her eyes. "Do you."

"Yeah. And I should probably say something like, 'This was a mistake.' Just so you have your out."

Before he settled into the cushions of the couch beside her, he reached down and picked up his shirt, draping it over her naked body.

Pulling the thing up to her chin, she studied his face. "By all measures, it was. It is."

Okay, ouch.

"But I just couldn't stop myself," she said softly.

"Temptation is like that." And he needed to get it through his head that that was probably all it was on her side.

Her eyes shifted to the floor next to the couch . . . where his wallet lay open, another condom clearly tucked into its flaps.

"I should probably go," she said roughly.

Christ, why had he always kept two in there?

And her leaving was the last thing he wanted—and the last thing he would get in the way of. "You're going to have to take my shirt. I broke yours."

Closing her eyes, she cursed softly. "I'm sorry."

"God, what for?"

"I don't know."

He believed that. Also knew she was going to figure out just exactly what and how much she was regretting soon enough.

As he stood up from the sofa, he cupped his sex with his hand; no reason for her to see that right now. And no reason for her to think of the evening as anything other than what she'd said it was: a mistake for her.

For him, on the other hand? Thanks to her, he'd had his first home-cooked meal in the twenty-first century, a ride home through the storm, and sex that came damn close to that dumb-ass overused phrase: making love.

Ironic how two people could come away from the same list of events with two totally different takes. Unfortunately, hers was the only one that counted.

In silence, he gathered her clothes one by one and handed them over. Going by the sounds, she drew her pants on, and then her socks and shoes. He assumed the bra went on as well, but that wouldn't make a lot of noise, would it. Holster was the last thing he gave her, and as she dealt with the leather strapping, he grabbed his pants and held them over his hips.

"I'll walk you to the door," he said, when she was finished.

No reason to draw out the awkward stuff. Besides, she'd already gone, anyway.

God, he felt like he'd been shot in the gut, he thought as he went into the front hall.

As Reilly came up to him, he focused over her shoulder. Which unfortunately brought his eyes to the couch.

"I don't want it to end this way," she said.

"It is what it is. And it's not like I don't get where you're coming from."

"It's not what you think."

"I can imagine."

"I don't want to . . . I really wanted this. But I guess it's hard to just be another woman in your bed."

Opening the door, he got slammed with a blast of cold and wet. "I would never take you upstairs. Trust me."

She blinked. Cleared her throat. "Okay. Ah . . . I'll see you in the morning."

"Yeah. Nine a.m."

As soon as she stepped through, he shut the door and went around to the kitchen to watch her get in her car and drive away through the rain.

"Motherfucker."

Bracing palms on the counter, he let his head hang for a moment. Then, disgusted with himself, he doubled back and hit the stairs at a jog. In his bedroom, he passed by his bed and thought, Nope, absolutely not. He'd never take Reilly there. That mattress, which he'd brought up with him from Manhattan, was where he'd banged the randoms he'd picked up in bars—some of whom he hadn't even gotten a name from, much less digits.

All of whom he'd booted out before the sweat was dry.

The woman he'd been lucky enough to be with tonight was not one of that less than august group, and even if she didn't feel the same way he did, he would never cheapen her by laying her on that soiled place.

Clean sheets didn't hide the stain of the way he'd been living.

In the bathroom, he snapped off the cold condom and tossed it in the wastepaper basket. As he looked at the shower, he thought about taking one. But in the end, he just threw on a pair of sweats and went down to the couch below, her delicate perfume still on him.

Pathetic.

One good thing about having logged three years of working various beats in Caldwell was that Reilly could get home from any neighborhood without thinking about it.

Handy on a night like tonight.

I would never take you upstairs. Trust me.

Yeah, boy, that little ditty was going to be with her for the rest of her natural life.

And of course, she wondered exactly what rarified class of females was welcome in that special space. God, how many women had he had on that couch? And how did you make the cut to get into his bedroom?

But she didn't blame him for any of the way she felt now. She had wanted exactly what had happened, and she was going to deal with the consequences—which, thanks to safe sex, were just going to be emotional: She'd chosen this outcome. . . . She'd followed him to his door; she'd pushed him into his house; she'd told him to get the wallet. So she was going to damn well be an adult and spend the next ten hours pulling herself together before she had to walk into the office at nine tomorrow morning.

It was what professionals did. And why professionals didn't let things like tonight happen.

Ten minutes of rain-soaked road later, she eased into her driveway, and hit the garage door opener. As she waited for the panels to up, up, and away, she thought, Oh, crap. Between dinner and what had gone down afterward, she hadn't checked her phone in hours.

When she took the thing out, she found that she had missed three calls. There was only one voice mail, but she didn't waste time getting it, considering who had been trying to find her.

She just hit José de la Cruz back.

One ring. Two rings. Three rings.

Shoot, maybe she'd be waking him. It was late—

His voice cut through the electronic *brrrrrring-ing*. "I was hoping it would be you."

"Sorry, I've been tied up." Wince. "What's going on?"

"I know you wanted to get in there and talk to Kroner, and I think you can and should now. Docs say he's even better than he was this morning, but the tide could turn, and I believe your doing an interview as a neutral third party will help Veck, both in fact and in the court of public opinion."

"When can I see him." Hell, she'd go tonight if she could.

"Tomorrow morning's probably best. I got an update about an hour ago and he was still resting comfortably. He's no longer intubated, is off sedation, and actually ate something—but last I heard, he's conked out."

Recalling the condition the guy had been in on that forest floor, it was crazy that he was still breathing, much less sucking back hospital food—and she had to think of Sissy Barten. So unfair. That Kroner was alive and that girl . . . well, she probably wasn't.

"I'll be there at nine tomorrow."

"There's twenty-four/seven security. I'll make sure they know you're coming. Hey, how're you and Veck getting along?"

She closed her eyes and kept a curse to herself. "Fine. Just perfect."

"Good. Don't bring him with you."

"I wasn't going to." For more than one reason.

"And check in with me afterward, if you don't mind."

"Detective, you'll be the first person I call."

After she hit *end*, she rubbed the back of her neck, easing a strain that she had a feeling was from the session on her partner's couch.

Releasing the brake, she let the engine's idle draw her forward into the garage. After she canned the ignition, she got out and—

Reilly stopped in the process of closing the driver's-side door. "Who's there," she called out, ducking her hand under her coat and palming her gun.

The overhead automatic light gave her a clear picture of her stand of rakes in the corner and her trash barrel and the bag of rock salt that she used on her front walk in the winter for the mailman. It also made her a sitting duck for whoever was watching her.

And someone was.

Moving fast, she went around the hood instead of the trunk and had her key ready before she got to the door. With quick, sure moves, she unlocked the dead bolt, shot into her house and hit the garage door at the same time. And the dead bolt was turned back as soon as she was inside.

Her ADT system immediately started beeping from the corner of the kitchen. Which meant the alarm was operational and she was the person who had triggered it.

Using her left hand, she punched in her code, and canned the noise.

Her gun was in her right.

Keeping the lights off, she went through her house, looking out of the windows. She saw nothing. Heard nothing.

But her instincts were screaming that she was being watched.

Reilly thought of those "FBI" agents and the fact that someone had been in or around Veck's house the night before. Police officers could be stalked. Were stalked. And though she hadn't done anything with the public for a number of years, she was tangled up with Veck.

And he was far from uncontroversial on so many levels.

In the office, she picked up the phone and checked for a dial tone. There was one. And ironically, the first person she thought of calling was Veck.

Not going to happen.

Besides, she was perfectly capable of defending herself.

Pulling the chair out from the desk, she oriented the thing in the corner so that she could see both the front door and the door that she'd come in through from the garage; then she dragged a side table over. In the closet, in a fireproof safe, there were three other guns and plenty of rounds of ammunition, and she palmed another autoloader, put in a clip, and flicked the safety off.

Sitting down with her back to the wall, she reached over for the cordless receiver to her landline and placed it on the table with the extra gun, keeping her cell phone in her pocket in case she needed to move fast.

Someone wanted her?

Fine. They could just come on in and see what kind of welcome they got.

CHAPTER
24

Downtown, in the marble lobby of the bank Jim had broken into, Adrian was losing blood and getting light-headed, but he refused to pass out.

Wasn't going to happen.

Over in a shaft of light that beamed in from outside, Jim put Eddie down gently on the hard, polished floor. The angel was still tucked into that tight ball, his huge body in a fetal position on his side, his dark braid snaking out like a rope.

"Can we get you on your back, buddy? See what's going on?" Jim said. Not questions—more like a warning to Eddie that more movement was coming up. And as the guy was eased over, the cursing was good to hear. It meant the big bastard was still breathing.

Except he stayed curled up around his belly. And his face was . . . not right. His normally darker-hued skin had faded to the color of snow, and his eyes were squeezed shut so tight that his features were distorted.

There was blood on his mouth, staining his lips red.

Blood . . . was coming out of his mouth.

Adrian started to pant, his fists curling in, sweat breaking out all over his body. "You're gonna be okay, Eddie. It's gonna be—"

"Ease yourself for me," Jim said. "I know it hurts like a bitch, but we've got to see."

"—okay. It's gonna be okay—"

"Oh, shit," Jim whispered.

Oh . . . shit . . . was right. The blood didn't just stain or leak from underneath where Eddie was holding his gut . . . it streamed out in pulses.

Jim ripped off his wet leather coat, wadded the thing up, and pushed Eddie's slippery, glossy red hands out of the way. Then he just froze.

Somehow that harpy's knife had penetrated Eddie's intestinal tract and then streaked to the side, slicing a hole long enough and deep enough that the loopy anatomy was exposed. But that wasn't the worst part: given the amount of blood coming from the injury, clearly one of the larger veins or arteries had been severed.

And that was what was going to kill him.

Jim shook himself and put the knot of jacket right on the wound. "Can you hold this for me, buddy?"

Eddie made an attempt to bring up his hands, but they moved only an inch or two.

Jim looked over. "Can he die?"

Adrian shook his head as his legs went numb. "I don't know."

Bullshit. He knew the answer. He just couldn't say it.

"Fucking hell." Jim leaned in toward Eddie's face. "Buddy, is there anything you can tell me?"

Adrian didn't so much get down as fall to his knees. Taking his best friend's hand, he was horrified at how cold it was. Cold and wet from the blood and the rain.

"Eddie . . . Eddie, look at me," Jim was saying.

This wasn't right. This heroic fighter, this warrior of the ages, couldn't be done in by a half-assed harpy with a knife. Eddie was blaze-of-glory material, a take-out-an-army-of-minions-on-his-way-to-the-exit kind of guy. Not this quiet leaching—and not tonight. . . .

Eddie let out a gasp, his big body jerking, his palm squeezing Adrian's.

"I'm here. . . ." Ad said roughly as he scrubbed his eyes with the back of his free hand. "I'm not going anywhere. You're not alone . . ."

Holy motherfucking shit. They were losing him.

And this was the inexplicable at work. As angels, they were and were not alive; they at once existed and were not bound by the flesh; they were immortal, but very capable of losing the slice of life they had been granted.

"Eddie, fucking hell . . . don't go. . . . You can fight this—" He looked up at Jim. "Do something!"

Jim cursed and glanced around, but come on—they were in a bank lobby, not a hospital. Besides, it wasn't as if the savior could grab a needle and thread and start suturing, could he?

Except then Jim closed his eyes and settled back on the floor, crossing his legs Indian style and going utterly calm. Just as Ad was ready to scream that now was not the time for a fucking meditation, the guy started to glow: from head to foot, a pure white light began to emanate from his head, body and hands.

A moment later, the savior reached forward . . . and placed his palms on the big, barreled chest of—

Eddie's torso bucked hard, as if he'd been hit with those cardiac paddles humans used, and then he sucked in a breath. Instantly, his red eyes blinked open . . . and focused on Adrian.

Feeling like a pussy for crying, Ad did another sweep of the eyes. "Hey." He had to clear his throat. "You gotta hang on and fight this. Heal yourself. Just use what Jim's giving you—"

Eddie shook his head a little and opened his mouth. All that came out was a groan.

"—hang on. Come on, man, just—"

"Listen . . . to me . . ." Ad went absolutely still; Eddie's voice was so weak, it didn't carry far. "You need . . . to stay . . . with Jim . . ."

"No. No fucking way. You are not leaving—"

"Stay . . . with Jim . . . do not—" He struggled for another breath. "Stay with Jim."

"It's not supposed to end like this! I'm the one who's supposed to go first—"

Eddie dragged his arm up and put his forefinger on Ad's lips, silencing him. "You be . . . smart . . . for once . . . okay? Promise me."

Adrian started to rock back and forth, his eyes flooding to the point where his vision blurred.

"Promise . . . on your honor . . ."

"No. I won't. Fuck you! You're not leaving me!"

The angel's lids slowly started shutting. "*Eddie! Fucking Eddie! Don't you fucking die on me! Fuck you!*"

As the echoes of the outburst faded, Eddie's breathing got more labored, his mouth stretching wide as if his jaw hoped that would help. And in the terrifying, silent moments that followed, Ad's heart hammered faster and faster, sure as if his boy's were slowing down.

Edward Lucifer Blackhawk died two breaths later.

It wasn't the abrupt lack of movement in the ribs or the way the body went lax or the fact that the hand in his lost what little grip it had had.

It was the scent of spring blooms that wafted up into the still air of the bank.

Adrian locked a grip on the front of Jim's shirt. "You can bring him back. Bring him back—for fuck's sake—put your . . . hands . . . back on him—"

For some reason, he couldn't speak anymore after that.

And then he couldn't see.

Momentarily confused, he looked around, thinking a choking, stinging fog had rolled in.

Oh, wait.

He was sobbing like a little bitch.

Not even pretending to give a shit, he grabbed Eddie around the chest and hauled him up, cradling to his heart the fallen angel who had been with him every step of the way on earth and in purgatory for centuries. And as he held him, the weight grew lighter in his arms, even as the vacated body's inches and feet stayed the same.

The essence of Eddie had moved on.

Adrian burrowed his face into that thick neck and rocked them back and forth, back and forth . . . back and forth. . . .

"Don't leave me . . . don't . . . oh, God, Eddie . . ."

Adrian wasn't sure how many minutes or hours passed, except even in his distraught state, he became aware that something had changed.

Glancing up over Eddie's head, he saw the savior . . . and had to blink a couple of times to make sure the picture made sense.

Jim Heron was in a crouch, teeth bared, huge body straining. His eyes were locked on Adrian and Eddie, and an unholy black glow emanated out of them, the buffering waves of evil pulsating through the bouqueted air.

It was vengeance and wrath and rage upright and walking. It was the promise of hell on earth. It was everything that Devina was . . . in the form and feature of the savior.

Adrian was strangely soothed by the show. Calmed. Centered.

He was not alone in feeling violated and stolen from.

He was not by himself as he went forward.

The path he would wear out in getting that demon for this would have two sets of footprints, not one—

At that moment, Jim opened his mouth and let out a roar that was louder than an airplane taking off, and the ripping sound was followed by a great explosion:

The glass windows of the bank lobby, all hundred feet of them, blew out at once, showering the street in front with a glittering snowfall of glass shards.

CHAPTER
25

Up in heaven, Nigel bolted out of his bed of satins and silks. He hadn't been at rest—he couldn't seem to close his eyes without Colin beside him—but waking or slumbering, the vision that came to him would have shocked him into alert no matter the circumstance.

With shaking hands, he drew his robe on over his nakedness Edward—oh, dearest, stoic Edward.

He had been lost. Just now and down below.

Oh, this was a terrible turn of events. An awful destabilization.

How could this have happened?

Indeed, the conception that one of those two warriors could take a fall was something he had not contemplated in any of his planning: He'd sent the fallen angels to help Jim because they were hard and resilient and so very proficient at defending the good that they so often downplayed in themselves. And out of the two of them, Eddie was supposed to survive: he was the prudent and smart one, who balanced his electric, eclectic, out-of-control comrade.

But destiny had corkscrewed on all of them.

"Damn it, damn it ... damn it ..."

And there was no bringing Edward back—at least not in

any fashion that Nigel could affect: Resurrection was up to the Creator, and the last time an angel had been returned had been . . . never.

Nigel patted his face with a linen handkerchief. He had wagered both Edward and Adrian, thrown them like dice—and now Adrian, the volatile one, was shipwrecked without his compass, his anchor, his captain. And Jim, who already had a distraction, was worse than on his own. He was going to have to look after the other angel.

This was ruinous.

And a fine maneuver on the demon's part—and yet how had it happened? Edward was always aware. What could have distracted him from his instincts?

Going over to his tea bar, Nigel set about warming the kettle. His hands were shaking as he thought about what he had wrought. Edward had been safely living in the nonsequestered part of this place that Nigel o'ersaw—he'd been waiting to be used, true, and thrilled to have been finally forgiven for breaking the rules and saving Adrian all those years ago. But still.

A fine male. Now he was gone.

It was not to have been thus.

You are not so powerful as you think, Nigel.

Bracing his hands on the marble-topped bombé chest, he could hardly bear the weight on his heart. If he had not sprung them both from their respective purgatories, this would not have happened.

. And he had been so arrogantly certain of his choice.

What had he done . . .?

Standing there, with no one behind him and no one in front of him, alone with his bad thoughts and the burden of his deeds lying heavily within his ribs, he thought of Adrian. Alone. In pain. In the war.

As Nigel struggled for breath he did not need, there was only one entity to turn to in this god-awful solitude. And the fact that Colin was not here, and sadder, that Nigel could not go to the other archangel, made him mourn the state Adrian was in. To have lost your other half was worse than death.

It was torture. Although it was instructive ...

In the passing course of all Nigel's faux days and faux nights, in the endless rotation of his pretend meals and his fake croquet games, within the construct of all this self-imposed structure that he engineered to keep him and his archangels from going mad in the infinity they existed in, he had never bent to another's will. It was not in his nature do to so.

And yet Colin had a part of him.

And unlike Adrian, he could go to his other half, seeking succor in the midst of this fear and loneliness and regret.

Adrian would never have that again: Barring a miracle that would be impossible to grant, he would be separate e'ermore from that other part of himself.

You are not so powerful as you think, Nigel.

When the shrill whistle of the pot broke through the tent, he left the water to carry on, his feet fleet as he took off out of his private quarters and crossed the grounds in a streak of robe.

Per the cycles he set and commanded, night had fallen like a cape of velvet o'er the landscape. Up ahead, flamed torches burned along the battlements and turrets of the castle, and it was toward the flickering glow that he ran over the grass.

Edward was lost.

Colin was here.

And there was too much lawn between them.

Following the manse's walls, he came to the westernmost corner of the fortification and looped to the right. Off in the distance, Colin's tent was set against the tree line, the squat, low-hung fixture made from heavy woolen tarps supported by squat poles. Unlike Nigel's private sanctuary, it was small and modest. No silks. No satins. No luxurious accoutrements: The archangel bathed in the rushing stream behind and slept not on a bedding platform, but a cot. One blanket. No pillows. Only books for amusement.

All of this was why Nigel had insisted that they share his

quarters, the other archangel having essentially moved in ages ago.

In fact, as he came up to the tent, Nigel realized he had never spent a "night" herein. It had always been Colin who transplanted himself.

When had he even been here last? Nigel wondered.

No jamb upon which to knock.

"Colin?" he said quietly.

When there was no reply, he repeated the name. And did it once more.

There appeared to be no light glowing within, so Nigel summoned a beacon upon his palm, calling up a glow for his eyes. Reaching out, he pulled the tarp aside and led with his hand, the illumination penetrating the dark interior.

Empty.

And indeed, if one didn't know better, one would think there had been a robbery. There was so little inside. Yes, yes . . . just that field cot with a steamer trunk at its foot. Some leather-bound books. An oil lamp. For the floor, there was not even a woven rug, but merely the grass of the lawn.

Bertie's and Byron's quarters, which were on the opposite end of the wall, were as luxurious as Nigel's own, just kitted out to their individual tastes. And Colin could have had more than this.

Colin could have had the world.

Turning away, Nigel left the tent and went around to the stream. There were towels hanging from tree branches and a set of footprints on the sandy shore.

"Colin . . ." he whispered.

The sound of his own mournful voice was what pulled him up short.

Abruptly, his desperation shocked him and recast his decision to come here in light of the reality of the war: he thought of Jim and Adrian and their weaknesses, weaknesses that were being exposed and exploited by the other side.

He himself was weak when it came to Colin. Which meant he had an unprotected flank.

On a burst of speed, Nigel wheeled about and rushed away, his feet carrying him through the night as he pulled his robes and pride back about him.

The destination of his own quarters was one he must not stray from again.

He was not Adrian. He would not be lost . . . as Adrian was. And he would not be compromised by his emotions as Jim was.

Duty called for such isolation and strength.

And heaven could afford nothing less.

CHAPTER

26

The following morning, Veck sat at his desk, and stared over his Starbucks mug at Bails. The guy's mouth was moving at a fast clip, his face animated, his hands motioning in circles.

"—the whole goddamn thing blew out." Bails paused and then waved in Veck's face. "Hello? Did you hear me?"

"Sorry, what?"

"The entire first floor of Caldwell Bank and Trust at Trade and Thirteenth is in the fucking street."

Veck shook himself into focus. "What do you mean, 'in the street'?"

"All the glass of the lobby windows was blown out. There isn't anything left but the steel frames. Happened sometime before midnight."

"Was it a bomb?"

"Damnedest bomb anyone's ever seen. No damage in the lobby—well, some of the waiting area's chairs had been blown back, but there's no evidence of a detonation—no ring of impact. There was some weird paint on the lobby floor, sparkly shit that looked like fingernail polish, and the place smelled like a florist's. But other than that, nothing."

"Officers on scene check the security tapes?"

"You better believe it, and guess what? The system flickered off at about eleven and stayed that way."

Veck frowned. "It just went dead?"

"Dead. Even though no power surge in the neighborhood was reported. The lobby lights appear to have been fritzed as well, although no other electricals, or systems, were affected in the place—including their alarm and their computer network. It's just too fucking weird. How do you lose your vid and nothing else?"

Veck's nape went tingly on him. For chrissakes, where had he heard that before . . .

"So yeah, it's weird."

"That's one word for it."

Bails tilted his head, his eyes narrowing. "Hey, are you okay?"

Veck turned to his computer and called up his e-mail. "Never been better."

"If you say so." There was a pause. "Guess your partner's going in with Kroner."

Veck jerked around. "She is?"

"You didn't know?" Bails shrugged. "De la Cruz texted me late last night. I wanted to go back in there again today, but IA is getting the next crack at him—no doubt to tie you up in a pretty bow of not-the-perp ribbon."

Fucking hell. The idea of Reilly anywhere near that monster made his blood run cold. "When?"

"Now, I guess."

And what do you know, his first instinct was to get over to St. Francis at a dead run. Which was no doubt why she hadn't stopped in this morning and told him where she was going.

"Anyway, I'll see you. Gotta get back to work."

On instinct, Veck grabbed his phone and checked it. Sure enough there was a text that he hadn't heard come in and it was from Reilly: *I'll be in late today. R.*

"Fuck."

He looked around, like that was going to do any good. Then he tried to focus on the screen in front of him.

Damn it ... no way in hell he could sit on his ass stewing while she interviewed a madman.

And, actually ... this was an opportunity, wasn't it.

Taking his coffee with him, he walked out of Homicide, hung a louie, and headed for the emergency exit. In the concrete stairwell, he went up two steps at a time, punched through the steel door, and beelined for the evidence room.

Inside, he checked in with the receptionist, did a little small talk—like this was all just routine—and then after an appropriate chat-up, he was inside the stacks.

As a beat cop down in Manhattan, he'd spent a good deal of time handling evidence like bags of drugs, cell phones, and impounded cash—things that were used. Now that he was in Homicide, it was more about bloodied clothes, weapons, and personal effects—things that were left behind.

Heading down the long rows of shelving, he zeroed in on the back of the huge facility where the tables were.

"Hey, Joe," he said, as he came around a six-foot-tall partition.

The veteran crime scene investigator looked up from a microscope. "Hey."

"How's it going?"

"Workin' our way through."

As the guy lifted his arms over his head and stretched hard, Veck leaned against the workstation, all casual. "How you holding up?"

"The night shift is easier than the day. Of course, after this week, both suck."

"There much longer till you're through it all?"

"Maybe forty-eight hours. There's a trio of us. We've been going around the clock except for last evening."

Veck looked over the collection of things that had been cataloged and sealed up, as well as the massive tray of pre-liminarily logged items that were still to be examined and properly bagged.

The investigator used tweezers to take what turned out

to be a hair tie from underneath the magnifying sight. After he placed the black twist in a plastic bag, he took a long, thin neon yellow sticker, and went up and over the opening. Then he made a notation with a blue pen on it, signed his initials, and tapped on a laptop's keyboard. Final step was to pass the bag's bar code over a reader, the beep signifying that the object was now officially in the system.

Veck took a sip of his coffee. "So I'm working a missing persons case. Young girl."

"You want to take a gander at what we got?"

"Would you mind?"

"Nope. Just don't take anything out of here."

Veck started at the far end of the low-slung shelving that had been temporarily set up. None of the collection had been given a permanent home yet, because everyone from CPDers to the FBI were going to be all over the objects.

Skipping the jars of skin samples—because Cecilia Barten hadn't had any tattoos—he focused on the multitude of rings, bracelets, barrettes, necklaces. . . .

Where are you, Sissy? he thought to himself.

Bending down, he picked up a clear plastic bag that was sealed with the signature of one of the other investigators. Inside, there was a stained leather wristband that had a skull's head for a "charm." Not Cecilia's style.

He moved on, picking up a silver hoop that had been logged in. In all the pictures at the Bartens' house, the girl had been wearing gold.

Where are you, Sissy . . . where the hell are you?

Over at St. Francis Hospital, Reilly was all business as she strode down one of the hospital's thousands of corridors. As she marched along, she passed white coats and blue orderlies and green nurses and casually dressed patients and families.

The ICU she was looking for was all the way down to the right, and she took her badge out as she approached the nurses' station. A quick conversation later and she was directed down farther, to the left. As she turned the final corner, the guard by the glass cage got to his feet.

"Officer Reilly?" he said.

"That's me." She showed him her badge. "How's he doing?"

The man shook his head. "Just had breakfast." The clipped answer dripped with disapproval—as if the guard wished the suspect would go on a hunger strike. Or maybe be starved to death. "Guess they're moving him out of here soon because he's doing so well. Do you want me in there with you?"

Reilly smiled as she put her badge away and took out a small pad. "I can handle him."

The private security officer seemed to measure her, but then he nodded. "Yeah, you look like you can."

"It's just not appearances. Trust me."

She opened the glass door, pushed back the pale green curtain—and froze at the sight of a nurse leaning over Kroner. "Oh, I'm sorry—"

The brunette looked over and smiled. "Please come in, Officer Reilly."

As Reilly stared into eyes that were so black, they appeared to have no iris at all, she felt an irrational bolt of terror: Every instinct in her body told her to run. Fast as she could go. As far away as she could get.

Except Kroner was the one she needed to be wary of—not some woman who was just doing her job.

"Ah . . . why don't I come back," Reilly said.

"No." The nurse smiled again, revealing perfect white teeth. "He's ready for you."

"Still, I'll just wait until you're—"

"Stay. I'm happy to leave you two together."

Reilly frowned, thinking, What, like the pair of them were dating?

The nurse turned back to Kroner, uttered something in a quiet voice and stroked his hand in a way that made Reilly slightly nauseous. And then the woman came forward, growing more and more beautiful—until she was so resplendent, you had to wonder why she wasn't a model.

And yet Reilly just wanted to get the hell away from her. Which made no sense.

The nurse paused at the door and smiled once more. "Take your time. He has everything you need."

And then she was gone.

Reilly blinked once. And again. Then she leaned out and looked around.

The guard glanced up from his seat. "You okay?"

The hallway was empty except for a crash cart, a rolling bin full of soiled linen, and a gurney with no one and nothing on it. Maybe the nurse had just gone into another room? Had to be it. There were units on either side of Kroner's.

"Yup, just fine."

Ducking back in, Reilly pulled it together, and focused on the patient, locking stares with a man who had killed at least a dozen young women across the country.

Bright eyes. That was her first thought. Smart, gleaming eyes, like you'd find on a hungry rat.

Second? He was so *small*. It was hard to believe he could lift a bag of groceries, much less overpower young, healthy women—but then again, he'd probably used drugs to help incapacitate his victims, cutting down on both the escape risk and the noise. At least initially.

Her final thought was . . . Man, that was a lot of bandage. He was all but mummified, strips of gauze wrapped around his skull and neck, square pads taped to his cheeks and jaw. And yet even though he looked like a work in progress out of Frankenstein's lab, he was alert, and his skin color was positively radiant.

Unnaturally so, actually. Maybe he had a fever?

As she approached the bed, she held up her identification. "I'm Officer Reilly from the Caldwell Police Department. I'd like to ask you some questions. I understand you've waived your right to have counsel present."

"Would you like to sit down?" His voice was soft, the tone respectful. "I have a chair."

As if she were in his living room or something.

"Thank you." She pulled the hard plastic seat over toward the bedside, getting close but not too close. "I want to talk to you about the other evening, when you were attacked."

"A detective already did that. Yesterday."

"I know. But I'm following up."

"I told him everything I remembered."

"Well, would you mind repeating it for me?"

"Surely." He pushed himself up weakly and then looked over as if he wanted her to ask whether he needed help. When she didn't, he cleared his throat. "I was in the woods. Walking slowly. Through the woods . . ."

She wasn't buying the acquiescence and accommodation for an instant. Someone like Kroner? No doubt he could turn on the poor-me for as long as it suited him to do so. That was how psychopaths like him worked. He could be normal, or certainly convince others, and maybe even himself for periods of time, that he was just like everyone else: a composite of good and bad—where the "bad" didn't go further than fudging on your taxes, or speeding on the highway, or maybe talking smack behind your mother-in-law's back.

Not killing young girls. Never that.

Masks never lasted, though.

"And you were headed where," she prompted.

His lids lowered. "You know where."

"Why don't you tell me."

"The Monroe Motel and Suites." There was a pause, his lips growing tight. "I wanted to go there. I had been robbed, you see."

"Your collection."

There was a long pause. "Yes." As he frowned, he covered up whatever was in his stare by looking down at his hands. "I was in the woods and something came at me. An animal. It was from out of nowhere. I tried to beat it off, but it was too strong. . . ."

How'd that feel, you bastard, she thought.

"There was a man there—he saw it happen. He can tell you. I picked him out of the photographs yesterday."

"What happened with the man?"

"He tried to help me." More with the frowning. "He called nine-one-one.... I don't remember ... much ... else—wait a minute." Those beady eyes got shrewd. "You were there. Weren't you."

"Is there anything you can tell me about the animal."

"You were there. You watched me get put into the ambulance."

"If we could stay with the animal—"

"And you were watching him, too." Kroner smiled, and the Mr. Nice-and-Normal pretense slipped a little, a strange calculation entering his eyes. "You were watching the man who'd been with me. Did you think he'd done it?"

"The animal. That's what I'm interested in."

"That's not allllllll you're interested in." The *all* had a singsong lilt to it. "It's okay, though. It's all right to want things."

"What kind of animal do you think it was?"

"A lion, a tiger, a bear—oh, my."

"This is not a joke, Mr. Kroner. We need to know whether we have a public safety issue."

Having studied interview techniques, she figured she'd give him an opening to be a hero. Sometimes suspects like him would play the game in hopes of ingratiating themselves, or trying to gain trust they would later enjoy violating.

Kroner's lids dropped low. "Oh, I think you've taken care of the public just fine. Haven't you."

Yeah, assuming he didn't flee this hospital, and the system slammed a prison door on him for the rest of his natural life. "It must have had fangs," she said.

"Yes ..." He touched his ruined face. "Fangs ... and big. Whatever it was—it was overpowering. I still don't know why I survived—but the man, he helped me. He's an old friend...."

Reilly made sure that her expression didn't change in the slightest. "Old friend? You know him?"

"Like recognizes like."

As a chill rippled down her spine, Kroner lifted a hand up and stopped her from speaking. "Wait—I'm supposed to tell you something."

"And what is that?"

Those bandages on his face crumpled up as if he were grimacing, and that hand went to his head. "I'm supposed to tell you . . ."

Considering he didn't know her at all, that was impossible. "Mr. Kroner—"

"She had long blond hair. Straight, long blond hair . . ." He took a labored breath and batted at his temple as if he were in pain. "He's stuck on the hair . . . that blond hair with the blood on it. She died in the tub—but that's not where her body is." Kroner's head went back and forth on the pillow. "Go to the quarry. She's there. In a cave—you've gotta go deep to get to her. . . ."

Reilly's heart started pounding. The scope of her interrogation was supposed to be limited to the night of the attack, but there was no way she wasn't following up on this one. And no reason why Kroner would know that Cecilia Barten was a case she was working on.

"Who are you talking about."

Kroner dropped his arm and suddenly his color took a turn toward the gray spectrum. "The one from the supermarket. I'm supposed to tell you this—she wants me to tell you. That's all I know—"

Abruptly, he started to shake, the trembling in his torso escalating until he jerked back into the pillows and his eyes rolled into his skull.

Reilly lunged forward and punched the call button and intercom. "We need help in here!"

From out of the seizure, Kroner shot a hold onto her wrist, those unholy eyes of his glowing. "Tell him she suffered. . . . He has to know . . . she suffered. . . ."

CHAPTER
27

Back at HQ, in the evidence room, Veck went through everything there was of Kroner's collection, filing away in his mind snapshots of the objects. Unfortunately, there was nothing that he'd seen in the photographs at the Bartens' that matched any of the jewelry or other things.

Stepping back, he crossed his arms over his chest. "Shit."

"There's still more," the investigator said. Without looking away from what he was doing, the guy threw back the drape that covered all that had yet to be cataloged.

Veck took a drink from his cold coffee, went over, and leaned in at the hips. No touching, of course, so good thing it had all been laid out side by side. More jewelry . . . more hair ties with strands of black and brown and pink stuck to—

His phone went off, and he pivoted away to answer it. "DelVecchio. Yeah, yup . . . uh-huh . . . yup, that's me. . . ."

It was Human Resources, verifying his information before they sent out his first paycheck. As he rushed through the questions, he thought, no offense, but he had better things to do.

When he was finally off with them, he turned back

around to the tray. He'd been so sure that Sissy had been taken by Kroner. Fucking hell—

From out of the investigator's latexed grip, a gold glint flashed as whatever it was got put under the microscope.

It was an earring. A small, birdlike earring. Like a dove or a sparrow.

"Can I see that?" Veck said hoarsely.

But even without the closer look, he recognized what it was ... from the Bartens' bookcase, that close-up of Sissy when she'd been unaware she'd been photographed. She had been wearing an earring just like it.

Maybe she'd been wearing that exact one.

His phone rang again just as the investigator held up the piece of evidence.

When Veck glanced at the screen and saw it was Reilly, he immediately accepted the call. "You'll never believe this—I'm looking at Sissy Barten's earring."

"In the Kroner evidence." It was a statement, not a question.

Veck frowned. Her voice sounded all wrong. "Are you all right? What happened with Kroner?"

There was a brief pause. "I ..."

Veck stepped away from the investigator, going into a corner and turning his back to the guy. Dropping his voice, he said, "What happened."

"I think he killed her. Sissy. He ... killed her."

Veck's grip squeezed down on the phone. "What did he say."

"He identified her by the hair and the Hannaford."

"Did you bring any photographs of her? Can we get a positive—"

"He went into a seizure in the middle of the interview. I'm outside the ICU right now and they're working on him. No telling whether they'll pull him through or not."

"Did he say anything else—"

"The body's somewhere in the quarry. According to him."

"Let's go—"

"I've already called de la Cruz. He's going over there with Bails—"

"I'm leaving right now."

"Veck," she bit out. "This case is no longer missing persons. You and I are off of it."

"The hell we are—she's still mine until they find a body. Meet me there so you can suspend me if you want. Or even better, come to lend a hand."

There was a long, long pause. "You're putting me in a terrible position."

Regret made him grind his molars. "I seem to excel at that when it comes to you. But I have to do this—and I promise not to be a pain in the ass."

"You excel at that, too."

"Stipulated. Look, I can't pull out of this until I at least know what happened to her. I don't have to be all up in Kroner's face if we find something and I won't touch a goddamn thing, but I've got to do this."

Another interminable pause. Then: "All right. I'm on my way. But if de la Cruz shuts us out, we're *not* fighting him, clear?"

"Crystal." Veck sent up a prayer of thanks. But then . . . "Did he say anything else? Kroner, that is?"

There was a rustling, like she was switching the phone from hand to hand. "He said he knew you."

"*What.*"

"Kroner said he knew you."

"That's a fucking lie. I've never met him before in my life." When there was nothing from her, he cursed. "Reilly, I swear. I don't know the guy."

"I believe you."

"You don't sound like it." And for some reason, her opinion didn't just matter; it was dispositive. "I'll take a polygraph."

Her exhale sounded exhausted. "Maybe Kroner was just screwing with me. It's hard to know."

"What did he say exactly?"

"Something along the lines of 'like recognizes like.' "

Veck went dead cold. "I'm not Kroner."

"I know. Here, let me get to my car and start driving. The quarry's on the far edge of town, and we might as well get in on the ground floor if de la Cruz will let us. I'll see you in a half hour."

As he hung up, the investigator glanced over from the microscope. "Get what you need?"

"I think so. Let me know if you find anything on that earring? I have a feeling it's from my missing girl."

"No problem."

"Where's the 'quarry'?"

"Take the Northway south about twenty miles. I don't know the exact exit, but it's marked. You can't miss it, and there are signs that'll take you in."

"Thanks, man."

"It's a good place to hide things, if you know what I mean."

"I do. Unfortunately."

Five minutes later, Veck was on his bike and roaring off toward the interstate. No reason to call de la Cruz ahead of time. They'd just do the showdown face-to-face when he arrived.

The exit in question appeared fifteen minutes later and read, THOMAS GREENFIELD QUARRY. The signs were easy to follow, and no more than a couple miles later, he was turning off and following a small dirt road that had trees tight to its flanks. In the summer, they would no doubt form a romantic canopy; at the moment, they looked like skeleton arms clawing at one another.

He cut the speed back as he rounded a fat right-hander that gradually climbed higher and higher. Wind whipped around, cold and stark, and the clouds seemed to close in as if to choke the ground. He was beginning to think he was lost when he crested the rise, and there it was.

Quarry? More like the Grand fucking Canyon.

And members of the CPD as well as the Caldwell Fire

Department had already gathered: Two search and rescue vehicles. A couple of squad cars. An unmarked that had to be de la Cruz. A K-9 unit.

Veck parked a ways away and made no bones about his approach as he came up to the huddle of men and women and dogs.

De la Cruz peeled off from the core and came toward him. The detective's permagrim expression didn't shift in the slightest. Then again, he couldn't be all that surprised, and the arrival was hardly happy news.

"Fancy meeting you here," de la Cruz muttered. But he put out his hand for a shake.

"This place is huge." Their palms met in a clap. "Betcha can use some help."

The quarry was easily a mile across and a half mile down—and more of a natural formation than anything left over from a mining operation. Three-quarters of its walls were solid drops, but the one to the south was a nasty-looking slope that was marked by boulders, scruffy brush . . . and a lot of dark holes that had to be caves.

"So are you going to let me work?" Veck demanded.

"Where's your partner."

"On her way."

De la Cruz glanced back at the tight band of colleagues. "We're keeping a light crew on here because we don't want any attention. The press gets word of this, we're going to have a field day with the rubberneckers."

"So is that a yes?"

De la Cruz nailed him right in the eye. "You don't touch a goddamn thing, and you don't go out until Reilly's here."

"Fair enough, Detective."

"Come on—you might as well join in the planning stage."

Jim's old place was not all that old and not his, either.

He'd rented the garage and its second-story studio apartment from an ancient guy in a butler's suit after he'd first come to Caldwell, and when he'd pulled out about a week ago, he'd assumed it was for the last time: His former boss, Matthias the Fucker, had been breathing down his neck, and he'd been Boston-bound to fight the next battle with Devina.

But really, what went according to plan? Matthias was no longer in the picture, Jim had returned to Caldwell, and he and Adrian needed a secure place to stay.

Hello, old haunts, as it were ... And it was time to pray that the owner hadn't gone in to find the rent money and key that had been left behind.

Pulling his F-150 into the long drive that led to the place, he checked to make sure Adrian was still behind him on that Harley—and the guy was. Together, they passed the owner's vacant but perfectly maintained farmhouse and continued down the lane, cutting through a rolling meadow that had to be a good twenty acres in size. The garage was far back on the property and had probably been used to house farming equipment and mowers, with a caretaker living above. He'd gotten the impression when he'd leased it, however, that it had been empty for a while.

Stopping grill first at the big double doors, he got out, grabbed one of the drag handles and threw his weight into it, wondering whether the place would be—

The panel rumbled open on its tracks, revealing a perfectly clean cement floor and a raw beam ceiling more than tall enough to park a horse trailer in.

Jim got back behind the wheel and let the engine's idle take him inside. And Adrian was right on his ass, parking the Harley and yanking the door shut behind them. As the gray light of day was cut off, Jim killed the motor, sprung his door—

The clean, fresh scent of flowers invaded the air. To the point where he nearly retched, even though the smell was arguably beautiful.

He and Adrian didn't say a word as they took up res on either side of the truck bed by the back. The tarp they'd bought at Home Depot an hour ago was secured by a half dozen bungee cords, and one by one they freed the hooks and bands. Rolling up the thick, blue cover, they revealed the sheet-wrapped body they had been so careful with.

They had left the lobby of the bank not long after Jim's fury had busted out all the windows, and they'd taken Eddie with them—which had been no struggle, as it had turned out; at least not physically. After the death, the body was light as a feather, as if all the critical mass had vacated the skin and bones, and what was left behind was nothing more than the outline drawing of what Eddie had once been.

Jim had had no clue where to go, but then Dog had appeared in their path...and led them to an abandoned three-story walk-up.

Leaving Adrian and the animal to guard their dead, Jim had returned to the hotel, packed up all their shit and loaded it into his truck. When he'd returned, he'd parked in an underground garage a couple blocks away, and flashed over with all sorts of plans to move to greater safety and collect the other vehicles and bikes that were still in the lot at the Marriott.

In the end, though, he'd just sat around, and given Adrian a break—because the guy had looked as if he were about to shatter.

Eventually, they'd had to relocate, however, and he'd decided that coming here was their best bet in the immediate short term. And Adrian had gone along without comment, except that was probably not a good sign—he was clearly still numbed out, but that wasn't going to last, and what was on the other side? Biblical wasn't going to cover the half of it, most likely.

Jim unlatched the back gate and let it fall. "Do you want to—"

Adrian sprang up and over the gunnels, landing deftly next to Eddie. Scooping up the shrouded remains, he stepped off the bed, and walked over to the side door. "Can you get this for us?"

"Yeah, sure."

With Dog leading the way again, Jim went over and opened the exit and then all three of them went up the exterior stairs. At the top, he used a lock pick, worked the doorknob in a matter of seconds, and stood to the side as Adrian went in.

The single bed was just the way it had been when Jim had left, the sheets tangled from the last bad night's sleep he'd had there. And yup, the money and the key were right where he'd put them on the counter of the galley kitchen. Sofa was still under the picture window, with the thin drapes pulled closed. Air smelled vaguely of hay, but that wasn't going to last.

Not with Eddie around.

As Jim looked over at Adrian, he knew there was no reason not to use this place. Matthias was in Devina's well of souls for eternity so it wasn't like he was any threat, and the rest of XOps was going to be busy scrambling to fill the leadership void the guy had left behind. Besides, Jim's only problem had been with his old boss.

Who he'd let down in the last round.

"There's a crawl space back here," Jim said, walking over to the kitchen.

Next to the refrigerator, there was a narrow half door that led into a shallow, Sheetrocked area under the eaves of the roof. Reaching in, he turned on the bald lightbulb and got out of the way.

As Adrian crouched down and went inside with his burden, Jim opened one of the drawers under the kitchen counter and took out a long knife.

He didn't hesitate as he put the blade against his palm and streaked it through his skin.

"*Fuck*," he hissed.

Adrian backed out of the crawl space. "What are you doing?"

Bright red, shimmering drops fell to the floor in a little trail as he walked over to where Eddie had been placed. The truth was, he wasn't entirely sure what was going on here, but his instincts were guiding him, pulling him forward, and putting his bleeding palm against the inside of the half door ... as well as on the body itself.

Before he retracted his dripping hand, he vowed, "I don't leave fallen soldiers behind. You're going to be with us—until you come back *to* us. Bet your ass on it."

Shutting the door, he looked over at Adrian, who had backed up against the counter and braced himself. The angel was staring at the linoleum like it was tea leaves . . . or a map . . . or a mirror . . . or maybe nothing at all.

Who the fuck knew.

"I need to know where you're at," Jim said. "You want to stay here with him or do you want to keep fighting?"

Vacant eyes rose from the floor. "It wasn't supposed to happen like this. He would have handled this better."

"Ain't no good way of dealing with it. And I'm not going to twist your arm about anything. You want to do nothing but mourn, that's perfectly fine with me. But I have to know what you're up for."

Shit, it was probably too early to ask the guy to think about what he wanted for lunch, much less whether he was tight to fight. But they didn't have the luxury to go all therapisty, explore-your-feelings. This was war.

When Adrian just mumbled something about how "not right" it all was, Jim knew he had to get the guy's attention.

"Listen to me," he said slowly and clearly, "Devina did this on purpose. She took him from you because she's depending on the loss incapacitating you. It's Strategy One-oh-one—isolation. Me from the two of you . . . you from the world. It's your choice whether it works or not."

Adrian shifted his stare over to the door Jim had shut. "How can something so . . . huge happen so fast?"

Jim went back in his own past, to a kitchen he had known so well, to a bloody scene he had never forgotten: his mother dying in a pool of her own blood, as she had told him to run as fast as he could, as far as he could . . .

He totally got the whiplash Adrian was dealing with, the horrible realization that the pylons you'd depended on to keep your sky from falling had turned out to be made of paper instead of rock.

"Bombs happen."

There was a period of silence, and then a soft ticking sound over the floor. Dog, who had mostly stayed out of the way, was limping over to Adrian, and when he got to the guy, he sat on the angel's combat boot, and lay his head against the angel's shin.

"I'm not mad," Adrian said finally. "I'm not ... anything."

That was going to change, Jim thought. The question was when.

"Stay here with him," Jim said. "I've got to go out into the field. I don't want DelVecchio on his own."

"Yeah ... yeah." Adrian bent down and picked up Dog. "Yeah."

The angel walked over and sat on the couch, putting the animal on his lap and keeping his eyes locked on the crawl space's door.

"Call me," Jim said, "and I'll be here in an instant."

"Yeah."

God, Ad was like an inanimate object that breathed. And Jim's last thought was, Devina was playing with fire. Adrian was going to wake up from this stupor ... and then there was going to be hell to pay.

After closing the door, Jim paused to light up a cigarette and look at the sky. Clouds were boiling up over the garage, and he found himself looking for an image or a sign in them.

None came.

He finished his Marlboro, and just as he was about to take off, he heard a radio inside the apartment get turned on.

A cappella. Bon Jovi's "Blaze of Glory."

How appropriate.

Jim took to the air, following the beacon that was DelVecchio. And he was about halfway to his target when he realized ...

He didn't own a radio.

CHAPTER
28

"Here, let me help you."

Reilly braced her stance between two boulders the size of wing chairs, and then bent down and reached her hand out.

Veck looked up at her for a moment. "Thanks."

Their palms met and clinched, and then Reilly cranked back, putting all her weight into the lift. Even with the ballast, he was like pulling a car up out of a ditch, and she had the very clear sense that if he hadn't jumped, he would have gone nowhere.

As he joined her on the plateau, they looked around. They'd been working the quarry's long slope for a number of hours, shining flashlights into shallow caves and outcroppings of rocks. The search and rescue officers were tackling the steep side and the other CPDers were far over on the left or going around the rim with the dogs. Minutes passed slowly, agonizingly, the sheer expanse of what there was to cover overwhelming her.

And the undercurrents with Veck, the things unsaid, didn't help.

God, she hated this whole thing. Especially the fact that they were trying to find the body of a young girl.

"There's another cave over here," she said, jumping off a boulder and landing in a crouch on the muddy ground.

The terrain had looked rough from the rim of the quarry. Up close, it was an obstacle course, the kind of landscape you wanted to wear hiking boots to tackle—so good thing extra outerwear and backup evidence kits weren't the only gear and supplies she kept in her trunk. Good thing also that the rain from the night before had stopped or this would have been beyond grueling. As it was, the tops of the rocks had already dried from the sun so at least they had some firm footing; the puddles and mud in the low spots slowed them down enough.

"You ever been here before?" Veck asked after he landed next to her. As usual, he didn't have enough clothes on—

Hold up, let's rephrase that, she thought: As usual, he *wasn't dressed warmly enough*, and his footwear was more office-bound than Outward Bound. Not that he seemed to care: Even though his shoes were no doubt ruined, and his black windbreaker had all the insulation of a sheet of paper against the cool breeze, he was soldiering on, sure as if he were perfectly comfortable.

Then again, they were working up a sweat.

Wait, what was the question . . . ?

"Like most people, I've known about the quarry forever." She glanced up to the rim. "But this is my first visit. Boy, it's like something ripped a giant divot out of the earth."

"Big something."

"They say it was created by glaciers."

"Either that or God was a golfer and the pin he was aiming for is in Pennsylvania."

She laughed a little. "Personally, I'll put my money on prehistoric ice. In fact, this is just called "the quarry"—it's never been one, just looks like one."

They surmounted another boulder, jumped off again, and pressed onward toward the dark maw of the cave she'd spotted. The one they were heading for looked larger than the others they'd been to already, and up close, its entrance seemed tall enough to get through without bending down—although there was no way Veck's shoulders were going to fit unless he turned sideways.

Shining her light in, there was nothing but a whole lot of rock wall and dirt floor, and God, the stink. Dank, musty. They all smelled the same, as if the place had one and only one kind of body odor.

"Nothing," she said. "But I can't see the end of it."

"Let me go in further."

Now would have been the perfect time to modern-woman it and hit him with a *Hell, no, I'll take care of this.* But heaven only knew what was in there, and she was not a huge fan of bats. Bears. Snakes. Spiders.

The great outdoors was the one area where she skewed solidly chick.

After she stepped aside, Veck pivoted and squeezed into the thin space. The fact that even his chest was a tight fit reminded her of just how much she knew about his body.

Glancing away, she tried to find the next target. Desperately.

"Nothing," Veck muttered as he reemerged and made a red X with spray paint on the stone.

"Wait, you have—" She rose up on her toes and brushed the cobweb from his hair. "There, much more presentable."

He snagged her hand as she went to turn away.

When she jerked in surprise and then looked around quickly, he said, "Don't worry, no one can see us."

Guess that was true: They were down in between three massive rocks. But that was hardly good news, because privacy was not what they needed. Spotlights. A stage. Bullhorns strapped to their faces, was more like it—

"Look, I know this isn't appropriate," he murmured in a voice that made her heart pound even harder. "But that shit that Kroner said—about knowing me?"

Reilly exhaled in relief. Thank God it wasn't about them. "Yes?"

Veck released his hold, and paced in a little circle. Then he took out a cigarette, lit it, and blew the smoke away from her. "I think on some level, that's what scares me most in this world."

Feeling like a fool for freaking out, she eased back on the sun-warmed flank of a boulder. "What do you mean?"

Veck stared up at the sky, the shadow of his strong chin falling on his chest and giving the appearance of a dark arch cut out of his torso. "Like recognizes like...."

"You really think you'd tried to kill him," she said softly.

"Look, this is going to sound crazy... but it feels like my father is always with me." He put his hand up to his sternum, right at that black shadow. "It's this... thing, that's a part of me, but not me. And I've always been terrified that it's going to get out—" He cut himself off with a curse. "Oh, Christ, listen to this bullshit—"

"It is *not* bullshit." When he looked over, she stared right back at him. "And you can talk to me. No judgments. No other audience, ever. Provided you haven't broken the law."

His mouth twitched bitterly. "I haven't done anything that can get me arrested. Although I really wondered if I had with Kroner in those woods."

"Well, if you have a fear that you're like your father, and there's a bloodbath in front of you, and you can't remember a thing—of course you would."

"I don't want to be like him. Ever."

"You aren't."

"You don't know me."

His hard expression put a chill through her, in spite of the fact that her feet were dry and toasty, and she was wearing a parka and gloves. And he was so sure of being a stranger to her, that she wondered why the truism hadn't stopped them in time the night before. Then again, sex and sexual attraction had a way of making you feel close, when in fact it was just about two bodies rubbing together.

How much did she really know about him? Not much other than what was in his H.R. file at work.

She was certain of one thing, however: He had not, in fact, hurt that man.

"You need to talk to someone who's a professional," she said. Because of course there had to be psychological repercussions to having a father like that. "Get this burden off of you."

"But that's the problem . . . it's inside me."

Something about the tone he used made that chill return—tenfold. Except now she was just thinking crazy. "And I'm telling you, you need to talk it out."

He resumed looking at the bright blue sky with its passing white streaks of cloud.

After a moment, he said, "I was relieved when you left so quickly last night."

Well, wasn't that a slap in the face to bring her back to her senses. "I'm happy to have obliged," she said with an edge.

"Because I could fall in love with you."

As her mouth eased open and she blinked like a fish, he tapped his cigarette and exhaled, the smoke rising up into the chilly spring air. "I know that's not helping anything. Both the fact that I said it now, and that it's true."

Too right. And yet, she couldn't help going there. "But last night . . . you told me you would never take me to your bed."

He shook his head, his upper lip curling in distaste. "Absolutely not. That's where I've been with women who don't matter. You did—you do." He cursed, low and deep. "You're not like the others."

Reilly took a deep breath. And another.

And she knew that now would be a good time to set them both straight with something along the lines of, "I'm really flattered, but . . ."

Instead, she just stared at him as he turned the cigarette around and looked at the little orange tip. Tracing the harsh and beautiful lines of his face, she tried to fight the pull toward him . . . and then gave up: In this pocket of privacy in front of the cave, with the breeze whistling between the boulders, and the sun on their faces, the gears between them started to slide back into place again . . .

and she realized the true reason she'd left his house so fast.

Screw the job issues: She felt the same way he did, and it had scared her off.

"But it's tied up in all the shit with my father."

"I'm sorry, what?" she heard herself say.

"This stuff with you . . . it's tied up with him as well." His eyes flashed over to her. "He was in love with my mother. And even so, he sliced her up while she was still breathing and made a heart out of her intestines on the floor beside her. I know, because I was the one who found her body."

As Reilly gasped, her hand went up to her throat, and she instinctively took a step back . . . only to find that she was trapped against the rock she'd been leaning against.

"Yeah . . ." he said. "So that's my family history."

Way to romance a woman, Veck thought as Reilly went snow white and tried to back away from him.

Taking a hard drag on his cigarette, he exhaled away from her. "I shouldn't have brought it up."

Reilly shook her head—maybe to clear it. "No . . . no, I'm glad you did. I'm just a little . . ."

"Shocked. Yeah. And that's only one of the reasons I don't talk about this shit."

She brushed a loose strand of hair from her eyes. "But I meant what I said. You can talk to me. I *want* you to talk to me."

He wasn't so sure she'd feel that way when he was through. But for some reason, he found himself opening his piehole.

"My mother was his thirteenth victim." Man, he envied those guys whose "bad history" stories involved beer bongs, the defacement of public property, and maybe pissing in someone's gas tank. "I was on summer vacation from high school, staying in a rental house on Cape Cod with friends. It was the last night we had the place, and I was the last person to go home, so I was alone. He brought her into the living room and did it there. Afterward, he must have come upstairs and checked in on me—when I woke up, there were two bloody prints on the doorjamb to my room. That was the only clue something evil had taken place. He'd put duct tape over her mouth so I never heard a thing."

"Oh . . . my God . . ."

Taking another deep drag, he talked through the exhale. "And you know, even back then, the first thing I did when I saw what was on the molding was look at my own hands. When there was nothing on them, I raced into my bathroom, checked the towels, checked my clothes—same thing I did after the Kroner thing, ironically. And then I realized . . . Shit, the victim. I called nine-one-one and was on the phone with them when I went downstairs."

"You found her."

"Yeah." He rubbed his eyes against images of red blood on a cheap blue rug, a heart made out of human parts. "Yeah, I did, and I *knew* it was him."

He could go no further than that, with her or himself. The memory had been shut off for so long that he had hoped it had decayed in a thoughtful, arguably healthful way. But no. The scene he had walked into was still drawn in shades of neon, as if the vapors of the panic and terror he'd felt had tempered and distorted everything about the mental photograph except for its clarity.

"I've read about your father—studied him in school," Reilly said softly.

"He's a popular topic."

"But there was nothing about . . ."

"I was seventeen, legally a minor, and my mother didn't have my last name, so you wouldn't have known from that. Funny, that was when law enforcement first talked to my father about a victim. Needless to say, they believed him when he said he was grief-stricken—and God knows he was good at faking emotions. Oh, and the prints on the doorjamb? He'd worn latex gloves, naturally, so there was nothing to go by."

"God, I'm so sorry."

Veck grew quiet, but didn't stay that way. "I didn't see

him much. And when he did come by, my mom would disappear with him. She could never get enough of him—he was her drug of choice, the only thing that mattered, the only thing she thought about. Looking back on it, I'm pretty damn sure he engineered her desperation, and it used to piss me off—until I realized what he was and saw that she hadn't stood a chance. As for his side of things? I guess the shit amused him, but the game got old after a while, apparently."

At that, he just petered out, like a sprinter who couldn't go the distance.

"Anyway, that's why we're never having dinner at my parents' house."

Lame attempt at a joke. Neither of them laughed.

When he got to the end of his cigarette, he ground the glowing tip out on the sole of his shoe—and noticed for the first time that his loafers were not going to come out of this mud bath alive. Reilly, on the other hand, had somehow managed to supply herself with a pair of hiking boots.

So like her. She was always prepared—

When he looked up, she was right in front of him. Her cheeks were pink from the wind and the exertion, and her eyes shone with the kind of warmth that came from not just a good heart, but an open one. Wisps pulling free of her ponytail gave her a red-tinted halo, and her perfume or shampoo or whatever it was reminded him of summer—the normal kind, not the last one he'd had as a "kid."

And then she stepped into him, put her arms around him, and just held on.

It took him a minute to get with the program, because that was the last thing he expected. But then he embraced her back.

The two of them stood there for God only knew how long.

"I'm not in the habit of dating," he said roughly.

"Coworkers, you mean?" She pulled back and looked up at him.

"Anyone." He smoothed her hair with his palms. "And you're way too good for me."

There was a brief pause and then she smiled a little. "So the couch is the preferred spot, huh."

"Call me Casanova."

"What am I going to do with you," she murmured, like she was talking to herself.

"Dead honest? I don't know. If I were a friend of yours, I'd tell you to run, don't walk, to the exit."

"They are not you, you know," she said. "Your parents don't define you."

"I'm not so sure about that. She was the sycophant of a psychopath. He's a demon in a dapper mask. And along came baby in a baby carriage. Let's face it, up until now, my life has revolved around avoiding the past, wasting the present, and refusing to think about the future—because I'm terrified I don't just share my father's name."

Reilly shook her head. "Listen, I used to be scared that the woman who gave birth to me was going to come back and claim me. For the longest time, I was convinced that whatever my dad did legally wasn't going to be enough if she wanted me back. It used to keep me up at night—and I still have nightmares that it happens. Matter of fact—and you want to talk about crazy—I still sleep with a copy of the court-certified adoption papers next to me in my bed-side table. My point? Just because you're afraid of something doesn't give it the power to come true. Fear isn't going to make it nonfiction."

There was another long silence.

He was the one who broke it: "Scratch what I said before. I think I *am* falling in love with you. Right here. Right now."

CHAPTER
29

As Jim stood a little ways off from Reilly and Veck, he made like a boulder and tried desperately not to overhear every single word they were saying to each other. And when they stepped in close, he turned his head away.

There were advantages to going invisi, but he was so not into the voyeurism thing.

And he was not pleased with this emo delay. They were looking for his Sissy—the lovey-dovey shit could wait until they found her or figured out that the location was a sham.

Stepping off the rock he'd been perched on, he landed in a puddle, the murky water splashing up on his leathers and his combats, but making no sound thanks to the little force-field he'd thrown up around himself. Man, this quarry was like something out of an old *Star Trek* episode, just without the red shirts and the transporters—

Abruptly, warmth bloomed on the side of his face, and the sensation brought his head up and to the right. A shaft of sunlight was streaming down on him, hitting him on the temple and the jaw.

What the hell, he thought, realizing it was coming from the wrong direction.

Frowning, he moved back and pivoted around, following the path of the lemon yellow stripe ... which led into the cave behind him.

Something flashed deep inside its dark belly.

"Oh, shit," Jim whispered as a premonition washed over him like cold rain.

Bracing himself, he walked to the ragged opening. No need to step aside; the illumination went right through him as if he weren't there.

The aperture was fairly large, about six feet tall, maybe three feet wide, although there was an internal turn almost immediately, so the question was, what had thrown the reflection?

Entering, the sunlight followed him, making him think of Dog in its quiet, comforting companionship. And he didn't stop to think about how the illumination managed to wrap around the corner or wonder why it seemed to direct him ...

"Oh ... God ..." He had to grab onto the rock wall to hold himself up as he stared at what the light had pulled from the darkness: Back against the fall wall of the cave, wrapped in a rough tarp, there was a body.

Lying there on the ground.

Like discarded garbage.

The glowing beam coalesced over the bundle at one end, and that was when he saw the length of hair.

Clean, it would have been blond.

Jim closed his eyes and collapsed against the rough flank of the cave. The sense that so much had been leading to this moment—shit, that maybe everything had—was like a blaring horn behind his head, going off incessantly, deafening him.

There are no coincidences, he heard Nigel saying.

When a hand landed on his shoulder, he wheeled around at the same time he took out his crystal dagger.

Immediately, he lowered his weapon. "Jesus, Adrian— you want to get stabbed?"

Bad question to ask on a day like today.

And the other angel didn't reply. He just looked over to

the light that floated above Sissy's head, a celestial crown of gold to mark her remains. In a low voice, he said, "I wanted to help you with your dead. You helped me with mine."

Jim stared at the other guy for a number of heartbeats. "Thanks, man."

Adrian nodded once, as if they had taken and exchanged a vow of some kind, and the accord they reached made Jim wonder ... If everything had a purpose, had Sissy died for this moment between the two of them? Had this been the reason they'd lost Eddie? Because as Adrian's dead eyes met his, the pair of them were in the same place, the two hotheads realigned by tragedies that were unrelated, and exactly the same.

Instead of going to his girl, Jim offered his palm to his partner. And when the angel accepted it, he pulled Adrian up against him and held the bastard hard. Over the guy's shoulder, he focused on Sissy.

Weighing the balance of the interests of the war against all who had lost the girl, as well as the head space where Adrian was at right now, it was a tough call whether those two losses were worth this unexpected unity: As far as Jim could see, the shit was fifty-fifty at best, with only a hair weighing in favor of the battle with Devina.

Except sometimes the straw broke the camel's back. And families lost their daughters. And best friends didn't come home at the end of the night.

And life didn't seem worth living.

But you went on anyway.

When they stepped back, Adrian put his finger on Sissy's necklace. "She *is* your girl."

Jim nodded. "And it's time to get her out of here."

Holy shit, Reilly thought. Veck was looking like he was going to kiss her.

And she was feeling like she was going to let him.

And then there was the "love" thing.

As she went stock-still, she wasn't sure what to say in response. She was falling in love with him, too. But she could barely handle the concept in her mind. Saying it out loud was way too naked.

There were other ways of replying, however.

Just as she leaned in toward his mouth, he eased down, heading for hers—

Someone appeared on the rock outcropping above them. Someone big, who loomed tall and blocked out the sun. As she jumped back from her partner, her immediate thought was, Oh, God, please let it not be anyone from HQ—

Her wish came true, unfortunately: It was the "FBI agent."

Veck moved so fast, she didn't know she'd been put behind a human shield until her hands rested on his back. Which was a gallant move, but she didn't need the cover. Tucking her hand into her coat and finding the butt of her weapon—just as he had done—she stepped back out with her gun pointed upward.

Except . . . the man staring down at them didn't seem aggressive in the slightest. He looked ruined. Positively destroyed.

"Sissy Barten is right there." He pointed behind himself. "Against the back wall of the next cave."

He's not going to hurt us, she thought with a conviction that came from the soul.

Redirecting the muzzle of her nine to the ground, she frowned. Around his body, there was a subtle glow, a radiance that might be explained by the fact that he was in a shaft of sunshine—except, wait a minute, he wasn't. It was too late in the day for where he was standing.

"Are you all right?" she heard herself ask the man.

His haunted eyes locked on her. "No. I'm not."

Veck spoke up, sharp and demanding. "How do you know where the body is."

"I just saw it."

"I called the FBI. They've never heard of you."

"Only the current administration." The tone was bored. "Are you going to go help her or waste time—"

"Impersonating a federal officer is a felony."

"So get out your cuffs and chase my ass—just come this way."

As the guy jumped off the rock and disappeared, Veck glared over his shoulder. "You stay here."

"To hell with that."

Something in her expression must have told him that arguing would be nothing but a time suck, because he cursed a blue streak—and got moving. Together, they scrambled up the boulder in front of them, surmounting it in clawing grabs. When they got to the top . . .

Jim Heron, or whoever he was, had disappeared.

There was, however, the opening to another large cave.

"Call for backup," Veck said, leaping down as he got out his flashlight. "I'm going in—and I need you to cover me from out here."

"Roger that." She palmed up her radio, but then barked at him, "*Stop!* You have to watch for footprints. Approach from the edges, okay?"

He looked back at her. "Good call."

"And be careful."

"You have my word."

Leading with the flashlight and his gun, he stepped into the cave, his broad shoulders barely fitting through the entrance. Almost immediately, he must have come to a corner, because the glow dimmed and then got cut off.

As she called for their colleagues and received confirmation that the others were on their way, she carefully lowered herself down to the muddy patch of ground that was the cave's welcome mat. She knew it was going to take some time for the others to arrive, and prayed that her instincts were right about that big blond man who evidently wasn't worried about lying or misrepresenting himself—and yet who seemed crushed when it came to Sissy Barten.

If anything happened to Veck on her watch, she'd never forgive herself—

"What . . . the hell?" she murmured.

Reilly frowned and sank down onto her haunches. Smack in the middle of the patch of soggy dirt, the impressions from where Veck had landed were like moon-craters. Likewise, around the rim, his path to thc opcning was dccp and obvious, the sunken impression of smooth-soled shoes dominating the ground and announcing that a man of some two hundred pounds had been by.

Rising up, Reilly braced her foot on a ledge and stretched high to look where Veck and she had crossed over. On the top of the shelf of stone, there were two sets of wet prints, hers and Veck's. That was it.

Surveying the expanse of the slope, she shook her head. No way Jim Heron or whoever he was could have gotten down here without having his feet get soaked. And no way he could have stood where he had without leaving damp prints behind, as she and Veck had done.

What the hell was going on here?

Behind her, Veck reappeared at the cave opening. "It's Sissy Barten. He's right."

Reilly swallowed hard as she got back down. "Anything else in there?"

"Not that I can see. Did you call us in?"

"Yes. Are you sure it's her?"

"I didn't touch anything, but there's blond hair showing and the body is where Kroner said it would be." Veck's brows dropped. "What's wrong?"

"Were there any other footprints on the floor of that cave?"

"Let me check." He disappeared. Came back. "Not really. But it's not the best surface for capturing them. It's relatively dry, with little soil depth. What are you—"

"It's like he just dropped out of the sky."

"Who? Heron?"

"There's no evidence he's been here, Veck. Where are his muddy footprints? On the ground? Up there?"

"Wait, aren't there—"

"Nothing."

He frowned and glanced around. "Son of a bitch."

"My feelings exactly."

Off in the distance, she heard the other officers approaching so she cupped her hands and called out, "Over here! We're over here!"

Maybe someone else could make sense of this. Because she was coming up with nothing ... and evidently, the same was true of Veck.

CHAPTER
30

As the last of the day's sunlight drained from the sky, Sissy Barten's remains were carefully bagged up and removed from the cave.

Veck was one of four guys who took the handles, bore her weight, and walked her out into the clean air. He'd stayed close as the afternoon had progressed, but kept his hands to himself, limiting his participation to taking his own photographs with his phone, talking with the coroner when the guy arrived, and helping wherever, and whenever he could with nonessentials.

Reilly had done the same.

And now the only thing left to do here was to get the body up the slope.

"Let's go this way," he said to the others. "It's the best shot we've got."

The four of them headed to the north, taking the least obstructed way—which was a relative term.

And there were plenty of people waiting for their arrival.

Naturally, the news crews had arrived and parked on the rim. God only knew who had tipped them off. No one in an official capacity at the site, that was for sure, but this was a public area and the whole town knew not only about Kroner's capture and recuperation at St. Francis, but also the victim in that motel, and the other dead girls. The fact that there were a dozen uniforms traipsing around a remote area with a lot of dark places probably didn't mean someone was having a birthday party at this pile of rocks. Plus now there was a body bag involved.

And God knew every idiot had a cell phone these days.

Which was precisely why, the moment after a positive identification had been made using photographs and birthmarks, de la Cruz had literally run up out of the scene and gone gunning for his car. Although the CPD would not release the name to the press until after the family had been notified, there had been numerous e-mails, texts, and phone calls back and forth with HQ—and there was no way of knowing who might have told their wife, who told her sister, who told someone at the television station.

Sometimes the information age sucked.

And no one wanted the Bartens to find out about their daughter on the evening news . . . or, heaven forbid, Facebook.

As Veck and the other three guys grunted and stretched and pulled and lifted, Reilly was right with them the whole way, clicking her flashlight on and shining the beam to give them something to go on as things got darker. And darker still.

Until it was pitch-black.

Nearly an hour later, they made it to the top and carefully placed the remains in the back of one of the search and rescue vehicles.

Veck and Reilly stood back as Sissy Barten was taken safely back to town.

As the other officers began to disperse and engines were started, Reilly said quietly, "I don't think—"

"Kroner didn't kill her," Veck agreed just as softly.

"The MO does not fit."

"Not at all."

And they weren't the only ones who'd noticed the discrepancy between Sissy and the other victims: This body had been suspended head over heels and drained of blood, and there had been some kind of design etched into the stomach. Further, even though she had been naked and picked clean of personal objects, no patches of skin had been removed and she hadn't been sexually assaulted—which had been another of Kroner's perversions.

"I just don't know how to explain the earring," he murmured.

"Or why Kroner knew where she was if he didn't kill her."

Veck glanced over at his partner. "You want to eat somewhere?"

Bracing her arms over her head, she stretched. "Yes, please. I'm starved. And stiff."

He took out his phone and texted her: *Ur place? Luks like u culd use a bath. Takeout n promise 2 b gent.*

There was a discreet *bing*, and after making some small talk, she surreptitiously got out her phone and glanced down at it.

"Perfect plan."

His impulse was to kiss her hard and quick. Except he nipped that in the bud, because they were not just not alone; they were around people they frickin' worked with, hello.

And he wanted to drive back with her, but they were going to have to tandem it, thanks to his damn bike. Shit, to think he used to like that thing.

Then again, it had gotten her to take him home last night.

"See you in twenty," he told her.

"Are you sure you don't want an extra coat?"

"I'll be fine."

As he walked off across the still spongy, muddy ground, he thought about Jim Heron and the lack of footprints. He'd spent more time looking for evidence that someone other than he and Reilly had been walking around that area, but there had been nothing. Yet he was very sure the man couldn't possibly have shown up nearly half a mile down the slope, having traversed wet, uneven terrain, without leaving any trace. And it wasn't as if Veck had imagined the guy's appearance.

Look down at your feet, Thomas DelVecchio. And then you call me when you get scared enough. I'm the only one who can help you.

Whatever, Heron.

Resisting the urge to shout at the shadows, he mounted up, started his engine, and waited as Reilly stood next to her open trunk and took off her caked, filthy boots. At least that made him smile. He was willing to bet she had either a plastic bag or a rubber mat in there so that she didn't put the dirty treads on the rug. And she'd take those nasty suckers out as soon as she parked in her garage, and wash them right away so they'd be ready for the next time.

He glanced down at his own feet. His loafers were ruined. The kind of thing that you addressed with a garbage bag, not a scrub brush and a hose.

Hard not to find some other parallels there.

Reilly took the lead, and he was on her all the way into town even though going seventy on a bike on a night like this made you feel like you were back in December. Windbreaker, his ass. He might as well have been wearing a muscle shirt and nothing else, the cold biting into him.

But it wasn't as if he dwelled on the temperature. In his mind, he went back to the shower he'd taken after that nightmare in the woods with Kroner, back to the dark presence that had wrapped around him and spoken to him and caressed him, back to his biggest fear up close and personal.

It was nothing of this world. Never had been.

And then he heard Reilly's voice: *It's like he just dropped out of the sky.*

Christ, he was losing his mind. Had to be. Because he wasn't actually thinking Jim Heron didn't exist.

Was he?

About ten minutes later, they got off the Northway and weeded their way over to Reilly's neighborhood, and it was a relief to see all the nice-and-normal in the form of houses with lights and TVs on inside, and cars going at slow paces, and corner stores with lottery signs in them.

All things that could be easily and concretely explained. And who'd have ever thought he'd crave that?

When they got to Reilly's place, he pulled in behind her and dismounted as she eased into the garage, the bright reds of her brake lights flaring and then disappearing as she cut the ignition.

"You should wear a helmet," she said as she got out, went around to her trunk, and snagged her muddy boots.

Sure enough, she flicked a light switch on, walked them over to the garden hose on the front corner of the garage, and washed off the dirt.

When she glanced back at him, she flushed a little. "What are you smiling for?"

"I had a feeling you were going to do that."

She laughed and refocused on the cleaning job. "Am I so predictable."

Eyeing her bent form, he thought "sexy as hell" would also cover it. Man, the woman could turn a mundane chore into something *so* worth watching.

"You're perfect," he murmured.

"Trust me, never that." Cutting off the water, she shook the boots, dried them with a chamois, and put them back into the trunk.

Together, they went into her cock-a-doodle-doo kitchen and more lights went on. First thing he looked at? The table.

The hard-on was instant. As was the replay of the night before last when he'd done so much more than kiss her on it.

But neither lasted.

Through the doorway into the office, he saw that she had rearranged the furniture in there: The armchair had been pulled into the far corner and angled outward, and a small table was next to it. Extrapolating, he figured that if you were sitting there, you could watch both the front and the rear doors with your back to a solid wall.

"You want to try for pizza again?" she asked from over by the phone.

Cranking his head around, he said roughly, "Why didn't you tell me."

"What?"

"That you were being watched, too."

Jim didn't wait around to follow Sissy's mortal remains out of the quarry and into town. Instead, he disengaged from Veck, leaving Adrian to stay with the guy, and proceeded to her family's house along with a shortish, intense-looking detective who muttered to himself in Spanish.

He said, "*Madre de Dios*" a lot. And made the sign of the cross so many times it was like his hand had a stutter.

What he did not do was notice that he had a passenger with him in his unmarked: Jim rode shotgun all the way back to Caldwell with the guy. Yeah, sure, he could have taken the fly-by-night route, but this gave him some time to get his shit together.

Plus the Spanish primer was educational.

Twenty minutes after they left the site, the detective pulled over in front of the Barten house, turned off the engine, and got out of the car. As he jacked up his slacks, his face was grim, but then, with the kind of news he had? Hardly time to be flashing your dental work.

Hitting the walkway, Jim stayed side by side with the man, unwilling to invade Sissy's mother's house even for a moment, and even though she would never know he was there.

At the door, the guy lifted his hand and put it under his tie, at his chest. There was a cross there. Had to be, especially as the man fell into Spanish as if he were praying—

Abruptly, the detective looked over.

And even though the guy couldn't see him, Jim met those tired, sad dark eyes. "You can do this. You're a good man, and you can do this. You're not alone."

De la Cruz looked back at the door and nodded sure as if he had heard the words.

Then he rang the bell.

Mrs. Barten opened up a moment later, as if she'd been expecting him. "Detective de la Cruz."

"May I come in, ma'am?"

"Yes. Please."

Before he stepped into the house, the detective kicked off his muddy shoes on the mat, and as the woman watched him, her hand crept to her throat. "You found her."

"Yes, ma'am. We have. Is there anyone else you'd like with you as we speak?"

"My husband's traveling—but he's on his way home. I called him right after I got off with you."

"Let's do this inside, ma'am."

She shook herself, as if she'd forgotten she was standing in the open doorway. "Of course."

Jim went inside with the guy, and then there they were, once again in the living room, with Mrs. Barten taking the same flower-printed armchair she'd sat in the other day. De la Cruz grabbed the couch, and Jim paced back and forth, his rage at Devina making it impossible for him to sit down.

"Tell me," Mrs. Barten said roughly.

The detective leaned forward and kept his eyes right on her tense, pale face. "We found her at the quarry."

Sissy's mother's lids went on lockdown, closing and staying there. Then her breath left her slowly, until there had to have been nothing left in her lungs at all.

This was the exodus of hope, Jim thought. She probably didn't even know she'd had any lingering, but here it was, squeezing out of her chest.

"Did she . . . Was she . . . suffer . . ."

De la Cruz spoke slowly and carefully. "We're not sure that she is part of the recent killings."

Mrs. Barten's eyes opened back up, her body going rigid. "What . . . Then who? Why?"

"I don't have those answers for you yet. But you have my word, ma'am—I will not stop until I find out everything and I get the bastard."

Jim couldn't stand it any longer. He went over to Sissy's mother and put his nonexistent hand on her shoulder. God . . . the pain she was in . . . . He could sense it clearly as if it were his own, and wanting to bear some of her burden for her, he pulled the emotion into himself and held it there until his knees knocked together and he felt light-headed.

Abruptly, as if she were strengthened, the woman squared her shoulders and lifted her chin. In a low, forceful voice, she said, "How did she die."

"Ma'am, we need the medical examiner to tell us that. She's going back with him now, and he's staying up all night to take care of her. She's in good hands, and after I leave here, I'm going right to her side. I won't leave her, ma'am. Not until she's through this part. That's my promise."

"Thank you." Mrs. Barten took a deep breath. "How will I know what's happening?"

De la Cruz took out a card and wrote something on it. "This is my cell. You call me anytime, night or day. My phone's always on and always with me. And as soon as the examiner's done, you'll be the first person I dial."

Mrs. Barten nodded and then shifted her focus, her eyes training on some infinite middle ground between her and the detective.

What part of Sissy's life was she remembering? Jim wondered. The birth . . . the birthdays . . . the Christmases or Easters? Was it Halloween or the Fourth of July, or no particular holiday, just some offhand recollection of a sweet moment between the two of them? Or maybe it was something witnessed between Sissy and someone else that showed the girl's kindness or empathy or humor. . . .

He wanted to see what she saw. Even if it was nothing good. Or nothing at all.

But he didn't intrude on her. Enough of her daughter had been stolen—

The vibration against his chest wall was not his heart going haywire on him. It was his phone on vibrate.

Taking the thing out, he read the text from Adrian: *Ben tryn 2 reach u—need u now.*

Jim didn't want to leave, but he was out of the house in a second. Speeding over to the east, he zeroed in on Adrian—

And flashed right into a fight on the back lawn of Veck's partner's house.

What the *fuck*?

Devina's minions had apparently boiled up out of the night, their smoky bodies circling Adrian like scavengers over a fresh corpse. But at least his boy wasn't dead—and wasn't about to be, given the way his deadly body was poised to do battle.

Jim upshifted immediately into full-on aggression and he didn't wait for the bell to ring. He jumped right in, throwing himself at the closest minion, tackling it hard. As the bastard screeched, that high-pitched sound was what got things rolling—between one second and the next, everything went shit-wild.

Holding the SOB down, Jim curled up a fist and pummeled the thing with a punch to the "head"—and then he took advantage of the split second of paralysis to look up and summon a visual and audio barrier around this freak show. This was a neighborhood, not a vacant field. And all the hand-to-hand was happening mere yards away from three other houses. All of which had plenty of phone lines that could call the police.

CPD uniforms were *not* what they needed right now.

Outing his crystal dagger, he offed the minion under him and then stabbed at everything in front of him, slashing and lunging, leading always with the sharp point of the weapon Eddie had given him and taught him about.

Everything came out in the violence, all his pain and his fury unleashed, until he didn't notice the acid blood from the enemy splashing his face. And he didn't care that the shit was eating through his leather jacket and beelining for more of his skin. In fact, he couldn't feel the earth beneath his feet as he powered from demon to demon; he was at once totally with it and utterly disappeared.

And in his wrath, they couldn't touch him: These were boys coming for a man's job, and they were getting served.

After Jim stabbed another black chest cavity, the acidy spray hitting his jaw and throat, he dumped the body and got ready for the next—

The blow across his back was a real tooth rattler, the kind of thing that made you see stars and hear birds chirping. But like the trained solider he was, Jim went with the momentum, letting himself fall to the ground and then curling at the shoulder at the last minute to avoid further injury.

When he stopped his roll and looked over, the minion who'd gone after him was ready for round two.

Well, hello there, yard man, he thought.

The bastard had gotten itself a shovel and obviously used the thing like a tennis racket, swinging and following through with the flat metal end. And it was hard to tell, but it seemed like laughter was coming out of the three-dimensional shadow.

Clearly, the dumb bitch thought he was in charge, and Jim was more than happy to teach Devina's lackey a life lesson in assuming shit. Staying down and playing like he was compromised, he waited for it to come on over—which it did, sure as if Jim were holding the strings to those oily arms and legs: Moving like a robot with stiff joints, the minion approached with the heavy tool balanced between both hands. Closer. Closer . . .

When it was in range, Jim jacked up his torso, double-palmed the handle, and yanked hard. The minion jerked forward and fell off balance, gravity grabbing that body and pulling it right on top of Jim.

Good thing it wasn't bleeding.

Jim's boot met the thing's pelvic bone to stop the descent, and then it was a case of rolling back and kicking the weight free—while keeping the shovel, of course.

As the minion went for a little joyride through thin air, Jim sprang up, stayed with it, and was the first to welcome it to its new home on the ground: Swinging the shovel around, he drove the business end into the bastard's shadowy chest.

The scream was satisfying. But even more fun was to step back and watch as it pinwheeled in slow-mo: Apparently, Jim had put so much into the strike, the tool had penetrated right into the ground—about three feet, going by how much of the wooden handle was showing. The minion was locked on its back, an insect mounted.

The thing looked up and snarled.

"Yeah? So come and get me." Jim gave it a second to get up. "No? Prefer being a welcome mat? Suits you, motherfucker."

Jim kicked it hard in the head, going soccer ball on that loose skull, and then left the SOB where it was; across the lawn, Adrian was about to get back-doored by a minion that had found a spade and was gunning for him at a dead run.

"What is this—Home fucking Depot night?" Jim muttered as he got out his dagger again. "Behind you!"

Adrian dropped to the grass just as the gardener from hell stabbed forward. Great timing—the minion caught one of his buddies right in the gut. Trouble? All that blood was going to golf-sprinkler Ad.

Jim was just about to pull a breathing tarp when Adrian took care of the problem, going combats-over-cranium and getting the fuck out of the way.

There were only two upright minions left and he and his buddy split the difference, Jim taking the one with the hoe-hoe-hoe and Adrian whipping up onto his feet and circling the other, crystal dagger in hand.

Unwilling to wait for a strike, Jim lunged forward, and grabbed onto the spade's handle, yanking it vertical and then snapping out so the tool's hardwood hello'd the minion in the frontal lobe. Cue the *duh* moment—which Jim exploited by stabbing the thing.

As he wheeled around, he got to watch Ad dust the other fucker by opening a trapdoor in its intestines, and then nailing it in the head.

After that, there was nothing but panting breath and steaming leather and stilled lawn supplies.

Jim glanced around, wondering where all the—Ah, yes, Reilly had a neighbor with one of those backyard shed things, and the squat box had been busted open. Too bad the lawn mower was still nestled in there—that would have been fun.

Coulda given a whole new meaning to a high-and-tight haircut.

"You okay?" he said to Ad.

Ad spit on the lawn. "Yeah."

They were both bleeding from scratches, but at least on Jim's side, he was feeling better. The fighting had blown the carbon out of his pistons, and he was more himself. Calmer. More capable of focusing.

Good timing, he thought as he went over and knelt down by the bastard who was nailed to the ground.

"You ever work one of these over for intel?" he said as he measured the thing. It was moving slowly, clearly still alive. Whatever the fuck that meant.

"Yup. They don't have anything to say. Can't talk."

"Probably why she likes them."

Ad came over and wiped his face with the bottom of his shirt. The glimmering red stain left behind looked like something a psychologist would ask her patient to interpret.

To Jim? It looked like the opening of a cave. A dense, dark cave that had the body of an innocent stashed against the back wall.

Yeah, like that interp was a shocker.

As a groaning sound bubbled up, Jim thought, Damn that demon. She was smart. If your subordinates were incapable of speaking about you, either because they were mute, dumb, or pain-resistant, it was damn good strategy—

"That was fun to watch."

At the sound of Devina's voice, Jim and Ad locked eyes. In silent agreement, they both made like her appearance was nothing unexpected. And as they rose to their feet and turned to her, Jim put himself in front of the other angel.

He was not losing another one to that bitch. Not tonight.

"Hiding from me, Jim?"

The demon's eyes all but reached out and grabbed him: They were so intense, it was like being physically struck.

Silly thing to say, though. He hadn't realized she couldn't find him.

"Radar not working, Devina?" So that was why Ad had gotten attacked. She'd wanted to draw Jim out.

The demon stepped delicately across the grass. She was wearing heels high enough to make him wonder how she handled the elevation sickness, and her skirt was the size of a napkin and the color of the Vegas strip.

Sounded ridiculous, looked hot—as long as you didn't know what she really was.

And Jim was never going to forget that.

Reaching behind, he put his hand on Ad's forearm. The other angel was hard as a concrete block, utterly immobile—and he was going to have to stay that way: He was not in the right frame of mind to tackle an out-and-out with the enemy.

Neither was Jim, to be honest. But she wasn't going to know that.

"Got something on your mind, Devina?"

She stopped when she came up to her undead soldier who'd been shish kebab'd. Staring down at the thing, she put her hand out, and with all the urgency of someone picking up a newspaper, summoned the form into her palm, drawing it up from the ground in a liquid rush and absorbing the stain into herself. When she was through, the shovel remained where it had been left, buried in the ground to the handle.

"How's Eddie doing?" She smiled. "Smelling like a rose?"

Jim wanted to curse. Of course she led with that.

It was the one thing guaranteed to make Adrian flip out.

Fucking hell—just when he'd thought this night couldn't get worse ...

CHAPTER
31

As Reilly met the hard eyes of her partner, she guessed the pair of them were going to miss another pizza opportunity: Standing across her kitchen, Veck was looking downright pissed off, and although she bristled at the caveman routine, it wasn't like she didn't know where he was coming from.

"Why didn't you tell me," Veck demanded again. "Or, shit, if not me, anyone else?"

"Who says I was stalked."

"Why else would you move the furniture into that arrangement."

See, this was why you didn't want to date a detective....

Linking her arms over her chest, she leaned back against the counter. "I didn't actually see anything." She shrugged. "If I'd had something to report, I would have told you. But I just sat in that chair all night, wondering if I was paranoid. Nothing happened."

"You should have called me." At that, she cocked a brow, and he cursed as if he were remembering how things had been left between them. "Okay, okay . . . but, damn it, I don't want you up alone for hours waiting for someone to break into your house."

"I was all right. I am all right now. And I *guarantee* you that if anyone had come into my house, I'd have taken care of the situation."

Muttering something about Dirty Harry, Veck went over and sat at the kitchen table. Bracing his arms on his elbows, he rubbed his head. "This shit is out of hand."

Which part? The idea that they were being stalked? The Kroner situation? The body they'd found?

The sex? The "love" thing?

So much to choose from.

As she took the chair across from him, she thought of her parents, sitting together at their table in that nice house of theirs. She'd bet they'd never had to stare at each other over this kind of—

A screech lit off from behind the house, and she and Veck were up on their feet before the high-pitched burst faded.

Guns came out as they both back-flatted on either side of the sliding door that opened to the backyard. Reilly nailed the overhead light switch, plunging the kitchen into darkness, before hitting the one that cranked the security lights on.

Her eyes searched the brightly illuminated yard.

There wasn't much to her back forty. It was more like a back four, and the only vista she had, such as it was, was of the boxy, suburban connect-the-dots of the other houses in the neighborhood.

Nothing was out there. That she could see.

Her instincts told her another story. And made her think of all the footprints "Jim Heron" hadn't left behind.

"I feel like I'm going crazy," she muttered.

"Funny, I'm worried we aren't."

When nothing else happened, they waited. And waited. And waited some more. Eventually, they both peeled off from the door and reholstered their weapons.

"We need food. And a shower," she muttered. "And a psych eval."

When there was no response, she glanced over at her

partner. Veck was pacing around, looking as if he were about to levitate off the floor.

It went without saying that there was going to be no talking him down. So she stepped in front of him, forcing him to stop or mow her over. He stopped.

"Food. Shower," she commanded. "In that order. We can skip the psych thing for now."

He smiled at her and brushed her cheek with his hand. "This your way of asking me for a date, Officer."

"Guess it is, Detective."

"Then how about we start with a shower," he said in the kind of deep voice that made her consider the value of cleanliness.

Meticulous, soapy, slow-going cleanliness.

She had to clear her throat. "Because I have a feeling we're going to be up there for a while."

"You don't say." He stepped in closer and put his hands on her hips. "You think we're that dirty."

"Try filthy," she said, focusing on his lips. "We are past dirty and into filthy territory."

Veck purred on a low throb as one of his palms went up to the small of her back. The other went down and gripped her, bringing her flush against him so that his erection was a hard, thick demand pushing into the front of her hips.

As he rolled his pelvis, he stroked her with exactly what she was breathless for.

And in response, Reilly rose onto her tiptoes, arched into him, and wrapped her arms around his neck. "Veck . . ."

"Yeah," he growled.

Tilting her head to the side, she put her mouth less than an inch from his. In her breathiest, sexiest voice, she murmured, "What do you want on your pizza . . ."

Then she sucked his lower lip in and bit it ever so slightly.

He groaned and tightened up all over. "Tease."

"I'll be your dessert—"

Turned out you didn't taunt a man like Veck. He backed her up against the wall, took both her hands, and held them out against the silly rooster paper. Pressing himself into her, so that she felt him from her thighs to her breasts, he worked a rhythm of retreat and advance until she was panting.

"You'd better order now," he said, licking up her throat. "Or I'm not going to let you get to the phone for a while."

He stretched out her arm, putting her in the vicinity of the receiver. But he didn't stop with the erotic riding, or the tongue. Instead, he pushed his leg between hers so the friction got worse ... or better, depending on how you looked at it.

God, she wasn't sure she could work the phone. Or remember the number of the place she called at least once a week.

Somehow, she snagged the receiver, and in a fit of inspiration hit redial—because the last number she'd called had been the one from two nights ago. As it was ringing? Veck amused himself by kissing his way down to her collarbone, which made speaking a little difficult.

Somehow, she squeezed out her name, address and the order for a pepperoni-and-sausage, large. And then it was a case of, "No. . . . no just the one . . . no . . . no Cinna Stix . . ."

She found herself burying her fingers in the thick hair at the nape of his neck and arching into him.

"No . . . God, *no*—" Okay, that sounded a little too porn-star, especially when it was about not wanting a half-priced liter of Coke product. In desperation, she croaked, "Just the pizza." *For the love of all that is holy, just the fucking pizza!* she wanted to scream. "T-t-thank you."

The phone was hung up on a wing and a prayer, and then it was all about the fast and the furious.

"How much time?" Veck growled against her throat.

"Twenty . . . minutes . . ." She latched onto his body, holding him as he had her before—by the hips. "Bathroom."

He grabbed onto the backs of her thighs and jacked her up off the floor. Locking on to his shoulders and linking her legs around him, she hung on as he made a mad rush for the hall bath.

The crowded little room shrank down to the size of a matchbox with both of them in it. But at least the sink had enough of a counter for him to put her on.

After he kicked the door shut, she went for the front of his slacks at the same moment he attacked the buttons on her shirt. . . .

Too many hands, not enough room.

"Let me," she said, putting him off and solving both problems in a matter of seconds by yanking her top over her head and doing an unzip at NASCAR speed.

He was already going for that wallet of his. Except then he frowned. "Last one."

She stopped in the middle of unhooking her bra. "I don't have anything in the house."

And this was just supposed to be a quickie before the main attraction of fully naked, in her bed, all over each other.

Damn it—she had never seen any virtue in being promiscuous, but at least if she'd had been worthy of all that stuff she'd bought at Victoria's Secret, she have condoms around. And on his side? It was chivalrous that he hadn't refilled the stash in the expectation of them, or anyone else he was with, being in this position. For chrissakes, though.

"Shit," she said.

Veck was breathing hard, his chest pumping, his body more than ready for what they'd started: His erection had taken advantage of being freed and was jutting out of those slacks of his, straining against his boxer briefs.

With a curse, he put his wallet back in his pocket. And then did the same disappear with his arousal, tucking himself away and rezipping, even though it was a struggle, given the size of that damn thing of his.

"Oh, no," she said roughly. "I—"

He came back at her lips, cutting her off as he owned her mouth with his tongue. With subtle pressure, he eased her into the wall by leaning forward, until she was jammed into the corner, her body semisprawled.

And that was when he started touching her.

He pushed the bra down and went for her nipples, tweaking them until she gasped against his lips. "Veck..."

"Shhh. Let me do you like this."

He bent further to get at what he'd exposed, sucking on her as his hands went other places, riding down her thighs, stroking her.

He moved with mind-scrambling laziness, juicing her up, but not going anywhere near that sweet spot that was aching. Meanwhile, his mouth was working miracles on her nipples, teasing and flicking, then sucking again, and, God, the sight of his dark head down to her naked skin was a turn-on.

Running her hands through his thick hair, she sawed her legs against his hips. "Veck—*please* . . .

"Tell me what you want," he said against her breast.

"Touch me."

He eased his head to the side and looked up at her. "I thought I was."

On that note, his pink tongue extended and ran a warm, wet circle around her nipple. Groaning, she tried to arch back, but there was no room.

"Where do you want me to go, Reilly?" he demanded. As she went for his hand, prepared to give him a guided frickin' tour, he held his arms away. "Nope. You have to say it."

"Veck . . ."

"Nice name." He put his lips next to her ear. "And even better, you sound like you're about to come when you say it. But I don't think you want me to touch myself."

"That'd get the job done," she moaned as she imagined his big fist gripping his shaft.

"Sorry, my focus is on you. Where, Reilly."

Screw this. Two could play at the teasing game. She gave him a subtle push and he obligingly inched back, no doubt ready to hear all kinds of fun things hit the airwaves. Instead, she lowered her lids, stared up at him . . . and put her own hand between her legs.

"I'm thinking of you," she said, rubbing herself. Then

she bit her lip and worked her hips as well—not because she wanted to show off, but because that was how she was feeling him. "Touching me ... I'm *feeling* you ... touching me...."

Veck's knees seemed to buckle. Either that or she threw off his center of gravity—either way, he sagged into the wall and had to throw out a palm to hold himself up.

Working her sex through her trousers, she watched him watch her—and it was gratifying to know this solo act wasn't going to last. His rabid eyes were locked on what she was doing, his body trembling like at any second he was going to snap and take over what she'd begun.

"Want to help?" she drawled.

He was on her in a flash, adding his hand to her minstrations, until she moved out of the way because it was more exciting for him to stroke her.

Under his quick and nimble fingers, her pants came undone and then he was pushing them down her thighs, his efforts aided when she braced her foot against the toilet seat and lifted her butt. With the waistband around her knees, he had access to her panties and—

"Oh, God!" she called out as he found her.

There was something so delicious about the combination of her being superslick and him doing the rubbing. And that was even before he ducked under the barrier and went skin-to-skin with her core.

Digging into his shoulders, she yanked him to her mouth as he focused on the top of her sex, driving her higher, and higher, and—

Reilly came hard, the force of the orgasm clenching her legs together around his talented hand, her body jerking in rhythmic pulses. He didn't stop what he was doing, however—he helped her ride out the cresting waves until she was a limp, panting bag of bliss.

As Veck pulled back and stared down at her, he might not have had a release himself, but he damn sure was looking satisfied.

"How was that for an hors d'oeuvre?" he murmured, his

low-lidded expression suggesting he knew every bit of how great he was.

When she'd recovered enough to move, she reached out and cupped his erection through his closed fly. "Payback is going to be a pleasure."

CHAPTER
32

Standing across from Devina, in the backyard of the Internal Affairs officer's house, Adrian was not reacting to a target for the first time in his unnatural, immortal life.

How's Eddie doing? Smelling like a rose?

As he stared over Jim's shoulder at that fake-ass glamour-puss piece of evil, the demon's words banged around his skull sure as if she'd put a minion under his chrome dome and the fucker was whaling at his brain with a sledgehammer.

The old Adrian would have trampled Jim, or anything else in his path, to lock his hands around her throat and squeeze until she didn't just suffocate, but he snapped her ugly head right off her spine.

That was, however, precisely what she expected. What she was banking on. The reason she'd spoken.

And he stayed in control as it dawned on him that his hothead routine was the reason his best friend had been murdered. Jim was right: Destabilization was the name of the game, and the demon had done what she had because she was sure it was going to help her in the war.

So, yeah, as much as it killed him, as much as it ground his molars and fisted his balls, he simply stood where he was.

He couldn't answer her, though. He didn't trust himself to open his mouth.

"Eddie's safe and sound," Jim said. "And we're taking care of him."

"New jobs as morticians. How quaint." Devina smiled broadly, as if she were truly, deeply happy. "But don't you miss him, Adrian? Never mind, I can feel you from here. You know, if you ever need a shoulder to cry on, I'm always available."

Just as he was about to tell her to shove the plastic sympathy so far up her ass she gagged on the shit, Jim tightened his hold on Ad's arm—until the guy was all but cutting off the circulation.

And the savior was right: If he reacted as Devina wanted him to, Eddie had died for fucking nothing. Which was the only thing worse than their losing him in the first place.

On that note, he put his other hand over Jim's so that they were both holding him in place.

Devina seemed momentarily nonplussed. But it didn't last. "Paralyzed by grief, Adrian?"

An eternity passed.

And sometime in those infinite heartbeats between her taunts and his nonreaction, he started to grow cold: His emotions ceased to run to any kind of extreme, as if they had burned out—and like a star that collapsed in on itself, he felt a turning tide that retracted him out of Devina's reach.

She would have been better off to just leave him alone and let him stew in his anger. But now that she'd pushed him into this arctic clarity, for the first time, he could respond solely with his mind and not his heart.

He released his grip on Jim and stepped away from the savior. As he separated them, Jim's head ripped around as if he were about to intercede, but Adrian just stood next the guy and faced the enemy.

"Did you want something, Devina?" Adrian said in a dark voice. "Or is this just a social call."

Cue another round of silence. This time, however, Devina started to fidget with her long hair, her short skirt, her gold bangles.

And for Ad, there was no satisfaction at ruining the demon's fun. There was just a deadly quiet in his chest, a resonate power that for all his ferocious warrior instincts, he had never gotten close to before.

It was as if he'd been reborn. And he'd be damned if he ever went back to who he had been.

Literally.

As Jim looked over at the other angel, he thought, Okay, who the fuck are you, and what have you done with Adrian Vogel.

The male beside him wasn't anything close to the guy he'd met and worked with for the last two rounds in the war. This was a robot who looked like Ad: utterly identical, but completely rewired from the original.

There was no emotion in his face, his body, his vibe.

Nothing.

And something told Jim the shift was permanent, like the guy's motherboard had been blown out and replaced. Hard to know if it was good news or bad, though. The lightning-quick temper was gone. The passion was gone. The heat was gone. In its place? Icy calculation—which made him untouchable in a way.

And that was a sword that cut both ways, didn't it. But whatever, there was time to worry about repercussions later.

Jim turned his head back to Devina. "So what's it going to be. Social? Or business."

Devina swept her brunette hair up and out, the waves bouncing with health like she was in a shampoo commercial. "I'm very busy."

"Then why are you standing here talking." Jim took out his Marlboros and shook free a cig. "If you're such a busy little girl."

"Oh, you have no idea how much I'm working on." Her nasty smile was the kind of thing horror movies tried to pull off and couldn't get anywhere near. "I'm all about the game changers. And I'm looking forward to this round being over."

"Because you like the taste of losing?" He took out his Bic and lit up. "Strange appetite you have there, sweetheart."

"I like the taste of you." She ran her hand down her body. "And I'm going to gorge myself soon enough."

"Doubt it."

"Have you forgotten our agreement?"

"Oh, I remember it."

"And I haven't lied."

"You must be so proud."

When Jim said nothing further, she played with her hair a little more ... and that was it. She just stood there in front of them, all girlie-girlie, going-nowhere. Hell, maybe she thought she was being admired. Maybe she was dumb-blonding it, even though she didn't really have hair. Maybe she was ...

Holy shit, she was having a girlfriend moment, wasn't she. Sulking because she hadn't been able to find him. That was the "why," wasn't it.

Fucked up. This was too fucked up.

Date from hell was right.

And even though he didn't know why she couldn't find him, sometimes luck was with you.

Abruptly, her gaze shifted over to the house. In the back window, in the kitchen, Veck and Reilly made an appearance. They were both looking disheveled, and it was clear a whole lot of somethin'-somethin' had just happened somewhere: They were both in the glow-zone, happy and satisfied, to the point where Jim was pretty damn sure if the lights were to go out, they'd be glowing in the dark.

"I fucking *hate* them," Devina said, crossing her arms over her breasts.

Bet you do, he thought. Because those were two people in love right there.

And the envy was killing her, her face screwing down tight, eyes lighting up with hatred. She wanted that with him.

Ha, ha.

"So did you need something," he asked in a low, deep voice.

Her head snapped around. "Do you."

To keep her going, the answer, of course, was not to be nice. And gee fuckin' whiz, that was so not hard.

"Not from you." Jim assumed a bored expression as he took a drag and exhaled. "Never from you."

The fury on her face made him happy. Until she growled, "Because of that fucking Sissy."

Wrong turn, he thought. Waaaaay wrong turn on that one.

"Sissy who."

"Don't toy with me."

"I'm not. At least, not at the moment." He let his lids go half-mast. "When I play with you, you'll know it."

Even though the words sickened him, it got her off the scent: Abruptly, she flushed as if she were remembering them together, and then she smiled, big and slow.

"Promise?" she said huskily.

"Promise."

At that, she did a little twirl of joy.

Great. Like his stomach wasn't already nauseous.

"Then again, maybe I'm a liar," he drawled. "Guess you'll have to wait and see."

"Guess so." Her eyes went up and down his body. "And I can't wait."

Frankly, the shit made Jim shrivel, but he blocked that from her. And he wasn't taking for granted that he had total control over the demon. Even infatuated, she was a deadly piece of work, and he couldn't be sure this weapon of his was going to last forever.

For however long he could, though, and at whatever cost to himself it required, he was going to try to keep this connection cultivated.

"Well, I think it's time to bring this round to a close, Jim." Devina did another pirouette. "I have to go back to work, but I'll be seeing you soon."

"If Veck's in this house, why do you need to be anywhere else."

"Like I said, I'm a busy girl, as you'll find out." She blew him a kiss. "Bye for now. And Adrian, call me if you need a shoulder to cry on."

On that note, she was off into the night, fogging up, fogging out.

Shit. If she wasn't here with Veck, he had to assume the fight was somewhere else.

"Fuck," he muttered, ready to hit something.

"No," Adrian said. "We stay here. We stay with Veck."

Jim looked over. Old Adrian? Would have been the one seething to cut loose and follow her. New Adrian? The icy motherfucker was tight as hell, his cold, dispassionate eyes shifting over to Jim's.

"She's not going to crack us," Ad announced. "We're going to stay focused and right here. Smoke and mirrors ain't going to move me."

Now, that's what I'm talking about, Jim thought, with respect.

At that moment, the sound of a car pulling up in front of the house broke through the night. Flashing out to the street with Adrian, Jim unsheathed his dagger—except then he saw the little Domino's sign glowing on the sedan's roof.

Oh, maaaaaaan. Pizza . . . and sex. Maybe Devina had a point.

Hard not to be envious.

The deliveryman got out of his beater and hoofed it up the walkway. Veck answered the door, paid cash, disappeared back inside. Car drove off.

In the moments that followed, Jim itched to go after Devina; he could sense her presence elsewhere in the city . . . but maybe that was what she wanted?

You could never trust her.

New Adrian was right: They stayed here and hung tough.

"Thanks, man," Jim said without looking away from the closed and locked front door of the house.

"No problem," was the terse answer.

CHAPTER
33

Veck didn't track what the pizza tasted like. For all he knew, the thing could have been topped with rubber tires and chunks of plaster.

He couldn't stop thinking of Reilly up on that bathroom counter, her legs spread, her hand brushing against her core.

Sitting next to her at the kitchen table, he was pretty sure she was thinking along similar lines, because there was a whole lot of efficiency in the way she ate. Nothing messy or unladylike—just neat and quick.

He was the same. Except less neat.

When they'd polished off everything but the last slice, he stretched back in his chair and looked to the ceiling.

"So where's your bathtub?" he asked, shooting for casual.

Cue that side smile of hers. The one that made him want to kiss her all over. "I'll show you. Are you going to finish that piece?"

"No." Hell, if it hadn't been for her empty stomach grumbling, he never would have slowed down longer than it took to send off the delivery guy. But he'd wanted to make sure she ate. "You?"

"I'm full."

And I'm ready to fill you up, he thought.

Getting to his feet, he held out his hand to her. "Lead the way."

She did just that, taking him up the stairs and into a room that was nothing like the barren box he slept in. Her private space had nice curtains made to fit the three windows, a bed with lots of pillows, and a duvet that looked thick enough to serve as a trampoline.

Perfect place to make love.

"The bathroom's through there," she murmured, pointing across the way.

He walked over, stepped into the darkness, and patted the wall for the switch. When he hit the thing, he nearly dropped to his knees with a prayer of thanks.

Claw-footed. Deep as a pond. Wide as that bed out there.

And what did you know, the faucet had enough pressure to power a fire hose.

As the hot water rushed out and the level began to rise, he pivoted around to call for—

"Holy . . . fuck . . ." he breathed.

Reilly had lost her clothes and was standing naked in the doorway.

Way to short a man's brain out: All he saw was beautiful skin, and perfect breasts, and the swell of those hips he was dying to lock onto.

As he tried to form a response that didn't involve more curses, or worse, actual drooling, she pulled the tie out of her hair and shook the gloriously red lengths free . . . which made those breasts of hers sway ever so slightly.

"Come here," he said in a rough voice.

She approached him with her head up and her eyes down . . . on the hard cock that was killing him to get to her.

Stepping into his body, Reilly eased up to nip on his earlobe. "Is the water warm enough yet?"

"You get in there"—he gripped her pelvic bones and squeezed—"and it's going to boil."

He kissed her, bending down and putting their mouths together. His clothes lasted another . . . oh, minute and a half.

And then, like the gentleman he wasn't feeling even close to, but was damn well determined to be, he picked her up and carried her into the tub with care, settling them so they faced each other. The steam rising up between their bodies smelled like that scent he associated with her, suggesting she did this frequently, maybe with some kind of bath mix thing.

More kissing and hands going everywhere through the currents of warm water. Except as soon as she found his erection, he jacked up and splashed a few hundred gallons onto the floor.

"Oh, shit . . . sorry—"

She came with him, pushing him back against the curved wall of the tub. "I'm not worried about the water."

As her hand locked on his cock and started stroking, he muttered through gritted teeth, "I'm not going to last if you keep that up."

"I don't want you to."

Well, good. Because the sight of her slick, buoyant breasts and that erotic look in her eyes was enough to make him come on their own. Add the friction? He was waaaay past his threshold.

His hips found a rhythm to counter her own and he let his head go loose until it fell back against the tub's curled edge. Which gave him a hell of a vantage point. The level of the water was recovering from the spill, and the rising, waving action lapped over her hard pink nipples and disappeared, only to lap back, and recede again. . . .

Leaving her glossy. So glossy. As if he'd been licking at her himself.

That was ultimately what kicked him off the ledge. His molars locked and he let out a loud groan as his arousal jerked and bucked against her palm, his body torquing hard.

In response, her smile was precious, the kind you put into your mental backpack and carried with you forever.

And for some reason ... even though it was a mood killer ... all he could think about was her sitting in that chair downstairs, no doubt armed, waiting for someone to come and get her.

They were safe here together tonight, but that was not going to last. Sooner or later, he would have to go home, and she was going to be alone again. Christ, both of them getting stalked? It was time to take control of this situation and keep this incredible woman and her heartbreaking smile safe.

Next time that Heron character showed up, he was going to take the bastard into custody. Even if it killed them both.

"Are you all right?" she asked, clearly sensing the shift in him.

"Oh, yeah. Very all right."

He dragged his head off the lip of the tub and stretched his leg out, turning the faucet off with his foot. Then he pulled her on top of him, unwilling to waste this opportunity to enjoy her.

"I liked that a lot," he said against her mouth. "But I have a feeling you're going to be even better."

They stayed long enough for the water to take an edge from the chill, kissing, touching. Not that he needed the recovery time. He'd been ready to go right after the orgasm she gave him.

He wanted her that much.

"Take me to your bed?" he said.

When she nodded, he offered her a steadying hand as she stood up and delicately stepped over the tub's high walls onto the tile.

"Watch it," he warned. "It's got to be wet."

"It is." She looked down. "I'll get some towels."

"And I'll pay if we ruined your ceiling downstairs."

She glanced back at him, her torso twisting gracefully. "It was so worth it."

"And you are so beautiful," he said softly, as he watched the light catch her curves.

With red cheeks, she turned away to the stack of towels on the counter and began throwing them on the floor around the tub's base.

Even though he was more than content to watch the show, he rose up from the water and got out. The mirror over the sink made him nervous, but he forced himself to look into it. Nothing but his reflection. No shadows. Nothing that moved other than his ribs from his breathing.

Relieved, he approached her from behind. Stepping against her warm, wet body, he bent down and kissed her shoulder.

"I'm not . . . used to this." She patted the last towel of that stack, as if impatient with herself. "I'm just . . . I don't know how to handle this."

"You handled me just fine." He ran his forefinger down her spine. "Better than anyone has."

She laughed in a little tense burst. "Somehow I doubt that."

"Don't. You're something else."

He put his hands on her neck and caressed her back all the way to her hips. Then his lips followed the trail he'd blazed, kissing and nipping down her torso . . . and going even lower.

Getting on his knees, Veck ran his lips up her thighs, gradually moving closer to that juncture he'd been keeping in mind the whole time. At his gentle urging, she bent over the counter, exposing that slit of flesh that drove him insane—

With a sudden surge, he nuzzled into her, and then sucked her into his mouth.

Sweet . . . and hot . . . and slick against his tongue. And she loved it, too, her arms bowing out to keep her balance against the marble, her breath falling into a sharp panting rhythm.

Using his hands, he spread her feet further to give him more room to work, and then he swept his palms up the front of her legs to grip her and keep her tight to his face.

Fast flicking. Deep sucking. Penetration with his tongue.

He took his time, because there was so much to explore,

and he kept her on the brink until he couldn't stand the suspense anymore. Snaking his hand up, he eased the pad of his thumb into the top of her sex at the same time he extended his tongue inside of her. Quick circles in the right place sent her flying, and he loved the way she clenched internally and kicked against him.

When she was finished, he eased back. Through her trembling legs, he got one fuck of a view of her breasts, the two of them hanging down, the tips brushing against the marble as they swung back and forth from her breathing.

Veck squeezed his eyes shut and needed to take a minute.

The next time he came, it was going to be where his tongue had just been.

Orgasm. Of. Her. Life.

As Reilly struggled to remain upright, her body was still cruising at full speed ahead—except there was nowhere to go, however, so all the muscles of her thighs did was twitch in place. And that wasn't the half of it. Her mind was blown, to the point where she wasn't exactly sure where she was.

Turning her head, she got a faceful of toothpaste and brushes.

Bathroom. Well, she guessed there were two locales in her house she would never look at in the same way—wait. Three. The downstairs loo as well as the kitchen.

As the world tilted and spun, she realized that Veck had picked her up. Good plan. She didn't think she could walk—and what a way to air-dry.

In her bedroom, he laid her out on her duvet and covered her with half of it. "I'll be right back."

She wasn't alone long, however, because he moved fast, going downstairs, rifling around in what sounded like the kitchen, coming back quickly. He canned the overhead light as he reentered, and at first she thought it was for her modesty—not that she needed it, considering what he'd done to her at that counter—but then she saw him put something on the bedside table.

His gun.

No, there were two. He'd brought hers as well. From where they'd disarmed at the table before dinner.

How romantic.

The stark reminder of the night before chilled her, but he took care of that, covering her with his hot, hard body.

"Don't think about it," he whispered. "Not now. There'll be plenty of time when we're through."

She touched his face and wished they were on vacation somewhere far, far away from the kind of work they did and the reason they had been brought together.

"You're right," she said. "And I don't want to wait a moment longer."

He nodded, and produced that last foil square he'd kept in his wallet. When he was finished taking care of things, he mounted her again, and as she spread her legs further, she felt the shift in him, in herself: everything slowed down.

As he entered her on a gentle glide, she welcomed him not just with her sex, but her soul, kissing him deeply.

Without words, without hesitations, without any reservations, they moved together, building momentum, gathering intensity. When the end came, it was at the same time, and they held on to each other, she with her nails digging into his back, he with his arms under her and squeezing.

It was the most perfect union. And afterward, even though he had to pull out and did, they lay together in the dark as close as they could get, their bodies forming a critical mass of warmth in the center of the bed.

"Will you let me stay the night?" he asked.

"Yes. Please, yes."

"I'll be right back. You get under the covers."

Good idea. Because as soon as he was up off of her, the cold rushed in and goose-pimpled her all over.

A few minutes later he came back from the bath and joined her. "Did I take your side?"

"Ah . . . no. I'm over here at night."

"Good."

She rolled over and they faced each other, heads on her

pillows, bodies warming up under the weight of the blankets.

He brushed his fingertip down her cheek ... across her jaw ... to her lips. "Thank you ..." he whispered.

God, she couldn't find her breath at this moment. "For what."

There was a pause. "The pizza. It was just the way I like it."

Reilly laughed. "Smart-ass."

"Come here. I need to hold on to you."

She felt the same way. And when there was no distance between them, it was like coming home.

With her head on his chest over his thumping heart, and his arms around her, and her leg thrown over his, she wasn't just comfortable; she was safe.

While he idly smoothed her hair, she closed her eyes. "This is just perfect."

She could hear the smile in his voice: "Which is how I want it to be for you. I want to make everything perfect for you."

As Reilly drifted off to sleep, her last thought was ... she couldn't wait to do it all over again. And not just the sex. This lovely, invaluable quiet was even better than the making love part.

Although that hadn't been half-bad, either.

CHAPTER

34

The following morning, as Veck walked into HQ, his number one priority was not grinning like a motherfucker.

Tough to pull off.

He was an hour late, because he and Reilly had engaged in acts that, had he had any more condoms, would have been termed "foreplay." As it stood, given that they'd been completely surrounded by no amount of latex, what went down was better than the best sex he'd had with anyone else—by about five thousand miles.

And he'd already hit a Walgreens and stocked up on the way into work.

As he strode through the lobby, he nodded to people, keeping it professional even though his inner sixteen-year-old had its swagger on like he'd won the Super Bowl, the World Series, and the Stanley Cup all in one night.

When he got to the top of the stairs, he prayed like hell that Britnae didn't morning-coffee him. That girl had nothing on his Reilly, and it was time to break her of the habit of coming on to him. He didn't need to worry, though. One of the night guys, who worked intake, was at her desk. Veck didn't know the officer all that well, but he was looking different somehow. Kind of like he'd gotten his Hugh Jackman on, in spite of the fact that on the surface he had more in common with Homer Simpson. And Britnae? Eating it up.

Which proved that what was inside was what counted—and who knew a girl like that would figure it out?

Down in Homicide, he sat at his desk and fired up his computer. And then struck by a romantic notion that was as unfamiliar as it was undeniable, he went into his e-mail, got Reilly out of his contacts, and got ready to send her something.

Lot of space to fill. Looooot of space.

In the end, he typed only a few words. And he hit *send* fast, before someone looked over his shoulder.

Afterward, he just sat there and stared at his screen, wondering if he'd done the right thing . . . until he realized he was looking at his in-box, and the report on Sissy Barten was already in from the ME.

Clearly, the guy had burned the midnight oil to do the autopsy.

Veck read through it all and looked at each one of the twenty or so photographs of the body. There was nothing in any of them that he hadn't seen for himself at the quarry, and when he got to the last shot of the ritualistic markings on the torso, he sat back, and tapped his forefinger on his mouse.

If Kroner didn't kill her, who did?

"Mail call."

Veck glanced up at the administrator with his rolling cart of envelopes and boxes. "Thanks, man."

Three pieces. Two interdepartmental. One U.S. mail . . . that happened to have a cancellation stamp from Connecticut. Return address? The federal corrections institution he had avoided for the past ten years.

Looking at the envelope, he felt like he'd gotten shrink-wrapped in broken glass.

His first impulse was to throw the thing out, but the pull of what might be inside made that impossible—and didn't that make him hate the mental power his father had always had over him.

Call me when you get scared enough.

Why Jim Heron's voice was in his head as he tore open the flap was nothing he was going to waste energy on.

Inside was a sheet of paper with three lines handwritten in an elegant, flowing script that was more the image of wealth that his father had sported than the guy's roots in the Midwest.

Dear Thomas: I hope this finds you well. I wish for you to come see me as soon as possible. The prison is allowing me a final visitor and I have chosen you. There are things to be said, son. Call the below. Love, Your Father

"Are you okay?"

Veck glanced up. Reilly was standing next to him, her coat still on, her purse hanging from her shoulder, her hair smooth and freshly shampooed.

If it hadn't been for the night before, he would have yeah-fine'd her and moved along. Instead, he just held the letter up to her.

She sat down in her chair as she read it, and he watched her eyes go left to right, left to right, left to right. Then she went back to the top and read it over again.

"What are you going to do," she asked when she finally looked up.

"It's mental suicide to see him." Veck rubbed his eyes to clear the imprint of those words. "Mental fucking suicide."

"Then don't do it," she said. "You don't need whatever he's going to say to stick in your head for the rest of your life."

"Yeah."

The trouble was, his father wasn't the only one with something on his mind. And sure, it would be great to be the big man and walk away, but he felt the need to look into those eyes one last time—at least to see if there really was anything in common in there. After all, he'd felt crazy all these years, covering up mirrors, double-checking shadows, staying up at night wondering whether it was paranoia or valid perception.

This could be the last chance to find out.

"Veck?" she said.

"Sorry."

"Are you going to go down?"

"I don't know." And that was the truth. Because she did have a point. "Hey, ah . . . the report on Sissy Barten came in. You need to take a look at it."

"Okay." Down with the purse. Off with the coat. "Anything surprising?"

"Everything is surprising about that case." Veck glanced over. "And I want to go to talk to Kroner."

She met him right in the eye. "You'll never get the clearance."

"I wasn't planning on asking for it."

Reilly cursed to herself. This was not how she'd planned for the morning meet-and-greet to go. After Veck had left her house, she'd enjoyed a long shower, shaved everything she had to run a razor over, and gone bag-diving into her new Victoria's Secret collection.

The black-and-red bra-and-panty set she had on reminded her of every single lick, suck, and stroke they'd shared—and put her in mind for more of the same as soon as possible. So she'd planned on coming in here, acting professional, and somehow discreetly tipping her hand to him about what was under her clothes.

Instead, she'd walked into a management issue.

Glaring at her partner, she shook her head. "Going off half-cocked is *not* the answer. And if you intend to follow through with this, you've put me in a hell of a position."

"Sissy Barten is what's important. Not bureaucratic rules. And I've been cleared from any involvement with that night at the motel—remember? You were the one who did it." He sat forward. "Kroner didn't kill her, and you know it. Serial killers do not vary their styles—they get sloppy sometimes, or stop in the middle if they're interrupted. But a guy who has been taking trophies off his victims does not suddenly start scratching symbols into their skin, or bleeding them out. What I need to find out is why that man knew what he did about the quarry and why the hell her earring is in the things from his truck. There's something we aren't seeing in all this."

She couldn't argue with him on any of that. It was his method that was the problem. "Someone else could ask him those questions."

"You?"

"Yes."

In the silence that followed, she thought, Well, at least they'd had the night and the early morning to be on the same page. Too bad it hadn't lasted. He was going to fight her on this, and she was going to get pissed, and then everything they'd shared before and after that damn pizza was going to go out the window—

"Okay," he said. As Reilly recoiled, his mouth tightened. "You don't have to look so surprised. Just take Bails with you this time. Or de la Cruz. The idea of you alone with that man, even though he's in a hospital bed and you're good with a gun, gives me the heebs."

God, she wanted to take his face in her hands and kiss him for being sensible.

Instead she smiled and took out her cell phone. "I'll check in with de la Cruz right now."

As she got the detective on the phone, she signed into her e-mail—and nearly lost focus on the conversation she was having with the man. Veck had left her something in her in-box, and she double-clicked on it just as some kind of update on Kroner's condition came over the line.

There were only three words: *I love you.*

Her head whipped around. But Veck was looking studiously busy with his computer.

"Hello?" de la Cruz said.

"Sorry. What?"

"Why don't you and Bails go together."

"Fine." Her eyes stayed on Veck's face as he stared at the screen in front of him. "I'm ready to head out when he is."

Some other things were said, but damned if she knew what they were. And when she hung up, she was at a loss.

There was no *I think* before the *I love you*. No stupid photo below the words of a cat and dog with computer-generated affection in their eyes. No other way of misinterpreting the statement.

"Just thought you should know," Veck said under his breath.

She wasn't aware of a conscious decision to hit *reply*, or of putting her hands on her keyboard. It just happened—

"What's going on here?"

Reilly cleared the screen with a quick click. Swiveling her chair around, she looked up at Bails. Crap. He was right behind her, looking tense.

"Did de la Cruz call you?" she said smoothly.

The guy glanced over to the back of Veck's head—where he got nothing, obviously. So his eyes returned to her. "Ah ... yeah, he did. Just a second ago."

Cue the *Jeopardy!* theme. And the likelihood that he'd read what had been on that e-mail.

"And when will you be ready to go over to the hospital with me?" she prompted.

"Ah ... I've got a suspect coming in for questioning right now. So after that?"

"Fine. I'll be here."

As she stared up at him, she met his narrowed gaze fully and without apology. She didn't know the guy well at all, but it was pretty clear he wasn't happy. And this was why you didn't date people from work. Possessive best buddies were bad enough if all you had to do was deal with them on the occasional poker night and during major sporting events. Seeing them nine-to-five?

Then again, as soon as Veck's probationary period was over, she was going to go back to IA.

The idea eased her. Much better all around—

Oh, *crap*. She was going to have to disclose this relationship, wasn't she. And once she did, they were going to take her off monitoring him—which was absolutely appropriate.

Well . . . it looked as if she wasn't going to have to wait for a month before she went back to her department.

"Hey, DelVecchio. Pick up your phone," someone called out.

Funny, she hadn't heard it ringing. Neither had he or Bails, apparently.

As Veck yeah'd and uh-huh'd his way through some kind of conversation, she could feel Bails hovering and wanted to shoo him off like a fly. Fortunately, the same woman who'd called out for Veck to get with the receiver came over and told the other detective that his suspect was down at intake.

"I'll stop by when I'm through," Bails said. After she nodded, he clapped Veck on the shoulder and walked off.

Veck hung up. "That was de la Cruz. He wants me downtown on a shooting that happened late last night. He needs an extra hand—and I think he wants to make sure I don't get any ideas about going to the hospital with you."

Made sense. "We're not heading off for a while, though."

"This is going to be a long day. We've got to cover an entire apartment complex."

Veck stood up, put on his coat, and patted his various pockets, no doubt checking for badge, gun, wallet, keys, cigarettes.

"You need to stop smoking," she blurted out.

As he froze, she thought, Damn it, way to sound like a girlfriend; those three words he'd sent her over e-mail didn't give her those rights. Step in that direction? Yeah. But not a door to drive a bus through.

The trouble was, she cared about him enough not to be comfortable with sitting by and watching him kill himself—

Veck took out his open pack of Marlboros . . . and crushed them in his hand.

"You're right." He tossed the wad into the wastepaper

basket under his desk. "If I get cranky for the next couple of days, I apologize."

Reilly couldn't stop the smile on her face. And in a whisper only he could hear, she said, "I'll think of some ways to distract you."

As she slowly uncrossed and recrossed her legs, his eyes flared. Which told her she might as well have revealed her Secrets, so to speak.

"I'm going to hold you to that." He winked like a bad boy who knew what to do with her body. Natch. "Stick with Bails—and call me when you're through, okay?"

"Deal."

She turned back to the desk she was using, but watched him walk out the door from the corner of her eye.

Dear Lord, that man looked good from behind....

CHAPTER
35

On some level, it felt great to be out doing his job, Veck thought a few hours later.

Okay, it was *not* great that some sorry bastard had gotten shot in the face, or that none of the neighbors wanted to say a word about what they might have seen, or that he and de la Cruz were likely wearing out the soles of their shoes for nothing. But this was normal-course-of-hard-business shit. This was not about his father or freaky, no-footprint-leaving, midnight-stalker shit.

The victim in question had been popped while parked and sitting in the driver's seat of his SUV at this twelve-building apartment complex known for its lively, illegal cash-and-carry commerce. Discovered this morning by the street-sweeping crews, there had been no drugs or cash on the body or in the vehicle, but they had found a list of names and dollar amounts on a crumpled piece of paper in the guy's coat, crack residue in a series of plastic bags in the back, and a total of five guns in the car.

None of which he'd evidently been able to get to fast enough.

Unless you assumed that the ones that had been easy-access had been lifted along with the rest of the valuables.

By noon, he and de la Cruz were well into their rounds of the buildings, knocking on doors, trying to get people who were suspicious of cops and rightfully scared of retaliation to talk.

As he went from door to door, he kept recalling the victim's frozen grimace as the kid sat slumped behind that wheel, the seat belt across his chest all that kept him upright, the facial features that had once identified him to his mother and his family and his buddies ruined to the point of putting him into dental records territory.

Thinking back to Kroner in those woods, Veck remembered his own urge to kill. The idea that he was going to take out an evildoer had made it seem more justifiable—at least, to one part of him—but did that really matter?

Hell, the motherfucker who'd shot this victim in the SUV no doubt had his or her reasons, however twisted they might have appeared on an objective moral scale. Except a murderous act was a murderous act, no matter the target's disposition.

Too bad none of that mattered to the dark side of him: That element didn't give a crap whether Kroner was a saint or a sinner—the killing, the taking had been the thing. The object of the wrath? Important only insofar as it was a target to hit.

Which was undoubtedly how his father felt about other people.

And what a happy thought that was.

As the sun started sinking, and the shadows grew longer, the warmth of the afternoon dwindled and the complex seemed even grungier. He and de la Cruz had split up and were focusing on the buildings around where the body was found, but given that there were six stories of apartments, they'd be lucky to wrap this part up by five o'clock.

Turning away from yet another no-answer, Veck hit the bald concrete stairs, descending to the lobby. The front doors were supposed to be locked, of course, but they'd been kicked open so many times, it was a wonder they shut at all.

Rubbing his face and wishing he had a cigarette, he turned to the east and headed for the last apartment building that was his responsibility. He was just at the door when his phone went off. The text from Reilly said that she was heading over to the hospital now with Bails.

Well, at least that gave him some more time to tie things up on this case.

And afterward, maybe take a little trip down to Connecticut, an inner voice suggested. *To see your father.*

He actually looked behind himself to see if someone was talking to him. But there was nothing except thin air and weak sunlight on his tail.

As well as the conviction that he was probably going to do just that. Soon.

With a curse, he turned back to the entrance, and as he pivoted, he happened to glance down at the cracked cement of the sidewalk.

What he saw stopped him dead.

He glanced over his shoulder again. The sun was setting right behind him, the single sun—as in one light source. And there was no huge reflective surface to throw a second illumination, no car with a lot of chrome, no stage light, for God's sake.

He looked back down at his feet. There were two shadows thrown by his body. Two separate and distinct shadows, one leading north, one leading south.

Graphic evidence of what he'd always felt—of two halves of him, cleaving apart, drawing him in opposite directions.

Look down at your feet, Thomas DelVecchio . . . and then you call me when you get scared enough.

As Jim Heron's voice shot through his mind, he thought of Reilly. He'd been confident of protecting her from any stalker, so fucking sure he could be what she needed. But all that cock and balls did not apply to this shit on the ground. He didn't understand it himself; how the hell could he fight it for her?

And Reilly *was* on the line. Otherwise she wouldn't

have spent the night before sitting up in a chair with a gun in her hand.

I'm the only one who can help you.

God knew if Heron had wanted to hurt either of them or get aggressive he could have. Instead, all the guy had done was point them in the right direction at the quarry . . . and disappear.

Decision made, Veck all but lunged for his phone. He'd saved Heron's number in his contacts for the incident report on the guy, and as he dialed it now, he prayed that the man who left no footprints would answer . . . and tell him about what was at his own feet.

The sound of a cell phone ringing out loud behind him ripped him around.

Jim Heron was standing three feet away from him, as if the guy had been there all along—which he had been, hadn't he.

Veck narrowed his eyes and took a careful visual picture of the man. The bastard seemed solid enough in his leather jacket and his fatigues. And as he exhaled smoke from his Marlboro, the shit floated over and tickled Veck's craving button.

But he wasn't real, was he.

Heart pounding in his chest, Veck hit *end* on his phone and the sound coming from Jim's pocket ceased.

"Time's growing short," the guy said.

And this made Veck think about his father: That note in the mail. That hourglass that was draining as they got closer and closer to the execution.

Which was coming so very soon, wasn't it.

This was it, he thought. Everything, his whole existence, had led up to this . . . whatever the fuck it was.

As Veck met the man's eyes, he felt as though the movie of his life had been out of focus without his even being aware the shit was blurry. The cameraman, however, had finally woken up and gotten with the program with his equipment . . . and it was a new fucking world.

Especially given the fact that the fading light of day was

coming from behind Jim Heron . . . and there was nothing at the guy's feet. No shadow at all.

"What the fuck are you," Veck demanded.

"I'm here to save your ass, that's what I am." The guy took a drag on his cig and exhaled slowly. "You ready to talk to me now?"

Veck stared at his own pair of outlines, both in the shape of his body. "Yeah. I am."

Reilly was behind the wheel of her unmarked as she and Bails went over to the St. Francis Hospital complex. Beside her, the detective was quiet in her passenger seat as she navigated heavy traffic and got stuck at red lights and then hit a detour that took her in the opposite direction.

"Any more of this and I'm going to start thinking someone doesn't want us talking to Kroner," she muttered.

Bails didn't even glance over. "Yeah."

More silence. To the point where she was going to ask him to just get it all out: The last thing they needed was this kind of tension when they were in front of that killer.

Bails spoke before she did, however. "I'm sorry I'm not talking. I just don't know what to do."

"About what?" When it was safe to take her eyes off the road, she spared him a quick look. The guy was drumming his fingers against the door, and staring out of the windshield as if he were searching for answers in the glass.

"I know you saw my e-mail," she said after a moment.

"If only that was the big problem." As she shot another glance across at him, he shrugged. "You know Veck and I are tight, yeah?"

"Yes."

"And you know that I've always been behind him one hundred percent. To the death. That boy is mine."

As he pounded over his heart, she said, "Okay."

"So, yeah, I saw the e-mail he sent you. I didn't mean to, but it was up on your screen when I came over to you two." He looked over. "I wasn't eavesdropping. It was just there."

Damn it.

That was all she had. *Damn* it.

"So now . . ." His fingers stilled and he shook his head. "I don't know what to do."

"No offense, but why is it your business. And I don't mean to be a bitch, but—"

"I know things about him that you don't, and I think he's done something illegal. And given that you're with him, I don't know who in Internal Affairs to go to. Good enough for you?"

As Reilly exhaled like she'd been punched in the gut, she wanted to pull over. Good thing they were finally at the hospital and she could park in the open lot in front of the emergency room.

When she turned off the engine, she faced him. "What are you talking about?"

Bails put a hand on the dashboard and ran his palm back and forth. Then he wiped the thin layer of dust he'd lifted on his thigh. "Look, I'm a cop because I want to protect people, and because I believe in the system. I don't think a civilized society can exist without the police and courts and jails. There are people out there who just do not belong in the general population. Period."

"You haven't said one word about Veck. FYI."

"Has he told you he has a record?"

As a cold shaft shot down her spine, she forced herself to remain composed. "No."

"I didn't think so."

This guy was full of crap, she thought. "Listen, I'm sorry to doubt your sources, but there's nothing in his personnel file—and you can't lie about that stuff. All HR has to do—and did—is run his name."

"Not when it's juvie shit."

Reilly blinked. Hard. "I beg your pardon."

"He has a juvenile record. A serious one."

"How do you know this?"

"I saw the thing. With my own two eyes." Bails let his

head fall back against the rest. "I first met Veck at the police academy. He was a loner who did everything right—I was the class clown. We just . . . clicked. After we got out, we stayed in touch even though we were assigned to different precincts down in Manhattan, and then I later moved up here. For all the years I've known him, he's always been tight in the head. In control. Tough, but fair. Matter of fact, he's one of the best cops I've ever met, and I recruited him to come to Caldie because I wanted to work with him." Bails cursed. "In all the time I've known him, I've never once thought he wasn't fit for the job because of that shit with his dad . . . until now. It started with him nailing that paparazzi guy. Then the Kroner thing out in the woods. It's like his wrapper's coming off—but I wasn't going to say anything, I really wasn't, until—"

"Wait. Stop." Reilly cleared her throat, thinking a dose of protocol might calm the headache she felt between her eyes. "In the interest of propriety, you should get in touch with my supervisor immediately if you have anything to say pertaining to Detective DelVecchio. You were right before you started . . . you shouldn't tell me these things. I shouldn't . . . be in the position I'm in now with respect to him. Matter of fact, I have an appointment with her when you and I get back from this interview so that I can properly disclose the relationship to my department."

Bails rubbed his eyes and nodded. "I'll do that . . . but I also think you need to know, too. Because if anything happened to you, I would never forgive myself."

At that, Reilly stiffened. "Why would you be worried about my safety?"

He raked his hand through his hair. "See, I helped him move into his house, you know, when he got up here. He had all these old boxes that needed to go into the attic. I was carrying one of them and the bottom fell out. Fucking papers went everywhere and I started to pick them up—and there it was. His juvi record from back in the mid-nineties."

"What did it say," she managed through a closed throat.

"He had every marker for psychotic, antisocial behavior there is." Bails frowned. "You know what I'm talking about, so I'm not going to list the shit he did."

Animal torture? Preoccupation with fire? Bed-wetting?

"All of it," Bails said, as if he were reading her mind.

"But he's never done anything as an adult," she countered—except it was less a statement than a question.

"Not that we know of. And, see, that's what's been worrying me. Psychopaths are really good at pretending to be normal. On the surface, they fit in—because they make it their business to. What if this stretch of relative peace and quiet up until now . . . is all he can manage? The end of the acting period and the time when the real him makes an appearance? You can't deny that his wheels have been coming off—hell, you wouldn't be his partner if things were going right." The conflict on Bails's face was plain to see. "Or worse . . . what if we just don't know what he's really been doing? I tell you, I couldn't sleep last night—I was trying to reconcile what I believe him to be . . . with what he might *actually* be. If that makes sense."

Reilly heard Veck's voice in her head: *I want to make everything perfect for you.*

And he had. He'd said the right things. Done the right things.

Thrown his cigarettes out for her—or at least had done so in front of her.

She'd fallen in love with him in four days.

Fortuitous accident? Or by design?

Except where would it get him? He'd been the one to argue for suspension . . . unless that had been a deliberate stance? She'd certainly taken care of championing his case and his reputation—which had more credibility than his doing so, didn't it.

Bails's voice drifted over. "You can't trust him. I'm learning that now."

"Just because he didn't tell you about what happened when he was younger?" she heard herself say. "And besides, keeping a sealed record to yourself isn't illegal."

"I think he planted evidence. Sissy Barten's earring, specifically. To make it look as if Kroner was responsible."

She didn't bother to hide her recoil. "*What?* And how?"

"He went up to her bedroom, didn't he. The day you two went over to the Barten house. He told me you were downstairs when he did. And he was in the evidence room yesterday morning—I talked to Joey, one of the crime scene investigators. He said Veck had been by—and he could have planted it then."

"But he said he'd found the earring in and among the evidence."

Bails rubbed his eyes again. "I checked the preliminary log of the items from the truck, the list that was made right after we got the vehicle. There wasn't any notation of an earring shaped like a dove. That's what I was double-checking right before I came and saw you two this morning."

So that was why he'd looked poleaxed.

She shook her head. "But what does he have to gain?" Unless . . .

Oh, God . . . what if he'd killed her. What if Kroner had somehow seen something in the course of his own evil work at that quarry?

"You've read the report on Sissy's body, right?" Bails said.

"Of course." She'd spent all morning on it—and the conclusion that she'd first come to when the body had been found was now inescapable: None of the victim's wounds matched those of Kroner's other killings—and that kind of change didn't happen, typically. Usually, the method and the fixations didn't alter.

"So you've got to know she wasn't defiled by Kroner. And maybe, after you add it all up . . . maybe Veck did it."

Good heavens, she couldn't breathe. Sure as if there were hands around her throat. "But . . . why?"

Although that was a dumb question to ask, she feared.

"How much do you know about Veck's father?" the detective said. "His murders?"

"Just what I studied in college."

Bails refocused out the front window. "Did you know that his father's first victim was bled out by the neck and wrists—having been hung by her feet. She'd also been marked up just like the Barten girl is. On the stomach."

Reilly reached for the handle and shoved open her door. It wasn't just for the fresh air. It was because she was seriously going to throw up.

"I'm so sorry," Bails said, his voice raw.

"So am I," she croaked, although that didn't begin to cover it.

As she stared at the pavement, she knew she had been snowed. Big-time. And of course Veck had made the effort. She was his advocate at headquarters, the one who was supposed to vet him carefully and yea or nay him to keep on the force: He'd wanted to keep working, and she'd been in the position to make that possible.

"Thank God for you," she choked out. Too bad she couldn't look at Bails—she was just too mortified that she'd been played so well. "Thank God you said something."

"So how 'bout you do some talking first."

As Veck spoke in a low voice, he kept an eye lock on Heron. The two of them had ducked around the corner of the apartment building and were standing in the shadows next to a scrubby bush.

Jim's stare was dead on and his voice was church-bell deep. "You know everything. All the answers you want?" The man put his forefinger on Veck's chest, right over his heart. "It's inside you."

Veck wanted to hit that one back with a racket full of *Whatever, a-hole*. But he couldn't.

"My father wants to see me," was his reply, instead.

Heron nodded and took out his cigs. When he tilted the pack forward, it was all Veck could do not to take one: "Nah, I quit."

"Smart." Heron lit up. "Here's the way it works. You're going to find yourself at a crossroads. There's going to be a decision you'll have to make, an action to be taken or not, a choice between polar opposites. All of what you are and what you have been and what you could be will be measured on your decision. And the consequences? They don't just affect you. They affect everyone. This is not simply life and death—it's about eternity. Yours. Others'. Do not underestimate how far this goes."

As the man spoke, Veck felt the two sides of him begin to split. One half was utterly repulsed. The other—

Veck frowned. Blinked a couple of times. Looked away and looked back. As God was his witness, he could have sworn that there was a shimmering glow over both of Heron's shoulders and around his head.

And the bizarre illusion gave this whole nightmare credibility. As did the fact that the moment he'd wanted the guy, the fucker had been right behind him ... and then there was the no-prints issue down at the quarry ... and the light show that had happened in the stairwell at the Barten house.

Veck put his palm up to his sternum and rubbed hard at the dark shadow in his chest. "I never volunteered for this."

"I know how that feels," Heron muttered. "In your case, you were born to it."

"Tell me what I am."

"You already know."

"Say it."

Heron exhaled slowly, the smoke rising up through that golden glow. "Evil. You are evil incarnate—or, at least, half of you is. And in the very near future, maybe tonight, maybe tomorrow, you're going to be asked to pick one side over the other." The guy pointed to himself with his smoking hand. "I'm here to try to get you to choose wisely."

"And if I don't."

"You lose."

"Right then and there?"

The man nodded slowly, his eyes narrowing. "And I've seen where you end up after that. It's not pretty."

"What are you."

Heron's expression didn't change. Neither did his stance. And he didn't even stop with the smoking. But one minute he was a man; the next ...

"Jesus ... Christ ..." Veck breathed.

"Not even close." He stubbed out his cig on the sole of his combat boot. "But I am what I am."

And that would be . . . an angel, evidently: In the weak and fading light of day, a refracted, gleaming show had appeared over his shoulders in the shape of giant wings, making him both magnificent and ethereal.

"I've been sent to help you." The man . . . angel . . . shit, whatever . . . refocused on Veck. "So when you go to see your father, I want to be with you."

"You already have been with me. Haven't you."

"Yup." The guy cleared his throat. "But not when you were . . . you know."

Veck's brows popped. "Oh, yeah. Good . . ."

Annnnnd cue them both looking anywhere and everywhere else.

Veck thought about that night with Kroner. "What if the crossroads has already happened?"

"The Kroner thing? Wasn't legal."

"Well, yeah, murder ain't."

"No, not like that. I'm not the only one who wants you, but the other side jumped the gun on that setup."

"Other side?"

"Like I said, it's not just me in this game. And trust me, the enemy is a real bitch—I'm sure you'll meet her soon, if you haven't already."

Oh, great, more good news, Veck thought.

And then he blurted, "I was going to kill him. Kroner, I mean." Damn, it felt good to get that out.

"You mean, *part* of you was going to. Let's get accurate— you didn't do the damage, and you also called nine-one-one, and if you hadn't done that, he'd have bled out right at your feet."

"So what attacked him?"

"You think you're surprised to be talking to an angel? You don't want to know what else is out there." Jim waved his hand dismissively. "But that's not what you and I need to worry about. We're going to go see your father. Together. ASAP."

Veck thought about that sensation of destiny's arrival, the one where he felt like his life had slipped into culmination mode. Not even remotely a hypothetical anymore, was it.

"Is that the crossroads?"

"Maybe. Maybe not."

Abruptly, Jim lowered his lids and tilted his head down. As he stared out of vicious slits, he was downright deadly—and precisely the kind of thing Veck was glad he had at his back: He had a feeling he was going to need another good fighter around if he was going to battle this side of himself.

And that was what this was. A fight to the death.

"We'll find out," the angel vowed, "when we get there."

Everything happened for a reason, Reilly thought as she and Bails walked away from Kroner's room a half an hour later.

Kroner's condition had degraded, almost as if his injuries were a sea that he had briefly surfaced out of, only to be pulled back underneath: He hadn't been able to focus, had mumbled replies that made no sense, and not long after they had arrived, she and Bails had given up.

"What's with the suffering thing?" Bails muttered as he held the door of the elevator open for her.

Reilly shook her head as they began the descent. "I don't know."

It had been the same as before. *He has to know she suffered. . . . He has to know she suffered. . . .*

She hadn't a clue on that one— and no idea what the connection was between Kroner and Veck. Hell, at this point, she didn't feel like she could trust her instincts when it came to her own name. Speculating on this mess? Total nonstarter.

As they stepped out into the lobby and headed for the revolving door to the parking lot, Bails checked his watch. "You want a drink? I'm due to go make my statement in a little over an hour, and I need one beforehand."

Yeah, because when one detective has information like he did on another, it wasn't the sort of thing that people waited around for. He'd called HQ right after they'd spoken, and within a minute and a half, the sergeant himself had set up a meeting of high-ups, even though it was going to happen well after business hours.

No wonder Bails wanted a beer.

"Thanks," she murmured, "but like I said, I've got my rendezvous with my supervisor right now."

So didn't that make them two peas in a pod.

Together, she and Bails walked into the rows of cars, got into her unmarked, and did up their seat belts. They were both silent during the trip back to headquarters. Not a lot to talk about, and Bails looked as betrayed and sick as she felt.

They parted ways on a hug, and as he headed to his own car, she watched him walk off. Veck had put them in the same boat, and that meant someone who had been a stranger was now a kind of friend—

As her phone went off in her purse, she knew who it was before she took the thing out.

Veck.

Now, this was what they made voice mail for, she thought.

Except he would probably come looking for her, and that was the last thing she wanted. Face-to-face was to be avoided at all costs.

She hit *send*. "Hello."

There was a whirring sound in the background, as if he were in a car. "Reilly ... what's wrong?"

In a dispassionate way, as if she were observing him from the far side of a two-way mirror, she thought, yup, this was how he'd seduced her: The emotion he was projecting in that deep voice was the perfect combination of concern and sharp-edged protection.

"I'm fine. Just out from seeing Kroner—we didn't get anything new." Not from the guy, of course. Bails was a different story.

"You don't sound right."

Which meant any aspirations she might have had for

becoming a psychopath were out the window. What a shame.

In fact, the idea that she couldn't hide things was a relief. She didn't want to be like Veck. Ever.

"Reilly . . . talk to me."

"I've been thinking a lot about my job today," she said. "It is not appropriate for us to have taken our relationship where it's gone. I've compromised the integrity of the force, my position, and myself. I'm going in to see my supervisor right now and I'm resigning from your case. There will probably be some reprimands on my side, but I'll deal with that—"

"Wait, what? Why are you—"

"—and I don't think we should see each other again."

There was a pause. And then he said, "Just like that."

Now he sounded cold, and that was what she wanted—the true him, the real him. Even though it just made her realize anew how stupid she'd been.

"It's for the best," she concluded.

When he didn't say anything further, she began to get rattled, because she had to wonder exactly what he was capable of. No doubt he'd been the one stalking her the night before last . . . But whatever, this conversation was over, and once she made her disclosures to her boss, and Bails went in and did his duty, Veck was going to have so many other problems, he was going to be too busy looking for a defense attorney to waste time on retaliation. Or at least, she hoped that was going to be the case.

Hell, even better, he'd been in custody.

"I have to go," she told him.

There was another pause, and then his voice was cool as a cucumber. "I won't bother you again."

"I'd appreciate that. Good-bye."

She didn't wait for him to respond. Wasn't interested in getting pulled into a long, drawn-out conversation where he tried to manipulate her again, or worse, dropped that mask entirely and threatened her.

Her hand was shaking so badly, it took her two tries to get the phone back in her purse.

Steadying herself against her car, she looked up at the butt-ugly back end of headquarters, and didn't feel like she had the strength to go in there and face her boss.

But she did what she had to do ... because that was how she was raised.

CHAPTER
37

As Veck hung up his cell phone, he stared at the screen and found it hard to believe that conversation with Reilly had just happened.

"What."

He glanced over at Heron. The guy, angel—who the fuck cared—was behind the wheel of the truck they were all in, and his friend, comrade in wings—Christ, how could this be real?—was in the backseat of the dual cab, taking up more than half the space.

The three of them were heading for the Northern Correctional Institution in Somers, Connecticut.

"Nothing," Veck said smoothly.

"Bullshit," came from the rear.

First word the other man had spoken. Which meant that and the fact that he was apparently breathing were the only clues he was alive.

Jim shifted his stare over. "There are no coincidences. When we get this close to the end, everything matters."

"It was ..." My girl? Ex-girl? Internal Affairs officer? "Reilly."

"What did she say?"

"She doesn't want to see me. Ever again."

The words were spoken factually, in a calm, deep voice—so at least his cock and balls were still with him. In the center of his chest, however, there was a big black hole of agony, as if he were a cartoon that had had a cannonball shot through him.

"Why? She give a reason?"

"Mind if I borrow a cigarette?" When Jim extended the pack, Veck took two, thinking that now was a perfect time to toss that I-quit thing right out the window.

"And the reason is?"

"Because I either smoke something right now or punch out the glass next to me."

"Good call on the Marlboro," came from the back. "We're going seventy and it's fucking cold outside."

Veck took the lighter that was offered, flicked the Bic, and cracked the window. As he inhaled, he thought it was a damn shame there were so many carcinogens in the bastards, because sure as shit, this made him feel a little better.

Wasn't going to last, though.

Unlike the pain behind his ribs. He had a feeling that was going to hang around for a looooong time. Like a perpetual heart attack.

Except, man, he should have known this was coming. The woman went into Internal Affairs because she liked things that were done right, done well. Banging him? So not on that list. Falling in love with him? Don't be f-in' ridiculous.

"Reason?" Jim barked.

"Conflict of interest."

"But why now? She had to know what was doing the whole time."

"I don't know. Don't care, either."

The good news was that they couldn't fire him from his job just because she had woken up and smelled the crappies, so to speak. They were two consenting adults, and yeah, it looked bad, but she was doing the right thing and it was game over.

Inevitably, he was going to be called in for questions of the human resources variety, and he was going to be a stand-up guy and say it was all his idea. Which it had been: He'd been the pursuer, as well as the fathead with the I-love-yous.

Dumb-ass. What a fucking dumb-ass he was . . .

Not much else was said during the rest of the trip, which was fine with him. The images in his head of Reilly and him together made him not trust his voice—and not because it was going to go sad-sack cracking on him. He was liable to bite anyone's head off at the moment.

When they got to within a mile of the prison, Jim pulled over in the town just before the institution and they traded places.

Now behind the wheel, Veck threw the truck in drive and assumed the role of what he was: a cop. "So no one is going to see you?"

Although it wasn't as if he didn't think the guy could go invisible. Heron had dogged him for days with nothing more than a whisper of instinct to tip that shit off.

"That's right."

"Just as long as—" Veck stopped talking as he looked over at the suddenly empty seat next to him. Quick check in the rearview mirror and the back was also completely filled by absolutely no big, tough guy.

"You SOBs ever think about robbing banks," he said dryly.

"Don't need the cash," Jim said from the ether beside him.

"Don't need the hassle," came from the back.

Veck rubbed his face, thinking it would probably be better to feel like he'd gone crazy as he carried on conversations with thin air. Trouble was, he'd been dueling and dealing with this alternate reality all his life. The idea that it was an actuality and not a function of madness was nuts, but also made him feel sane.

Although . . . this was assuming he wasn't *Beautiful Mind*-ing it entirely.

Then again, it was homicidal impulses and not schizophrenia that ran in his family, so he likely hadn't lost his marbles, after all.

What. A. Relief.

Before leaving Caldwell, Veck had called ahead to the prison—not the number his father had provided, but the general line—and identified himself. It was not even close to visiting hours, but courtesies were extended in light of his professional occupation—as well as the fact that his father was going to be in a grave in about forty-eight hours. There was also undoubtedly the curiosity factor, something which Veck had no delusions about: in no time, this death-bed visit was going to show up everywhere . . . on the Internet, the television, the radio.

It was probably going to hit the Net before he even left to go back to New York State.

And what do you know.

As he zeroed in on the drive that ran up to the penitentiary's walls, there was a small army gathered on both sides of the surrounding field.

His father's fans.

There were at least a hundred of them, even though it was eight at night, dark as the inside of a hat, and chilly. They were prepared, however, with flashlights and candles and placards protesting the execution—and the moment they saw his vehicle, they rushed forward to the very edges of the asphalt, shouting, roaring, the din pressing into the truck even though they didn't get close.

Clearly they'd had training on civil disobedience, in spite of their Sex Pistols style of dress and the rabid way they carried on: No one blocked or touched his vehicle, and he slowed down only to get a look at them.

Big mistake.

One of the men leaned in to Veck's window, and obviously recognized him: As the guy hollered and pointed, the god-awful rapture that came over his features made Veck want to put down the glass between them and smack some sense into the sonofabitch.

But what a waste of knuckles that would be. Fidiot had the anarchy symbol scratched into his forehead. Try reasoning with that.

"It's him! It's him!"

The crowd tightened up and rushed at the truck.

"What is wrong with these people," Veck muttered as he gunned it, prepared to turn them into hood ornaments if he had to.

"This is what she does," Jim said out of the thin air.

"Who's 'she'?"

"Exactly what we're going to try to get out of you."

No time to follow up on that one. He turned in to the lane that law enforcement used and stopped at the gate-house. Looking up at the guard, he put the window down and flashed his badge and creds. "DelVecchio, Thomas—Jr."

In the background, the crowd was chanting his name—or his father's. Both of theirs, actually, and how frickin' efficient.

The guard's eyes dropped to the ID, and came back to Veck's face. There was a measure of distrust in that stare, but he'd no doubt been holding the hard line against the loonies for the last week.

Still, the guy hit the gate switch and the iron bars rolled back. "Stop as soon as you are clear. I'm going to have to search your vehicle, Detective."

"No problem." And good call not to do it on the outside. God only knew how long that crowd would stay put.

Veck followed protocol, idling into the compound and putting the brakes on the moment his rear bumper was on the far side of this first barrier. When he got out, he took Heron's pack of Marlboros with him and put them to good use, lighting up while the gates reclosed and the officer crawled around with a flashlight.

As he smoked, he knew the angels were not far. He could sense them hovering, and he was glad they had his back—especially as he stared through the bars at the crowd of crazies. The energy in those nutjobs was the kind of thing that made him grateful for what separated the bunch of them.

"You're free to proceed, Detective," the officer said, his attitude dialed down. "Go up to your first left and park by the door for security purposes. A guard is waiting for you."

"Thanks, man."

"No smoking indoors. So you may want to take your time."

"Good tip."

Back in the truck. Pausing at the second gate. And then they were in the facility proper.

Maximum-security prisons were nothing like they were in the movies. No age-washed stone walls with gargoyles eyeballing your ass. No steeped-in-history, Al Capone–laid-his-head-*here*. No guided tours.

This was the very modern business of keeping people like his father isolated and out of the gen pop. This was about bright xenon lights at night, and video cameras, and computerized monitoring. There were still guards with guns, and enough barbed wire to run a circle around the whole city of Caldwell, but procedure was executed with pass cards and computers and automated cell doors.

He'd been in a number of these places, but never this one: As soon as his father had been sentenced, a letter had been hand-delivered to the frat house Veck was living in at college as a senior. He should never have opened the damn envelope, but he'd never suspected his father could get someone to sneak the note out of jail. Retrospect? How fucking naive.

Then again, at least it had told him where *not* to go.

So yeah, there was a good goddamn reason Veck didn't work in Connecticut, and had gone into the police force instead of the Federal Bureau of Investigation. No out-of-state for him, thank you very much.

And yet here he was.

As promised, the moment he got out of the truck, a re-inforced door opened wide and a guard met him and led him into the sparkling clean, well-lit environs. As an officer of the law, normally, he would have been allowed to keep his badge and cell phone and weapon, provided he didn't go into the cell blocks, but he wasn't here in an official capacity, and that meant everything got checked in.

While he was turning his phone over, he saw that the

thing had a couple of messages. Clearly, the trip down had taken them into some no-service areas, because he hadn't heard it ring, but he wasn't going to stop and listen now. Whatever it was would be waiting for him when he got out of here. Besides, he had a feeling what they were about. He was no doubt going to get assigned another IA person—oh, joy. And Bails was probably checking in on him. The guy did that, especially if he'd texted and Veck didn't reply.

After he'd signed in and given all his stuff to the guard, he was taken down a series of halls with not much more than footfalls between him and the prison officer. But what the hell were they going to talk about?

Here to say good-bye to your dad? Oh, cool . . .

Yeah, first time I've seen him in years, last time in this life . . .

Have fun with it, then.

Thanks, man.

Yup. Big hurry to have that one.

About a hundred yards through the prison's maze later, Veck was shown into a visiting area that was the size of a small cafeteria, and made up like one as well, with long tables that had seats on both sides. The thing was lit like a jeweler's display case, with great panels of fluorescents screwed into the ceiling, and the floor was a speckled brown, the kind of thing that hid dirt well, but was kept buffed and shined anyway. There were no windows, no plants, and only one mural of what appeared to be the Connecticut statehouse.

Although the bank of four vending machines did add a little color.

"He's being brought over now," the guard said. "We've put you both in the contact visiting area as a courtesy, but I'm going to have to ask you to keep seated with both hands on the table at all times, Detective."

"No problem. You care where I park it?"

"Nope. And good luck."

The guy backed up and stood against the door they'd come through, crossing his arms and focusing on the bare wall across the way like he had a lot of experience with the pose.

Veck sat at the table in front of him and linked his hands together on the smooth surface.

Closing his eyes, he felt the presence of the two angels. They were to the left and the right of him, standing much as the guard did, still and watchful—

The door at the far end of the room opened without a sound . . . and then there was shuffling.

His father came through the jamb with a smile on his handsome face, and shackles on his wrists and ankles. In spite of the fact that he was in a baggy orange jumpsuit, he was elegant, with his dark gray hair brushed back off his forehead and his ambassador attitude out like a royal flag.

But Veck didn't give a shit about those kinds of appearances; he looked to the floor. His father threw a shadow, all right, a single shadow that pooled around his feet like black ink. The fact that it was darker than any other on the linoleum seemed logical in the new paradigm.

"Hello, son."

The voice was as deep and grave as Veck's own, and as he lifted his eyes to his father's, it was like looking in the mirror—twenty or thirty years from now.

"No greeting for me?" the elder DelVecchio said as he came forward with tight little steps, the guard who brought him in riding his ass so close he might as well have had another jumpsuit on his back.

"I'm here, aren't I."

"You know, it's a shame we have to be chaperoned." His father sat down across from him and put his hands on the table . . . in the precise position Veck's were. "But we can keep our voices low." The planes and angles of that face eased into an expression of warmth—that Veck didn't buy for a second. "I'm touched that you're here."

"Don't be."

"Well, I am, son." The saddened shake of the head was so appropriate Veck wanted to roll his eyes. "God, look at you . . . you're so much older. And tired. Work been tough? I've heard you're in law enforcement."

"Yeah."

"In Caldwell."

"Yeah."

His father eased forward. "I'm allowed to read the newspapers and I've heard you have a little fiend at work up there. But you caught him, didn't you. In the woods." Gone was the benevolent-father lie. In its place? An intensity in the man's expression that made Veck want to stand up and walk out. "Didn't you. Son."

If eyes were the windows of the soul, then Veck found himself staring into an abyss . . . and in the same way that leaning over a ledge and looking down created a vertigo-induced increase in gravity, he felt a pull.

"What a hero you are, son. I'm so proud of you."

The words warped in Veck's ears, his senses getting muddled, so it was as if he both heard them and felt them as a brush over his skin.

You should have killed him when you had the chance, though.

Veck frowned as he realized his father had spoken without moving his lips.

Shaking his head, Veck broke the connection. "This is bullshit."

"Because I complimented you? I meant it. As God is my witness."

"God has nothing to do with you."

"Oh, no?" His father quickly reached into his jumpsuit and pulled out a cross before the guards could get a hard-on about the hands rules. "I can assure you He does. I'm very much a religious man."

"Because it looks better for you, no doubt."

"I have nothing to prove to anybody." Now those eyes glinted. "I let my actions speak for me—have you been to your mother's grave lately?"

"Don't you dare go there."

His father laughed a little and lifted his hands, showing

off the steel cuffs. "Of course, I can't. I'm not allowed out—this is a prison, not the Four Seasons. And even though I've been falsely accused, falsely tried, and falsely sentenced to death, I'm held just as everyone else is."

"There is nothing false about where you're at."

"You actually think I murdered all those women."

"Let's be more accurate—I think you *butchered* all those women. And others."

More with the head shaking. "Son, I don't know where you get your ideas. For example . . ." His father's stare lifted to the ceiling, as if he were faced with a complex math equation. "Did you read about the death of Suzie Bussman?"

"I'm not one of your fans. So no, I don't keep up with your work."

"She was not the first girl they accused me of, but the first one they thought I killed. She was found in a drainage ditch. Her throat had been cut, her wrists had been slashed, and her stomach had been inscribed with all of these symbols."

As his father fell silent, he leveled his chin and stared at Veck.

Sissy Barten. Found in a cave. Her throat cut, her wrists slashed, her stomach inscribed with ritual symbols.

"Now, son, as you know, serial killers have patterns they like to follow. It's like a style of clothing or an area of the country to live in or a professional pursuit. It's where you feel most comfortable expressing yourself . . . it's the sweet spot in the center of the racket and the perfectly cooked piece of tenderloin and the room that is decorated to your taste and no one else's. It is home, son—where you belong."

"So you're saying that all those other women couldn't have been your work—in spite of the evidence at the scenes—because your first one didn't match the pattern?"

"Oh, I didn't kill anyone."

"So how do you know about the sweet spot."

"I'm a good little reader, and I like pathology."

"I'll bet."

His father leaned in and dropped his voice to a whisper. "I know how you feel, how apart you are, how desperate it can be to be lost. But I was shown the way and was all the better for it, and the same is going to be true for you. You can be saved—you *will* be saved. Just look inside of yourself and follow that inner core that we both know you have."

"So I can grow up and be a serial killer just like my father? No fucking thank you."

His father backed off and offered his palms to the ceiling. "Oh, not that, never that . . . I'm talking about religion. Naturally."

Yeah. Right.

Veck glanced around at the security cameras in the corners of the room. His father had cleverly not implicated himself in anything, even though the subtext was Las Vegas–obvious.

"Find your God, son. . . ." Those eyes grew luminous once again. "Embrace who you are. That impulse you have is going to take you where you need to go. Trust me. I've been saved."

As he spoke, the voice morphed into a dark symphony in Veck's ears, as if his father's words were being set to epic movie music.

Veck slanted forward, bringing them so close together he could see every one of the flecks of black in his father's deep blue irises. In a whisper, he said with a smile, "I'm pretty sure you're going to hell."

"And I'm taking you with me, son. You can't fight what you are, and you're going to be put in a position you can't win." His father tilted his face, like someone would a gun when they had it right up to your forehead. "You and I are the same."

"You sure about that? I'm walking out of here, and you've got a date with a needle on Wednesday. No 'same' there."

The pair of them stared at each other for a while, until his father was the one who ended up backing off.

"Oh, son, I think you'll find me alive and well come the

end of the week." Lot of satisfaction in that tone. "You'll read about it in the papers."

"How the hell are you going to manage that."

"I have friends in low places, as it were."

"That I believe."

The charming, slightly haughty smile returned, and his father's voice eased back into gracious territory. "In spite of how . . . acrimonious . . . this is, I'm glad to see you."

"Me, too. You're less impressive than I remember."

The twitch in the left eye told him he'd hit a mark. "Would you do something for me?"

"Probably not."

"Go see your mother's grave for me and bring her a red rose. I loved that woman to *death*, I really did."

Veck's hands curled into fists.

"Tell you what." Veck smiled. "I'll put my cigarette out on your headstone. How about that, *Father*."

The elder DelVecchio eased back, his expression going cold. Clearly, the meet-and-greet was not rolling the way he'd expected.

"This wasn't just about you, by the way," his father announced.

As Veck frowned, the man focused on the blank space behind Veck's shoulder. "She wants you to know that she suffered. Horribly."

Jesus . . . exactly what Kroner had said . . .

Veck caught himself before he looked up and over at Jim, but the angel's response was clear: A cold draft boiled up and drifted over Veck's head, crossing the table and causing the skin on the back of his father's hands to go goose bumps.

His father smiled into the thin air where Jim was standing. "You don't honestly think you're going to win this, do you? Because you can't take her out of him—an exorcism isn't going to work because he was born with it—it's not in him, but *of* him."

His father glanced back over at Veck. "And didn't you think I'd know you brought friends? Silly, silly boy."

Veck stood up. "We're done."

Yup, it was definitely time to go: Given the arctic-blast thing going on, Jim Heron, the angel, was about to raise hell on his dad. Fun to watch, but aftermath-wise? File that under not-here-not-now.

"No hug," his father drawled.

Veck didn't bother replying to that one. He was through wasting his breath and his time on the sonofabitch. In fact, he wasn't sure why he'd come—just to trade potshots? There was no crossroads he could see here ... Then again, maybe the point had been that message to Heron?

As Veck turned and walked over to the guard, the other guy opened the door quickly, like he didn't want to be in the enclosed space a moment longer, either.

"Thomas," his father called out. "I'll see you in the mirror, son. Every day."

The closing door cut off the words.

"You okay?" the guard asked.

"Just fine. Thanks."

Following the other man, Veck headed in the direction they'd come from. "When's the execution scheduled for?"

"First thing in the morning, Wednesday. If you petition the warden, I think you can get a seat."

"Good to know."

As he strode along, Veck could feel his father's presence with him, as if the battery that kept that evil lamp inside of him on had been plugged into its charger and regained a strength it hadn't had for years.

In the center of his chest, that dark anger flared to life ... and spread.

"You sure you're okay, Detective?"

Veck wasn't certain which part of him was answering as he replied, "Never felt better in my life."

CHAPTER
38

"**Y**ou did the right thing."

Reilly glanced over the felt lip of her cubicle. Her supervisor was leaning against the partition, her coat on, her briefcase in one hand, her keys dangling from the other.

"And you should go home."

Reilly smiled a little. "Just catching up."

"No offense, but bullshit—I'm not going to stop you, though."

"Thank you." Reilly stretched her arms over her head. "I've just got to do this. For my own sanity."

On the screen of her computer was that preliminary list of evidence that had come out of Kroner's impounded truck. She'd done a word search on *earring* and was now scanning the descriptions and first-impression photos one by one.

She had about fifteen more to go, and then she was going to comb through the master list, which had been finalized just this afternoon.

Stuff like this she had to see for herself.

Her supervisor nodded. "No, I get it. And FYI, DelVecchio hasn't returned my calls—and I just talked to the sergeant again. Nothing there, either."

"When are you going to issue an arrest warrant for him?"

"Noontime tomorrow if he hasn't turned himself in for questioning before then."

The charge would be tampering with evidence. Both she and her supervisor, as well as the sergeant, had screened the security video of the evidence room from the day before—and they had watched as Veck had gone in, looked through all the cataloged objects, and then rifled through the box of things that had yet to be logged in. That was his opportunity, and he had made several passes in and out of his pocket with his left hand.

It was not ironclad proof, but paired with Bails's statements and the discrepancy in the list, it was enough to at least arrest him. Besides, if he wasn't responding to calls, there was a good chance they were right.

"Be honest with me," her boss said. "Do you fear for your own personal safety."

"No." Maybe.

"Do you want me to put a patrol on your house?"

"Actually, I'll be with my parents tonight. I'm going to stay with them."

"Good idea. And consider the patrol done." The woman put her hand on Reilly's shoulder. "Don't blame yourself for any of this."

"How can I not?"

"You can't control other people."

But she could choose whether or not to sleep with them, for god's sakes. Changing the subject, she said, "So are you finished talking to Bails?"

"Yup, his statement's on file. You can read it if you like—it's exactly what he told you. He just left a little while ago."

"I'll do that. And before you say it, yes, I promise to go home before midnight."

Her boss was almost at the door when Reilly called out, "When are you going to talk to the Bartens about this?"

"Not until our ducks are in a row. Those poor people have been through hell and back, and the idea that a cop might have slaughtered their daughter is going to make it so much worse. Especially with the name DelVecchio associated with the case."

And in light of the fact that Veck had been in their house.

At that moment, his own words replayed in her head. *I took that man into a victim's home.*

God, he was such a liar.

"Call me if you want to talk," her boss murmured.

"I will. And thanks again."

As she was left by herself, she thought of Jim Heron, the "FBI" agent, the one who had "shown" them the cave where Sissy's remains had been found.

Veck had played that scene brilliantly. So surprised when it happened. So professional thereafter.

And as for the lack of muddy footprints on the rock? Heron could have been camping down there for hours as he waited for Veck to lead her in the right direction, the soles of his shoes drying off until he raced away in another direction. And they'd all been so transfixed by finding the body, no one had looked for him. Which had been a major mistake.

It was clear that Heron and Veck had to be working together.

Reilly cursed and refocused on her screen. The last of the preliminary earring entries took no time to go through, and as she'd expected, there was no dove anything to be found. Just as Bails had said.

After she moved over to the final version, with its precise photographs taken with a microscope, the cataloging was so succinct it was the work of a moment to find the earring. The discrepancy hadn't been noted; it would be soon, however.

"What a mess," she murmured, as she went over to Sissy's file to review the autopsy pictures again.

God, they were physically painful to look at.

In the course of her years on the force, she had seen a lot of gruesome things, but the situation with Sissy got to her.

Maybe because she'd become personally involved, thanks to some criminally stupid decisions on her own part.

Unsettled, but unable to leave yet, she decided to waste some time on the Internet. Entering the name "Thomas DelVecchio Sr." into Google gave her over one million references in seventeen seconds. Mousing down through the tally, she clicked over and scanned some of the blogs and the Web sites—only to become seriously unimpressed with humanity.

Not that she needed the help in that department.

There was just so much adoration for the wrong reasons, and she had to wonder how many of these people would think it was fun if their daughter or mother had been one of the victims. Or if they themselves had fallen into DelVecchio's hands . . . and knives.

Refining her search to victims, she found plenty of references to the first woman who had been killed, including some with autopsy photos. And doing a side-by-side comparison between Sissy Barten and Suzie Bussman told her what she already knew: The method and markings were the same.

What a way to pay homage to your father. God, even the names were eerily similar.

Reclining deeply into her chair, her eyes went back and forth between the two halves of the screen—and she found herself praying that they found enough to nail Veck. All they had to go on right now was the planted earring, Kroner's statements with regard to the quarry, and the fact that Veck had been in the Barten house. Then again, everyone had approached the case as if Kroner had done it. No one had been looking at Veck—and that was changing now. His desk, computer, and locker had already been searched and everything in them seized. His home was being cased. And as soon as he showed up, he was going straight into interrogation.

Although maybe he'd gone on the run—

Reilly jerked up and wrenched around in her chair.

Her heartbeat roared in her ears, drowning out the

sound of the heat coming through the ceiling vents, and the whirring of computer equipment . . . and the creak she'd heard behind her.

Glancing to the ceiling, she looked at the security camera in the far corner. The red light on its belly was slowly blinking, the lazy cycle of flashes telling her it was operational.

"Who's there."

Of course no one answered. Because there was no one there.

Right?

She listened to her own breathing for a while, and then thought, Okay, this is bullshit. She was not going to be bullied in her own goddamn department.

Bursting out of her chair, she marched down the lane of empty cubicles and checked the conference rooms and offices. On the trip back, she went all the way to the main door, pushed it open, and looked down the hall both ways.

Pivoting quickly, she half expected to find someone behind her.

No one.

Cursing under her breath, she returned to her desk, sat down, and—

When her cell phone went off, she jumped and put her hand to her throat. "Oh, shut *up*."

Hard to tell whether she was addressing her BlackBerry or her adrenal gland.

Grabbing the thing and accepting the call, she barked, "Reilly."

"How're you doing."

At the sound of Detective de la Cruz's voice, she took a deep breath. "I've been better."

"Sarge called me."

"What a mess." Apparently, that was her new theme song.

"Yup."

There was a long pause, filled by the same kind of silence that had marked the drive back from the hospital for

hcr and Bails: *What the hell happened* was all over the line
without a word being spoken.

"Did anyone tell you the other part of it?" she asked.

"That you and Veck were ... ah ..."

She had to grimace. "It was incredibly poor judgment on
my part. I thought I knew him, I really did."

"And that's the rub, isn't it." This was said with the kind
of exhaustion that came from personal experience. "In the
end, you can only really know yourself."

"You're so right ... and I'm glad you callcd. When this
gets out—and it's going to—"

"All people are going to do is think he's an asshole. And
that's a best-case scenario for him."

Killer was the other word they would be batting around,
no doubt.

"You're going to get through this," de la Cruz said. "I
just wanted you to know you can call me if you need any-
thing."

"You're being really ... kind."

"Partners are tricky shit. I've been through a few."

Bet you've never slept with one, though, she thought.
"Thanks, Detectlve."

After Reilly cut off the connection, she stared into
space. God, had that story about Veck finding his mother
murdered even been true? Or had it just been another way
to play on her emotions?

Well, there was one way to find out ...

It didn't take long for her to locate some amateur blog
entries that covered that particular chapter in DelVecchio
family history. She read all about how Veck had discovered
the body, been questioned, and been cleared of any in-
volvement based on the physical evidence: Although his
fingerprints were all over the house, there had been none
on the victim; there also had been no blood under his nails,
on his clothes, or in and around his bathroom or bed.

Sissy Barten's body was the same: no evidence to tie him
to the killing.

Then again, Veck was a detective who knew exactly

what to do to leave nothing behind. Which made her wonder about his mother. And worry.

God . . . what if he got away with this? The threshold for being fired for planting evidence was so much lower than that of a successfully prosecuted murder charge. He could be out of a job, but free on the streets. And if he was building on his father's foundation of slipping out of the hands of law enforcement, then it could be years before anything stuck to him.

Disgusted with so much, and apparently looking for more to get sick about, she went to Facebook and typed in Thomas Delvecc—

She didn't have to go any farther than that to find a line of results. Idly going from page to page, she stared at the fan clubs Veck had spoken about.

At least he hadn't lied on this one.

The largest group had twenty thousand members, and she went to the wall and looked at the lineup of photographs on the top and then the postings that ran vertically. All about the execution. All about the adoration.

She sat back and just stared at the screen.

It was a long time before she shut her computer down and grabbed her coat.

"Who is the 'she,'" Veck demanded from behind the wheel of Heron's truck. "The one that my father went on about?"

As Jim sat beside the guy, he didn't look over. They had at least another hour before they were back in Caldwell, so there was plenty of time to frickin' chat it up—but he wasn't in a big hurry to talk about the weather, much less Devina and Sissy.

She wants you to know she suffered.

That demon was such a bitch.

Veck cursed hard. "Damn it, one of the pair of you had better get talking. And if you don't want to tell me about the chick, then you'd better fucking explain that exorcism reference."

Jim tapped the tip of his cigarette out the crack of the

window, and decided to tackle the latter rather than the former. "You're not our first trip through the park. The first soul we saved—we did it by serving Devina an eviction notice."

"Devina?"

"Devil in a blue dress, buddy."

"Is she the one who suffered?"

"We wish," Adrian muttered from the back.

Jim couldn't agree more on that one. "Here's the way it works. Devina is a demon—and if you need more of an explanation about that, think of collective wisdom and you've got a pretty good picture of it. She gets into a person and gradually takes over, influencing their choices and decisions. Eventually, you get to your crossroads, and you have to pick. Depending on the way you go, what you follow, what action you take—that determines where you're going to end up. And downstairs is a roasty, toasty fucking place, if you get what I'm saying."

"Hell."

"You got it."

On that note, Jim thought about the guy's father. Man, that one was pure evil. And if that was what bound Veck's flesh?

"Am I going to end up there?" Veck said softly, as if he were talking to himself.

"Not if we can help it."

Although how the hell were they going to pull that off? Especially given that Veck had seemed darker since he'd left that visiting room. Angrier. Farther away even though he was just as close by.

Why the hell did Eddie have to die, Jim thought. They needed him on this one.

Devina was *such* a bitch.

"Is Reilly in danger," Veck asked harshly.

"The more distance between the two of you, the better."

The man cursed again, and muttered, "Mission accomplished there."

"It really is safer. She'd be nothing more than collateral damage, and Devina's into that shit."

At the side of the highway, a green sign with white lettering read, CALDWELL 55.

How many cigarettes did he have left?

"So who is the 'she.' The one who suffered?"

Oh, yay. That question was *so* going to help his mood. "Someone I care about."

"Sissy Barten." Veck looked over. "Right? Kroner said the same thing, in exactly the same words, when he was talking to Reilly about her. And you already told me it was personal."

"That I did."

"So what were those markings on the girl's stomach?"

"Devina doesn't know from ADT. She uses virgins." Jim stretched in his seat, his muscles going rigid as the urge to kill rang his motherfucking bell. "What you saw on Sissy was the way she does it."

"Fucking . . . hell. So my father's first victim . . ."

"Maybe Devina made him do it for her as a pledge of faith. Maybe he just helped her work. Who knows."

"How long has this been going on? Between you and the . . ." The pause that followed suggested the man was still getting used to the word *demon* on his tongue.

"Only a couple of weeks. But there were people before me—and going to be none after me unless I make sure that you don't go the way she wants you to."

Jim glanced over at the detective's hands. They were wrapped so tightly around the steering wheel, it was a wonder the damn thing hadn't snapped off.

Okay, that kind of pissed was *not* going to work in their favor: It gave Devina a flashpoint—if she hit the vein correctly, they'd be dealing with an explosion. And Veck was a big, powerful guy who was capable, and probably trained, to kill with his bare hands.

Goddamn it, Jim hated this waiting around. "By the way, we're staying with you tonight."

"I figured. I only have one bed, but I got a couch."

"I'm mostly interested in some version of a 7-Eleven." He flipped open the box of Marlboros. "Running low."

"There's a Stewart's close to my house."

"Cool."

Veck reached into his pocket and took out his cell phone. "Might as well turn this back on."

While Jim seethed in frustration, he looked out the side window at the highway's dark shoulder, wondering when in the hell things were going to—

"What the hell," Veck muttered. "My damn phone blew up."

As Jim slowly cranked his head around, he thought, *Waiting's over; here we go. . . .*

CHAPTER
39

U p in Heaven, Nigel was playing with himself.
Chess, that was.

In truth, it was a bit boring, even though he found his opponent smashingly dressed and incredibly astute: Fellow had all the same moves he did, so the lack of surprise presented no challenge a'tall, really—in spite of the flamboyantly brilliant strategies.

"Checkmate," he said out loud to the silence of his private quarters.

When there was no cursing, no accusations of unfair practice, no stamping about and demands for a rematch, he was reminded again as to why playing with Colin was much more gratifying.

Rising to his feet, he stepped away from the table and left the pieces as they were, with only two on the board, a white queen and a black king.

The urge to leave his tent and go wandering across the lawn toward the castle, toward the river, toward where Colin slept, was such a compelling impulse, it went beyond the mental to border upon the physical.

But he had lowered himself to that folly once, and been spared embarrassment. He would not do so again.

Distracted by the ache in his chest, he went 'round the bed and into the bath and then came back out once more. In truth, he hadn't properly focused in . . . well, since that horrid meal . . . when Colin's honesty had fired a shot directly at Nigel's arrogant, pissy little ego.

Strange the way one's position changed, wasn't it. As time had drifted by like a lazy current in a vast and largely still stream, his initial hotheaded, defensive reaction had faded into a more moderated response . . . one that might even make him prepared to apologize, provided an apology was tendered in return.

Which was proof positive that miracles could happen.

Unfortunately, he was entirely unsure what he would receive in reply, and knowing himself, as well as the other archangel, he recognized that another round of arguing would benefit neither of them.

Still, Colin could be the one to offer the olive branch.

In fact, although Nigel would admit it to no one, he had been skipping the last several meals, and passing time herein, in hopes of that archangel coming forward. This was wearing thin, however. Such passivity was not in his nature, and patience was a virtue he had little of—

"Nigel?" came a voice from the far side of the flaps.

Nigel gritted his teeth, but kept his curse to himself as he double-checked his cravat. The last thing he needed was a visitor of the non-Colin variety. It was hardly proper to punish a well-intended innocent, however.

"Byron, old boy," he muttered, heading for the entrance, "how fare thee—"

The moment he drew back the satin weight and saw the other archangel's face, he stopped dead. "Tell me."

"Is . . . Colin herein?"

"No."

"We cannae find him." Byron fiddled with the brass buttons on the sleeves of his club jacket. "When he did not present himself for the evening meal, we assumed he was studying and left him be. But afore I was going to turn in, I went to search him out with some provisions. He was not in his tent. Not at the water's edge. Not in the castle . . . and not here, either, apparently."

Nigel shook his head at the same time he stretched out his senses—and found no sign of the angel. Indeed, if he had not been so preoccupied with himself, he would have recognized previously what he noted clearly now: Colin was not on the premises.

There was a brief urge to give in to panic, but Nigel controlled the emotional response. And considering things logically, he knew there was but one place the sod would go.

Why had he not seen this coming?

"Worry not," Nigel said grimly. "I shall go and retrieve him."

"Would you care for aid in this?"

"No." For he was not going to be responsible for the ass-lashing he gave the archangel. Personality conflict was one thing; rank insubordination was another altogether. And the latter was not going to be indulged in any fashion.

Upon his will, his robing and monogrammed slippers morphed into a suit of dove gray, a shirt of bright white, a pale tartan tie, and a pair of wingtips.

"Go forth and comfort Bertie and Tarquin," he told the other archangel. "Undoubtedly, they shall be worried. And know that I shan't be long."

"Wherever will you go?"

"Where he is."

With that Nigel was off, traveling through the barrier to the world down below. And when he resumed his corporeal form, it was before a two-story garage of modest distinction set within farmland country.

He thought of Edward resting therein.

How common a marker for such an extraordinary soul.

With grim focus, Nigel surmounted the narrow exterior staircase and passed through the door as if it were naught but a veil of fog.

No reason to be throwing the panels open; he had announced himself sure enough.

And Colin did not seem shocked at the intrusion. The archangel was sitting on a ragtag sofa beneath a picture window, lounging with one arm running across the top of the cushions and his legs crossed knee to ankle.

Nigel recommitted to memory every angle and line of the male's harsh, handsome face. And then recast them with a black eye and a fat lip of his doing. "Did you not think your absence would be noted?"

"Do I appear surprised at your arrival?"

"The proper course of these things is to ask permission before taking your leave."

"Perhaps for Byron and Bertie. But not I."

"I would not have denied you."

"How could I have known that."

Nigel frowned, his anger abruptly abating, exhaustion taking its place. How did humans stand this emotional turmoil? And why ever had he allowed it into his heart?

This was no good. Moreover, this could not go on.

When he next addressed the archangel, it was with composure. "Colin, it would appear that you and I have reached our own crossroads. As much as I was prepared to recognize certain ... errors of judgment on my part ... I fear that will be insufficient for you, as water shall not do when blood is sought. Further, I believe that in your thrust to embrace a logical stance, you have missed the truth about yourself. Your passions rule you far more than you realize, and they take you in directions that jeopardize our collective interests."

Colin's eyes shifted away.

"Therefore, I say unto you, let us put into the past any assignations that may have occurred, and move forward into a proper distance. Mayhap over time, we shall work together in harmony anew. However, until that occurs, I expect you to behave appropriately or I shall remove you from any influence over these proceedings."

When there was no immediate reply, Nigel walked over to a galley kitchen and stood before a short, squat door. Behind the flimsy barrier, Edward lay in state, neither breathing nor in decay, the angel's body a vase sporting the scent of flowers that were not there.

Colin was wise to be here, he thought. With Jim and Adrian engaged in heated warring with Devina, this vessel was not safe—and if it were broken or compromised, there was no restoring the seat of Edward's soul.

Although even if it remained pristine, there was no way of knowing whether he would return. Things of this nature were within the purview of the Creator alone.

Moreover, it would be an unprecedented occurrence.

But still, Colin should have—

"I should have told you where I was going," the arch-angel said brusquely. "You are correct in that."

Nigel turned about. The angel was still on the couch, still sprawled, but those eyes were focused upward, meeting his own.

"Is that an apology," Nigel said.

"Take it as you will."

Nigel shook his head and thought to himself, Not good enough, old friend. 'Tis just not good enough, I'm afraid.

Tugging at the sleeves of his shirt, he pulled down upon his gold cuff links, and stated once again, "I am endeavoring to win this vital contest the best way I know how—and that is within the bounds of proper gamesmanship. I cannot subscribe to the tenet that two wrongs make a right. I will not."

"Do not kid yourself," Colin murmured as he lifted his palm and flexed his fingers. "Clean hands, as you say."

"And look at how that turned out. Edward is dead."

"You are not to blame for this."

"I am." Nigel shook his head. "That is what you do not understand. All of this is my responsibility. You can have your opinions and your contrariness and your anger, but at the end of it, your shoulders shall not bear the burden of defeat if that is what arises. That is for me, and me alone. So whilst you despise my control, you view things from the advantaged position of commentary without consequence."

On that note, Nigel walked over to the door. "I'm glad you are here, and I know you will guard well what is precious."

"Nigel."

He glanced over his shoulder. "Colin."

There was a long moment of silence.

When nothing further appeared to be forthcoming, Nigel looked over to the kitchen, and thought of the nature of loss: Some you chose—and could unchoose. Some was forced upon one. And . . . some was permanent.

"I shall see you anon," Nigel said, before he ended things by walking out.

CHAPTER
40

The next morning, Reilly went into work from her parents' house on a full stomach: fresh orange juice, two homemade cinnamon buns, a cup of coffee, and a strip and a half of bacon that she had purloined from her father's plate.

As she parked her car in the lot behind HQ, every ounce of the yummy-yummy turned to lead: Veck's motorcycle was angled in against the building.

He'd obviously turned himself in and was being questioned.

Looking up the ugly rear flank of where she worked, she was tempted to turn the unmarked's engine back on and head off to . . . anywhere.

But she did not run. Never had. Never would.

Getting out, she blinked in the bright sunlight, and wished that God would hit the dimmer switch: Instead of lifting her mood, the cheery-spring thing drove it down even farther into the sewer.

"Beautiful day, ain't it," someone called out.

Glancing over her shoulder, she said, "Morning, Bails."

The detective was wending his way through the cars and

trucks and SUVs, and as she watched him, she squinted, the light abruptly going glare on her.

Maybe she was getting a migraine.

"You okay?" he asked.

"Not even close. You?"

As he came up, he took off his sunglasses. "Same boat." He nodded over at the bike. "So he's here."

Reilly rubbed her eyes. "Yes, he is."

"Where are your lenses?" he said, tapping his aviators. "Summer's coming, and so are cataracts."

As he put his darks back on, she tilted her head and looked up at him. The light was so bright around the guy, it seemed as if he were made of chrome.

Okay, she was losing her mind, going total gaga. Next thing she knew, she'd be wearing meat to work.

"I said . . . are you going to watch the interrogation?"

Shaking herself, she murmured, "God, no. And sorry, I'm just off today."

He put his arm around her shoulders as a friend would, nothing more. "I get that. Come on, let's go in and try to pretend we're working."

"Good plan."

They walked in together, headed out to the lobby and hit the stairs. On the second-floor landing, the admin pool was not at their desks, but over in the back corner, clustered together. As soon as one of them saw Reilly, all of them looked over.

Ducking her head, she muttered a see-you-later and hurried off to her department. In Internal Affairs, she had more eyes on her, but at least here her colleagues came over, said good morning, and acknowledged the situation: awkward, but better than hushed whispers—and folks were supportive.

Then again, most people at one time or another had gotten snowed. It was an occupational hazard of breathing.

When the chat-ups dwindled, she sat down at her desk,

logged into her computer and lasted about . . . a minute and a half.

Out of her department. Down the hall. Into Homicide.

And as if it were supposed to happen, the first person she ran into was de la Cruz.

"I was wondering if you'd show," he said, coming forward and offering his hand.

Shaking his palm, she cleared her throat. "How's it going."

"They're just getting started. You want to watch?"

"Yes," she said hoarsely.

"Come with me." As he led her past the desks, he lifted up his coffee cup. "I just made a caffeine run, you want some?"

"I'm jittery enough—thanks, though."

The interrogation rooms ran down a narrow corridor that was entered through its own doorway, but there was a cut-through at the rear of the department, and de la Cruz held the back door open for her.

"There's a monitor in here."

The tiny conference room had old carpet, but a new round table—on which was a screen showing black-and-white feed from a ten-foot-by-fifteen-foot room. The camera was trained on Veck, who was sitting in a chair against the corner, and she felt a physical shock at seeing him. Man, he was big, especially looking as coldly aggressive as he was: his arms were crossed over his chest, and his eyes were narrowed and focused on the detective who was questioning him.

Kind of like the guy was a dartboard.

Reilly pulled out a chair and sat down, her legs feeling unreliable.

"Here, let me turn the sound on," de la Cruz said as he settled in and reached forward.

". . . did not plant that earring as evidence," Veck clipped out. "You have video—watch the damn recording. I didn't plant the fucking—"

"But you were over by the Kroner evidence—"

"Just like every other detective in the house."

"And Officer Reilly indicated that you were hoping to find a tie to the Barten case."

Veck showed no reaction to her name. "And I did. But how does that correlate with planting something?"

The other detective—his name was Browne, if she remembered correctly—leaned in over his legal pad. "Your hand was in and out of your pocket."

"You ever hear of change? Quarters, dimes, nickels?"

"You had been up in Sissy Barten's bedroom."

"As had others. I'm not the only rep from this department who's been through that house."

"Look, Veck, just tell me what happened."

Veck leaned in as well, his face flat-out furious. "I went to Sissy's house to speak to her mother. I went upstairs, yeah, sure, but I didn't take anything out of there, and I did not plant any evidence. You've already proved that I didn't hurt Kroner. Why would I want to frame the guy—for a murder, incidentally, that I did not commit?"

"I'm not sure what we've proved with Kroner."

Veck sat back again. "You're fucking kidding me."

"Maybe you staged the attack precisely so you could put the Barten murder around his neck."

"So you think I travel with trained mountain lions or some shit? Besides, Kroner knew where the body in the quarry was, not me."

"On the contrary, Kroner mentioned the quarry. *You* found the body."

"No, I didn't. That was ..."

"Who?"

At that, he reached into the pocket of the fleece he had on and pulled out a pack of Marlboros.

Ah, so he'd lied about quitting as well.

The other detective shook his head. "No smoking in here."

Veck muttered under his breath as he disappeared the pack. "Look, you want my statement? It's simple. I didn't do it—the murder, the earring, any of it. Someone is trying to frame me."

"Can you prove that, Veck."

God, she could practically feel a cold rush of air as Veck bit out, "The question is more, can *you* prove it."

"He killed her," Reilly said roughly. "Oh, my God, he killed her, didn't he."

He knew how the system worked, knew the ways to get away with murder—he was a detective, after all. He'd been trained on the limits of the law and evidence and proof.

De la Cruz glanced over. "I'm not going to lie. This doesn't look good, any of it."

She thought back to the quarry, to Jim Heron, to Veck finding the body . . . it was the perfect staging piece.

And Kroner? Veck could have gone out to those woods with the plan of killing the guy, only to have a wild animal cut him off.

Luck, after all, didn't just play in favor of the righteous.

If Kroner had died by that motel as he was supposed to, and the earring had been planted successfully, and Bails hadn't seen those juvie records, Veck would have gotten away with murder—just like his father.

And he would have killed again.

That was what psychopaths like him did.

Reilly's hand crept up to her throat. To think she could have fallen in love with a killer . . . just like Veck's mother had.

"The most important thing," she heard herself say, "is that the charges stick. We can't let someone like him get loose—or it's his father all over again."

"We're going to need stronger evidence. Right now, he's technically just a person of interest."

"We have to get into his house."

"We're lining up the warrant as we speak."

She refocused on the screen. "I want to be there."

Sitting on the "other side" of the interrogation table, Veck was on the edge of violence.

Someone, or something, was lining him up to take a fall, and, man, they'd done their homework. Between the condition of Sissy's body, the bullshit about this earring, and the connection with his father, he was looking at a crossroads, all right.

No choice for him, though.

It was like the autopilot on his life had recalibrated a course right into the side of a mountain, and he couldn't get the controls back. And the ass-slapper? His colleague across the way here, Detective Stan Browne, was using all the standard interrogation techniques. Hell, Veck could write the dialogue, and he knew the tricks; how the interviewer could shade things or suggest the truth even if there were gray areas. So there was no way to be sure exactly how much hard evidence they had against him.

At this point, he had one and only one thing going for him: he actually was innocent and the law favored innocent men.

"Don't bother to get a warrant," Veck said as he took his keys out and put them on the table. "Go through my house. Search my shit. You will not find a single thing that will tie me to Sissy Barten or Kroner."

Assuming whoever was after him hadn't planted their own version of a dove earring.

Shit.

Browne reached across and took the keys. "Do you want counsel?"

"I don't need it. Because this is going nowhere."

The other detective rubbed over his eyebrow with the pad of his thumb. "You sound very sure of that."

"I am."

"So how do you explain the fact that the earring was not accounted for immediately after the truck was impounded and searched, and that it showed up after you'd been in the evidence room?"

"Like I said, how many people were in and out of there over the last few days? Have you looked at all the digital files from the security cameras?"

"We will. We're just starting our investigation."

"Well, you better get going. Because what I don't see, Browne, is anything concrete."

"Yet."

"Ever."

"Will you take a lie detector test?"

Veck paused on that one. If they asked him whether he intended to hurt Kroner that night? How was he going to handle that?

"Yeah. Sure."

Browne turned the page on his pad, even though he'd done nothing but scribble circles on the top sheet. "Okay, good. And I appreciate your giving your consent to go through your house."

As if he had a choice? They were going to get permission from a judge anyway. What he really wanted to know was who the hell had implicated him in this—

Reilly, he thought. That was what the conversation had been about last night—she'd already turned him in at that point. Either that, or she'd been about to.

But why the hell did she think he'd taken any earring? And she'd been there at the quarry with him when Jim had shown them where Sissy was. They'd both been surprised.

Unless she didn't believe any of it. And if that was true, what had been the tipping point?

Fuck that . . . more like *who*.

"Would you mind doing the lie detector now?"

The subtext being: *while we search your house*.

Would Reilly go with them? he wondered. Probably. That was what he would have done in her shoes.

Veck lifted his eyes to the camera that was focused on him . . . and knew she was on the other side of it.

"Get the machine," he said to the lens.

Browne rose to his feet. "It'll take us a little time to get set up. You sit tight."

"Like I have a choice."

"Coffee?"

"No, thanks."

As Browne left, Veck kept staring up at the little black eye on the buff-colored unit in the corner.

In slow motion, he mouthed, *I'm . . . being . . . framed.*

He was dead clear on the fact that she wouldn't believe him, but he wasn't the type not to fight. And after that mute salvo, he refocused on the door. It didn't take a crystal ball to know that he wasn't walking away from this one with a reprimand letter or a really beautiful shadow from IA. His career in law enforcement was over, even if he were cleared.

Which, given how thorough this setup appeared to be, wasn't a given.

As he chewed on this new reality he had going on, that anger, that dark, vicious anger, took another crank behind his sternum. Tighter. Tighter still.

"So what do you think, Jim," he said softly.

The angel had been standing in the opposite corner the whole time, looming behind Browne—to the point that when the detective had first sat down, the guy had looked over his shoulder as if he'd sensed the presence.

Jim's voice echoed in his head. *This is just the setup. The question is, where is this taking us. And you need to lie on the test. You tell them you went out there to kill Kroner and you're fucked—they may not let you out of here, and that makes my job harder.*

In the silence that followed, the fury multiplied yet again in the center of Veck's chest, and in a terrible moment of clarity, he realized he was fully capable of killing someone. Right here. Right now. With the chair he was sitting on. With that blue-and-gold CPD pen Browne had left behind by mistake. With his bare hands.

And it would not be murder as in a "go apeshit, lose your mind, and white out" kind of event—as he'd assumed had happened with Kroner. This would be a very calculated murder, the sort of thing that would leave him in control of himself and his victim.

The sort of thing that took you away from this furious impotence and made you feel like a god.

No wonder his father had been addicted to the rush.

And weaklings like Kroner craved it. The ultimate power was to take away life, to see someone beg, to hold in your hands the future of another person and their family and their community . . . and then crush all of it.

Fear was the master and pain was the weapon.

And in Veck's current state, even with the angel right behind and sticking with him, he was only a step away from filling his father's shoes.

Sweet spot, indeed.

CHAPTER
41

A s Reilly drove over to Veck's house with half a dozen other officers, she was prepared to let her colleagues' fingers do the walking.

She was in observational mode and going to stay that way: eyes peeled, but hands staying in her pockets. Frankly, she was lucky to be allowed to come along at all.

By the time the various cars were parked in Veck's driveway, it looked like a cop convention, and as she got out of her unmarked, she caught sight of a couple of neighbors peeking through blinds. His reputation in his neighborhood was not her concern anymore, however.

Now, she was worried about keeping these people safe from him.

As the front door was opened with his own keys, the talk of her colleagues faded into background music for her, everything receding from notice as she entered behind the others.

The first thing she did was look at the couch. There was a pillow down at the far end, as if Veck had spent the night there, but no blanket, even though it was still cold at night. An ashtray full of butts along with two crushed packs of

Marlboros and a red Bic were on the floor ... right where his wallet had landed three nights ago.

Reilly fled that scene fast, and headed into the kitchen, not out of any design, but just because that was where her feet took her.

Cursing to herself, she knew she had to put her detective hat on. Boxes ... where would the moving boxes be?

"Is this the cellar?" someone asked as they opened the door to the hall bath.

She almost pointed the guy in the right direction, but held off. The last thing she needed to do was demonstrate how well she knew the house.

"It's over here," somebody else replied as they opened a different door and hit a light switch.

Reilly went over and followed that officer downward. As she stepped off onto the concrete floor below, the musty air tickled her nose and the chill made her pull her coat in closer.

"And I thought the upstairs was empty," the officer muttered, his voice echoing around.

You got that right, she agreed. Aside from the furnace, and the hot water heater, there didn't appear to be anything in the basement.

Even still, they walked around, taking separate routes, and then she stood to the side as he took a flashlight out to check behind the HVAC stuff.

"Nothing?" she said.

"Nada."

After they returned to the first floor, she stayed in the kitchen, and got a look at the back of every cupboard Veck hadn't used and the bottoms of all the drawers he hadn't filled and the empty rods of the closet he hadn't hung anything in. Officers were taking photographs of all the vacancies, and there were the sounds of people walking up above on the bare floors.

God, had she ever really been with this man? she wondered.

No, she thought. She'd been with the image he'd wanted her to see.

With a shudder, she went up the stairs and glanced into the master suite. The bed was messy and there was another pack of Marlboros and an ashtray on the side table. Two duffel bags were in the corner, and she went over and nudged open the one that was unzipped with her foot. Leathers. Fatigues. What looked like a black AC/DC shirt. Black socks.

The kind of stuff you'd take for an overnight, except nothing that she'd seen Veck wear before—but like that counted?

Frowning, she edged past the other officers and leaned into the bathroom. Two toothbrushes on the counter with a tube of toothpaste. A third brush standing upright in a glass.

Who the hell else was staying here?

And why was there a towel over the mirror . . . ?

As a flashbulb went off from behind her, the flare was caught in the panes of the window she'd seen him through that first night.

Grimly, she wheeled away and went out into the hallway. There were two other bedrooms with nothing in them, and another bath. With nothing in it.

"Been up in the attic yet?" she called to the other officers. When they shook their heads, she reached up with a gloved hand and pulled down the folding stairs.

Stepping aside, she let a colleague go up first with his flashlight. God, with this much available storage space, you'd think no one would bother to take anything to the third floor, but Bails had said he'd humped boxes on stairs—and there was nowhere else to check.

"Nothing," came the male voice from above.

Reilly took to the ladder-like steps, clawing up them with her hands and following with her feet. In the attic proper, the other officer had turned a bald lightbulb on, and the thing was swinging on its tether, going back and forth and pulling shadows out from the rafters.

After glancing around, she knelt down and ran a finger across the wooden planks that had been laid over the insulation. Dust. Lots of dust.

Frowning, she inspected the flooring that was around the opening they'd come up through. Her footfalls and those of the other officer left a distinctive pattern in the thick, pristine layer of particles.

What the hell? she thought.

Not only was there nothing up here; nothing had *been* up here since well before Veck had moved in.

" 'Scuse me," she murmured, before slipping back down the folding stairs.

She went into the first guest room she got to. Inside, there was only wall-to-wall carpet with footprints on it—no indentations left from boxes having been stacked anywhere. And in the bottom of the closet? More of the same: smooth, unmarked rug, the kind of thing you got when you'd vacuumed a while ago and left the fibers alone to recover from the tracks of your Dyson.

Getting up on her tiptoes, she looked at the shelf. No streaks from things having been pulled off and removed.

The other bedroom was the same.

Downstairs, she went into the kitchen, passed through the mudroom and headed out the far side into the garage. No lawn equipment or tools or birdseed. Just two bins for garbage, both of which were empty.

"When's the trash pickup?" she asked, not expecting anyone to answer.

It was a fact worth knowing, and no doubt someone would be finding out soon enough.

Returning to the kitchen, she stood in front of the open cupboards and drawers. It was clear that he'd given permission for them to search the house because he'd known damn well they wouldn't find anything—and she'd been aware of that coming over here.

But she had the sense that nothing had been here to begin with. She hadn't seen any boxes anywhere when she'd been over, but more to the point, there appeared to be no evidence that anything much had been moved in. Yeah, sure, he'd had a good twelve hours to get rid of stuff ... but you couldn't manufacture things like layers of dust and unscarred carpets.

Maybe Veck had tweaked to the juvie report's falling out of something ... and thrown the documents out. Except what the hell had Bails been talking about when it came to the boxes? And why would he have lied? The two were well-known for being friends, and the guy had been legitimately crushed.

God, there were just too many black holes everywhere.

With a curse, she checked her watch, then took out her phone and dialed de la Cruz's number. The detective had stayed behind at the station house, and when she got voice mail, she didn't bother leaving a message.

He'd know what she was looking for.

Outside, she got into her car and sat behind the wheel. Eventually, she looked over at the house. In the bright sunlight, the shadows were nearly black—

Her cell phone went off and she answered it without checking who it was. "Reilly."

"I have the results of the polygraph." De la Cruz sounded as tired as she felt. "Just came in—and I figured that was why you called."

"It was. Can you tell me?"

"He passed everything—all of it."

"*What?*"

"You heard me."

"How is that possible?" Except the instant she asked the question, she knew it was BS. A good liar, an exceptional liar, could fool the machine. It was rare, but not impossible.

With a groan, she rubbed the bridge of her nose. "Hold on, just to be clear, they asked him about the visit to the Bartens', the earring, the evidence room—"

"Everything."

"And he denied it all, and the machine said he was telling the truth."

"Yup. Except for one question."

So he was a stupendous liar— "Wait, he failed a question?"

"No, he didn't deny something. The examiner asked him whether he'd intended to kill Kroner that night by the motel. And he said yes, he had."

Reilly shook her head. "That doesn't make sense. Why would that be the only thing he admitted to?"

If he was lying about everything else, why wouldn't he cover his ass on that one as well?

"I don't know," de la Cruz muttered. "I got no answer for that. . . ."

CHAPTER
42

"Couldn't they shut the goddamn cupboards?"

As Adrian stood in Veck's kitchen, he stared across the empty, all-open everything, watching as the poor bastard closed shit with hard claps.

On some level, it was hard to get jazzed about anything—and that included not just someone else's drawers, cabinets and closets, but the war in general. The only thing likely to get his attention was if Devina showed up again, but that demon seemed to have gone into hiding.

Never a good thing.

Next to him, Jim was hanging back as well, letting Veck do his thing to put the house back together. When the detective went upstairs, the savior glanced over.

"Devina had better make her fucking move soon or his head's going to explode."

Ad grunted in agreement. "But not much we can do about it."

He and Jim had also backseated it during the interrogation and the lie detector test and the further interro, until Ad had become convinced that they were never getting out of the police station. In the end, however, Veck had been released. All the cops had against him was circumstantial shit, and with the results of the polygraph in, there was not enough to charge him or even put him on a forty-eight-hour detainer.

Good news on some level—better to have the show-down with Devina away from all those uniforms. But the detective was pushed to his limit, and Adrian knew all too well what that was like.

Abruptly unable to stay still, Ad went over to the refrig-erator and cracked the thing. Not much inside—no surprise there—but even if there had been a boatload of lo mein, he didn't have any impulse to actually eat.

Even breathing was just something he did out of habit at this point.

Matter of fact, he'd heard once that there were stages of grief. Was he in depression now? He certainly wasn't as pissed off as he had been when Eddie had first . . . whatevered. At the moment, all he had was a cage of pain around his lungs and the sense that he was dragging a river barge behind him.

Shaking his head, he deliberately put that shit out of his mind. Introspection was not his friend right now—

Too bad the resolution didn't stick.

Glancing over at Jim, he said, "Do you think he's all right left alone?"

"Veck needs the space."

"Wasn't talking about him."

"You mean Eddie?" Jim crossed his arms and cursed. After a moment, he said, "Actually, yeah, I think he'll be all right. Devina's not incented to fuck with him because as long as he's with us, it's an open wound that won't heal. She takes the body or compromises it? That's a short-term thing."

Ad walked over to the window and looked out. Five o'clock and the light was just starting to drain from the sky.

Man, he was jumpy all of a sudden. "She has to know where he's being kept."

"But I marked that door. Anyone gets in there"—the guy pounded his chest with his fist—"I'm going to know."

Ad paced around a little, feeling like he had ants on the inside of his skin. Eventually, he muttered, "Look, I'm just going to head over there and check on him. I'll be right back—"

Jim stepped in front of him. "Eddie is okay. And I need you here. Shit is about to go down."

"Ten minutes."

"This is exactly what she wants. You need to realize that."

Adrian didn't want to throw down with the guy. They already had enough tempers flaring, thanks to Veck going WWE with the attitude—and Ad had enough sense to know that he was unstable himself, capable of flaring up or burning out with the flip of a coin.

But he couldn't shake the abrupt need to return to the garage.

"Look, I'll be right back. Promise." He met the savior's eyes with his own. "I swear on Eddie's soul."

"Goddamn it," Jim muttered.

"I couldn't agree more."

Without waiting for another round of disagreement, Ad spirited himself out of that house. And as soon as he took form on the garage's front lawn, he knew he'd been right to come: there was another presence inside the apartment with Eddie.

Instantly falling into fight mode, he outed his crystal dagger and—

"What the hell?" he muttered, lowering his weapon.

At that moment, Colin opened the door at the top of the staircase and stepped out onto the landing. "That would be 'Heaven,' thank you very much."

The archangel was not in namby-pamby whites, but the kind of clothes you could fight in: loose pants and a tight shirt. And he was alone, at least as far as Ad could sense.

"What are you doing here?" Ad asked, even though he knew there was only one explanation.

"Watching TV."

Adrian went over to the bottom of the stairwell. "Jim doesn't have cable."

"So one can imagine how dissatisfied I am."

"Nigel's let you guard him?"

"He knows I'm here, yes—"

The wind abruptly changed direction, shifting so it came out of the east—and it brought bad news with it: Riding along the invisible currents, weaving in and out of the gusts, was a subtle groaning sound.

"Fucking. Bitch." Adrian nailed Colin with his stare. "You stay with Eddie."

"Thank you for the order," Colin said dryly. "But that is why I came."

"Yeah. Sorry."

There was no time to kiss ass any further: As the wind intensified and the moaning sounds turned into shrieks, Ad didn't just curse Devina and her warlords—he wanted to kick himself in the head. This was precisely what Jim had said was going to happen: The pair of them apart, him dealing with a bunch of soulless, boneless bastards as Jim undoubtedly handled the actual crossroads.

He'd played right into the demon's hands.

And he was going to have to stay in her palm.

He sure as shit wasn't leaving now: Colin was powerful, but there were limits—and they'd already lost Eddie once.

Not going to happen again.

Moving fast, Adrian flashed into the garage. Over in the truck, there was a duffel full of leather riding gear, and he quickly yanked on studded gloves that went all the way up his forearms, and then pulled out the black duster Eddie had used for long trips on the bike.

On his way out, he passed by a pitchfork—and doubled back to grab it. Shit knew he felt like stabbing the crap out of something—and he'd just seen how much fun lawn tools could be.

When he stepped outside again, Colin was nowhere in sight, which was good timing and exactly what he wanted:

All around, minions were pulling up out of the shadows, forming into eyeless killers that were just his fucking cup of tea.

Adrian inflated his lungs until his chest stung and then he let out a war cry that shook the tree limbs around the garage, blowing them back so far a few of them even snapped.

And then he went in.

Locking a death grip on the worn wooden handle, he lunged forward, nailing the closest minion right in the gut before angling the tool heavenward—until it jacked right into the rib structure of the torso. With the tines locking in place, it was a case of up-and-over as he slung the bastard into left field like it was a bale of hay. Then it was the small matter of tucking the business end under his arm so that he caught the SOB riding up on his ass in the thighs.

Adrian wheeled around, yanked out the tool, and went over the head, bringing the curved spikes down laterally on the crippled bastard. They penetrated through the face, such as it was, and went into the chest cavity from above, reducing Devina's fighter to a mud puddle.

The squeal was so fucking satisfying.

Disengaging again, Adrian widened his stance and angled himself so that the pair of minions that were trying to split his attention got what they were asking for: Keeping his head straight forward, he measured them in the peripheral vision of both eyes.

He was banking on a third coming from behind.

It was just too cocksucking obvi.

Flexing his knees, he threw himself into the air, backflipping over the one he'd guessed right about—and then stabbing it in the back and twisting hard. As the impact registered, the minion went into a full-body spasm, acidic blood going flying to the point where he had to disengage and get gone. Diving around the side of the thing, he ducked into himself and hit the ground on a roll.

When he sprang up onto his feet, he was prepared to take on the other two.

Instead, he faced an army.

Minions had boiled up from every shadow in the yard and they surrounded him, their numbers so deep, they were in and among the trees on the edges of the garage's lot.

There must have been thirty. Forty. Fifty.

Facing the overwhelming force, a resonant calm flooded through him, kind of like he was bleeding out. Eddie was going to be okay; Colin was going to make sure of that. And Ad was going to give that archangel enough time and space to get the pair of them out of here.

As for him? He wasn't getting out of this in one piece, and he was just fine with the way he was going to go.

This was the way to die: defending your territory and taking out a fuckload of the enemy on the way to your grave.

This was honorable.

As Adrian got ready to go into the thick of it, he thought, for what was going to be the last time, that he wished his friend was with still him. At least they wouldn't be separated for much longer, however.

Downtown at HQ, Reilly found herself on the verge of leaving and going home. For about an hour and a half.

There was nothing for her to do. She hadn't been assigned a new case yet; she'd finished up her work on her other ones; and God knew she was off Veck's. And yet she was sitting at her desk as though someone had superglued her butt to her chair, her colleagues having filed out a while ago.

Unfortunately, she wasn't just staring into space. She was back on Veck's father's Facebook page like some nutjob addict.

Going into the links section, she clicked through to a few sites, but none of them gave her what she was looking for. Then again, nothing with www. was going to help her out: Her answers as to why Veck had seduced her, and why she'd fallen for it, and why he had to be just like his father, were not on the Web.

She went to the videos section. God, these things were positively repulsive, most taken at fan rallies—

She frowned and leaned in toward her screen. One of the newest had been shot within the last couple days or so from in front of the prison where the elder DelVecchio was housed. In the bright sun, the signs were plainly visible and the slogans were ridiculous.

Some even rhymed.

Execution. Persecution. How original.

She watched the video again. And again. And again. Until she'd memorized the two-minute clip's pans and close-ups, as well as the part where that flashbulb went off from the back—

Wait.

Not a flashbulb.

She backed the file up and let it resume. In the back row, standing off to the side, was a man . . . with a pair of mirrored sunglasses on.

There was no way of zooming in, so she just replayed.

"Oh . . . God . . ."

Again with the replay.

"Oh . . . my . . . *God*."

It was . . . Bails?

It had to be him . . . standing in and among the deranged devotees. As the camera panned, he was speaking to the guy next to him—until he saw that he was on the video and turned away.

She went back to the wall on the page. Searching the membership was useless: Not only was there no way to screen the data, more to the point, she didn't know what she was looking for in terms of a name. In fact, if she typed in "John Bails" in the Facebook directory, it brought up a guy in Arizona who was sixty, and someone in New Mexico who was seventeen, and three other people who weren't a match.

On a burst of paranoia, she paused and checked over her shoulder. No one was behind her . . . or even in the department.

Back to the video.

As she watched over and over again, she wasn't absolutely sure it was him. After all, there were a million pairs of mirrored sunglasses out in the world. But the hair . . . the build . . . the coloring . . . all of that was dead-on.

Abruptly, she thought of those "boxes" he'd talked about . . . as well as the fact that Veck had passed his lie detector test. Yes, it was possible to dupe the machine, and given how cool Veck could get, he seemed like a perfect candidate for that rarified class of fibbers. But why, then, would he have admitted intent when it came to hurting Kroner? It didn't make sense.

Unless, of course . . . he'd simply told the truth.

Reilly went through every video there was . . . and found two other sightings of the man who appeared to be Bails. He always wore sunglasses, even at night, but not exclusively those mirrored jobs.

She sat back in her chair. Kicked her foot and sent herself on a leisurely spin.

Was it possible that Bails had a relationship with Veck's father?

Then again, if Bails was one of the legions of fans that madman had, he didn't have to actually know the guy. But why frame Veck?

As the momentum of her chair slowed, she found herself looking at the page again, and thought, Well, duh . . .

If the father was executed, how did they keep the love going? Simple—someone created the illusion that the family tradition was carrying on. Maybe even got Veck jailed. Maybe even drove him to kill.

She thought of that polygraph, and considered the idea that Veck actually had a murderous impulse. If pushed hard enough, if put under enough stress, it was possible that someone could snap and act in ways they wouldn't normally. Hello, that was why police departments had homicide divisions.

As for what happened in the woods? Veck might have gone there with the thought of killing Kroner on his mind, but given the way he'd behaved with the paparazzo he'd hit, it was conceivable he'd approached it as retaliation for what the man had done—which was still illegal, immoral, and inexcusable if he acted on it, but different from singling out an innocent woman and defiling her. Make that twenty-five innocent women.

Besides, Veck had not, in fact, harmed Kroner.

He had, in fact, called 911.

She thought of how Veck had been around her, the way he'd talked and acted and touched her.

Then she recalled Bails by her car, looking forlorn and betrayed by his "best friend."

Psychopaths could be very convincing. That was at the core of how they caused the damage they did.

The question was, Between those two men, who was the liar?

As she thought more about Bails's great reveal in her unmarked in front of the hospital, she had to wonder . . . how had he known about the earring's discrepancy? There were hundreds of pieces of evidence in the preliminary report. Hundreds. As a detective on the case, he would have looked that list over once, maybe twice. Kind of hard to believe he'd remember a single entry.

What had prompted him to compare the two lists around that particular object? The fact that Veck had recognized the earring as Sissy Barten's?

Or maybe because Bails was the guy doing the framing?

There was only one way to know for sure. Unfortunately, it was not legal.

Reilly stood up and walked through her department, striding all the way to the rear and looking in the conference rooms; then returning to the front to check reception;

before doubling back and peeking into her boss's office even though she knew the woman had left.

Over at her desk once more, she picked up her phone and dialed the one person she knew could help her.

When the call was answered, she said softly, "I need some help, but it's walking the line."

De la Cruz's voice was steady. "What kind of line we talking about?"

"The only one that counts."

CHAPTER
43

A drian Vogel was a bloody fucking lunatic.

Staring out the picture window from the flat above the garage, the archangel Colin measured the battlefield down below. Previously, the quarter acre had been nothing but a dirt drive and a squat piece of lawn. The moment those minions had showed their oily faces, however, an alteration of purpose had been affected, and now Adrian was facing a legion of Devina's bastards.

This had catastrophe stamped all over it: Even though Colin had no respect for the denizens of the demon's lair, they were very dangerous, especially in these kinds of numbers. And that daft son of a bitch was facing off at them with nothing but a thin suit of leather and a farming tool.

Colin closed his eyes briefly and cursed. The angel was not going to make it out of this. He was an extraordinary fighter—as good as even the savior who was a master. But the sheer numbers he was facing? It was a swarm.

Except there was no leaving Eddie to go down there and help. Devina would want the body undefended, for one thing, and Jim had only a notification spell up with that bloody handprint of his. If something broke in here? It would only trigger a signal to the savior—and pulling Jim away from his work with the soul in question was not what anyone needed.

Moreover, if Colin assumed arms and went down upon the ground, he'd have to deal with Nigel for interfering—and less strife betwixt them rather than more was advisable at this point.

Except one couldn't stand by and just watch the massacre, could one.

Getting up and going over to the door, Colin opened up the fragile, worthless barrier. Immediately, the wafting stench of acid blood tingled in his nose, and the shouts and grunts of fighting burned in his ears.

Adrian was astonishing, wielding the hay fork with piercing success even as the tide of the enemy pressed forward and threatened to close ranks to surround him. Stabbing front-wise, then angling left, then right, then returning to center, he was picking off minions with such capability that for a moment, one had to reconsider involvement.

But then a minion, backed up a mate, came in low whilst Adrian was working at the chest level.

The bastard was going for the angel's feet, trying to get him off balance and then on the ground—at which point they would all seize control and own him like a dog.

Colin ducked back into the house and looked around.

Mirror. He needed a mirror.

A quick survey of the premises yielded one that hung over the sink in the bathroom. Unfortunately, it was part of a built-in unit upon the wall, not something he could take down from a hook. He would, however, make it work.

Focusing upon his forefinger, he gathered a coldness upon the tip, intensifying the energy, building it up and keeping it harnessed.

When he made contact with the reflective glass, the pane shattered but held itself within its frame, the cracks emanating from where he had touched. Glancing around, he found a publication upon the back of the toilet marked *Car and Driver*, and picking it up, he pressed the folios flat against that which he had splintered.

With a drawing force of will, he called the shards forward, separating them from their backing, affixing them temporarily upon the face of what he held to them.

When he removed the stack of papers, the pieces stuck as if they had been glued, the rest free-falling into the white sink in a tinkling, sparkling rush.

He was zip-quick as he raced back through the flat and went out upon the landing of the exterior stairs once again.

Adrian was nearly surrounded. He had done incredible work, however. With just the lowly hay fork, he had incapacitated so many, the lawn and drive were an obstacle course of black writhing bodies. Steam, from where he'd been splattered with that corrosive blood, rose off his leather outerwear, giving him a foggy shadow as he jabbed and whirled.

Holding the magazine flat in his palm, Colin commanded the mirrored shards to rise and fly, sending them in a group out to Adrian. When they arrived at their destination, they rotated en masse so that their reflective surfaces faced him and then began to circle him, picking up his image . . . and throwing it.

One Adrian became two. Two became four. Four became sixteen. Sixteen became a countless army to meet a finite force.

Each had the leather coat. Every had the pitchfork. All were the proficient killer.

They were Adrian multiplied, perfect reproductions who fought and thought exactly as he did. And as he looked around at himselves, he lost his rhythm for a moment as he realized he had backup of an unexpected kind.

He was not one to waste time in the heat of battle, however, and as he reengaged, the others of him fell into fighting stances and then made good on the preparation, engaging the minions.

"Now 'tis fair," Colin murmured as he shut himself back in the garage and resumed his perch at the window.

It was a full-blown melee down below, a ground war of proper dimension with well-matched combatants. The minions snapped out their expandable limbs, their fangs flashing white in featureless, noir faces whilst they sought for purchase upon angel arms and legs. And in return, the Adrians engaged with no less aplomb, striking with vicious accuracy and a kind of brutal elegance of movement, that humble farming tool transformed into a most worthy weapon. As time passed, the angel brigade lengthened their territory, cutting off any avenues for rear-flank dominance, and then they began to conquer their foes, squeezing the minions into a wedge as they closed in from the sides, leaving contorted bodies underfoot.

'Twas so very satisfying to watch, but even better to be a part of, Colin thought with envy.

Up above in heaven, this war was of grave importance, yes, but there was a staunch lack of visceral feel. Here . . . this was where it was happening.

Here was where he wished he was.

Abruptly, he thought of Nigel and wondered whether the archangel was correct. Colin had long seen himself as a logical being, rising above all base emotion—and that was a big part of what defined him.

He had passion in his gut, however. Deep rivers of it.

And it made him want to fight, not play witness.

Alas, he wanted to be in Adrian's combat boots . . .

CHAPTER
44

As Reilly sat at her desk and stared at her phone, she didn't think de la Cruz was going to pull it off.

Yes, he was the only person she could think of who could get into a sealed juvenile file that was fifteen years old and no doubt buried in the basement of some suburb of New York City. But that was a tall order, even for a miracle worker like him.

For one thing, "sealed" meant "lose your job" if you went there. For another, most old records were tossed after a number of years, given that computerized files were not all that prevalent in the nineties, especially in smaller municipalities. And finally, the guy hadn't worked in Manhattan for years and years. Who knew if he had any contacts left down south?

Still, it had been a relief to lay everything out to the detective, even the stuff about Bails: She didn't like feeling crazy all by herself. And at least he didn't seem to think her suspicions were totally unfounded.

Glancing at the clock across the office, she knew that he wouldn't be getting back to her tonight . . . so it was probably time to go home before she ossified in her chair.

Rising to her feet, she stretched hard—which was less

about loosening her body and more about finding an excuse to look behind herself. Again.

Man, you knew paranoia was bad when you had to make excuses for it to yourself.

After shutting down her computer, she picked up her coat, pulled it on, and grabbed her purse. Before she left IA, she checked her gun in its holster under her arm and got out her cell phone.

Just in case.

As she stepped out into the hallway, she looked both ways and took a listen. Off in the distance, past Homicide, she heard a vacuum running, and down below in the foyer someone was using a floor buffer.

She glanced behind her. There was no one around.

Walking fast for the main stairs, she reminded herself that even though it was after hours, the lights were still on everywhere and there were twenty or thirty night-shift people working in the building—

When her phone went off, she nearly dropped the damn thing. And then almost lost it again when she saw it was de la Cruz. Accepting the call, she whispered, "Don't tell me you found the juvie record?"

"That's what you asked me to do."

Her feet slowed. "My God . . ."

"My brother-in-law's cousin's husband, actually."

"Tell me."

"Truancy. That's it."

She stopped at the head of the stairs, and kept her voice low. "What do you mean 'that's it.' "

"The Garrison County records department has a single listing in 'ninety-six for a Thomas DelVecchio Jr. He was brought in for skipping school repeatedly."

"And there is no other reference? No psych evals? No—"

"Nothing. The backlog of cases were digitalized in two thousand five—and they saved ten years of files, so we just made it inside the safe zone. DelVecchio was fourteen at the time he was brought in—and if he'd had earlier trips through the justice system, they would have been noted in that entry."

"And there was nothing afterward."

"Not a thing."

There was a long silence. And then she felt compelled to ask, "There is no way something was missed?"

"If for some reason he got into trouble in another jurisdiction, well, then yeah. But real estate records show that his mother owned a house in the same town for twenty years and I know Veck's résumé's been vetted—and he has on it that he graduated from the Garrison County High School in two thousand. So I think it's safe to assume he stayed in that area."

Reilly put her hand on her head as her mind reeled. "He's being framed."

"Sure looks that way."

"God*damn* it."

Now she got moving, racing down the stairs, her heels clipping loudly on the marble.

"Another thing," de la Cruz said. "While I was waiting for the callback, I got on that Facebook page that you sent me the link to."

"And you saw Bails?"

"Yup, I think that's him, too. Where are you?"

"Just leaving the station house. I'm going over to Veck's right now."

As she passed by the housekeeping staff, she watched her footing on the wet marble and then shot down the back hallway.

"There's only one problem," de la Cruz said. "We can't use the juvie record to prove anything. We should never have gotten this information."

She punched the bar on the rear exit and burst out into the night. "I have the Bails images on Facebook—I took screen shots of them in case they get taken down and I found the alias he's using. I think we have enough to get a warrant to force Facebook to give us the account details and the Internet service provider. We can link him that way."

"Proving that he's a fan of DelVecchio Sr. isn't enough."

"It's a start."

"Agreed, but there has to be something more. And before you ask, yes, I'll call the sergeant—unless you want to?"

"I'm going to be busy with Veck. Maybe he'll have some ideas."

"Roger that—"

"I don't know *how* you pulled this off."

"Officially, I didn't."

"Well, I really owe you. You're a lifesaver."

She ended the call and got out the keys to her unmarked—

"Actually, that's not quite the word I would have used."

Reilly didn't get a chance to spin around. A hand grabbed the back of her head and slammed her face-first into the car's hard contours, the top of the door catching her right at the browline.

As her lights went out and her knees buckled, all she heard was Bails's voice in her ear: "You really should have looked behind you."

Adrian slayed the last minion with an arcing slice that went from high to low, the pitchfork's tines piercing an oily black chest, all knife-through-butter.

At least . . . he thought he was the one who did it.

As the body fell to the ground with a wet thud, he looked around . . . at all the others of him. Who, at the very same moment, turned and looked in his direction.

He spun the pitchfork around and stabbed the ground—and the other dozens of himselves did the same thing a mere split second later.

If Eddie were here, he thought, the guy would have been pissing in his pants. Too many openings for a good ass-slapping.

Shit, Eddie . . . why hadn't he been the one with the nine lives?

At that moment, the face of every Adrian grew tight, those mouths that he knew so well flattening out, those pierced brows lowering ... until he was surrounded, literally, by his own grief.

The sound of slow clapping brought their collective faces up and around. Colin had come out of the apartment and was standing on the top landing of the stairwell.

"Well-done, lad, well-done."

"I had help."

Huh. None of the other Adrians spoke up, so this had to be him—and what a thing to be relieved about.

For fuck's sake, this shit was going to give him a disorder.

"I would have joined you," Colin said as he floated down the stairs and then walked across the steaming, black-stained ground. "But as you pointed out, I am here to take care of our dearly departed."

"Eddie okay?"

"Yes."

Ad shook his head. "Thank God you were here."

"Indeed."

As the archangel strode through the remains of all those minions, his boots remained pristine even though the ground was a sloppy mess.

He and the other Adrians all looked impressed. And then he realized that they were steaming: Every Adrian had tendrils of smoke rising from their shoulders and backs, the corrosive blood eating through the leather, heading for skin.

On that note ... Adrian ripped off the duster—

Not even a split second afterward, a chorus of flapping went off, like a flock of geese had gotten goosed and taken to the sky. And then the Adrians tossed their coats down on the ground with disgust just as he had.

Colin stopped in front of them all. "Would you like to keep your little friends?"

Adrian looked around at himselves. "They're great backup—I wonder if they do windows? And if you don't mind me asking, how'd you pull this off?"

Colin extended his hand. At some kind of command from him, the surface of the inky sludge covering the driveway and lawn began to vibrate, and then here and there, tiny objects rose, dripping with—

They were shards, Adrian realized, as they shed their coating of minion. Glass—no, mirrored shards.

"Tricky, tricky," Ad murmured.

"Say good-bye to your crew, mate."

He glanced around. And found that he wanted to tell himselves thank you—

In perfect synchronization, all of the other Adrians put their right palms up to their hearts, those dark heads dipping gravely.

And then they were gone, along with their coats.

"Can I have them back if I need them again," Ad asked. "Like if I have to lay some carpet, or move a piano."

"You know where to find me."

"I do." He reached out, but then dropped his hand when he saw the condition of his gloves. "I gotta know something."

"What."

"Why'd you do it?"

"You were going to lose."

"Are you going to tell Nigel?"

"Probably. I subscribe to the notion that it is better to apologize than ask permission."

"Know that one well."

There was a period of silence. "Thank you," Adrian said roughly.

The archangel bowed with grace. " 'Twas a pleasure. Now, I think we should get this cleaned up. Not many neighbors about, but it would be hard to explain, don't you think?"

Good point: If there was just a skirmish, there wasn't a lot of reason to worry about the icky aftermath. God knew that humans left plenty of oily messes around, and smudges on the ground soon disappeared with enough sunlight. This?

"The only option," he muttered, "would be to tell people an oil tanker exploded on the front lawn."

"And does that not require a permit or some such?"

"Probably. As well as a lot of gunpowder." He shook his head. "Damn, we're going to need a lot of—"

Cleaning solution was the term he was going to use, as he started to wonder how much of that witch hazel concoction he could pull together. Enough for a fire truck would do the job.

Colin, however, took care of it all: Sweeping his hand in a circle, he disappeared every trace of the tremendous fight.

Adrian whistled under his breath. "You wouldn't be in the market for a second job, would you?"

Colin smiled with a dark edge. "That would be against the rules, dear boy."

"And God forbid we bust those bitches."

Adrian yanked off one of his gloves and matched the archangel's cynical expression as the pair of them clapped palms and shook hard.

"Jim's probably waiting for me," Ad murmured, glancing up toward the garage.

"And at the moment, I have nothing better to do."

The relief that Eddie wasn't alone was so profound, he was tempted to hug the motherfucker. "Then I'll just get back to work now."

"And so shall I."

As Adrian nodded and took to the air, he was prepared for Devina in ways he hadn't been before.

Good thing, as it turned out, considering what he walked in on when he got to Veck's.

CHAPTER
45

When Veck's phone went off at quarter to nine, he was so keyed up, he almost didn't bother answering the fucking thing.

He'd been marching around his house, waiting for something, anything to go down with Heron, that he was practically vibrating off the floor, all live wire with nothing to plug into.

"Aren't you going to answer it," Jim asked from the other end of the kitchen. The angel had been smoking quietly in the chair he'd sat down in, like, frickin' days ago.

Okay, it hadn't been days. This stretch of nothing happening felt like *decades*.

As the ringer went off again, Veck glanced over. He'd tossed the cell on the counter and it was on vibrate, the thing inching closer and closer to the edge with every trembling ring-a-ding-ding.

He was quite content to let the POS walk itself right off into a free fall. Except then he saw that the screen had one word on it: *Reilly*.

Veck all but dived across the countertop. "Hello! Hello? *Hello!?*"

He had no idea why she would be calling him, but he

didn't care. Maybe she'd misdialed, or maybe she needed the pizza guy's number. Or, hell, even if she just wanted to cuss him out, he was down for—

"You sound so pent-up there, DelVecchio."

He frowned at the male voice. "Bails?"

"Have I told you how much I love your name? DelVecchio . . ." The guy drew out the syllables. "Mmm, just the sound of it gets me off."

"What the fuck are you talking about?"

"DeeelllVeccccchiooo."

Abruptly, Veck felt a shot of blind aggression nail him in the heart. "Why are you on Reilly's phone?"

Although it wasn't as if he couldn't guess. Christ, here it was again, he thought. Another snow job by someone he'd assumed he could trust—only this time, he was terrified of the consequences.

He looked over to Heron, who had put his cig out in the ashtray and gotten up—as if this was what he'd been biding his time for. "Why, Bails?"

There was a grunt and a scraping noise . . . the kind of thing that a pair of feet made over the earth.

"Sorry, just moving the body."

Veck squeezed the phone so hard, one of the dial keys went off with a screech. "*I'm going to kill you. If you hurt her—*"

There was a slapping sound. And then a groan. "Wake up, bitch. I want you to talk to him."

"*Reilly.*" So help them both, Veck was going to rip Bails's head off his shoulders and bowl with it. Then he was going to disembowel the body and cut off the arms and legs.

But first, he'd castrate the motherfucker.

"*Reilly—*"

"I'm . . . sorry . . ." a weak voice said.

Veck closed his eyes. "Reilly, I'm going to get you—"

"I didn't . . . believe you . . . so sorry . . ."

The words were slurred, as if she had a swollen mouth, or maybe—God forbid—had had some teeth knocked out.

"I'm going to come and get you. Don't worry—I'll—"

She cut him off. "I know ... you didn't ... do it.... Bails ... lied—"

Her scream was so loud, Veck had to jerk the phone away from his ear.

"Reilly!" he shouted, his voice ringing around his kitchen. "Reilly—"

"Sorry," Bails cut in. "I had to introduce her to my girl-friend. They're going to have some fun together—at least until you come join us."

"Tell me where you are, motherfucker."

"Oh, I will, but I have someone who wants to say hello first. But not to you. She says for you to give Heron the phone now."

"Fuck that—"

There was a rustle and then a female came on the line. "Hello, little Tommy."

Oh, shit, that voice was ... all wrong. Like someone had one of those distortion filters over the receiver. But that wasn't the only problem.

His father had called him that when he was young.

"Now listen, Tommy, I want you to give the phone over to that big, beautiful man who's standing across your kitchen from you. Then I want you to grab your coat and get nice and armed—I'm talking your guns, your knives, whatever you like. By the time you come back to where you've been pacing around for the last few hours, Heron will tell you where to go."

"Who are you?" he gritted out.

"You know *exactly* who I am." The laugh that followed was blade-sharp. "One note, by the way—those towels you keep putting up? They might stop you from seeing me, but it's not a vice versa kind of thing. I've always had my eye on you."

Veck shifted his stare over to Jim. The angel was shaking his head from side to side slowly, as if he knew exactly what was being said even though the cell was all but stapled to Veck's ear.

"Before you throw the phone to Jim," the woman, or whatever the fuck it was, said, "you should know that if anyone comes with you, I'll kill her. I'll take the knife I have right now in my hand and I'll start with her face. Are you aware of how long someone can live without a mouth? Long time. Ears? Teeth? She can be alive, but praying to be dead if you know what I mean. And I won't stop there . . . I'll go down to her fingers. Just to the first knuckles. I'm good at walking the line, keeping them alive if I want to—who do you think taught your father all of his tricks?"

"If you touch her—"

"Who said I haven't already. Now be a good boy and throw the phone."

"Catch," Veck barked, as he tossed the thing over.

He didn't wait to see whether there was a safe landing. Racing for the stairs, he took them three at a time, the soles of his shoes squeaking, especially as he hard-cornered it on the second-floor landing.

The closet in his bedroom was full of weapons. Guns, ammo, knives—how that bitch knew about it all, he didn't want to think—

"Motherfucker!" he shouted as he opened the doors.

The shelves were empty.

But of course. The police had come and taken everything he had into evidence.

"That's not what you're going to need."

He wheeled around—and recoiled. Standing in the doorway of his room, Heron's partner, Adrian, was looking like a hot mess: His shirt had been rotted through in places and . . . Christ, the *smell*.

Whatever, though, the guy was alive and breathing, and with the way things were going, that was the only data screen that counted.

"Guns aren't going to work," Adrian said.

"The hell they won't."

Rushing out of the room, Veck pushed past the man, his eyes watering from that acrid stench. Downstairs, he checked the other two obvious places he'd kept autoloaders: in the kitchen under the sink, and under the couch.

Gone.

Only one stash left.

As Jim Heron's angry voice drifted in from the kitchen, Veck went into the utility hall that connected the garage to the house. The washer and dryer were behind a pair of louvered doors, and he busted both sides open before squatting down. The dryer unit had been dropped during his last move, the bottom panel becoming loose enough so that if you knew where to press, it . . .

Snapped. Right. Off.

And there they were. Two nines with fully loaded clips, with everything stored in plastic bags to keep them lint free.

"Thank you, Jesus."

"Those are not what you need."

Veck looked up. Jim was standing over him, that cell phone in his hand. The angel was so pissed off, a flush had ridden up his throat and nailed him in the face, but that wasn't the only glow he had going on: There was a fierce light emanating from his body, like he was a Lava lamp in the *on* position.

Veck leaped to his feet, images of Reilly being defaced giving him a very precise picture of what in fact *was* required. Ripping the guns out of those Ziplocs, he double-checked their actions, and then went down low again for the two extra clips.

"Where is she?" he demanded as he loaded up his pockets.

"If you go in there half-cocked, you're going to choose the wrong path."

"Fuck that, I'm fully cocked." He grabbed the guns, and shoved Heron out of the way.

His spare holster was hanging from the coatrack by the back door, and he slipped the straps over his shoulders. Both weapons went in perfectly, because he was a one-size-fits-all kind of guy, and then a light windbreaker covered the show.

"Where is she," he snapped.

"We need to talk first."

"Not on my list of things to do. Sorry."

At that, he unsheathed the pair of autoloaders and pointed one barrel at Jim Heron's chest and the other at Adrian's.

"Now, where is my woman."

CHAPTER
46

Well, this was going fucking great, Jim thought, as he stared into the business end of a nine.

"You tell me where she is," Veck bit out, "or I'll shoot you."

The guy meant it: He was cucumber cool, icebox ready. Kinda made you respect the bastard. Except he wasn't thinking straight, was he.

"You kill me," Jim pointed out levelly, "and I can't tell you where to go. You kill him"—he nodded in Ad's direction—"and I'm going to strangle you with your own colon."

There was a brief pause and then the gun pointed at him shifted no more than a millimeter to Jim's left.

The SOB pulled the trigger and buried a bullet into the molding right by Jim's ear.

"Who said anything about killing?" Veck subtly moved the muzzle lower. "Pain works wonders on tight lips. Besides, I'll bet if I did a callback they'd pick up."

Triangulating where the next bullet was going to land made Jim fear a new career as a falsetto—assuming he didn't want to take for granted the whole bullets-can't-touch-me thing. Then again, at least it wasn't Adrian's 'nads on the line—given how much that guy could not sing.

"You might think this shit over, Jim," the other angel muttered. "We know the guy's got good aim."

Jim shook his head. "You don't know what you're walking into, Veck."

"Have I mentioned time is flying? God only knows what's happening to her."

"True, but she's not the one I'm worried about." Jim glanced over at Ad. "And I need to go with him. Any clue how I can do that?"

The other angel cursed softly. "That was Eddie's department."

"*No* one's coming with me," Veck barked. "Or that woman is going to kill her. *And will you stop wasting time—*"

"Devina is not going to do shit to her! She needs you there, and Reilly alive is the only way to make sure you show up. Now will you give me a moment to think, asshole?"

As Jim began pacing, Veck started spouting off, all, "Stop moving or I'll shoot," but he ignored the guy—

The second shot went into the floor at Jim's feet, and halted him. Pegging the Clint Eastwood motherfucker with a glare, he said, "That was, like, an inch from my boot, man."

"Next time it's your goddamn ankle."

"Better than your balls," Ad pointed out.

Jim turned to face the detective, ready to paint the true picture of Devina . . . when he happened to glance down at the guy's bifurcated shadow on the tiled floor.

That pair of dark patterns looked like two trees in the forest . . .

And you could stand behind trees, couldn't you. Hide behind them. Camouflage yourself to appear to be part of the environment such that anyone, like, say, your enemy, could look around . . . and notice nothing.

After all, Devina had seemed to suggest she couldn't find him—but was he really willing to take a chance on something he didn't quite get?

Except then he thought about that shit with the badge. Granted, it had nearly split his own self in two, but was there any other solution? Short of sending this pistol-packing, pissed-off sonofabitch into the showdown alone?

"I have to get inside you," Jim said in a deep voice.

Veck frowned hard. "Sorry, you're not my type."

"We could put a wig and a dress on him," Adrian suggested. And as he got the hairy eyeball from everybody in the room, the angel shrugged. "They gotta make that crap in tarp size, right?"

"And to think I'm actually glad your smart ass is coming back," Jim muttered before refocusing on Veck. "I've got to come with you—and she can't know I'm there. So if you'll excuse me . . ."

Jim closed his eyes and instinctively let the corporeal part of himself go, shedding his suit of skin and bones until he was nothing but the light source that animated his body from within.

The dissolve went off without a glitch—it was exactly what he had done but hadn't been able to control down in Devina's lair when he'd exploded in fury at her.

"Brace yourself, big boy," he said into the air.

Clearly, Veck heard him, because the guy recoiled, his eyes rolling around like peas in a jar at the prospect of being possessed. But this was the only way to protect him, and he must have known that because he didn't run.

Given that Jim had no clue what the hell he was doing, he approached carefully. The last time he'd done this, he'd blown Devina apart—not exactly the happy ending he or Veck needed in this case.

Good news, though. As he pressed forward, Veck became nothing more than a sieve, offering only a passing resistance. Inside the shell? Jim fought for room in a metaphysical landscape that had nothing to do with the molecules that made the man, and everything to do with the space in between them. And what do you know, he got a crystal-clear on why Eddie had said no-go for an exorcism. Veck was a goddamn Moon Pie, all half-and-half: Every inch of his soul was yin-and-yang, with good and evil spliced together.

No way to operate and excise. You'd destroy him.

Except two could play at this takeover game: on instinct, Jim suffused the man's interior being, becoming a fog that turned it into a threesome situation. . . .

Man, that sounded dirty.

But the fact of the matter was, just as Devina's "DNA" was pervasive, Jim became the same—and he hid not behind the good side, but the bad one. Better coverage that way—

Huh. From this vantage point, he could look out of Veck's eyes.

"How'm I doin'?" Jim asked in his own voice—hey, he could talk out of the bastard's mouth, too.

Across the way, Adrian shrugged. "Pretty damn good—I can't sense you. But I gotta ask—the pair of you want a cigarette? Or are you going for a twofer?"

"Fuck off," Jim and Veck answered at the same time.

Standing in his utility room, Veck felt vaguely nauseous, like he'd eaten a two-day-old Philly cheese steak, washed it down with lukewarm beer, and had a cherry slushie for dessert: too full of shit that didn't get along.

And as for hearing Jim's voice coming out of his own lips? He could do without that, thank you very much.

"So where are we going?" he asked.

Well, didn't this give a whole new meaning to "talking to yourself."

"The quarry."

"The *quarry*? For fuck's sake, it'll take forever to—"

"Get the cigarettes," Jim said.

"Screw that, we need my bike—it'll take us a half hour—"

"Come on, sport. Get the Marlboros—I'll take care of the travel arrangements."

Cursing a blue streak, he beat feet over to the kitchen table, grabbed the pack and the lighter, and shoved them in with the backup bullet clips.

"And take this," Adrian said, unsheathing what looked like a glass knife.

"No offense, I'll stick with bullets."

"Silly subhuman." The angel shoved the dagger into Veck's belt. "You can trigger up anything you like—it's for Jim."

"Tell me this isn't permanent?"

"No, you have to give me my weapon back at the end." Har-har, hardy-har-har. "I'm talking to Jim."

"No, it's not," the angel answered from out of Veck's mouth. "I can get free as easily as I got in."

"You sure about that?"

"Nope."

"Fabulous." Veck looked around to meet Heron in the eye and realized that was pointless—without a frickin' mirror. "So how are you going to get us—"

Next stop was the quarry. Literally.

And there was no bus ride or train trip or car crawl to compare: One moment Veck was in his house; the next he was in the center of the quarry's long slope.

Don't address me out loud, Jim said in his head.

Is this what schizophrenics experience, Veck wondered.

Couldn't tell you. Just make sure you stay tight.

"Like I have a choice with you in here, too," Veck muttered, as he looked around.

Wait, before you head in. There was a pause. *Veck, this is your show. I'm just going to make sure you live long enough to have a shot—but everything is on you. I won't interfere or intercede—we clear? You've got to make your mind up on your own. But you've got to do the right thing, whatever that is.*

"Yeah. Sure."

I just want you to remember—evil is usually the easy way out. And your fate is your own and no one else's.

As if on cue, a glow emanated out of the mouth of a cave about one hundred and fifty yards off to the right.

Enough with the fucking chatter.

Unsheathing both guns, Veck moved like the damn wind, leaping from boulder to boulder, jumping down, jumping up, scrambling. As his body went on full flip-out to get him to Reilly, his eyes stayed locked on that light. With every obstacle he threw himself over, horrible visions ran through his head, the gruesome, bloody nightmares making his chest burn with a fury that gave him power beyond the physical sum of his muscles and strength.

The cave in question had an entrance large enough so that he didn't have to duck down, and wide enough so that he didn't have to squeeze through. And then the nature-made corridor he found himself in stretched out ahead, penetrating far into the belly of the earth.

Dropping into a crouch, he ran as fast as he could toward the flickering glow.

All around him, the walls were wet and rough, the ceiling dripping, the floor puddled up. In a panic, he tried to filter out the pounding sound of his own footsteps so he could hear what was up ahead: Screams? Heavy breathing? Painful moaning?

Nothing.

It was too fucking quiet.

And then he turned the final corner.

The cave opened up to what appeared to be a low-walled space about the size of a big living room. It was impossible to get a true sense of its breadth, however, because the place was lit with candles, outside of which there was nothing but darkness.

In the center, there was a body strung up by the arms, the deadweight hanging from the ceiling.

It was not Reilly. It was what appeared to be a man with short sandy blond hair.

Veck glanced around for Bails and that bitch woman. But all there was ... was the body. And it was turned to face the far wall.

Was that ... a hospital johnny? he thought as he stepped forward, keeping the guns up.

"Reilly!" he shouted.

The echoing name roused whoever was hanging, and as the head jerked, a scraping sound rose up into the still, dank air. The person was slowly turning himself around, using the tips of his bare, muddy feet to change his position.

When Veck saw who it was, he cursed: The victim's identity was clear, in spite of the fact that the guy had obviously been punched in the face recently: His forehead was swollen and going black-and-blue, but the features were well known.

"Kroner . . ." Veck muttered, wondering how in the fuck the bastard had been brought here. Then again, abductions from hospitals were improbable but not impossible.

The serial killer struggled to lift his chin, his mouth working slowly. He was trying to talk, but Veck didn't give a shit what the fucker had to say.

"Reilly!" he called out, hoping that the darkness beyond the candles meant that there was another chamber where she was—

Someone stepped out of the shadows toward him.

He blinked once, and when the vision didn't change, he realized it was, in fact, a woman. Although what someone like her was doing here—

"Hello, Veck." It was the voice from his phone, live and in person. "Welcome to the party."

The brunette made Angelina Jolie look like a librarian: She was lush and dangerous, an upright jungle dressed in stilettos and a short skirt that belonged in a café downtown, or an elegant private club . . . anywhere but this stank-ass cave.

"Did you come alone?" she asked him, her plump, juicy lips pursing.

"Yes."

"Good." She moved around him, circling, smiling. "You're just like your father—taking direction well."

"Where is Reilly?"

"Your devotion to the woman is"—her voice got tense— "enviable. And because I can imagine how anxious you are to find her, I'll say that I'm prepared to tell you."

"So do it."

She eyed the guns. "Do you honestly think those are going to work against me?" Her laugh was wind chime–beautiful—and nonetheless rang falsely in the ear. "And, oh, look, they gave you a dagger, too. Hope does spring eternal, I suppose. By the way, did Jim tell you he used to be a killer?"

"I don't give a shit what he was."

"Right, right, it's all about the girl." That voice grew bitter again. "How lucky she is. And she should know how you feel about her, don't you think."

At that, the woman idly turned toward Kroner and strolled across to the guy. Speaking over her shoulder, she said, "Yes, tell her how you feel, why don't you."

Veck looked into the shadows. "I love you, Reilly! I'm here!"

"So romantic," the brunette said dryly.

As the woman stayed fixated on the serial killer, Veck decided to hedge his bets: He put one of his guns away . . . and palmed up that glass dagger he'd been given. None of this was making sense—which gave some credibility to Adrian's advice.

"Where the fuck is she?" he growled.

"I'll tell you—but you have to do something for me."

"What."

The brunette smiled and stepped back from Kroner. "Kill him."

Veck narrowed his eyes on the woman.

In response, she smiled more deeply. "It's what you were going to do all along. You waited for him in those woods, biding your time until he showed up among the trees next to that motel. You were going to act . . . but you were denied your chance."

Facing off at her, Veck's body began to vibrate, that rage that had sprung loose at the prison coalescing in his torso, tightening his muscles.

"This is my gift to you, little Tommy. You kill him, and I'll show you where your woman is. It's what you want. It's what you're here for. It's your destiny."

From out of nowhere, a reflection of light pierced the darkness, and illuminated the shadows, revealing . . . Bails.

The guy was sitting on the floor of the cave, leaning back

against the wet wall. A gunshot marked his forehead be-
tween his wide-open eyes, the smallest trail of blood seep-
ing out and dripping down his nose. His mouth was lax; his
skin pale gray.

"Don't worry about him," the brunette said dismissively.
"He was nothing but a pawn. You, on the other hand . . . are
the prize. And all you have to do is act. Kill him . . . and I'll
make sure you see your girl."

Abruptly, Veck realized where the shaft of light was
coming from.

His hand had risen up, and that glass dagger had caught
the butter soft candlelight, sending a shaft of it across the
cave to zero in on his supposed friend.

"Time's wasting, little Tommy. Let's get through this, so
we can come out the other side. Listen to your gut. Do what
you know is right. Take out this piece-of-shit, amoral killer
and find what you seek. It's such an obvious path, such a
simple trade—everything that Reilly is, for this murdering
madman. It's all in your hands. . . ."

"Is Reilly alive?" he heard himself say.

"She is."

"Will you let us both out of here alive?"

"Probably. Depends on what you do, doesn't it." The
brunette's voice dropped to a seductive whisper. "You can
see her the moment you take care of business. I swear to it.
It's all in your hands. . . ."

CHAPTER
47

As Reilly hung from the cave's ceiling, she still could not believe the image she was showing to Veck: The hospital johnny and the flat chest and the dangling legs were not her own.

Yet through the screaming pain in her head, through her confusion and panic, she could move these limbs that were not hers, could draw breath through a throat she did not know, could fill lungs that were someone else's.

All of which gave credibility to what Veck thought he was looking at.

And so he was going to kill her, she thought in horror and disbelief.

Struggling to speak, she whispered in a rasping voice that was not her own, "I'm ... me ... please ..."

"... It's such an obvious path, a simple trade—everything that Reilly is, for this murdering madman. It's all in your hands. ..."

The brunette who was talking was not in fact a woman. Reilly had seen what that thing was—it had shown her its true vileness while Bails got Veck on the phone, and that was why she had screamed.

Then afterward, she had watched as it had gotten into Bails's mind and made him turn his own gun on himself.

The great liar, she thought. Who knew that that was so true about the devil.

"Veck . . ." Reilly tried to marshal more breath, dragging air down into a frozen rib cage. "Veck . . . no . . ."

But she wasn't reaching him—and she wasn't going to: The louder she spoke, the more she sounded like Kroner, as if his voice box had replaced hers. And she was losing what little strength she had: Bails had dragged her down the quarry's slope, and her lower legs were contused badly—to the point where she knew she'd lost blood. She was also very sure she had a concussion, and she had grown weak from having hung in the cold for God only knew how long.

A hot tear slid down her cheek, and then a second . . . and then a rush of them.

At one time or another, like most people, she had entertained morbid thoughts about what death was waiting for her: A slow-growing disease? A quick car accident? Some genetic weakness that predisposed her to a bad heart? Or maybe an attack from a criminal where she'd fight back, perhaps shoot him as he shot her. Real blaze-of-glory stuff.

What was happening in this frigid, damp cave? Not it.

Staring across at Veck's cold, furious face, she started to see double, and her eyes were incapable of bringing the two halves of him together . . . so she had more than enough opportunity to find that there was no compassion, no emotion, no doubt in his expression . . .

As that glinting crystal dagger lifted, she realized she was looking into his father's face.

This was the son living up to the father's legacy.

Images of her own parents made the tears come harder. She hadn't had a chance to say good-bye. To tell them one last time that she loved them, and that they'd changed not just her life, but so many others'. . . .

And she hadn't been able to tell Veck properly that she believed him, that she knew he was innocent . . . and that she loved him.

Of course, the grand irony was that he was about to kill her under the guise of saving her.

"I know you didn't do it," she said on a harsh breath that didn't carry far. "The evidence ... it was Bails. ..."

Why that was important to say given the amount of time she had left—which was nearly none—she hadn't a clue.

Better get on with it: "I love ... you. ..."

And then she closed her eyes, turned her head away, and braced herself. He was going to go for the heart. With a dagger—that was the most efficient way—and Veck was not going to want to waste time if he thought her life was hanging in the balance.

Terror choked her and her body began to shake.

Her mouth opened as she started to sob.

Tears flowed ... as her blood soon would.

Nights ago, in those woods, by that motel, Veck had been prepared to take this piece of shit Kroner out.

Granted, it hadn't been for society's benefit—although he'd been prepared to maintain that it was. And after the opportunity had come and gone, he'd been relieved that he hadn't done it.

Now? He had the only justification that mattered: his Reilly. He didn't care that she thought he'd tampered with evidence or that she wouldn't have anything to do with him after this.

Saving her life was enough.

The brunette was right; such a simple trade.

Veck focused on his victim. As Kroner hung from the cave's ceiling, his mouth was moving, and given the tears that were pouring out of his eyes, he was no doubt begging for mercy, the killer reduced to begging for everything he hadn't granted his prey.

Christ, he was so fucking pathetic, that hospital gown marked with blood as if he'd been pulled headfirst down the slope, his skin so white it had slipped into snow territory, his face all distorted from swelling.

Veck had a passing urge to put the dagger away and

punch the guy until the motherfucker had a coronary. The man's victims had had to go slowly . . . had been conscious as he'd taken his godforsaken bits and pieces from them . . . it seemed like karma to have him know on an up-close-and-personal level what it felt like to be out of control, in pain, and at the mercy of another.

But Reilly's life was at stake.

Veck craned his arm up higher over his shoulder and angled the glass dagger's point at Kroner's chest. One vicious stab was all it was going to take, and fuck knew that Veck had the strength to get the job done—

Just as the weapon reached the apex of the arc, in the second before he was going to put all his upper-body power into the downward thrust, one of the weapon's facets caught the candlelight and shot a beam onto Kroner's face.

Veck frowned as he got a clear picture of those ratlike features: Kroner had closed his eyes and turned his face to the side, his frail body trembling as he braced himself for death.

"What's the matter," the brunette barked. "Do it—and you'll have her."

This is not my life to take, Veck thought with a sudden, inexplicable conviction.

"Do it!"

This is . . . *not my life to take.*

His father . . . Kroner himself . . . men like that . . . they thought that all lives, all people, all things, were theirs for the taking, and it was just a case of whim-based design who they decided to choose, who became the next notch on their belt. And the trophies were about keeping a slice of this moment now, when they had all the power, when they were in control, when they were God—because like an orgasm, this pleasure point was fleeting, and the memory wasn't a patch on the actual experience.

Which was why they did it again and again.

And as for him? On some level, this was the perfect beginning, the stripe of poison ivy itching on his arm that, if he scratched it, would bloom and take over his entire body.

This is not my life to take.

"Just fucking do it!" the brunette demanded.

Veck shifted his eyes over to the woman. Her black stare called out to him even more than her words did, offering him a temptation that went beyond this cave, this split second, this on-the-verge—

"Reilly or him," she hissed. "Pick now."

Veck's arm began to tremble, his rock-hard muscles poised to strike and unable to bear the dead-space tension between decision and action.

"I don't believe you," Veck heard himself say.

"What."

Veck slowly lowered the weapon to his side. In a hoarse, cracking voice, he said, "I don't trust you. And I'm not . . ." He had to clear his throat. "I'm not going to kill him."

Bails was already dead, and there were no other sounds in the cave. And this woman . . . whatever she was . . . was a liar: Reilly had been alive at some point—it had absolutely been her on the phone—but there was no one else who was breathing in this damp hellhole with them, and given how weak she had sounded, it was doubtful she could have gotten herself free.

Chances were good she was already dead.

And although that made him mad-crazy with grief and the urge for vengeance, Kroner, in his condition, had most certainly not done the deed.

"You miserable little *shit*," the woman spat. "You pathetic, spineless, cocksucking *pussy*. Your father didn't hesitate—years ago, when it was his time, he leaped at the goddamn chance I gave him."

For some reason, Veck thought of that dinner with Reilly's true parents, the ones who had taken her in and ushered her into adulthood, the ones who were not blood, but who were better to her than those who had brought her into this world.

"I'm not my father," he said roughly.

As the words registered in his ears, he felt stronger: "I am *not* my father."

From across the way, a hot breeze hit him, as if the brunette were a heating unit on overdrive.

"You're saying *that*"—she pointed to Kroner—"is worth more than the woman you love."

"No, I'm saying I won't kill him. I don't think Reilly is—" His voice broke, but he quickly recovered. "I don't think she's alive. And I don't know why the hell you want me to nail him, but if the last thing I do in this life is piss you off? I'm good with that. Bitch."

The roar that lit off was so violent that he was thrown off his feet, his body sailing through the foul air and slamming into the cave wall behind him. As he slumped for a split second, he could feel the earth shaking beneath him, and hear the boulders of the slope vibrating up above as dirt and small rocks fell from the ceiling of the cave. On impulse, he sheltered his head, for all the good that would do—

The candles went out on a oner.

And then in the pitch-black, the wind came from out of nowhere, the violent gale carrying on its back a vicious, ear-splitting noise. In the midst of the fury, heavier and heavier stones fell on him, until he tucked into a ball and thought . . . shit, he wasn't getting out of this one alive.

No fucking way.

Off in the distance, he heard more great rocks shifting, but knew that in reality, it was probably not far away at all and just a case of the earth muffling the sounds: The whole quarry slope was a Swiss-cheese mine field of subterranean cutouts, incapable of withstanding this kind of blast—

Abruptly the hurricane sucked out of the cave, taking the screeching noise with it.

In the aftermath, soft sobs cut through the rumbling of the slope.

Feminine sobs.

Not like Kroner's at all.

"Reilly?" he shouted. *"Reilly!"*

He jumped up— "Fuck!" he muttered as he hit something overhead.

Rubbing his skull and crouching down so he didn't bang

the ceiling again, he shoved the dagger back into his belt and patted his pockets for his flashlight. Shit. He hadn't brought one.

Cursing a blue streak, he tried to zero in on the sounds of her. "Talk to me, Reilly! Help me find you!"

"I'm ... over ... here. ..."

"Reilly!" he hollered, throwing out his arms in front of him and sweeping them from side to side—

All at once he had his own mini-earthquake, his body going haywire as Jim Heron separated the pair of them, and stepped out, revealing himself.

Perfect timing: Suddenly there was plenty of light in the cave, the angel's form glowing fiercely as he stood off to the side.

For a moment, all Veck could do was stare at what he saw.

It made no fucking sense.

Reilly was hanging from the ceiling, in exactly the place Kroner had been, her arms stretched over her head, her feet barely touching the earthen floor. Her face was swollen and her legs were bleeding, her panty hose shredded, her skirt covered in mud, her shoes God only knew where.

"Reilly?" he breathed.

She struggled to lift up her head. Through her dirt-caked hair, her blurry eyes sought his. "I'm ... me. ..."

A shower of rock fragments fell from the ceiling and snapped Veck into action. Now was not the time to question any of this shit. He had to get her out of here before the slope collapsed on them both.

Thank God for Heron's guiding light.

Veck used it to shoot over to Reilly, except when he got a look at what she was strung up by, he knew they were in trouble: The iron links had been screwed into the rock ceiling, and the thick iron cuffs clamped to her wrists were bolted onto the damn chains.

Shit, this was not the first time this cave had been put to use, was it.

"Fucking hell," he muttered as he tried to find a release.

"Use the dagger," Jim said.

"It's just glass—"

"Use the goddamn thing."

Veck took out the blade and put it against the links. He didn't expect much—other than the "weapon" shattering—

The metal cleaved apart under the crystal, not just slicing in two, but getting ripped free of itself: He barely had time to catch Reilly and keep her off the ground.

Crushing her against him, he felt her shudder, and he allowed himself one treacherous moment of bliss to know that she was alive—and then he was all about getting her out.

As he swung her up into his arms, Jim led the way to the snaking corridor with his light.

Just as they came up to Bails, Veck had to stop.

"We're leaving him," Jim pronounced.

"You got that right." God only knew who his "friend" really was, but one thing was clear: Who the fuck cared. Anyone who so much as cut Reilly off in traffic was on his shit list. Endanger her life?

The bastard was lucky to have already been shot in the head—

Behind them, the ceiling began to crumble, the rush of sound and rocks and cold air all but palming his ass and ushering him the fuck out.

Veck broke into a run, his body charging forward at breakneck speed. As the chute they were racing through started collapsing on his heels, this was Indiana Jones, except it was real. Shit, the way in hadn't seemed this long—

Veck burst out of the tunnel into the fresh air, narrowly missing a body slam by leaping up onto the boulder in front of him.

There was no time for thanking God or Heron or anyone else. If that cave had just bitten it, there was a good chance that there was going to be an avalanche.

Zagging sharply to the left, he didn't bother measuring the distance he had to go to get them to the lip of the quarry, and he didn't waste time looking behind himself to see all the rolling, car-sized hunks of quartz barreling down on top of them.

Even if it killed him, he was going to get her up this goddamn slope.

He *was* going to save her—and all the odds that were against him from the obstacle course he faced, to the half mile up, to the burning fatigue that was already squeezing his thighs and his chest, weren't going to stop him.

He'd had the chance to sell his soul and had walked away from the negotiating table.

And that triumph paled in comparison to what it was going to feel like to make sure Sophia Reilly got to see tomorrow morning's sunrise.

CHAPTER
48

Reilly must have lost consciousness after Veck got her down from the chains in the cave, because when she came to again, there were red lights flashing all around and she was stretched out on something relatively soft.

"Veck . . . ?"

"Ma'am?"

Definitely not Veck's voice. Frowning, she forced her eyes to try to focus . . . and got the blurry picture of an EMT leaning over her.

"Ma'am? What's your name?"

He did it, she thought. Veck had somehow gotten them out.

"Ma'am? Can you hear me?"

"Reilly. Sophia . . . Reilly."

"Do you know what year it is?" After she told him, there were a couple more how-many-of-your-marbles-have-you-lost questions.

"Where is . . . Veck?" Why the hell wouldn't her eyes work—

A brilliant light exploded on one side of her vision. "Hey!"

"Just checking your pupils again, ma'am."

She fought to bring her hand up, and found that they'd run an IV into her arm vein.

"We'd like to take you to St. Francis," the man said. "You're on the verge of shock, you may need a transfusion, and you have a concussion."

"Where is . . ."

She turned her head . . . and there he was.

Veck was standing off to the side, just on the verge of being outside of the light thrown by the open double doors of the ambulance. His forearms were crossed in front of his chest and he was staring at the ground at his feet. He looked like he had been through a war, big patches of sweat staining his shirt, his pants splashed with dirt and ripped in places, his hair sticking straight up. Dimly, she had to wonder where his windbreaker had gone.

A CPD officer with an open pad was next to him, obviously taking a statement, and there were several members of Search and Rescue who looked like they were about to go down into the quarry.

To get Bails, no doubt.

Veck was shaking his head. Then nodding. Then speaking.

Tears cheated her of the sight of him.

He had carried her out of there. And he had done the right thing . . . he was not a killer at heart.

As if he felt her eyes on him, he lifted his stare and met her own: Instantly, she was back to that night in the woods, when they had looked at each other over Kroner's body.

When he seemed to hesitate, as if unsure of whether she'd want him, she tried to reach out her hand. "Veck . . ."

He took a step forward. Then another.

The police officer let him go and the medic got out of the way and then he was beside her in a rush, taking her palm in a squeeze that faded to a gentle holding.

"How you doing?" he asked in a ragged voice, as if he had screamed a lot, or maybe panted like a racehorse getting her up the rough slope.

"Head . . ." She tried to lift her free hand and found that her arm weighed four hundred pounds. "You? Are you . . ."

"Fine."

He didn't look fine. He looked gaunt and washed-out. Matter of fact, if it had been any other man, she would have said that he was . . . lost.

"Bails," she said, and then tried to swallow. Her throat was so dry, she felt like she had been in a forest fire, breathing smoke. "He shot himself—"

"Don't worry about—"

"*No.*" Now she was the one squeezing. "He set you . . . up. Said . . . juvie record . . . Facebook . . ."

"Shh—"

"He was at the prison. For your father. He was . . ."

An abiding cynicism eclipsed Veck's exhaustion. "One of the legions."

"I know . . . you didn't plant the earring. Bails . . . Had to have been him. He shot himself . . . in front of me. . . ."

"None of that matters—"

"I'm sorry." Those damn tears returned, but she did nothing to stop them. "I'm so very sorry—"

"Shh." He placed his fingertip on her lips. "Let's get you out of here."

"You already did."

"Not far enough."

For a long moment, they just stared at each other.

"I'll call your parents." He brushed her hair back. "And tell them to meet you at the hospital."

"And what about you—"

"I'll make sure they're there." He stepped back and glanced at the medic. "You'd better get going."

Not a request. A demand.

"Veck . . . ?" she whispered.

His eyes avoided hers. "I'll call your parents."

"*Veck.*"

As she started to try to sit up, the medic and his partner began rolling her to their vehicle. Meanwhile, Veck just took another step back.

There was a bump and a smoother roll as she was packed inside.

"I love you," she shouted as loud as she could. Which turned out to not be very loud.

The last thing she saw before the doors were shut was Veck's expression of pain . . . and then him slowly shaking his head back and forth . . . back and forth.

Good-bye, she realized in a cold rush, didn't have to be spoken in order to be real.

Veck breathed in sweet diesel fumes as the ambulance trundled off the shoulder and onto the dirt road that led away from the quarry. As it took off, its engine growled loud and then settled into a softer hum that gradually disappeared.

"Detective?" his fellow CPDer said behind him. "I just have a couple more questions."

Good luck with that, he thought. He wasn't sure he could remember how to speak English.

"When you arrived, Bails was holding Officer Reilly—"

"She was strung up," he gritted. "By the wrists."

"And then what happened. After you arrived."

Yeah, how to explain all that. "I was set up . . . to kill her."

"Officer Reilly?"

"Yes."

"But why?"

In this he could tell the truth: "Because like everyone else . . . he wondered how much like my father I am. I disappointed him. Gravely."

Might as well leave out the woman. Obviously, she didn't really exist—at least, not in the conventional, 3-D, police-report kind of way.

"You said Bails was dead when you left the cave."

"He was dead when I got there. Shot in the head."

"By who?"

"Reilly just said he did it himself."

The officer nodded and scribbled.

Man, Veck thought, he was so done with being on this side of the law.

"Well, that's all I've got for now." The officer looked up. "I imagine you'll want to get to the hospital. Can I give you a lift?"

Veck shook his head. "I'm just going to go home."

Except, shit, how was he going to accomplish that, given the way Jim Heron had brought him out here? And where was the guy, anyway?

At that moment, an unmarked pulled up, and Detective de la Cruz got out, the brisk wind blowing at the man's coat and hair.

"Okay, Detective," the other officer said. "Take care. And no doubt there will be others from your own department with questions."

"I think one's just arrived."

As the uni walked off to his squad car, de la Cruz strolled over, his head shaking back and forth on the approach.

"We've got to stop meeting like this." De la Cruz offered his palm. "How you doing?"

Veck shook the hand that was offered briefly, and became aware that he was getting cold. "I'm okay."

"You look it," the guy said dryly. "You need a ride back into town?"

"Yeah." On that note, how was he going to explain how he got out here?

Oh, who the hell cared anymore, he thought.

"So Reilly went to the hospital," he said.

"I heard. Also heard you saved her."

More like she saved him. Not that anyone was counting.

"She was the one, by the way," de la Cruz continued. "The one who found out about Bails. We think that's why he targeted her. She found him on your father's thing on that Facebook what's-it. Then she followed up on something he'd lied about concerning your past—with a little help from someone else."

Given the dark light in the detective's eyes, it was not a stretch to wonder what role the man had played on that front.

"Thank you," Veck said softly.

Casual shrug. "I wouldn't know, of course."

"Of course."

"Listen, I called her parents on the way in. Let them know she was going to St. Francis."

"That's good." It meant he didn't have to bother them. "You want to question me?"

The detective's weary eyes met his own. "I want to take you to the hospital. You're shivering in case you haven't noticed."

"Am I?"

"Come on, St. Francis has a stethoscope waiting for you—"

"Reilly doesn't need to see me now. Or ever."

"Don't you think that's her call?"

Not in the slightest. There was too much that couldn't be explained—and the context of that vast informational void was not pixie dust or unicorns or leprechauns. It was demons and evil and double shadows. It was what he had been seeing in mirrors all of his life. It was nothing that you wanted anyone you truly loved even reading about, much less being around.

"Mind if we get in your car, Detective? I think you're right, I'm fucking freezing all of a sudden."

"Yeah. Sure."

Good plan. Except when Veck tried to walk forward, the heavy muscles of his legs locked up tight against his bones, the lactic acid buildup from the sprint to the rim compromising not only his ability to walk, but challenging his pain tolerance.

"Legs hurt?" de la Cruz asked as he measured the hobbling.

"Nah, they feel great."

De la Cruz laughed. "Like I said, you need the hospital."

"It's nothing that a good stretch and some Motrin can't cure. Just take me home, cool?"

They both got into the unmarked, and as soon as de la

Cruz fired up the engine, the good detective cranked the heat. Which somehow made the ice cold in the core of Veck's body worse.

"Ffff-uck," he muttered, grabbing his forearms.

"No wonder you don't want to take that bike of yours back."

"Huh?"

De la Cruz put the car in drive and eased forward around the lane's first corner . . . and there was Veck's ride. Parked safely off to the side.

"Hold up," Veck said roughly. "I want to get the key."

"Guess you were distracted when you got here."

"You could say that."

As Veck went to get out, the blast of cold wind eased the deep freeze in his bones—which probably meant he was into hypothermia territory—and to protect the other man from the gust, he shut the door.

Sure enough, the key was in the bike's ignition.

"Nice touch, Heron," he whispered, looking around at the brush.

Over on the left, a soft glow illuminated the budding trees.

Veck took a deep breath. "There you are. I thought you'd blown this Popsicle stand."

"That's usually my MO." Heron stepped out, and Veck frowned as a shaggy little dog limped forward with him. "I'm making an exception in your case, though."

"Lucky me." Veck tempered the reply with a half smile. "That your dog?"

"He's everyone's, really."

Veck nodded, even though there was no question to answer. "So I think I need to thank you."

"Not in the slightest. As I said going in, s'all you, buddy."

"And I guess I passed. That whole crossroads thing."

"You did. Flying colors." The angel stretched out his pack of smokes. "Cig?"

"Thank you, baby Jesus." Veck slipped one free and then

leaned into Heron's lighter. "Oh, man . . . this is better than a parka."

"Yeah, no offense, but your lips are blue."

"Just the makeup. I wanted to look pretty for you."

Heron grinned. "Asshole."

"Actually"—Veck exhaled—"I'm going to be looking for a new job soon—thought I'd try auditioning for the Michelin man. You saying I need to go more silver?"

"Yeah. That's it." The angel got serious. "You're free now. You can put this shit behind you. She's never going to bother you again."

Obviously, the "she" was not Reilly. "What was that brunette?"

"A devil of a woman."

"You got that right."

"So now you need to go to that Reilly of yours." This was all said in the tone of *What are you waiting for, idiot.*

Veck stared at the glowing tip of his cigarette. "I think she's dealt with enough."

"You're free."

"And so is she."

Jim cursed under his breath. "Look down."

"Excuse me?" When the angel pointed at the rough earth of the road's shoulder, Veck obliged—only to roll his eyes when he saw nothing. "What."

"Behind you, jackass."

Veck muttered something vile, and looked over his—

On the ground, stretching behind him . . . was a single shadow.

"Like I said, you're free."

Veck stared at the nice-and-normal for what felt like ages. Then he refocused on the angel. "My father . . . he thinks the execution is going to get stayed. He told me he was going to live."

"Not a bet I'd take." Jim shook his head. "Maybe that was true if you'd have made a different choice, but thanks to the way things worked out . . . I think you'll like what you see in the papers soon enough. It's what my boss has told me all along—there are no coincidences."

"I thought you were the boss."

"I wish."

"Veck? Who're you talking to?"

Veck glanced at de la Cruz, who'd craned out of the unmarked. "Ah . . ." When he looked back, Heron had disappeared, as if he had never been there. The little animal, too. "Ah . . . no one."

"Look, I don't care if you smoke in the car. Especially if it'll save you from frostbite."

Veck looked back to where Jim had been standing. The man was gone, the glow had faded . . . and yet the presence remained somehow.

Go to your woman, you moron, Jim declared into his head.

"Veck?" de la Cruz said. "Come on, you can smoke in here."

"Nah," Veck replied after a moment. Then he stabbed the ember out on the sole of his boot. "I think I'm quitting."

"Again."

Veck snagged the motorcycle's key and got back in the unmarked. As he and the other man closed their doors, Veck stared across the front seat.

"Do you believe in God, Detective."

De la Cruz made the sign of the cross over his chest. "Absolutely."

"So does that mean that demons exist?"

"Hell is real. Unless you've forgotten that girl we found at the motel? Or what happened to Sissy Barten."

"I haven't forgotten."

De la Cruz nodded and began driving off. "But yeah, I got the faith. And I believe that sinners go to Satan's living room for eternity and the just go to Heaven and the mighty Lord provides. I attend Mass with my family every week, and the Good Book"—he pounded on the glove compartment, the door flipped open, and a little red Bible glowed in the tiny light—"is always with me. If there's one thing that life's taught me, God takes care of us, my man."

"So you think . . . people can be saved."

"No, I know it. And once you got the faith—and I don't care what kind it is—it transforms you. There's no going back, and no one and nothing can take it away from you. You open the heart, and it comes in, and that's when you know shit's going to be all right."

Veck nodded and fell silent as he stared out the front window.

Together, they bumped along the dirt lane. Got out to the county road and hung a left. Angled over for the highway.

After they were on the Northway and headed toward Caldwell, Veck said, "Permanently."

"Huh?"

"I'm quitting permanently."

De la Cruz looked over. "You know . . . this time, I believe you."

"Take me to the hospital."

"Emergency room or inpatient."

Veck smiled a little. "Wherever my partner is."

De la Cruz grinned and clapped him on the chest. "Now you talkin', my man. Now you makin' some sense."

CHAPTER
49

Far above, in Heaven's lap, as Jim stood at the foot of the manse of souls and stared up at the second flag waving lazily on the parapet, he thought . . . two more to go.

If he managed to get two more of those flappy bastards on top of that wall, he could quit this shit.

And his mother would be safe forever.

And Sissy would be free. If he hadn't sprung her before then.

"You have done well."

Nigel's autocratic English accent didn't seem quite so annoying.

"Yeah, but I'm not stopping now."

"In this you are correct."

Jim nodded, and then looked over at his boss. The guy was dressed in a pretty damn sharp suit, this time black with pinstripes. Matter of fact, he looked like an elegant gangster as he stood beside a table set with fancy-schmancy plates and crap. Two of the other archangels and the big Irish wolfhound were seated, clearly waiting with patience for the go-ahead on the dessert that was all laid out.

"On that note," Jim murmured, "I'm going back down. Next round will be starting soon."

Or at least, he hoped it would.

"Won't you stay for an after-dinner sweet? We have a seat for you."

"Thanks," Jim said. "But I've got someone I have to see."

"Very well."

Except before he could disappear, Nigel drew him aside, out of the earshot of the others. "We are not yet finished, you and I."

"Sorry, I'm really not hungry."

"With regard to this agreement you had with Devina—"

"You mean who the soul was."

The archangel cleared his throat. "Yes, indeed. I would caution you—"

Jim clapped the guy on the back and ignored the glare he got in response. "I got this, Nigel. Trust me."

As he cocked a half smile, the odd, noncolor eyes of his boss narrowed. "Sometimes I wonder if that is wise."

"Trusting my ass? Well, you picked me."

"I am e'er reminded." The angel caught Jim's arm. "But I would tell you something."

"Blah, blah, blah—"

"The next soul. You will recognize him as both an old friend and an old foe who you have seen of late. The path could not be more obvious if it were spotlit."

Jim rolled his eyes. "Nice road map, Nigel. As usual, you put a real sharp point on 'obtuse.'"

"Trust me."

As Jim cocked an eyebrow, one side of the archangel's mouth lifted in a smile.

Jim had to laugh. "You know, it's a wonder we don't get along better."

"I would have to agree."

On that note, Nigel sent him back, and the trip was easier than the first couple of times he'd gone up and down to earth.

At least this time, he didn't have to die to get his travel ticket stamped.

Taking form in front of the garage he now lived in again,

he looked up. The windows of the apartment were dark, and with no exterior lights on, the night extended through the yard, past the forest, and out to the rolling field beyond. But all was not black. Off in the distance, the white farmhouse had its two lanterns on the front porch glowing, the beacons throwing off a pair of peachy flushes, as if the structure were blushing a little.

Man, it was frickin' cold. No moon out, either.

Looked like it was going to snow—

"And so you won."

Turning around, he greeted Devina's arrival with a broad smile. "And that would be 'again.' Come to watch me gloat?"

"No."

"Pity, it's a hell of a show. I'll even give you an intermission in case you want to get more popcorn."

As usual, she was looking fine as a brand-new dollar bill, all put together in one of her outfits that left nothing to the imagination: Tonight, those curves of hers were wrapped up tight in bright red.

"You know why I'm here," she said.

"Nowhere to go, huh. So sad."

"Our deal, Heron." Now she smiled. And as she walked forward, her hips moved like she was ready to be ridden hard. "I kept up my end of the bargain. In spite of what you think of me, I told you who the soul was—I didn't lie. So you'll be coming with me now."

Jim let her saunter on over. And he let her have her little moment of satisfaction.

And when she was right in front of him, he let her reach out and cup him between the legs.

But as she opened her mouth, he cut her off. "I did."

She laughed, a lovely sound that suggested that in her mind, they were already fucking. "I believe, in the human marriage tradition, the response is 'I do.' Is that what you're after, my love?"

He pointedly removed her hand. "I lied, Devina." He leaned in and put his mouth right next to her ear. "Fibbed.

Falsified. Fabricated. You know allllll about it, don't you. So how's it feel being on the other side, bitch."

When he stepped back, the confusion on her face was something for the history books. If only he had a camera . . .

"Do I need to draw you a picture?" he murmured.

Abruptly, her expression changed, her features darkening to the point of violence.

"Intent is irrelevant," she said in a low tone. "You were very clear."

"Oh, I think you'll find intent is everything. You can't take what's not yours, and I didn't let you in—I led you *on*."

"You . . . bastard," she spat.

"All's fair in love and war. And don't pretend you didn't write that playbook."

She hauled back and slapped him across the face. "*Don't you forget your place.*"

Jim laughed at her. "Never for a minute." Except then he got serious. "But, Devina, you and I need to be clear on something—if you go back and mistreat . . . anyone . . . I'll make sure you never get a piece of me again."

"I already know you don't keep your promises."

"That's a vow." He pounded his chest and then put his forefinger right between her breasts. "From me . . . to you. You hurt anyone down there, I'll never fuck you again."

For a split second, her mask slipped, that monstrous visage with its rotting skin and jutting ridges of bones making an appearance.

Jim cocked his head. "You know, demon, anger suits you. To a T."

There was a long moment of tense silence, and then she seemed to get herself under control, the fake beauty covering up the evil underneath once more.

"I will never trust you again," she announced.

"Sounds good to me." He lifted up his hand and waved. "Bye-bye, Devina."

"This is not over."

"Predictable parting shot. Just what I've come to expect from you."

He was aware he was pushing his luck, but flush with winning another round, he didn't give a crap.

Devina, however, was finished playing, apparently. She tilted her chin down and looked at him from under her carefully sculpted brows. "See you soon, Heron."

And just like that, she was out of there, ethering away.

In the aftermath, Jim shook a cigarette from his pack and lit up. On the exhale, he laughed again, enjoying the buzz going through him. It was kind of like he'd just had sex—the good kind.

Turning to the garage, he strode over to the stairs, figuring he'd check in with Adrian before he went—

As he exhaled, he frowned and wondered if he was hearing things. But no. That radio he did not own was playing again. . . .

An a cappella version of Train's "Calling All Angels."

What the hell?

Mounting the stairs quickly, he put the cigarette between his lips as he pushed open the door. . . .

Sitting on the floor, with his back against the crawl space's entryway, Adrian had his head in his hands. With soft, perfect pitch, he carried the lyrics slowly, beautifully . . . as if he had been born for the microphone.

"I thought you couldn't sing," Jim said.

Adrian didn't lift his head, but he stopped and shrugged. "I just did that to piss him off. You, too, matter of fact."

Jim exhaled a steady stream of smoke. "You got a nice voice."

Funny that he preferred the off-key, annoying shit.

When there was no reply, he said to the angel, "You going to be okay if I do a quick errand?"

"Yeah. We're fine. I'm just going to sit with him."

Jim nodded even though there was no eye contact. "You need anything?"

"Nah. We're good."

Staring across at the massive figure of the angel—whose heavy legs were curled up, and powerful arms were resting loosely on the knees—Jim was beyond ready for the next round: Adrian had seemed alive again for a while tonight, animated, engaged. This resolute stillness, on the other hand, was too close to Eddie's condition for his liking.

"I'll be back."

"Take your time."

The separation wasn't good, but Jim had to do this. Some things were a choice ... others were a matter of necessity if you had any honor at all in your bones.

Turning around, he went out the way he'd come in, quietly closing the door behind him. Before he left, he put his palm on the wall of the garage and closed his eyes.

With hard concentration, he called up the memory of Adrian and Eddie in their hotel room at the Marriott, the pair of them arguing back and forth, and trading potshots. He imagined them doing that again, seeing Eddie's red eyes squaring off at Adrian's theatrics, while the other angel threw his arms up in exasperation.

They were back together again in this vision he created in his mind.

They were safe and whole.

They were both alive.

When he opened his lids, there was a subtle glow around the entire building, a phosphorescent illumination that threw no shadows, but was more powerful than stadium lighting.

Just as Jim retracted his hand, the first snowflake fell from the sky ... which was his cue to disappear into the thin, cold air.

CHAPTER
50

It was two and a half hours after Veck arrived at St. Francis Hospital before he was finally free to go see Reilly ... *two and a half frickin' hours*.

Then again, when de la Cruz had pulled up to the entrance next to the emergency room to drop him off, he'd thrown open the car door and found that he wasn't able to stand up.

Kind of a rate-limiting issue.

So instead of going through the revolving doors of the inpatient building and heading up to Reilly's room—which he had the number of thanks to a call into hospital information—he'd ended up in the ER himself. Where, of course, they wouldn't give him any details about her or her condition.

Damn HIPAA rules.

And, man, they crawled all over him.

After he'd been poked, prodded, and X-rayed, they'd tried to suggest he needed an IV for fluids, but he'd shot that one down and informed them he was leaving. By way of compromise, they'd wrapped an Ace bandage around the thigh that hurt more, thrown another mummy special on his opposite ankle, and told him to go home and expect to feel worse the following day.

Thanks, Doc.

The cane was helpful, however. And as the elevator dinged and he stepped off onto the seventh floor of the inpatient building, he used the thing to help get his sorry ass out into the corridor.

He looked in both directions. Had no idea which way to go.

At random, he picked right and figured that at some point he'd run into a staff member or a map or the unit he was looking for.

As he hobbled along, he glanced down at his clothes. Filthy. Sweated out. Torn. Hell of an outfit, but it wasn't like he was going to take time to go back home and change.

And when he got to the nursing station, he had no intention of being hit with any kind of no-visiting-hours, come-back-later crap.

Reilly had told him she loved him.

And he'd shut his woman down.

Yeah, okay, he hadn't been the one to actually slam the door in her face—technically, that had been the medics. But he'd let her go—and that was the sort of mistake you wanted to rectify as soon as you got the chance.

Even if you needed a cane to get there and looked like you should be hosed off.

Turning another corner, he faced off against a long corridor that had directions in both English and Spanish, as well as a lot of arrows, and a map. Too bad none of the shit made any sense—and not just because he was exhausted. Did they purposely make patients hard to find here—

Down at the far end of the hall, a huge, dark figure appeared and began striding toward him.

Closer. Closer still. Until Veck could make out the leather pants, and the shitkickers, and the black coat.

Instantly, a sharpshooter drove through his brain. To the point where he wondered whether he hadn't thrown a clot with all that running up the quarry slope.

Except . . . as he looked up into a hard face, he knew who it was. This was . . .

Veck cursed and listed into the wall as the pounder in his head wiped out all thought.

And meanwhile, the man just kept approaching. Until he stopped right in front of Veck.

As Veck focused through his pain on that incredible face, he knew he would never forget it.

"I'm going to make it right," the man said in a foreign accent that wasn't quite French, wasn't quite Hungarian. "Worry not, my friend."

God, those rolling Rs were pleasing in the ear, curiously smooth and aristocratic.

And then Veck realized who the guy was talking about: "Kroner . . ."

With a gallant, affirming nod, the foreigner resumed his walk, the footfalls of his boots a death knell if Veck had ever heard it. And then halfway down the hall, the figure flat-out disappeared . . . like a ghost.

More likely, though, he'd just turned another corner.

To go find Kroner . . . holy *shit*.

Veck rubbed his eyes, thought about the cave, and realized he'd missed a piece in all of this: He'd seen the serial killer hanging in front of him, except that hadn't been anything but an image, had it. An image projected onto his Reilly.

That was the only explanation. Because she had been the one hanging from those cuffs after the dust settled, and God knew there hadn't been time to switch the pair of them.

Abruptly weak-kneed, he leaned hard onto the cane as it dawned on him exactly what had gone on. Or rather, what could have. If he had stabbed who he had believed was Kroner . . . he would have killed her.

In the rush and panic of the aftermath, that hadn't even dawned on him.

Christ, his choice at that crossroads had saved both of them, hadn't it. Because he never would have recovered if he'd done what he'd been set up to do.

And as for Kroner . . .

Jerking his head over his shoulder, Veck refocused on the direction that figure of death had gone in. The serial killer must still be alive and in his hospital bed, then—and how much you want to bet, his room was down there somewhere?

By all rights, Kroner's life was still not Veck's to take. But that didn't mean he was going to stop whatever was about to happen. Shit, angels, demons, small dogs with bad perms ... the world was full of crap he'd only heard rumors about before. So for all he knew? That was the Grim Reaper upright and in person—and in that case, Kroner's life was being snatched the right way.

Just to be sure, though, Veck limped over to a ceiling light and checked his shadow—even though he felt like a fool.

Only one.

"Ready for this to be over," he muttered to himself. "Soooooo ready."

Eventually, he found the right ward, and fortunately, maybe because the nurses took pity on him, he didn't get any no-visitors backchat. He was just sent down five doors and told if he needed anything to holler.

Like maybe they expected him to fall over in a dead heap at any moment.

When he got to Reilly's room, he didn't rush inside in case she was asleep. He just leaned in a little so he could peek past the door.

In the dim glow seeping from the bathroom, it was clear she was out like a light: Even though her head was turned away from him, her breathing was deep and even, her body small and still under the blankets. She was on an IV, and there was a monitor attached to her that was beeping regularly. Probably her heart—

Her head whipped around on the pillow—and then she winced, her hand coming up to her temple. "Veck ..."

As he rushed over, he said, "Are you all right?" What a dumb-ass question, he thought.

"You're here." Then she obviously saw the wristband he'd been given. "Are *you* okay?"

"Just don't ask me to run a marathon tomorrow." When she tried to sit up, he pulled a chair over to the bed. "No, no, lie back. I'm going to park it right here."

"I didn't think you were coming," she said.

As he thought about a response to that, she murmured, "Neither did you, huh."

He shook his head. "I . . ." God, where to start? "You know, since the first moment I met you, I've brought a lot of shit into your life. And then I nearly got you killed tonight—"

"No, you didn't. We both got set up by Bails and that . . . Who was that woman?"

"I don't know. But I can tell you this: She's not coming back." He believed Jim on that one. "Ever."

"You took care of that, didn't you."

"Guess so."

"I didn't mention her when I was questioned."

"Neither did I."

Cue a pause. And then he cleared his throat, eager to talk about something, anything other than what had happened in the cave. Maybe later, with distance, they could cover all that what-the-fuck-happened, but not tonight.

"Did your parents come by?"

"They wondered where you were."

"So you didn't tell them about me."

"Oh, I told them everything. How you were framed, how you came after me—"

"I love you."

That stopped her dead. To the point where he wondered if maybe he shouldn't apologize. Except then she teared up and reached for his face.

"I love you, too."

Bending down, so she could reach him more easily, he murmured, "I just want to do right by you. It's all I've ever wanted for us."

"Then, as you said"—her voice was rough—"no running tomorrow. Or ever."

"That's what a friend of mine told me."

"Jim . . ." When he nodded, she whispered, "That man is an angel."

"You got that right."

He didn't mean to intrude, but somehow he ended up crawling onto the bed and lying next to her. She fit against him so perfectly, and as he held her, he shuddered. They had nearly missed this—not just with what had happened in that cave, but the rest of the shit Bails had been trying to engineer.

Leaning in, Veck kissed her carefully and then just stared into her eyes for the longest time. He'd never had a clean slate before. Hadn't even been born with one. But at this moment? He saw the fresh start he'd never expected to get in the hazel flecks of those perfect green eyes of hers.

And it was then that he noticed the weight was gone. He'd lived with his heavy burden for so long, it had become something that he wasn't aware of anymore. Now, though, in the absence of that taxing pressure inside every square inch of him, he felt . . . free. Fresh. Reborn.

The only trouble was that that new-man syndrome had him thinking crazy things, and deciding they seemed entirely reasonable.

Smoothing her beautiful red hair back, he said softly, "So your father asked me a question that night I went for dinner with you all."

Reilly smiled. "Did he? I just remember him telling you he knew CPR."

"It was right before that," he whispered. "You think maybe I could give him an answer someday?"

Her breath hitched. And then a brilliant joy shone out of her face. "If I understand what you're saying, I think you're going to have to ask him something first."

"Your parents free for dinner tomorrow night?"

She started laughing and then so did he. "I think I can arrange that."

"Perfect." He got serious. "You're just . . . perfect."

Cradling her against his chest, Veck let a peaceful exhaustion claim him: All was right in his world. He had his woman, his life, and his soul back.

Didn't get any better than this.

Up in heaven, Nigel's feet took him on a trip around the castle. The ambulation was not to admire the unfurled grace of Jim's latest victory. Nor was it to check for security. Nor was it to take the air.

Although if asked about his stroll, he would have offered all of those lies in response.

Indeed, perhaps Jim and he were closer than he thought.

And yet if he had proffered such explanations to any person or dog, what he held upon his flattened palm would have announced him as a liar: He carried with him a plate with a damask napkin draped over it—and beneath the fine cloth, there was a currant scone, two biscuits, and a fresh strawberry.

As he walked along with his pastry load, he had in his heart a vague sense of distaste at this butler-like activity. But he needed a tangible excuse to go where he was headed, not just for any others with inquiring minds, but for the intended recipient of what had been plated.

That being said, however, it was not just sweets for the not-so-sweet that he was bringing with him. He had news to share.

Approaching Colin's tent, he felt like a royal arse, but the archangel had not presented himself for the collective gathering and had missed the missive, so to speak. He was also likely to be hungry after his time away.

Excuses, excuses ... Nigel wanted to see the jammy sod.

Damn them both.

And so much for clean breaks.

At the entry flap, he cleared his throat. "Colin."

Waiting for a response, he tugged at the damask napkin to make sure it was still covering the goodies.

"Colin."

Oh, enough with this polite restraint.

He pushed his way inside and stopped. Upon the modest cot, there were three suits laid out, each with coordinating ascots, stockings, and shoes.

The middle combination of black and pale grays would compliment him best, Nigel thought.

Putting the plate down, he reached out to stroke the fine cloth of the sleeve. Odd that the archangel had lined these up. Colin was not particular about his vestments.

Turning away, Nigel looked at the leather-bound books. The trunk. The oil lamp that burned with gentle light.

Where was the angel going with such dress?

And then he recalled: Colin had been down with Edward, and wherever Edward was, so too was Adrian.

That cocksure angel with the fetish for piercings had never been known to affiliate with members of his own sex before, but it wasn't as if Nigel got into that portion of his subordinates' lives in any detail. Besides, Colin was irresistible. Which was what had landed Nigel in the position he was in now.

Such a fool he was, Nigel thought. *Such* a fool.

He strode out, but closed the flap behind him softly. The last thing he needed to do was get caught—

A cheerful whistling tune brought his head about.

Sneaking behind the tent, his breath caught. In the midst of the stream's rushing current, Colin stood with his back to the bank, a soft rubbing cloth passing over his shoulders and leaving a trail of suds that eased between the winged muscles of his torso, following a path e'er downward. . . .

Colin's head came 'round, and then the top half of him followed.

Nigel swallowed hard as their eyes met. The male was a vision such as he had seen afore, and yet was e'er new.

"Good evening," the other archangel said, before resuming his soapy ministrations across his chest.

As Colin worked his skin over, he didn't swivel away, but instead continued that soft cloth down, down . . . down. . . .

"Going somewhere?" Nigel said bitterly.

"Yes."

"Where?"

The archangel pivoted all the way about ... and given what the male's body was up to, Nigel felt like cursing. The outfits. This washing. Skipping the meal as if he were preparing for something special.

That arousal.

If it wasn't Adrian, could it be a human suitor? Or a soul on the safe side of the castle walls, mayhap?

"I have news," Nigel forced himself to say smoothly. "That was shared over dessert, in fact."

"I'm sorry I wasn't there."

"Indeed."

As they conversed, Nigel's peripheral vision was proving achingly acute: Although he focused upon Colin's face, he was all too well aware of the careful attention the archangel was paying to his manhood.

And to think cleanliness was a virtue.

More like a torture.

"Nigel?"

"You also missed the victory flagging, and Jim's appearance."

"For which I give my apologies." Colin hissed a little in pleasure and then seemed to refocus. "Now, tell me, what is your news."

"The Creator has decreed for whom the next bell tolls. It is not whom we were told at first."

This got the archangel's attention—and froze that damnable cloth. "I thought all the souls were agreed upon before the game began?"

"They were. And it was assumed, at least by me, that there were but six because one side or the other would win early."

"But now?"

"Oh, this soul was approved of. I was just unaware that there would be a second inning upon him."

Colin's surprise was satisfying; at least it proved Nigel could still get a reaction out of him.

With a powerful thrust, the archangel took a smooth dive into the waters and then stepped out of the river. As he emerged, dripping and still hard in that essential place, Nigel obligingly proffered the male the toweling that hung upon the closest branch—it was not to save the archangel from a chill, however.

More because Nigel did not need to incinerate on the spot.

However, although Colin did dry off, the bastard merely looped the thing around the back of his neck when he was finished.

"Weren't you getting dressed?" Nigel interjected.

"Aye."

"Now?" Please.

"Who is the soul?"

"Matthias."

Colin frowned. "Is the Creator redacting Devina's victory, then?"

"The decision from on high is that the loss to her shall stand, but that Jim will have a second attempt to influence the man."

"This is unprecedented."

"The game is unprecedented."

As the pair of them stared at each other, Nigel's heart ached to the point of actual pain. Which was his cue to leave, wasn't it.

"At any rate, I thought you should like to know," he said briskly. "I bid you adieu, and . . . good evening. Clearly, you intend to have one."

"I do." Colin's lids went low. "Indeed I shall."

Nigel nodded stiffly and walked with no greater grace back to his tent. As he passed the tea table that had since been cleared, he was glad that the other two and that grand dog had returned to their quarters. He did not wish for even Tarquin's canine stare to witness this walk of private humiliation.

He had gone o'er to present a gift, only to witness preparations for a tryst that obviously didn't involve him.

Stupid.

Fool.

In his quarters, Nigel stripped down, but he did not retire to the bath—too many memories. Instead, he donned a new satin robe that he had never worn in the presence of Colin and stretched out upon his chaise longue, looking about his luxurious appointments.

Even with all the colorful drapery and the comfortable bedding, it seemed such an empty place.

Beside him, the flame atop a beeswax candle idly wafted to and fro, and he envied it its easy job. Unfortunately, the thing offered little in the way of company, so he just watched it cannibalize itself in silence, the tears of consumption dripping slowly down its ever-shrinking body.

How depressing: Even something as romantic as candlelight he interpreted in a vocabulary of loss—

"This scone is fantastic."

Nigel looked up. Colin was standing in the entryway of the tent, his strong arm holding the tarp curtain aside, his long, lean form filling the space.

He was wearing the black and the gray.

Nigel went back to focusing on the candle. "I am glad it sustains you."

"Thoughtful of you." The archangel came in whilst finishing the thing. "You know, you haven't paid me a visit in quite a while."

Actually it had been very recently, but that hardly served to be mentioned.

"Were you not heading out somewhere?" Nigel muttered.

"Oh, aye." When Nigel glanced over, Colin circled in a masculine way. "Do you like this?"

"The clothing?" Nigel waved his hand. "Not for me to judge."

"I wore it for you."

Nigel's eyes shot back. "Surely you don't mean to be that cruel."

"Cruel?" The archangel seemed honestly confused. "For whom else would I wear such useless garb?"

Nigel frowned. "I thought maybe Adrian or . . ."

Colin's laugh was immediate. And grating as all get-out. "You think that angel . . . and I . . .?"

"He is fit."

"Aye. But he is not whom I want."

Nigel swallowed hard, and tried to hide his reaction by looking away. "It . . . is for me?"

"Aye. So what say you, lover mine."

Eventually, he swung his eyes back and the two of them stared at each other for the longest time.

Then Nigel sat forward and brushed his hair back with a shaking hand: The desire for composure did not win, not here and in private. Not with Colin.

Never with that archangel, he feared.

Reaching out his hand to his love, Nigel said hoarsely, "I say . . . it was the one I would have chosen."

The archangel came forward with a smile. "And that," Colin murmured, "was why I put it on."

CHAPTER
51

Down below, in an attractive suburb of Caldwell, Susan Barten sat in her living room, wide-awake even though it was four a.m. Upstairs, her husband and her remaining daughter were sleeping in their respective beds, and all was quiet above, around, and below her.

She was used to this silent, painful sitting in the dark. The last stretch of uninterrupted rest she had gotten had been the night before ... "it" had happened.

As usual, she sat in the armchair next to her couch, with her eyes trained on the front door. This was her perch, the branch she locked her feet onto as the winds of fate blew gales at her loved ones, peeling off layers of who she was and what her family was and how she'd expected to pass her time on earth.

She always faced the door Sissy had once gone in and out of so regularly—and this had been true even after the first couple of nights, when the initial hope had bled out, leaving nothing but a paralyzing fear behind. It was still true even now, when there was a concrete reason to know that her daughter was never, ever returning home again.

God, to think she felt lucky there was something for them to bury.

At the thought, tears itched in the corners of her eyes, and she found herself thinking about that Dr. Seuss book, the one that had been so ubiquitous at the high school graduation, the one they had bought for Sissy along with those dove earrings and that dove necklace and that dove braclet.

Oh, the Places You'll Go!

An early grave was not what any of them had contemplated.

Why couldn't this destination of hers have been medical school? Or Europe? Or New York City?

Or just to a hair salon in downtown Caldwell, or a vet's office, or an elementary school to teach?

Why couldn't it have been what all of her classmates had been granted?

Why did it have to have been that Hannaford supermarket on that particular night . . .

Susan balanced on the tipping edge of madness as the hundreds of different avenues open to her elder daughter presented themselves in a list . . . and she wondered yet again why, when the dice had been rolled, had they come up with—

A shout erupted out of her mouth before she was conscious of making the sound, and her legs were the same—doing their duty to get her out of the chair and around behind the thing before she was aware of moving.

A man had come through the door.

A huge man with blond hair had entered her house without actually opening the way in, and he was now standing in her front hall.

Staring at her.

Wait . . . she knew him. He was the one she had given that necklace to. He was the one who had looked devastated along with her.

And he was devastated still.

"What are you doing here?" she asked softly, strangely aware that however he had arrived, he was not here to hurt her or what was left of her family. "Why have you come?"

The man just stared at her without answering, his harsh

face saddened to the point where it seemed as if he were on the same edge she was.

Feeling unsteady, Susan rounded the armchair and all but fell back into it. Then she placed her hands on her knees, and rocked back and forth slowly.

"I already know they found her," she said. "I know they found . . . my daughter. . . ."

The man came forward as she began to sob, and after she tried to wipe her eyes, she found that he had crouched down at her feet.

"You said you were going to bring her back," she choked out.

When he nodded to her, she took that to mean he still intended to make good on the promise, but surely he knew such a thing was impossible.

"I'm glad you came," she murmured, thinking out loud.

He remained silent, and as she looked into his strange eyes, she voiced the guilt she had not spoken to anyone else: "I killed my daughter. I sent her out for those groceries. I asked her to go . . . and if she hadn't . . . she wouldn't have . . ."

There was no going any further as she began weeping. And as she cried her heart out, the massive warrior stayed with her, sharing her pain and her solitude and her regrets, his big hand coming to rest on her shoulder and easing her, his presence a balm over the raw burns that covered her even though her skin was outwardly still intact.

When she calmed down some, he put his hands on hers.

At the contact, magical warmth entered her and traveled up both sides of her arms, the tide moving into the chasm in her chest, filling her.

It was then that she saw he had wings. Great gossamer wings that rose over his huge shoulders and caught the light, even though she had left the house in darkness.

"You're an angel," she whispered, transfixed. "You are . . . an *angel*. . . ."

He showed no reaction, just kept staring up at her, his beautiful eyes and his healing touch elevating her even though she remained seated.

Eventually, he removed his hands from hers, but the warmth he had given her stayed inside her body.

"You have to go?" she said sadly.

He nodded, but before he rose to his great height, he pulled open his shirt. There, at his throat, was the delicate necklace she had given him, the dove of peace suspended from its little chain.

She reached out and touched the links that were warm against his glimmering skin. "I know you will take care of her."

He nodded once . . . and then he was gone. Instantly.

With jerky movements, Susan jumped out of the chair and rushed across to the front door. Unlocking it and throwing it wide, she leaped onto the cold concrete of the stoop.

No sign of him. But he had been there.

The warmth he had given her was still with her.

As she looked up to heaven, she saw that it was snowing: Little white flakes were drifting down slowly from the sky, their weaving paths like that of the destinies of people, ever changing, never the same, moving around obstacles seen and unseen.

Letting her head fall back, she felt the tiny spots on her forehead and cheeks as if they were small, kind hands sent to brush her tears away.

The angel would be back, she thought.

And Sissy, wherever she was, was not alone. . . .

It was a long time before Susan stepped back into the house, shut the door, and quietly made her way up to the bed she and her husband had shared for decades. As she slid inside the sheets, he roused briefly.

"You all right?"

"We have an angel," she told him. "He's watching over us. Over Sissy."

"You think?"

"No," she said, going into her husband's arms and closing her eyes in exhaustion. "I *know*."

And with that, she fell into a deep, abiding sleep . . .

EPILOGUE

Two weeks after Reilly got out of the hospital, she stood at her bureau in her bedroom and wondered if it was morally wrong to wear lingerie under your clothes—assuming you were going to your parents' for Sunday dinner.

Maybe she'd just throw on the black lace. Sexy, but nothing peekaboo—

"What you doin'," Veck said as he came up behind her and put his arms around her.

He was naked, as usual, and very glad to see her—as usual.

Glancing over her shoulder, she smiled and held up the bra in question. "The black. I was thinking the black. What say you?"

"Good choice. It's one of my favorite sets to take off of you."

As he kissed her slow and deep, and rubbed that arousal against the back of her bathrobe, Reilly gave herself over—but only for a moment.

Inching away, she shook her head. "We're already late."

"Won't take me long," he murmured, going for the tie in front. "Promise."

"But I'll have to explain to my father why we delayed dinner."

Veck stepped back sharply. Cleared his throat. All but glanced behind himself to see if the man in question was in the room with them. "Good God, why aren't you dressed yet, woman. Come on—shake a leg."

She laughed as he headed over to the suitcase in the corner and started throwing on clothes like the house was on fire.

Her partner was still the tough-cored, straight-talking, sexy man she'd fallen in love with: Ever the dogged detective. Always alert and very protective of her. Precisely the kind of guy who never backed down, rarely gave an inch, and somehow managed to still cater to her.

But if there was one person on the face of the planet who could snap his BVDs, it was her father.

Veck and Big Tom, as Veck called him, were cut from the same cloth, but Veck never overstepped, and was always on his best behavior. And the fact the pair got along so well was just one more reason to love both of the men in her life.

"You're still in that robe, Reilly," he shot over while he yanked his pants on.

"I love you, you know that?"

He didn't even pause, the flapping continuing as he pulled on a button-down. "That's nice, honey. Now come on, get dressed."

Reilly laughed again, grabbed her Victoria's Secret, and did her own, toned-down version of the DelVecchio shuffle in the bathroom.

It was amazing how much had changed ... and how little. Bails's body had been found in the rubble of the quarry three days later, and the cause of death had been ruled a suicide, as the gun he'd used had still been locked in the grip of his cold hand. Kroner had also woken up dead: Medical staff at the hospital had discovered that very night of the quarry collapse that he'd stopped breathing and they'd been unable to revive him, something which had not been a surprise, given the extent of his injuries.

As for Sissy Barten, her death had been unofficially hung around Bails's neck: Her body had yielded no DNA to tie the two together, but forensic IT specialists had gotten into the man's various computers and found a web, literally, of madness and scheming—all of which revolved around Veck and Veck's dad. Turned out Bails had often spoken in his postings online of killing someone just as Sissy had been killed, using precisely those techniques and markings, as a way to honor Veck's father.

Needless to say, Veck had been cleared of all suspicion—in fact, an audit of the security camera files from the evidence room showed that the system had conked out for a period of time one night between when the Kroner stuff had come in and when Bails had put forth his false accusation. The implication that Bails had somehow engineered the malfunction was obvious.

And that . . . was that.

In the aftermath of it all, Veck didn't talk much about what had happened—or remark on the fact that his father had been executed on schedule, or seem to dwell on that moment in the cave when the wrong decision on his part could have ended both their lives. But there had been enough nights when she and he had lain together and he'd said a few words here and there. She was giving him time, and he was taking it, but she'd never gotten the feeling that he'd hidden, or would hide, anything from her.

God willing, they had the next fifty years to keep up the dialogue.

"Are we ready?" he called out from the bedroom.

"Yup! Coming!"

A quick brush of her hair, a spritz of that perfume Veck liked, and she rushed out of the bath—

In the center of her room, right by the bed they shared, he was down on one knee, with a little velvet box on his outstretched palm.

Talk about skidding to a halt.

Putting her hand to her beating heart, Reilly blinked like an idiot for a moment.

"Two guesses what I'm going to ask you," he murmured, flipping the top open.

For a long moment, she just stood there in shock. Except then she got with the program, all but floating over to him.

Looking down, she saw a small, perfect diamond in a simple pronged setting.

"Just so you know," Veck murmured, "I asked your father a week ago. He gave me his permission—and vowed to beat me to a bloody pulp and bury me in your mother's rose garden if I ever do wrong by you."

Reilly got down on her own knees with him, tears waving everything up. "It's . . . really like him to say that."

They both laughed.

"Yeah. So." Veck cleared his throat. "Sophia Maria Reilly, will you be my wife? Please?"

She nodded, because she didn't trust her voice—and forget about the rock; she threw her arms around him and held on hard. "I love you. . . ."

Veck crushed her to him, and then eased back. With hands that shook ever so slightly, he took the ring out of its velvet slot . . . and slid it on her finger. "Fits perfectly."

She took some time to admire the winking, flashing brilliance. The stone was incredibly bright and lively, almost impossibly so.

"It's not big," Veck said, "but it's flawless. That was important to me. I wanted to give you something . . . flawless."

She pressed her lips to his. "You already have, though. And it's nothing you could buy me in a jewelry store."

Veck kissed her back for the longest time . . . forever it seemed, and that was just barely enough for her.

And then, with his mouth still against hers, he whispered, "Now do you mind if we get in your car and break the speed limit? Much as I love your mother's garden, I'd prefer not to be Miracle-Gro, especially on a night like this."

Laughing, Reilly got to her feet and helped her . . . holy crap, *fiancée* . . . to stand up. "You know what I just realized? We both go by our last names."

"And neither one of us can cook."

"See," she said as they raced for the stairs side by side. "We were meant to be together."

Halfway down, he tugged her to a stop, pulled her into his arms, and kissed her again. "Amen to that, my love. *Amen*."

One last kiss ... and then just like that, they were out the door ...

And off into their future.

Read on for a sneak peek of

LOVER UNLEASHED

from J. R. Ward's
#1 *New York Times* bestselling
Black Dagger Brotherhood series.

Available now!

Manny Manello didn't like other people driving his Porsche. In fact, short of his mechanic, no one else ever did.

Tonight, however, Jane Whitcomb was behind the wheel because: One, she was competent and could shift without grinding his transmission into a stump; two, she'd maintained the only way she could take him where they were going was if she were doing the ten-and-two routine; and three, he was still reeling from seeing someone he'd buried pop out of the bushes to hi-how're-ya him.

So many questions. Lot of pissed off, too. And yeah, sure, he was hoping to get to a place of peace and light and sunshine and all that namby-pamby bullshit, but he wasn't holding his breath for it. Which was kind of ironic. How many times had he stared up at his ceiling at night, all nestled in his beddy-bye with some Lagavulin, praying that his former chief of Trauma would come back to him?

Manny glanced over at her profile. Illuminated in the glow of the dash, she was still smart. Still strong.

Still his kind of woman.

But that was never happening now. Aside from the

whole liar-liar-pants-on-fire about her death, there was a gunmetal gray ring on her left hand.

"You got married," he said.

She didn't look at him, just kept driving. "Yes. I did."

The headache that had sprouted the instant she'd stepped out from behind her grave instantly went from grouchy to gruesome, and shadowy memories Loch Ness'd below the surface of his conscious mind, tantalizing him, making him want to work for the full reveal.

He had to cut that cognitive search and rescue off, though, before he popped an aneurism from the strain: As maddening as being lost in his own mind was, he had the sense that he could do permanent damage to himself if he kept struggling.

As he looked out the car window, fluffy pine trees and budding oaks stood tall in the moonlight, the forest that ran around Caldwell's edges growing thicker as they headed north from the city proper and the twin bridges of downtown.

"You died out here," he said grimly. "Or at least pretended you did."

They'd found her Audi in and among the trees on a stretch of road not far from here, the car having careened off the shoulder. No body, though, because of the fire.

Jane cleared her throat. "I feel like all I've got is 'I'm sorry.' And that just sucks."

"Not a party on my end, either."

Silence. Lot of silence. But he wasn't one to keep asking when all he got in return was *I'm sorry.* Besides, he wasn't totally in the dark. He knew she had a patient she wanted him to treat and he knew . . . Well, that was about it, wasn't it.

Eventually, she took a right hand turn off onto . . . a dirt road?

"FYI," he muttered, "this car was built for racetracks, not roughing it."

"This is the only way in."

To where, he wondered. "You're going to owe me for this."

"You're the only one who can save her."

Manny flashed his eyes over. "You didn't say it was a 'her.'"

"Should it matter?"

"Given how much I don't get about all of this, *everything* matters."

A mere ten yards in and they went through the first of countless puddles that were as deep as frickin' lakes, and as the Porsche splashed through, he gritted, "And screw this patient. I want payback for what you're doing to my undercarriage."

Jane let out a little laugh, and for some reason, that made the center of his chest ache—but nothing good was going to come from dwelling on the emotional crap. It wasn't like the pair of them had ever been together—yeah, there had been attraction on his part. Big attraction. And, like, one kiss. That was it, however.

And now she was Mrs. Someone Else.

About five minutes later, they came up to a gate that looked like it had been erected during the Punic Wars. The thing was hanging at Alice in Wonderland angles, the chain link rusted to shit and broken in places, the fence that it bisected nothing more than six feet of barbed cattle wire that had seen better days.

Yet the thing opened smoothly. And as they went past it, he saw the first of the video cameras.

While they progressed at a snail's pace, a strange fog rolled in from nowhere in particular, the landscape blurring until he couldn't see more than twelve inches ahead of the car's grille. Christ, it was like they were in a *Scooby-Doo* episode out here.

The next gate was in slightly better condition, and the one after that was even newer, and so was the one after that.

The last gate they came to was spit-and-shine sparkling, and all about the Alcatraz: Fucker reached twenty-five feet off the ground and had High Voltage warnings all over it. And as for the wall it cut into? That shit was nothing for cattle, more like velociraptors, and what do you want to bet that concrete face fronted a solid twelve or twenty-four inches of solid horizontal stone.

Manny swiveled his head around at her as they passed through and began a descent underground into a tunnel that could have had a "Holland" or "Lincoln" sign tacked on it for all its sturdiness and lighting. The farther down they went, the more that big question that had been plaguing him since he'd first seen her loomed: Why fake her death? Why cause the kind of chaos she had in his life and the lives of the other people she'd worked with at St. Francis? She'd never been cruel, never been a liar, and had no financial problems and nothing to run from.

Now he knew without her saying a word:

U.S. government.

This kind of setup, with this sort of security ... hidden on the outskirts of what was a big-enough city, but nothing so huge as New York, L.A. or Chicago? Had to be the government. Who else could afford this?

And who the hell was this women he was treating?

The tunnel terminated in a parking garage that was standard issue with its pylons and little yellow painted spots, and yet as large as it appeared to be, there were just a couple of nondescript vans with darkened windows and a small bus that also had blackouts for glass.

Before she even had his Porsche in park, a steel door was thrown open and—

One look at the huge guy who stepped out and Manny's head exploded, the pain behind his eyes going so intense, he went limp in the bucket seat, his arms falling to the sides, his face twitching from the agony.

Jane said something to him. A door was opened. Then his own was cracked.

The air that hit him smelled dry and vaguely like earth ... but there was something else. Cologne. A very woody spice that was at once expensive and pleasing, but also something he had a curious urge to get away from.

Manny forced his lids to open. His vision was wonky as hell, but it was amazing what you could pull out of your ass if you had to, and as the face in front of him came into focus, he found himself staring up at the goateed motherfucker who had ...

On a wave of pain, his eyes rolled back into his head and he nearly threw up.

"You've got to release the memories," he heard Jane say.

There was some conversating at that point, his former colleague's voice mixing with the deep tones of that guy with the tattoos at his temple.

"It's killing him—"

"There's too much risk—"

"How the hell is he going to operate like this?"

There was a long silence. And then all of a sudden, the pain lifted as if it were a veil drawn back, and memories flooded his mind.

Jane's patient. From back at St. Francis. The man with the goatee and ... the six-chambered heart.

Manny popped open his eyes and lasered in on that cruel face. "I know you."

The guy had shown up in his office and taken the files on that heart of his.

"You get him out of the car," was the only response from Goatee. "I don't trust myself to touch him."

Hell of a welcome wagon.

As Manny's brain struggled to catch up with everything, at least his feet and legs seemed to work just fine. And after Jane helped him to the vertical, he followed her and the goateed hater into a facility that was as nondescript and clean as any hospital: Corridors were uncluttered, lights were paneled fluorescents on the ceiling, everything smelled like Lysol.

There were also the bubbled fixtures of security cameras at regular intervals, like the building was a monster with many eyes.

While they walked along, Manny knew better than to ask any questions. Well, that and he was so screwed in the membrane, he was pretty fucking sure ambulation was the extent of his capabilities at this point.

Doors. They passed many doors. All of which were closed and no doubt locked.

Yeah, this sure as hell put the "undisclosed location" in "National Security," didn't it.

Jane eventually stopped outside a pair of double flappers. She was nervous, and didn't that make him feel like he had a gun to his head: In the OR, in countless trauma messes, she'd always kept her cool. That had been her trademark.

This was personal, he thought. Somehow, whatever was on the other side hit close to home for her.

"I've got good facilities here," she said, "but not everything. No MRI. Just CAT scans. But the OR should be adequate, and not only can I assist, but I've got an excellent nurse."

Manny took a deep breath, reaching down deep, pulling himself together. Whether it was his years of training and experience, or who he was as a man, he ditched all the baggage and the lingering ow-ow-ow in his head and the strangeness of this descent into 007 land, and got with the program.

First thing on the list? Ditch the pissed-off peanut gallery.

He glanced over his shoulder at Goatee. "You need to back off, my man. I want you out in the hall."

The response he got to that news flash was ... just fangtastic. The bastard bared a pair of shockingly long canines and growled, natch, like a dog.

"Fine," Jane said, getting in between them. "That's fine. Vishous will wait out here."

Vishous? Had he heard that right?

Then again this boy's mama sure hit the nail on the head, assuming the little dental show Manny was getting wasn't just a figment of this situation, but the motherfucker's personality.

But whatever. He had a job to do, and maybe the bastard could go chew on a rawhide or something.

Manny pushed into the examination room—

Oh . . . dear God.

Oh . . . Lord above.

The patient on the table was lying still as water and . . . she was probably the most beautiful anything he'd ever seen. Hair was jet-black and braided into a thick rope that hung free next to her head. Skin was a golden brown, as if she were of Italian descent and had recently been in the sun. Eyes . . . Her eyes were like diamonds, which was to say both colorless and brilliant, with nothing but a dark rim around the iris.

"Manny?"

Jane's voice was right behind him, and yet he felt as if she were miles away. In fact, the whole world was somewhere else, nothing existing except for the stare of his patient as she looked up at him from the table.

It finally happened, he thought. All his life he'd wondered why he'd never fallen in love and now he knew the answer to that. He'd been waiting for this moment, this woman, this time.

This female is mine, he thought.

"Are you the healer?" she said in a low voice that stopped his heart, her words gorgeously accented, and also a little surprised.

"Yeah." He wrenched off his sport coat and threw it into a corner, not giving a shit where the thing landed. "That's what I'm here to do."

As he approached her, those stunning icy eyes slicked with tears. "My legs . . . They feel as though they are moving, but they do not."

Phantom pain. Not a surprise if she were paralyzed.

Manny stopped next to her and glanced at her body, which was covered with a sheet. She was tall. Had to be at least six feet. And she was built with sleek power.

This was a soldier, he thought, staring at the strength in her upper arms. This was a fighter.

God, the loss of mobility to someone like her took his breath away. Then again, even if you were a couch potato, life in a wheelchair was a bitch and a half.

He reached out and took her hand, and the instant he

made contact, his whole body went wakie-wakie on him, as if she were the socket to his inner plug.

"I'm going to take care of you," he told her as he looked her right in the eye. "I want you to trust me."

She swallowed hard as one crystal tear slipped out to trail down her temple. On instinct, he reached forward with his free hand and caught it—

The growl that percolated up from the doorway broke the spell that had bound him and turned him into a kind of prey. And as he glanced over at Goatee, he felt like snarling right back at the sonofabitch. Which of course made no sense.

Still holding his patient's hand, he barked at Jane, "Get that miserable bastard out of my operating room. And I want to see the goddamn scans. *Now.*"

Even if it killed him, he was going to save this woman.

And as Goatee's eyes flashed with pure hatred, he thought, well, shit, it might just come down to that. . . .

Watch out for titles in the Black Dagger Brotherhood *series by J. R. Ward*

DARK LOVER

In the shadows of the night in Caldwell, New York, there's a deadly turf war going on between vampires and their slayers. There exists a secret band of brothers like no other-six vampire warriors, defenders of their race. Yet none of them relishes killing more than Wrath, the blind leader of the Black Dagger Brotherhood.

The only purebred vampire left on earth, Wrath has a score to settle with the slayers who murdered his parents centuries ago. But, when one of his most trusted fighters is killed – leaving his half-breed daughter unaware of his existence or her fate – Wrath must usher her into the world of the undead – a world beyond her wildest dreams . . .

978-0-7499-5522-9

LOVER ETERNAL

Within the brotherhood, Rhage is the vampire with the strongest appetites. He's the best fighter, the quickest to act on his impulses, and the most voracious lover – for inside him burns a ferocious curse cast by the Scribe Virgin. Possessed by this dark side, Rhage fears the times when his inner dragon is unleashed, making him a danger to everyone around him.

Mary Luce, a survivor of many hardships, is unwittingly thrown into the vampire world and reliant on Rhage's protection. With a life-threatening curse of her own, Mary is not looking for love. Her faith in miracles was lost years ago. But when Rhage's intense animal attraction turns into something more emotional, he knows that he must make Mary his alone. And while their enemies close in, Mary fights desperately to gain life eternal with the one she loves . . .

978-0-7499-5527-4

Do you love fiction with a supernatural twist?

Want the chance to hear news about your favourite authors (and the chance to win free books)?

Keri Arthur
S. G. Browne
P.C. Cast
Christine Feehan
Jacquelyn Frank
Larissa Ione
Sherrilyn Kenyon
Jackie Kessler
Jayne Ann Krentz and Jayne Castle
Martin Millar
Kat Richardson
J.R. Ward
David Wellington

Then visit the Piatkus website and blog
www.piatkus.co.uk | www.piatkusbooks.net

And follow us on Facebook and Twitter
www.facebook.com/piatkusfiction | www.twitter.com/piatkusbooks

piatkus